In Memory of Araella Renee Bornmann
20 Dec 1997 – 15 April 2018
We lost our Rae of sunshine too soon, but the Universe
has gained a beautiful new star.

PRAISE FOR MARIA V. SNYDER

"Smart, witty, and full of heart, *Navigating the Stars* had me hooked from the very first page!" Lynette Noni, bestselling author of *Whisper*

"This is one of those rare books that will keep readers dreaming long after they've read it." *Publishers Weekly*, starred review on *Poison Study*

"Snyder deftly weaves information about glassblowing into her tale of magic and murder." *Library Journal* on *Storm Glass*

"Filled with Snyder's trademark sarcastic humor, fast-paced action, and creepy villainy, *Touch of Power* is a spellbinding fantasy adventure." *USA TODAY*

"This deftly plotted story will engage readers of both genders with its fresh story line." *Kirkus Reviews* on *Storm Watcher*

"A wonderful, thoughtful book full of vivid characters and a place—Inside—that is by turns alien, and breathtakingly familiar." Rachael Caine, etc.... on *Inside Out*

ALSO BY MARIA V. SNYDER

Study Series

POISON STUDY
MAGIC STUDY
FIRE STUDY
SHADOW STUDY
NIGHT STUDY
DAWN STUDY
ICE STUDY (Available
as an ebook)

Glass Series

STORM GLASS
SEA GLASS
SPY GLASS

Healer Series

TOUCH OF POWER
SCENT OF MAGIC
TASTE OF DARKNESS

Inside Series

INSIDE OUT
OUTSIDE IN
(collected as INSIDE)

Standalone Titles

STORM WATCHER

Discover other titles by Maria V. Snyder at
MariaVSnyder.com

NAVIGATING

THE

STARS

MARIA V. SNYDER

This is a work of science fiction. Names, characters, places, and incidents are a product of the author's imagination. Locales and public names are sometimes used for atmospheric purposes. Any resemblance to actual people, living or dead, or to businesses, companies, events, institutions, or locales is completely coincidental.

Navigating the Stars / Maria V. Snyder—1st edition
Cover design by Design by Committee
Crinkle space graphic by Louise Summerton
Published by Maria V. Snyder

Print ISBN 978-1-946381-01-9
Digital ISBN 978-1-946381-02-6

2471:333

"The answer is no, Lyra." My mother utters her favorite—I swear—phrase.

"But—"

"End of discussion."

Arguing is usually futile. But I'm not about to give up. Not this time.

We are having dinner in our housing unit. I'm picking at my reconstituted mashed potatoes, wilted broccoli and mystery protein...er...meat...while my dad scans his list of packing supplies on his portable, only half-listening to my mother's efforts to convince me that traveling to the new planet will be a grand adventure.

"Besides," Mom says, almost breathless. "We'll be the *first* archaeologists to assess the discovery. This new site on Planet Yulin has the potential to explain *who* transported the Terracotta Warriors to twenty-two different planets. We're getting close to an answer."

I gotta admit, my parents are the experts with a capital E on the life-sized Warriors. It's why they've been asked to relocate to the new planet. As for finding an answer to one of the Galaxy's great mysteries, I'm not as confident.

"Think about it, Lyra," Mom continues. "Over two million Warriors were custom-made on Earth by ancient Chinese craftsmen and transported by an unknown alien race to other worlds. We're bound to find evidence of who they were—or are—and why they used Earth's clay and people to create the Warriors. Why not make their own?"

Dad looks up. "The clay's from Earth, but there's no evidence they were made *on* Earth."

"The Chinese calligraphy on them is all the evidence you need," Mom retorts and they launch into an all-too-familiar debate.

I tune them out. Too bad the archaeologists don't know why the aliens needed all those Warriors throughout the Galaxy. Since we've yet to discover any other alien artifacts or sentient beings, we don't have anyone to ask.

And this recent discovery is all the way out on the edge of Explored Space. Yeah, you gotta say it with those capital letters since it's such a big deal that we've traveled so far from Earth. But what really boggles the mind is we're still in the Milky Way Galaxy. Space is big. Really big.

When my parents finish, it's my turn. I ensure they are both paying attention by clearing my throat. Loudly.

In a reasonable tone, I say, "It's exciting that you have a new site to research. You'll have all the top scientists eager to explore with you so you don't need me. I can remain here while you travel to Yulin. After all, I'm seventeen Actual years old—only a mere A-year until I'm of legal age."

Mom bangs her fork on the table. "I said end—"

I keep right on going. "Staying on planet Xinji, I'll be closer to the university—onsite learning is much more effective than distance. Dr. Wendland's research on learning strategies has proven it. And Lan's parents have already agreed to let me stay with them."

Mom and Dad exchange a look, which means they are doing that silent communication thing that parents do. I study them while I wait, sitting on the edge of my seat and resisting the urge to jiggle my leg with nervous energy.

My dad runs a big hand through his short sandy-brown hair, making it stick up at various angles. He normally appears younger than his forty-six A-years, but a sadness pulls on his face, aging him. "We're going to lose her in a couple A-years anyway, maybe we should consider her—"

"Absolutely not." Mom's brown-eyed gaze focuses on my father with such intensity, I'm surprised he doesn't burst into flames. Even though she is younger than my father by two A-years, my mother is in charge of our family. "I can't…not so soon after…Phoenix."

Before you ask, yes, my parents named me and my brother after constellations. Kinda funny considering we can't see either of those constellations unless we're on Earth, which, by the way, neither of us was born on. My parents have some really strange ideas at times.

The mention of Phoenix effectively kills any support I might have gotten from my father. He ducks his head and I wilt.

"Don't ask again," Mom says in the I've-decided-and-nothing-will-change-my-mind tone.

It's not fair, but arguing is pointless and will result in me cataloging thousands of broken Warrior shards as punishment. Appetite ruined, I push my now cold food away and head to my bedroom.

"Li—" my father calls after me.

I keep going. Our unit is small and narrow with a kitchen, common room, two bedrooms and the washroom. Not much space is allocated for housing in the base. The majority of the place is occupied by the scientists' labs, which is where most of the people living here spend all of their time anyway. We aren't a colony, but a research facility charged with assessing the entire planet. The base is filled with chemists, biologists, geologists, physicists, astrophysicists, meteorologists... Pick any "ologist" you can think of and they're probably here, including archaeologists like my parents.

And those ologists have been drooling happy since the announcement of the New Discovery. As for me? Not so much. While they've been talking in excited, high-pitched voices and making plans for the trip, I've been dreading launch day. Don't get me wrong, I'm glad for my parents. They've dedicated their lives to puzzling out this great Warrior mystery and I've no doubt that they'll eventually solve it.

Well...maybe a little doubt.

However, I'm tired of leaving my friends behind and I need to find my own passion. Not sure what that is yet, but I'm pretty sure it doesn't include researching ancient artifacts.

My room consists of a narrow bed, a few drawers, a desk, a chair, a screen and a terminal to access the Quantum net...well, a fraction of it—it's like being confined to the shallow end of the pool—very frustrating.

When the Quantum net—Q-net—was invented back in 2066, it changed everything. Earth's technology advanced at a sizzling pace, and inventions like the Crinkler engine, which allows us to travel through space super fast, were designed using the Q-net. Now it's used to keep track of...well, everything, but it's most important for knowing the precise location (and time) of all the space ships. Oh, and all the information collected from all the planets is stored within its amazing vastness.

But admittance to this scientific wonder is limited. Since I'm underage, I'm allowed to access the school programs, game programs, entertainment, and communications. At least the Q-net is able to send text-based communications between planets in Actual time. Can you imagine waiting decades for a reply?

I flop onto my bed and stare at the images of my friends from the other planets my parents dragged me to before Xinji. They fill the screen. The reality of space travel—the dreaded time dilation—stares back at me. Many of my friends have died of old age by now, and my two friends from our last assignment on Planet Wu'an are now in their fifties. Thanks, Einstein.

A musical ping sounds. The images fade into the background as the screen displays an incoming communication from a Miss Lan Maddrey.

"Accept," I say.

The words disappear and my best friend's face appears.

"What did they say?" Lan asks, but she notices my morose expression. "Oh, sorry, Li-Li!"

Only my father and closest of close friends call me that. I used to love pandas, okay? My father thought it was cute and that's how I got the nickname.

Her eyebrows smash together and furrow her brow. "Did you tell them about Dr. Wendland's research? I can send them the Q-cluster location to the paper. And my parents—"

"Won't matter," I say.

"Did your mother utter the three dreaded words?" she asks.

"Yes."

We share a moment of silence. Lan's blue eyes shine more than normal as she nibbles on the blond hair at the end of her French braid. She's fifteen, but soon to be sixteen—a little over a year younger than me, but we bonded over our mutual love of Diamond Rockler— the greatest singer in the Galaxy. Our only disagreement was over who he was going to marry, me or Lan, and that was three A-years ago. I wouldn't have gotten so close to her except my parents assured me that this was their last assignment. Sigh.

"My brother works for the port," Lan says. "You can sneak

off the shuttle and he'll hide you until it takes off. By the time they discover you're missing, they can't return."

An interesting idea. My heart races with the possibilities. I could start my own life. I hope to attend Brighton University on Planet Rho, a mere four Earth-years away. We measure distance between planets by how much E-time passes while you're traveling, not by how many Actual years pass. Which means if I stay here, I'll be fifty A-years older when my parents arrive at Yulin, but they'll only be ninety days older. Crazy right?

Regardless, I'd never see my parents again, which is why they won't leave me behind. Not yet anyway. They're still grieving over Phoenix and hoping I'll catch the science bug and stay with them, but I am tired of hanging around ancient things that have been buried for thousands of E-years. My excitement over running away fades.

"Thanks, Lan, but I can't do that to my parents."

She nods and gives me a watery smile. "I understand." She heaves a sigh, then lowers her voice. "When should we plan your..." Lan hesitates. "You-know-what."

I glance at my door. It's closed, but I sit at my desk and insert the entanglers into my ears—they resemble little round plugs, but they allow me to link directly to the Q-net through the terminal. Then I engage the privacy mode. If my parents walk into my room, they'd see a blank screen, but I can still see and hear Lan—another super cool invention courtesy of the Q-net.

How about at my last required soch-time? Do you think Jarren can fool the snoops? I think.

Of course. Who do you think created the dead zone in the back corner of the supply bay?

I laugh. *You mean the kissing zone? I heard Jarren took Belle there for a smooch fest.*

He did not! Lan's cheeks turn pink.

Oh? Do you have better intel?

Shut up.

A knock at my door prevents me from replying. Lan says good-bye and I disconnect and return to my flopped position on the bed. I might be resigned to leaving, but that doesn't mean I'll let my parents off easy. "Display wall art," I say to the screen. Only when it once again shows images of my old friends, do I say, "Come in."

Dad pokes his head inside as if expecting to be ambushed. "Is it safe?"

I huff. My temper isn't that bad. Well…not since I was seven A-years. "Only if you brought something sweet."

He holds his hand out, revealing a plate of chocolate chip cookies. A warm sugary scent wafts off them— fresh baked! My empty stomach groans in appreciation.

"Then it's safe." I'm not above bribery.

He enters and sets the plate down on my desk. He has a box tucked under his right arm. "You okay?"

"I'm gonna have to be. Right? Unless you're here to tell me you changed your mind?" I sit up at the thought.

"Sorry, Li-Li. We're not ready to lose you." My father hunches over slightly as grief flares in his brown eyes.

My older brother decided to leave for Earth two years ago

when he turned eighteen A-years. Earth is about ninety-five E-years away. So by the time Phoenix arrives on Earth, we will all be dead and Phoenix will still be eighteen.

Guilt over my earlier snit burns in my stomach.

"You just have to go on one more assignment with us, then you can decide what you want to do," Dad says.

"It's all right." I gesture to the box. "What's in there?"

He sets it down on my desk. "A puzzle."

I've fallen for that before. "Are you sure it isn't a bunch of random rubble?"

"No. We think we have all the pieces, but my assistant swears no one can possibly put it back together." He raises a slender eyebrow.

Appealing to my ego, he knows me so well. "Let's see."

Dad opens the box and pours out what appears to be shards of pottery—all terracotta, ranging in sizes from a thumbnail to six centimeters. I scan the pieces. They'd once formed a specific shape, and I can already see it has edges. Could be a piece of armor. Or a shield. Intrigued, I sort through the fragments, flipping them over and matching colors.

My father hands me the adhesive. "I'll let you prove Gavin wrong." He pulls my straight black hair back behind my shoulders and plants a kiss on my temple. "Thanks, Li-Li."

"Uh huh." The air pulses as he leaves. I arrange the pieces—about a thousand or so. There are markings on most of them. Odd. I group the ones that appear similar together. Reconstructing artifacts is actually fun. Not I-want-to-do-this-for-the-rest-of-my-life fun, but challenging and satisfying to make something whole again.

No one was more surprised than I. Trust me. I was roped into helping my parents a few years ago when they noticed that, after attending my required socialization time, or rather soch-time, and doing my school lessons, I had plenty of free time. I argued there was a reason it was called "free." It went over as well as my bid to stay on Xinji.

I was assigned all the chores no one else wanted to do, like sweeping and running the 3D digitizers—each of the thousands of Warriors has to be scanned and cataloged. But one night I found a half-finished reconstruction of a face and, well, I finished it in a couple hours. My parents made a big deal about it and now when there's a jumble of fragments that is declared "impossible" by the team, it comes to me. Not that I'm that great. There have been plenty of boxes filled with bits that I couldn't get to go together. A 3D digitizer could do it in minutes, but we only have four so using them for repairing broken pottery is not the priority.

This piece is tricky. Usually once I connect the edges, the rest is easier to match. But the shape is…octangular? Strange. Lan messages me while I'm working.

"It's all set," she says. "All our friends have been informed." Her voice is heavy with dismay.

I glance at her. "Thanks."

There's an awkward silence.

"What's that?" she asks.

"At this point, I've no idea."

"No. The markings on it."

I peer at the symbols etched into it. Silver lines the grooves so they stand out from the reddish orange clay. Lan should recognize them. Her parents are the base's language experts and cryptologists. While life-sized and made of terracotta, the extraterrestrial Warriors have quite a few differences from those discovered in China. One is they are covered with alien symbols that no one has been able to translate.

"Uh...it's Chinese calligraphy. Probably the name of the craftsman who built it."

"That's not Chinese."

"Are you sure?"

"Lyra." Her flat tone indicates she's insulted.

"Okay, okay. So it's one of those other alien symbols."

She shrugs. "I haven't seen markings like those before."

"Well consider two million Warriors with what... sixty some markings per Warrior, makes that..." Ugh, I suck at math.

"The symbols are not all unique. And they still haven't cataloged them all."

"Don't give my mother any ideas," I say, pressing my hand to my chest in mock horror. But the reality is that with limited funds, personnel and equipment, the Warrior Project is a slow-moving beast.

Lan laughs. I'm gonna miss that light trill.

"Seriously, Li-Li. It's different. It might be important."

"Important enough to keep my parents on Xinji?" Hope bubbles up my throat.

Lan straightens with enthusiasm. "Maybe. When you finish it, bring it to my mom."

"Will do."

It takes me the rest of the night to complete the piece. I'm not exaggerating. The faint smell of coffee wafts under my door as my parents get ready for their day. I stare at the...shield—for lack of a better word— because it's a meter wide and a meter long, three centimeters thick and octagonal (of course—the aliens have a serious addiction to the shape...maybe they are sentient octagons? Hmmm).

The shield has a spiderweb of fine cracks and a few fragments missing here and there—standard for reconstructed objects, but the eight rows of markings are clear. Each row has eight different symbols, but they appear to be similar—like they're siblings, with similar swoops or curls. Then another row also has eight unique glyphs that complement each other— sorry, it's hard to explain. But one row looks like Chinese calligraphy, but I'm not sure.

What I'm certain of is, I've been living on Warrior planets all my life, but I've never seen anything like this before. Excited, I rush out to get my dad. He's sitting at the table, sipping coffee and reading from his portable. My mother is at the counter.

Dad spots me. "You're up early."

"Come on." I tug on his hand. "You have to see this!"

He follows me to my room.

Mom trails after us. "Lyra, did you stay up all night?"

Her tone is disapproving so I don't answer her. Instead, I sweep my hands toward the octagon with a flourish. "Ta da!"

Both my parents gape at it in stunned silence for a solid minute. My father reaches toward it, but I stop him.

"It's not dry."

He snatches his arm back as if he's been burned. When my parents still don't say anything, I say, "This is important. Right? Something different?"

The silence stretches. Now it's getting weird.

"Yes," my mother says finally. "Different."

"Lan said her mom, Dr. Maddrey, would want to see it."

"Oh, yes," my dad says. His voice is rough. "I expect there will be *lots* of people who would want to see this."

There is a great deal of excitement from the scientists in our base over the strange object with the rows of markings. Theories about them fly faster than a Crinkler engine through space. The one that generates the most gossip is the possibility that the octagon is an alien Rosetta Stone even though it's made of the same baked clay as the Warriors. Lan's parents are put in charge of figuring out the mystery.

"I hardly see them," Lan complains one night.

She's lying on her bed and I'm sitting on her chair as we listen to Diamond Rockler. His voice is like honey— smooth with a thick sweetness. Rockler's heart-melting lyrics fill the small room as a video of him plays on her screen. He's talented and gorgeous and intelligent— that's just not fair. Some people don't even get one of those qualities.

"If anyone's going to figure out what it means, it's them," I say. Frankly, I wouldn't mind seeing less of my parents. They've been asking me to join the crews of people searching through the million fragment piles in hope of finding more octagons. *More data, more data,* my mom's always saying. They're drowning in data, but no one's made any connections. I think they have too much data, but that's me.

"Messages were sent to the other active Warrior planets," Lan says. "The other language experts might have some ideas on how to translate it and they're all looking for their own Rosetta Octagon."

"As long as it keeps everyone busy," I say, smiling.

Lan sits up. "Lyra Daniels, you're not thinking—"

"I am." I insert my tangs into my ears and access the Q-net via the two sensors that were implanted in my brain when I turned ten A-years old. Staying entangled in the Q-net for long periods of time is flirting with insanity. So everyone must be able to completely disentangle. It's the reason terminals are needed to interact with the Q-net. It's funny, to me anyway, that the terminal is a bland plate built into the desk. It's some type of rare metal, but otherwise it's boring in appearance.

Lan's terminal has the same limits as mine, but I've learned how to mask my identity and bypass a few security barriers.

"You're going to get into trouble,' Lan says. But it doesn't stop her from inserting her own tangs to trail me.

"Don't you want to find out who Belle's been hanging out with?" I don't listen to her answer. Instead I concentrate. I view the Q-net as a sphere with a zillion layers, like a universe-sized ball of yarn. And, while I'm blocked from most of the layers, I can find...holes...in the security, almost by feel—it's a strange sensation— and wriggle into an area that I'm not "technically" supposed to be able to access. We call it *worming*.

Video feeds from the cameras around the base pop up.

"Oh my stars, Lyra! You're going to end up in detention if security discovers you."

"Big if. Look, Mom, no ripples."

"How did you..." She sighs. "Jarren, right? He taught you? You're getting better at worming."

I scan the images. People bustle through the hallways. Some stop to talk. The labs techs are busy doing whatever they do. No sound. That would be too creepy. And no cameras in private units. That's an invasion of privacy.

"Found Belle." I hone in on the camera in the canteen. "She's flirting with that chemistry tech— what's-his-name."

"Trevor, but he's too old for her. He's like twenty-three A-years," Lan says. "How do you know she's flirting?"

"She's flipping her hair and eyeing him as if she wants to eat him for dessert."

"For dessert? Really? That's gross."

"Ah youth. So innocent."

She smacks me on the arm with her pillow. "And you shouldn't be spying on your friends."

"Oh? Should I spy on someone else?"

"No." She pulls out her tangs. "We should be planning Jarren's surprise sixteenth birthday party."

I groan. "That's not for another hundred and eighty days."

"Planning," she says with authority, "will be the key to success."

I disentangle from the Q-net and we brainstorm a few ideas. "I think we should have it in a spot he'd never suspect," I say. "Like the middle of a hallway. Or outside the base!"

Just then, Dr. Maddrey pokes her head into Lan's room. "Have you finished your school work?" she presumably asks Lan, but she gives me a pointed look when Lan shakes her head no. Dr. Maddrey leaves the door ajar when she retreats.

My cue to leave. "Better get going, I've a physics test tomorrow that I need to ace now that I'm applying to Brighton University."

"It's two years until the next Interstellar Class ship, what are you going to do for that extra year?" Lan asks.

"I think I'll intern in a bunch of the labs and see if anything catches my interest. Chemistry and biology might be fun. Dr. Nese says he always needs help with keeping the weather instruments clean." And any chance to go outside is always taken. "I'm sure I'll find plenty to do." Even if I have to spend the year reconstructing damaged Warriors. It'll be worth it. And once I get my degree, I could be assigned to a colony planet and interact with normal people.

Lan bounces on her bed. "And my parents already agreed that we can attend the university together even though I won't be eighteen yet!"

The best part. We share a grin. Then I wave a goodbye to the Maddreys and return to my housing unit. The place is empty. Not a surprise, my parents have been busy with the new find.

I settle next to the terminal and access the physics lectures.

After two hours, I'm doing head bobs and my stomach growls. However, my parents are still not back. I check their work schedules—yes, they've given me permission—to see if I should wait to have dinner with them or just go to the canteen. Scientists tend to get engrossed in their work so the base has a cafeteria for those too busy to cook a meal. I've seen techs carrying trays back to labs for their bosses.

They both have late meetings and a few "evening" appointments. It doesn't matter that Xinji's sun is still high in the sky, every single colony planet and Warrior planet, as well as the people traveling in space ships, all follow Earth's clock. Days have twenty-four hours. Years have three hundred and sixty-five days (yes, we do the leap years as well). The base's lights and window shutters are programmed to keep Earth time. However, we stopped using the names of the months and days— that would be silly. Instead, we track the year and day. Today is the three hundredth and fortieth day of the year 2471, otherwise referred to as 2471:340.

I was born on 2337:314, and I'm seventeen Actual years old, which means I've lived seventeen of Earth's years. But since I've traveled to two different planets and made two time jumps, one hundred and thirty-four E-years have passed during those seventeen years I've been alive. Boggles the mind, doesn't it?

I scan my parents' agendas idly, noting it'll be a couple days before we have another family meal. Odd that they should be *that* busy. And why are they meeting with Dr. Gage and Dr. Jeffries tomorrow, they don't normally interact. I straighten as my heart sinks. My guts churn as I study their itineraries, trying to dismiss my suspicions. When I reach 2471:360, I'm on my feet. I yank my tangs out and sprint from my room.

I'm breathless by the time I reach the archaeology lab. My mother is in her office with Dr. Bernstein. He's a meteorologist. What the heck? I interrupt them. Manners are the least of my worries.

Mom's annoyance changes to concern when she sees my face. "I'm sorry, Ben. Can we finish this later?"

"No need, Ming. You've already convinced me."

My mother shakes his hand. "I'll send you the contract."

"Great." He gives us a jaunty wave.

Mom's polite demeanor drops as soon as he's out the door. She shuts it and turns to me. "Lyra, what—"

"Tell me we're not still going to Yulin," I practically shout.

"Of course we are, why did you think we weren't?"

"Because of the find. I thought you and Dad would want to study it."

"It's exciting, but other than authenticating and dating it, it's not our area of expertise."

"But…" A tight knot forms in my throat, cutting off the rest of my protest.

"That's why we have linguists and cryptologists, Lyra. And I'm hoping the find will allow the Warrior Project to hire more. Besides, Dr. Natalia can handle directing the techs with the reconstruction of the damaged statues on Xinji and searching for more octagons. We've uncovered all sixty-four Warrior pits and found no other artifacts alien or otherwise on Xinji. But on Yulin..." Her eyes shine.

I stop listening as despair claws at my heart with its sharp talons. The pain is making it difficult to breathe.

We're leaving.

We're really leaving.

And there's not a damn thing I can do about it.

I've no memory of the trip back to my room. It took every bit of effort not to burst into tears. But once alone, I dive onto my bed and cry into my pillow. Lan and I will never attend university together. She'll have to plan Jarren's party without me. I'll never see her again.

When I gain control of my emotions, I message Lan. She takes one look at me. "What happened?"

By the time I spit out the news, we're both crying.

"This is worse than before," she sniffs. "It's just cruel to give us hope and then yank it away."

I agree. "To be fair—I know, not helping—but my parents never said we were staying. I just assumed we would."

"So did I." She wipes her face. "I'll let our friends know it's back on."

"Thanks."

Why is it when you're dreading something, the time just flies right on by? I swear I blinked and my last twenty-one days on

Xinji disappeared. The Interstellar Class space ship entered Xinji's orbit today—the dreaded 2471:360. I've a day left before I board the shuttle. It only takes me an hour to pack my stuff.

Now all I have left to do is attend my funeral.

2471:360

The children of planet-hopping parents have figured out long ago that, despite being able to communicate with our friends left behind via the Q-net, the time dilation is too hard to overcome.

The math just isn't in our favor. It will take me ninety days to reach Yulin, which is fifty E-years away. That means Lan will be sixty-six A-years old (that is, if she remains on Xinji) when I arrive, while I will only be ninety days older. Yeah, it sucks. Which is why we hold funerals for the person leaving and cut all ties. It's easier for all of us.

The adults don't know about the funerals and every effort is made to keep it that way. Otherwise the psychologists would descend on us en masse.

This will be my second funeral—I was too young when we left Ulanqab. If only the explorers would stop exploring. Each time they—the Department of Explored Space (DES), which was formed when interstellar travel became possible—expand the edges of Explored Space, they discover yet another exoplanet with Terracotta Warriors, which wreaks havoc on my social life. Overall, I know it's a good thing. They also find exoplanets without Warriors that are potential candidates for colonization. Earthlings and their drive to seek new worlds for their ever-growing population... plus the constant need for resources because Earth is tapped out.

It's just hard to adapt. There are plenty of people out there who relish the adventure of being time travelers, but I'm not one. Or I don't think I am. I've never been given a choice and that sucks the most. I've no living aunts or uncles or grandparents. There's a couple of my fourth or fifth cousins living on a colony on Planet Beta, but I'll never meet them. Phoenix is a memory. He wouldn't let me come to his funeral. We both knew I'd sob through it and unhinge his efforts to remain stoic. Leaving us cost him just as much as it hurt us.

Heck, it takes a toll from everyone, and our idea of family and our traditions is just not the same as those who stay in one place their entire lives. We are Earthlings, but we have no emotional connection to our ancestors or cultural traditions. Instead, we have our own warped research base traditions like the annual desk chair race and landing day celebrations.

I carry a bag through the narrow and featureless corridors of Xinji's Central Base. It's basically a giant rectangle. It resembles Wu'an's base, which resembles Ulanqab's, which resembles Taishan's. You get the idea— one size fits all. I was born on Planet Ulanqab and my brother on Taishan. A tightness circles my chest. Will Phoenix think of me when he gazes up at the stars when he reaches Earth?

The soch-area is filled with bright colors, soft pillows, big couches, thick carpets, entertainment cubbies, screens on the walls, the clean scent of baby powder and a couple facilitators—a.k.a. babysitters—who ensure we all play nice. All residents under the Actual age of eighteen are required to spend the same two hours a day in here. Most of the younger kids stay much longer, but those of us sixteen and older prefer to hang out in other locations. Like the kissing zone. I smile when I spot Lan standing close to Jarren. Belle is staring at Jarren as if she'd like to strangle him, her face almost the same color as her bright red hair. Knowing Jarren, he probably deserves it. He's gotten into more trouble than the rest of us combined.

With a tilt of her head, Lan indicates the back game room. All the kids know that room is for the older teens for the next two hours. After that, anyone can use it. I follow Belle inside. Cyril is already there. He's all legs as he lounges in an armchair and his black hair is buzzed short. Jarren and Lan come in soon after. That's it for our age group. A grand total of five.

Lan shuts the door. Privacy is an illusion and we all instinctively glance at the cameras. The babysitters can watch us, but not hear us.

"Relax," Jarren says with a smirk. He flips his shaggy brown hair from his forehead, revealing his light brown eyes. "I've been taught by the best."

Jarren can't let an opportunity go by without gushing over his friend, Warrick Nolt, who Jarren learned all his worming tricks from back when they were on Planet Kaiping together. We all give him an exasperated look.

"Don't worry. The babysitters are watching our required soch-time from twenty-one days ago," he says.

Ah, that explains why he'd messaged us with instructions on what to wear today and for Cyril's recent haircut. Not that we had a ton of clothing options— mostly just hand-me-down jeans, sweatshirts, T-shirts, and sweaters—it's cold on Xinji. But anything is better than the nerdy jumpsuits and lab coats the adults wear. I tug my black sweater over my waist. The color is fitting for the occasion.

Lan takes up position in front of the large screen we use for gaming—all Q-net activities must be visible during soch-time so the babysitters know we're socializing and not ignoring each other. The others sit in chairs, facing her. I have the position of honor and settle into the oversized armchair next to Lan. Setting my bag down on the floor near my feet, I try to relax.

As my best friend, she is in charge of my funeral. "We are gathered here today to remember our friend Lyra Tian Daniels."

Before you ask, Tian means "sky" in Chinese.

"When I first met Lyra, I hated her."

I glance at her. This is new.

Lan flashes me a smile. "When I arrived here from Planet Heshan, I thought she was perfect. With her glossy black hair that didn't have a hint of frizz, no pimples and hazel eyes, I called her the Warrior Princess since she resembled the Chinese Warriors."

Over the years, lots of people have commented on how

much I look like my mother. When they mistake us for sisters, Mom preens and is quite obnoxious about it.

"I despised her on sight," Lan continues.

Interesting. I'd no idea.

"Then I made the mistake of talking to her." Lan sighs dramatically. "And it was impossible to hate her. She went out of her way to help others and she also had the audacity to prove that she wasn't perfect. Oh no, she was far from it."

"Thanks," I say with plenty of sarcasm.

"Hush," Lan scolds. "You're not allowed to talk." She taps a long finger on her cheek. "Where was I?"

"Not perfect," Jarren says helpfully.

"Right. Along with her delusion that Diamond Rockler would pick her over me to marry, Lyra has a number of faults. Remember the time we all had to clean out the lavatories for seven days because Lyra wormed into the base's security?"

I bite down on a protest. The roasting has begun and the roastee—me—must endure it in silence.

Lan continues with her eulogy of my misdeeds. "...adhesive everywhere, took poor Lucas hours to get free. Then she wormed the doors and lights of the soch-area and all our babysitters thought the place was haunted."

Jarren laughs. "That was classic."

"Despite her propensity for practical jokes, she was a perfect friend and I'm gonna miss her very much." Lan sniffs and digs in her pocket for a tissue.

Pressure builds behind my eyes and my throat tightens. I'm gonna miss her more.

"Would anyone else like to speak?" Lan asks.

Jarren hops to his feet and shoots me a sly smile. "I've a confession. While Lyra has proven herself to be rather adept at worming, she didn't breach the base's security systems so we could sneak outside. That was me, but I had so many demerits at that time—"

"You still have them," Belle mutters.

He flashes her a grin. "I gotta maintain my reputation. However, one more demerit would have sent me to detention for seven days. And we all know how horrible it is to be locked up in a white room that long." At everyone's blank looks, Jarren says, "Nobody? Really?" He sighs. "Trust me, it's terrible, so I'm eternally grateful that Lyra took the blame for the worm. She was good that way."

We share a sad smile. Nice of him to fess up. I swipe my eyes. He taught me a great deal about worming in the Q-net, and most of my pranks were to impress him.

"Anyone else?" Lan asks.

Belle tells a story about how I helped her with calculus and Cyril describes our epic space battle that we'd fought for so long the Q-net called it a tie and shut us both out of the game cluster for three days.

When they finish, Lan resumes her role. "Lyra Tian Daniels, may you rest in peace," she says in a heavy tone. There's a moment of silence. "Now for the reading of her will." Lan sits down.

I pick up my bag and stand. "For Belle, who often commented on the beauty of the ancient Warriors despite being covered in red dust daily..." Digging into the bag, I pull out a terracotta vase about fifteen centimeters tall that I constructed with a variety of discarded pieces and then sealed so it wouldn't leak. "I leave this vase." I set it in her hands.

"This is beautiful! Thank you." She cradles it with reverence.

"For Cyril, who is the King of *Mutant Zombies from Planet Nine*, I leave a file describing all my best moves and a list of cheats that I've discovered."

"Sweet," he says.

"For Jarren, who is the most likely to wind up in detention again—"

"Hey!" he protests.

I wait.

Then his cocky grin returns. "Probably right."

"I leave the passcode to the soch-files."

For once Jarren is speechless. The passcode will allow him to access his disciplinary records and erase demerits. Took me at least thirty days to worm around all the safeguards, but worth it to surprise him.

I whisper the code into his ear. "I suggest you be subtle and only delete one or two at a time."

He hugs me. "Thank you, thank you, thank you."

Only one thing left. "And for Lan, a kindred soul who is the sweetest person in the Galaxy. I leave..." I take out a glossy colored photograph printed on precious paper. I planned to give it to her at her surprise sixteenth birthday on 2472:022—a mere twenty-seven days away. "Diamond Rockler. He's all yours."

She shrieks when she sees her name and his autograph scrawled over his bare muscular chest. "How did you get this? You shouldn't have—this is too much. I love it!" Her words tumble over each other.

It set me back a few...er...a hundred credits, but I did get paid for my hours helping in the archaeology lab. Besides, I would have spent more just to witness her reaction.

With that last gift, my funeral officially ends. There is no good-bye or we'll be in touch. I hug Lan and leave the room with only my memories and a couple photographs to add to my collection.

Emotionally drained, I head back to our housing unit. Each step an effort of will. By the time I reach my bedroom, I make a promise.

No more friends. Ever.

2471:361

Launch day isn't as exciting as it sounds.

Last to be shuttled up to the ship are the scientists who are voluntarily relocating to Yulin. The port occupies about a third of the research base and is filled with people saying good-bye. The port's roof is retracted all the way open to allow the shuttle access. The entire base can be pressurized with breathable air if necessary, but, so far, all the Warrior planets have air similar to Earth's. I weave through the groups, avoiding eye contact. The various surface vehicles the scientists use when doing field work have been pushed to the sides along with piles of equipment, in order to leave room for the passenger shuttle.

Before embarking, I gaze at the light purple sky of Xinji and the massive forest that keeps trying to reclaim the land the base occupies. The native trees are so determined, Dr. Natab's team has to clean saplings off the roof every fourteen days. Breathing in the thick moist aroma of living green mixed with a spicy coffee odor, I try to hold in Xinji's particular scent. The same one I complained to my parents about when we first arrived. Now I'd bottle it and take it with me if I could. Instead, I step into the long oblong of the shuttle's main compartment and find my seat. All without having to talk to anyone. Bonus.

It takes forever for everyone to board. I scan the passengers. About a dozen kids—most under twelve A-years old—are going to Yulin. They appear as miserable as I feel, but a quartet of fourteen A-year-old girls are sitting close together and excitedly chatting. Lucky them.

My father is doing a final check as my mother settles next to me. She squeezes my hand. "Sorry your friends didn't come see you off."

I shrug. "We said good-bye yesterday."

"I know, I just thought—"

"Am I going to have my own room on board the ship?" I ask. I'm not in the mood to discuss my feelings.

"Yes. And since your father and I are in charge at Yulin, our housing unit will be four times the size of the one here."

Wait. "You're in charge of *all* the research teams?"

"Yes, DES asked us to be the lead scientists after we discovered the alien octagon. Your father will oversee the base's operations and I'll be directing personnel."

That's cool for them. "Does that mean you can use all the 3D digitizers on the broken pieces instead of cataloging the Warriors with them?" It'll be so much faster than a group of people trying to glue the shards together. "You might find another alien artifact."

"That would be ideal, but we still have to assess the *entire* planet, not just the Warriors." Mom's expression pinches tight.

"What's wrong?" I ask.

"Not everyone believes the octagon is alien."

I'm not surprised. Other than the strange markings, there's no other evidence it was made by an extraterrestrial instead of one of the craftsmen on Earth. That's one of the theories about the Warriors—made on Earth, transported to the stars by...something. "Maybe it's like one of those practice boards. You know, so they can learn how to do it right before they carve the symbol on a Warrior." Some of those glyphs have complex designs.

Mom huffs with amusement, but then sobers. "A few people think it's a hoax."

"Why would they think that?"

"It's been a couple centuries of Earth time since we discovered the Warriors on other planets and, in all that time, we don't have any credible theories on why they are there." Mom presses her lips together in frustration. "A number of naysayers think we planted the alien artifact so DES continues funding our research."

Oh. "Are they going to shut down the Warrior Project?" An interesting thought. "We could return to Earth and catch up with Phoenix!"

I regret my outburst when my mom flinches and gazes down at her hands. They're now clutched together in her lap.

"Phoenix made his choice, Lyra," she says, so quiet I have to lean closer. Then she glances at me. "DES will still fund the project, but they might reduce the budget. We're already understaffed and have only a few people to analyze the data so the likelihood of discovering any new clues will diminish."

Unwilling to hurt my mom's feelings again, I refrain from reminding her that the archaeology teams haven't discovered why the Warriors are on other planets since explorers found the first group on Planet Xi'an. At that time, they marveled over the sheer number of Warriors—about ninety-three thousand— the alien symbols on the armor, and the fact that the Warriors were modeled after the Chinese like the original find on Earth back in 1974. But each new Warrior planet, so far, matched Planet Xi'an, which was named after the city in China where the original Terracotta Army was discovered. Ever since, the Warrior planets have been named after cities in China, unlike the colony planets that are named using the Greek alphabet.

My father bounds onto the shuttle. "Everyone's here, we're good to go," he says to the pilots.

We strap in and soon Xinji is falling away along with my heart. Grief burns in the empty space in the middle of my chest. To fill the hole, I imagine inserting a titanium heart complete with gears and valves—functional and impenetrable.

The artificial gravity kicks in when we clear the atmosphere.

Yesterday, they transported supplies and equipment for Yulin to the Big Fat Frog in orbit... Oh, excuse me, it's a state-of-the-art Interstellar Class space ship with a Bucherer-Plank Crinkler engine that just happens to resemble a big fat frog. Since it doesn't travel through an atmosphere, there's no need for it to be aerodynamic. But it would have been nice if it at least looked sleek.

This morning, they conveyed all our gear up. The trip doesn't take long. Within thirty minutes, we dock with the Big Fat Frog. As I disembark and follow my parents to the passenger quarters, memories of my last trip bubble in my mind. All Interstellar Class ships have the same design. Cargo bays, medical bays, living quarters, dining areas, rec areas, etc... Of course the engine room, bridge and crew quarters are off limits to us. I remember how boredom drove my ten-A-year-old self to explore every inch. I expect this trip will be equally as boring. Well...maybe not. This time I know how to worm into a few restricted clusters of the Q-net. Maybe there's some hope for excitement.

Our quarters have a common area, washroom, and two bedrooms. It doesn't take me long to unpack. My room has a standard terminal and screen which is fine for doing school work, accessing my personal files, and messages. I can bypass some of my terminal's limits. If I used my parents' terminal, then I'd be able to go deeper, but if I'm caught I'll be in big trouble. Hmmm....boredom might trump trouble.

The ship vibrates and hums as it leaves orbit. We are traveling to a crinkle point—or rather a safe place where they can engage the BP Crinkler engine. If the ship is too close to a planet or a sun or a black hole or another ship that is also crinkling space when it starts the engine, bad things will happen. When the captain engages the BPC, the space around us will crinkle and we'll travel from one point in the Galaxy to another in seconds instead of decades. Then the engine is shut down and space smooths out. Warping space has a cost—the time dilation.

Yeah, it's hard to imagine, so on the next page are a few diagrams drawn by yours truly (I need to find a hobby).

Since it's too dangerous to crinkle a vast amount of space at one time, the ship does a series of small crinkles all in a row (crinkle, smooth, crinkle, smooth, crinkle, smooth, etc...). All of our Actual time will be spent traveling to and from the crinkle point—twenty days to the point and then seventy to Yulin. That gives me ninety days to see just how deep into the Q-net I can go without causing ripples. Fun.

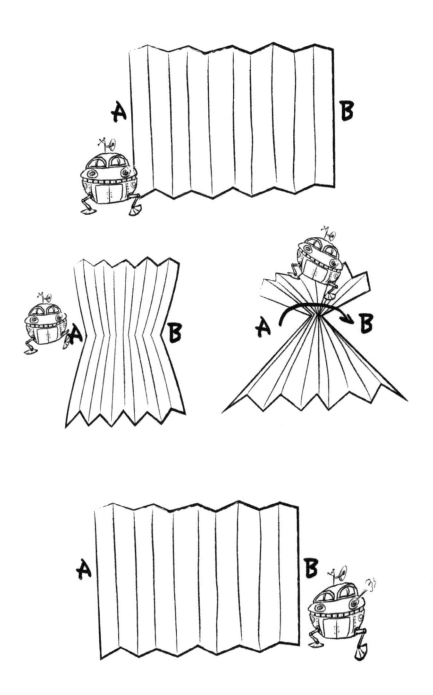

I get my first nasty surprise on the second day of the trip. "I should be exempt from soch-time," I say to my mother. "There's no one my age on board."

"It's required by law, Lyra. You know that. Besides, some of the crew have kids. Maybe one of them will be older."

I bite my lip—no way to win this argument. And I'm not going to tell her that I've no interest in befriending a crew kid only to be separated in eighty-nine days or she'll lecture me on the scientific research behind the socialization requirement for children. Instead, I keep my comment to myself and report for soch-time in the recreation bay. The area is off limits to anyone over eighteen A-years old for the next two hours. The babysitter is the only exception—she looks about forty A-years old. Her face is creased with lines as if she's already exhausted. I tell her my name so she can check me off. She starts to explain the rules, but I wave her off. I can recite the rules by heart.

As expected, the place is filled with noisy little kids, awkward pre-teens and the quartet of giggling girls from the shuttle. Oh joy. I head straight for the back wall. There's a game terminal and screen there, but during soch-time you can't play by yourself—that would defeat the whole purpose of *socialization* time. That's okay, I'm aiming for the group of comfy chairs facing it, thinking of taking a nap. But I stop in my tracks.

A guy is already there. He looks older than eighteen, but he's not wearing a crew uniform. And his black hair is longer than the buzzed fuzz of the other male crew members. He's sketching a picture of something leafy in an actual paper book with a stick of some sort—old Earth stuff—and I wonder if he was born on Earth, but I'm not curious enough to actually ask, despite the fact he's kind of handsome with his straight nose and angular jaw.

I turn to find another spot to nap, but the babysitter hustles up to me. She shoves a portable screen at me. The flat twenty-five-by-fifteen centimeter device can download files and run basic programs so you can do work without being entangled with the Q-net. 'Cause of that whole spend-too-much-time-and-go-insane caveat. You have to be in the Q-net for over twelve hours at a time for that to happen, but some of these scientists are serious workaholics.

"You need to state that you understand the regulations," she says.

Reciting my name and the fact that I'm well aware of the regs, I hand it back to her.

She glances at the boy. Oh no. Before I can retreat, she grabs my elbow. "Let me introduce you." She tows me closer. "Niall."

He pulls his gaze from his sketch reluctantly. His eyes are a blue-green. Annoyance pulses from him.

The babysitter is not affected by his glower. "This is Lyra Daniels. She's your age."

A slight nod of greeting.

"Lyra, this is Niall Radcliff."

I nod in return. The babysitter mutters something

uncomplimentary under her breath about teenagers and goes to yell at two kids fighting over a toy. Niall returns his attention to his drawing and I search for another quiet corner. Except I can't find one. And, after observing the kids, I notice that there is this invisible barrier between them and Niall. Even the kids from Xinji have picked up on this and avoid going near him. He's surrounded by calm and comfortable chairs.

I'm not about to suffer with the younger kids so I claim a seat near Niall. He ignores me and I return the favor. Except, I try to imagine what it'd be like to live on an Interstellar Class space ship. Due to time jumping, I'm one hundred and thirty-four Earth years old. Space brats who grow up on the ships can be as old as the dawn of crinkle travel—about four hundred plus E-years. It all depends on where they go. Having friends on a space ship must be really hard. Lots of things can happen—crews change, parents decide to settle on a planet and the passengers are all temporary.

"Are you done?" Niall asks me in an irritated tone.

"What are you talking about?" I ask.

"Staring. Are you done?"

Oops. I'd apologize, but his hostile glare pisses me off. "No, I'm not. What's that you're drawing with?"

He sighs—and on a scale of one to ten in teenaged aggrieved sighs, I'd give it a ten. "It's a pencil."

"Okay, now I'm done."

"Good, because I've no intention of becoming *friends*." He says the last word with disgust. "You passengers come on board and act like you own the place. You don't. You're a temporary nuisance and, as far as I'm concerned, the sooner you're gone the better."

Gee, what a sweetheart. "Don't worry, Mr. Nasty, I've no intentions of socializing with you either."

"Then we're in agreement. Excellent." He returns his attention to his sketch.

I glance away. My pulse taps out a fast beat—so much for my nap.

After a few minutes, I'm bored. I insert my tangs and turn on the game terminal. When *Mutant Zombies from Planet Nine* fills the screen, I smile, thinking of Cyril—he never could beat Jarren no matter how much he practiced. My heart kicks me hard, reminding me to not think about my friends. Once I confirm the babysitter's attention is elsewhere, I worm into the game controls and override a few restrictions. I hope outsmarting zombies will make the time go faster as I start the game.

Sometime...later, the babysitter's voice breaks my concentration and my avatar falls into a tar pit. I swallow a curse.

"You're not allowed to play alone," she says.

"I'm not." I gesture to the left corner of the screen. "There's Niall's player right there. See?"

She peers at it, then at Niall whose attention is focused on his sketch. Good thing his hair covers his ears so she can't see he's not wearing entanglers.

"He's waiting for the next wave of zombies," I say. "The tar slows things down."

"Oh. All right." She returns to the others.

Too easy. I switch my focus to "Niall's" avatar and continue to play by myself. When the tone sounds to end soch-time, I stand and stretch. Niall is already gone.

Niall and I have no difficulties ignoring each other. Plus I'm determined not to initiate a conversation with him. Ever. So I spend my soch-time fooling around with the game system. Of course tricking the system becomes boring and by the fourth day, I test how deep into the Q-net the game terminal will allow me to go.

My biggest problem is the screen. During soch-time, the screen must show what's going on—game, video, music—it's all visible, including worming. I need to squish my worming activities into a tiny section of the screen which would be still showing attacking zombies. I study the babysitter, noting the places she frequents. Then I take a stroll around the rec center, marking angles. Eventually, I figure out if she sits at her desk, she can't see the bottom right-hand corner of the screen.

It takes me a couple soch-time sessions to manage to have both and as soon as the babysitter is at her desk, I worm into the ship's schematics. I just need a few minutes to find a terminal that's been forgotten.

When I glance over my shoulder to check on the babysitter, I catch Niall staring at me. I. Can't. Resist.

"Are you done?" I ask.

He scowls at me.

"Staring. Are you done?" I ask again, but this time I'm more smug.

"Passengers are not allowed to access that information," he says.

I quickly exit the data cluster and the game fills the entire screen. "What information?"

He stands up. He's tall and lean, but his shoulders are tense. Is he planning on ratting me out to the babysitter?

"There's a reason passengers are barred from those areas. You could endanger the ship and kill us all, you idiot."

Seriously? An idiot? "Look, Mr. Drama King, I've barely scratched the surface and can't get deep enough to affect the operation of the ship. You should know that." I cock my head to the side. "Or do you need me to teach you about the Q-net? The Q stands for quantum."

His fingers curl into fists. "Worming is illegal and if you're caught you'll be tossed into the brig for the rest of the trip. That's B for brig."

"Oh you can spell, your mother must be so proud."

Niall takes a step toward me and unease rolls up my spine. Did I hit a nerve?

But he stops. "I should report you, but you'd just deny it."

Plus he wouldn't have any proof. Although I believe he wouldn't hesitate to rat me out to the babysitter if he catches me again.

When I don't respond, he says, "Consider this a warning. Don't do it again."

"Aye aye, Captain." I just couldn't resist the sarcasm— who does this guy think he is? I'm rewarded with a nasty glare before he resumes pretending I don't exist. I don't press my luck and return to just tricking the games during soch-time, but that doesn't mean I plan to stop worming.

After soch-time, I find the forgotten terminal. According to Jarren, the research bases and colonies always have a couple that are installed in areas the designers think people will use, but end up being forgotten. I'd figured it was the same with an Interstellar Class ship, and I was right. It's in a quiet out-of-the-way part of the ship not used by the crew or passengers—a perfect place to worm deeper into the Q-net.

The terminal is similar to the one in my room with a seat and screen, except this one doesn't have as many restrictions, and, as long as I don't broadcast my identity, I should be able to access deeper data clusters. Inserting my tangs, I keep the screen blank as I worm past the initial inquiry as to who I am.

Since my parents dodged my questions regarding my new home planet—which I suspect must be bad, otherwise why not tell me?—my first foray is to pull up the classified file on Planet Yulin. When the explorers in their Explorer Class space ships find a potential exoplanet in the Goldilocks Zone, their primary objective is to do a preliminary assessment and search for any sentient beings. If there are none (although everyone is ever hopeful), then the next step is to hunt for alien artifacts and

Warriors.

After that, it's up to the scientists to locate and catalog the native species and determine if a planet is a good candidate for colonization. The Warrior planets are not open for colonies. At least, not yet. Once all the Warriors are uncovered and inventoried, the data is sent to DES. Then the planet is closed and protected from looters until DES decides what to do with it.

Thinking about it, almost all the information from a new planet is stored within DES's secure database. Everything and everyone who's not on Earth is governed by DES. It's funded and run by all the countries of Earth. Once the Q-net was invented, there was one thing the entire world could finally agree on—when we're off planet, we are not Mexican, Russian, Egyptian, or any "ian", we are Earthlings.

After the explorers leave a new discovery, first responders are sent to construct the base and prep it for the scientists' arrival. They've done this for...at least a hundred planets so far.

Good thing for me, Jarren taught me how to worm into the cluster where DES keeps the survey information. I asked him because I hate not being in the loop. I scan the stats for Yulin. It's the fourth exoplanet orbiting around a G1V star. It's size is about one and a half times the mass of Earth. However, the planet is sixty-eight percent desert. And guess where the Warriors were discovered? Yup. Right in the middle of freaking nowhere...or thirty-four percent from anywhere the least bit interesting. No wonder my parents kept changing the subject.

Small consolation that the air is breathable and the climate is warmer than Xinji. All the Warrior planets have been found in what's called the Goldilocks Zone. Just the right distance from their suns so they aren't too hot or too cold for life. The experts figure that the aliens who transported the Warriors are probably biologically close to humans since it appears their ideal zone matches ours. And yes, the theory is that they are aliens. Unless the dinosaurs developed a way to cross the Galaxy, there's no evidence early man had the ability to ship millions of Warriors hundreds of light years away from Earth.

The other thirty-two percent of Yulin is forests with a variety of insects, flowers, small mammals, etc... I'm sure the biologists are drooling with excitement. The natural resource list is quite small. In fact, the file itself is sparse in details.

I dig for more information and find the personnel list for Yulin. More scientists are traveling from other Warrior planets and will arrive at some future point in time, depending on where they're traveling from. Maybe one of my friends from Wu'an became a scientist and volunteered for Yulin. A girl could hope. Of course, she'd be decades older than me, but a familiar face is always welcome.

Scanning the list of names, I jump when the door behind me hisses open.

"I found the worm," a male voice says.

Oops. I disentangle. My pulse speeds up as I swivel around. A security officer stands in the threshold. The officer is near my parents' age...I think. There's gray in his bristle-short black hair. He seems familiar.

He taps on the portable he's holding. "No back up needed.

Radcliff, out."

I flip between being insulted and being relieved over his comment. Then there's the chagrin mixed with fear over getting caught. Guess I'm not as subtle as I'd thought. Or...the name Radcliff rings a bell. Niall! Figures. He must have ratted me out to his father or uncle or older brother or it could be his great grandfather— with the time dilation you never know.

Officer Radcliff studies me. "Do you realize what you're doing is highly illegal?"

"I wouldn't call it *highly*. I'm not meddling with any of the ship's systems." I try to downplay it before he yells at me for endangering lives or something equally dramatic.

His expression hardens. He is not amused. "Let me ask you another question. Do you want to be confined to your quarters for the rest of the trip?"

Ah. "No." That would be torture.

"Then don't worm into the Q-net again. Understand?"

"Yes."

He waits.

"Uh, yes, sir."

"Good." He sweeps a hand out, gesturing to the hallway. "Allow me to escort you back to your parents."

It's not a request. We walk in silence. When we arrive, my mother is not happy to see us (an understatement). She keeps her temper in check until Officer Radcliff leaves.

"Lyra, it's only been seven days, you can't be bored *already*."

"It's your fault," I say.

"Excuse me?"

Her tone is scarier than getting caught worming. I should have kept my big mouth shut. "I was curious about Yulin."

She softens a bit. "Well now you know what to expect. And now you can help us. *That'll* keep you out of trouble."

Oh no.

"Your father and I have a ton of things to do before we reach Yulin. Seeing as you're so good using the Q-net, you can take over all the tedious tasks."

At that moment, I consider doing something *highly* illegal. Maybe Officer Radcliff would throw me into the brig for the rest of the trip. A girl could hope.

"Lyra?"

I suppress a sigh. "What do you need me to do?"

Turns out it's quite a bit. While the research base is the same rectangle as the others, my parents have to assign labs and decide on housing. In other words, organizing lots and lots of little details. And that is okay. The work makes the days go faster. It keeps me from counting down to the time when I lose my friends forever, and makes my soch-time an actual break where I find creative ways to annoy Niall, like having his avatar tell the zombies that eating people is illegal and they'll be thrown into the brig with a capital B.

When we arrive at the crinkle point on 2472:016, the thrusters are shut down. An eerie silence steals through the ship. It's creepy. Everyone is required to strap into their bunks. I lie in mine, staring at the ceiling, and say good-bye to Lan, Jarren, Belle, and Cyril. A klaxon cuts through the silence, warning us that the BP Crinkler engine is about to be engaged. A second later my world blurs and spins. I close my eyes as nausea swirls in my stomach and I clutch the straps. This repeats a dozen times or so. It's too fast to count and all my energy is on keeping my breakfast down.

We fly fifty years into the future without a sound. Strange, right? You'd think there'd be a boom or a roar. Even a click or snap would be satisfying at least. No. There's nothing.

That is until the Crinkler engine is turned off. As soon as the spinning stops and the walls solidify, fifty E-years' worth of messages, news and important information flood the ship's Q-net. My screen pings and flashes as the thrusters fire up and we sail toward Yulin. I'm reluctant to read what I missed and learn who died—Diamond Rockler is over seventy A-years by now—because once I know, I can't unknow and it becomes real. Now I can still believe nothing has changed.

Yeah, I understand all about denial. What's your point?

Then I realize there is one good thing about the time dilation. It's now 2522:016. I'm fifty E-years closer to my brother. When the next Interstellar Class ship arrives at Yulin in four E-years, it'll probably be heading back toward the other planets since this is the furthest point of populated space. I could eventually travel to the university on Rho. By then Phoenix would be on Earth and I'll be able to actually communicate with him in real time.

My father is sitting at the terminal in our living area with my mother hovering over his shoulder. If they noticed me, they don't show it. The screen is filled with messages, data files, and various information.

"Any new discoveries?" she asks.

"No new Warrior planets," he says, scrolling through the reports. "But they completely reconstructed the damaged Warriors in half of the pits on Xinji."

That's pretty good. Even though the robotic diggers are programmed to clear the sand and dirt from around the Warriors without harming them, they've been buried for over two thousand E-years and, during that time, cave-ins and partial collapses of some of the pits happen.

"What about alien artifacts? Did they find more? Or translate the markings?" She's clutching the back of his chair as if her will alone will bring good news. She could insert her own tangs, but I think she'd rather not be overwhelmed with too much information at once.

"Not that I can find. But don't worry, Ming, there are hundreds of files here, some are encrypted." He hums to himself. "They haven't improved on the BP Crinkler engine yet. We need another scientific breakthrough that fixes the time dilation."

I silently agree.

"What about that file?" Mom points to the screen. "It's marked high importance."

"Dated 2520:289. It might actually be relevant," Dad says.

The desire to bolt pulses through me. Those red arrows never mean good news. But curiosity keeps me in place as my father reads the message.

"Oh no." Dismay colors his voice.

An uneasy feeling swirls in my stomach.

"What's wrong?" Mom leans closer. "Spencer, tell me."

"There hasn't been any communication from Xinji in over an E-year."

My parents exchange a horrified glance. I step toward them on unsteady legs. Did I hear that right?

"No communications at all?" Mom asks.

My dad shakes his head. "No. Xinji has gone silent."

"What do you mean by silent?" I ask, joining them by the terminal. A burning nausea rolls up my throat.

My parents blink at me as if I'd appeared from nowhere.

"Er..." My father clears his throat. "It's probably a communication glitch, Li-Li, nothing to worry about."

I exchange a look with my mother and she raises her eyebrows as if to say "he's only trying to protect you."

But my bubble of denial has already burst. "Planet Gamma went silent and when the Protector Class space ship arrived, they found everyone dead."

"That was due to an incurable disease," Dad says. Spotting my expression, he hurries to add, "There could be a million different explanations. Let me read through these files and see what I can discover." The screen goes blank.

My mother rests her hand on my shoulder. "Did you read through your messages? Maybe your friends mentioned if they were having problems."

I squeeze her hand, grateful for the distraction, even though I haven't received any messages from my Xinji friends before we crinkled. Dead is dead after all and I kept to my side of the agreement and didn't send them any either. But I return to my room.

Not bothering with my tangs, I say, "Show me personal messages sent during crinkle time."

Expecting to see nothing, I'm surprised when messages fill my screen—all from Lan. The first one is dated 2473:364—roughly two E-years after I left—and the most recent one is dated 2520:161—about one and a half E-years ago.

With my heart tapping out distress signals, I select Lan's first message. Might as well read them in order.

2473:364: Hi, Li-Li! I know I'm not supposed to message, but I'm so devastated and I've no one else to talk to! Jarren left today! <sob> His parents finished their biological categorization thingy and they're going to Planet Suzhou to help in the jungles. And just like you, he's not old enough to stay behind. And I can't go with him as I'm not eighteen yet. My parents won't give me permission because DES changed the schedule. This one is going to Suzhou and the next blasted ship (coming in another two E-years from now!) is going to Planet Rho. We couldn't have a funeral for him, because he was put into detention—Jarren was caught worming. Once we figured out there was no way for us to "catch up" to each other, he tried to change the schedule of the Interstellar Class ships so the one to Suzhou wouldn't stop at Xinji until after his eighteenth birthday. Isn't that romantic? <sigh> Yeah, we've been dating this last year (Cyril and Belle hooked up, too). Security escorted Jarren to the shuttle— he's going to spend the trip to Suzhou in the brig! We only had a moment together before he left! <sob> My heart is a pile of shards. Guess I should sweep them into a box, label it and store it on a shelf. I'm not going to be needing it anymore.

Poor Lan. Even though we all know not to get involved in relationships just for that very reason, sometimes the heart refuses to listen. Suzhou is twenty-eight E-years from Xinji. By the time he arrives, she'll be forty-five A-years old if she stays on Xinji. I'm not surprised Jarren ended up in the brig—trying to alter the schedule of an Interstellar Class space ship is what I'd consider *highly* illegal. Plus people could die.

2480:123: Me again. Sorry for the drama in my last message. It's just... tough. Which you know! You're probably not even reading this, but it helps me to get it all out. <shrug> I'm at Brighton University on Planet Rho just about to start my first year. Nervous doesn't even begin to describe my state of mind! And it feels like my intestines have wrapped around my stomach and twisted into a huge knot. <deep breath> Here's something funny... in fact, I can already "hear" your goofy chuckle. Despite my prior adamant claims, I am studying cryptology like my parents. Yeah, I know. But something about those markings on that octagon you found... I just can't shake.

I laugh over her career choice—it's not a goofy chuckle, trust me—and I'm glad she was accepted into the university.

2484:349: Graduation! I made it even though this last year was touch and go for a while. <whew> I'm staying on Rho for the next four E-years since my fiancé, Vint, is continuing his studies. He graduated with a materials science degree—they think they can match the clay in the various Warriors to an exact location on Earth. Not sure why that's important, but he's really cute when he's excited. About his work! You have a dirty mind, Li-Li. Just teasing! Besides I wouldn't use the word "cute" for that, more like steamy.

My chest tightens and I'm not sure if it's embarrassment or jealousy. When I factor in the time dilation for her trip to Rho, Lan was twenty-four A-years when she sent the message.

2492:184: We've been assigned to Xinji! Can you believe it? The place hasn't changed and I keep expecting to run into you. Weird. And just FYI—the kissing zone is still in use. I caught a couple teens there the other day. The boy turned scarlet! Fun.

Fun? I huff. She would have been mortified if she'd been caught.

2503:111: Oh my, I just received a message from Jarren! Remember him? My old love. The poor boy was finally released from two years in detention after arriving at Planet Suzhou and is still in love with me. He's almost twenty and I'm thirty-nine A-years old and have two children! I hated to break his heart again, but it had to be done. Poor boy. Oh, and don't worry, Li-Li, I won't be taking my children away from their friends. We plan to stay on Xinji until the youngest is eighteen A-years old. Too bad I can't convince some of my friends to stay. How can they put their desires over their children? I'm sick of hearing, "we survived and so will they." Have we survived? I'm sure Jarren doesn't think so right now.

Poor Jarren, indeed. If he stayed on Suzhou, he'd be thirty-seven A-years right now. If not, I've no idea of his age. It's enough to give anyone a headache. No wonder DES leaves keeping track of all that up to the Q-net.

2520:161: Exciting news, Li-Li! I figured out what that octagon of yours means! No one believes me. I'm to send my research notes to the other "experts." I'm sure your parents will get the official report with all the details so I won't bore you, but it's been so long since we had any progress on that question mark. I hope when you arrive at Yulin in two E-years, the full mystery will be solved. My life's work has been on figuring out those symbols and I'm sending you my research notes—you might find them amusing since they're like a code within a code—remember when we made up silly codes so Jarren and Cyril didn't know what we were saying? Anyway, I believe I deciphered this hidden code and I will be able to "read" the symbols and find out why the Warriors were transported to so many other planets! I just need the "experts" to agree with me so I can get more funding. <argh> Now I'm sounding just like our mothers. <grin>

I'm so glad Vint and I decided to stay on Xinji after our kids left for university. I'd love if you could send me a message when you get to Yulin. That is if you even read mine and want to communicate with me. I'll be fifty-eight A-years old by then. <ugh> I'm older than your parents so I'll understand if you'd rather not.

I stare at the screen. Thoughts and emotions roll through me. Lan was on Xinji when it went silent. A new type of grief burns in my chest. It's one thing to pretend your friends don't exist, quite another to learn it's true. I slam my palm on my leg. This is why we cut all ties. Pressure builds behind my eyes, threatening to send tears racing down my cheeks. I place my crossed arms on the desk and rest my forehead on them. Letting the sadness wash through me, I consider Lan's life. At least she married and had children. I'm surprised that knowledge actually helps to lessen the grief. Huh? And who knows, maybe there was a communication glitch and she's fine. Ahhh...there's that denial I know and love.

Wiping my eyes, I push to my feet and go back to the living area. My parents are bent close and talking in low voices. I move closer and they jerk back as if caught smooching in the kissing zone. Odd.

"Did you learn anything about Xinji?" Mom asks.

"Lan mentions that she deciphered a code for the alien symbols and might be able to read them, but she didn't explain. She said you were sent a report with all the details. Did you find it?"

Mom's face lights up with excitement. "Not yet."

"Do you know when this was?" my dad asks as he scans through the files.

"The message was dated 2520:161."

"Okay, I'll start at 2518."

"Why so early?" I ask, thinking about the artifact and how quickly the news spread.

He shoots me a sly smile. "Sometimes discoveries are kept secret until more information can be collected. We couldn't do that with your octagon. Your friend Lan told everyone before we could validate the find. And then told them again after we certified it as genuine."

Oops. Dad searches through the files as Mom hovers nervously over his shoulder. If he finds the report, I wonder if he'll share the details with me. I could worm into his messages, that would be easy. But the thought makes me queasy. That would be personal versus worming into DES or the ship's net, which is impersonal. Plus it's DES's fault for leaving those holes in their security for me to worm through.

"Anything?" Mom asks after a couple minutes.

Dad blows out a breath. "Nope. Are you sure of the date, Li-Li?"

"Yes."

"Well maybe it was encrypted. Those take longer to come through."

"What did Lan say *exactly*?" Mom asks.

"Come see for yourself."

She trails me into my room and I open Lan's last missive. I study her as she reads the screen. Her long black hair is pulled back into a sloppy bun and there's dark smudges under her eyes. Except for the color, my eyes are the same as hers. My mother can trace her family tree back to China on Earth. Phoenix takes after Dad, whose family originated in England.

They met in Xi'an, China, Earth. All the archaeologists who wish to be assigned to a Warrior planet have to complete a two-year apprenticeship at Emperor Qin Shi Huang's necropolis, working with the original Terracotta Army. My mother likes to tease my father that she is more of an expert on the Warriors because her ancestors built them—a source of pride.

"She discovered a code," Mom says, more to herself than me. "A code as in those symbols are a language, or a code as a way to decipher the symbols?"

I realize she's asking me. "I don't know."

"Do you still have those codes you created with Lan?"

"Probably. Why?"

"It will give us an insight into how Lan thought. It might help us figure out how Lan approached the puzzle. What may have triggered her epiphany. Might is the key word. We're assuming Lan didn't change much as she matured. We've no idea who Lan the adult was."

Was. I grab her arm. "Did you find out...are they all...dead?"

"I don't know what happened. I didn't mean to imply that."

"But you think it?"

She rubs a hand over her face. "I do. I'm sorry."

"Why are you sorry? It's the truth." My throat tightens as I clamp down on my emotions.

Crouching next to me, she says, "It's a mom thing. I don't want to cause you pain and there's a chance I'm wrong. In fact, I'd *love* to be wrong." She lowers her voice. "Don't tell your father that."

"I won't." We share a sad smile.

Mom glances at the time. "You better hurry, Lyra. You don't want to be late for soch-time."

No way I'm leaving now.

When I open my mouth to protest, Mom raises a slender eyebrow. "Unless you enjoyed cleaning out the galley's food trap?"

I bite down on a growl. That happened seven days ago and I still can't wash the stink of rotten food from my sweater. "It was only three minutes. Don't you think that's an excessive punishment for being three minutes late?"

"Late is late, Lyra." She shoos me out.

Arriving at the rec room two minutes early—and where's my reward for being there early? If you're going to punish lateness, then you should reward earlyness. My mother's practical voice sounds in my head. *Not being punished* is *your reward, Lyra.* And then she adds, *Earlyness is not a word.* Pah.

The mood is downright grim among the older kids from Xinji. The quartet of girls sit in a circle and lean so close together their foreheads are almost touching. Niall is in his spot reading from a portable.

Playing a game holds no appeal for me and the babysitter is busy tending to the younger kids who don't know what's going on, but can sense the change in atmosphere and are cranky. I take advantage of her distraction and worm into DES's database through the game system, looking for information on Xinji. Shrinking the image down to the right bottom corner, I pull up a random game to cover the rest.

I'm extra careful this time, covering my tracks. My first discovery—there's thousands of files, messages, and data that was sent to DES from Xinji before it went silent. Ugh. My second—they named the octagon after me—well, sort of. It has an official designation, but in parenthesis is "LTD's octagonal artifact." I'm rather proud, until my imagination kicks in. What if Lan translated the alien script on the artifact and it led them to some forgotten chamber that was booby trapped with a fatal virus and it killed everyone on the planet? It would be my fault. Now, I'm horrified.

"You just can't stop, can you?" Niall asks.

No longer reading, Niall is looming over me. He's wearing

black jeans and a tight T-shirt—a good look for him except for the I'm-pissed-off-crease dug into his brow. "You've no idea just how dangerous it is to worm into DES. You could endanger everyone's life."

"That's bull. My activities are far from the ship's systems."

"It's all connected, you—"

I jump to my feet, cutting him off. "Watch it or you might say something you'll regret." He's about thirteen centimeters taller than me, but I get close enough to smell his shampoo—sage grass.

A spark of...anger?...surprise?...exasperation?... maybe all three flashes in his blue-green eyes. The muscles along his shoulders and arms tighten. "Fine. You'll be in the brig soon anyway."

"Because you're going to report me?"

He huffs in derision. "No need, security will figure out what you're doing, and then I won't have to see you ever again." He sits in his chair, pulls out his sketchbook and proceeds to ignore me.

I consider his comments. I've no desire to spend the rest of the voyage in the brig, so I retreat, careful not to leave a trail. Then I pull up my own personal files which include Lan's research file. Now if I'm caught, I'm only breaking soch-time rules.

Reading through the research notes—maybe there's a clue here why Xinji went silent, you never know—I scan page after page and learn that cryptology is...well, cryptic, and I would need a four-year university degree to translate her...er...translations. Why did she think I'd find them amusing? And she flagged what appears to be hundreds of symbols—not just the original sixty-four on the artifact.

I'm scrolling through when a symbol catches my attention. It's...different. It's hard to explain, but after helping my parents with the Warriors for three years, I'm well acquainted with the style of the markings on their uniforms and armor. And this one just clanks. Another page has a series of those strange symbols. I wonder...I pull up the image of my octagon with the eight rows of symbols.

One row on the artifact matches a couple of Lan's symbols. The others appear as if the same...person (for lack of a better word) drew them.

"What's an octagonal artifact?" Niall asks.

I turn my head and meet his questioning gaze. It's better than hostile, and it's the first time he's shown any interest in anything other than his sketches. A snarky retort perches on the tip of my tongue, but maybe he won't report me if I'm nice. Worth a try. "It was found on Xinji and is believed to be extraterrestrial." Best to downplay my involvement.

He huffs. "Yeah, right. And I have a piece of crystalized universe to sell you."

Niall's sarcasm isn't sharp, but I give him extra points for the speed and creativity of his reply.

"Fine. Believe what you want. I really don't care." I return to my search.

After a few moments, he says, "It has to be a hoax. No one has found anything out here except those Warriors."

There's a touch of disappointment in his tone, but I ignore him and decide to access the public cluster about the Warriors, seeking a report or file about the symbols. Nothing. I'm not too surprised. The Warrior Project's been collecting vast amounts of data but they don't have enough people to analyze it.

Silence alerts me that soch-time is over. Exiting the Q-net, I stand and stretch my back. Then I freeze. Niall is still in his chair. He's always the first person to bolt. Yet he's staring at me.

"That was interesting," he says.

I shrug. "Like you said, it's a hoax."

"Then why did you risk going to the brig to investigate it?"

Another shrug despite the spike in my heart rate over *brig*. "Boredom."

"Being in my company isn't entertaining enough?"

His outrageous comment surprises a laugh from me. "No, your company is far from entertaining."

"Ouch," he deadpans.

"You'll live." I leave before he can counter. What was that all about? Did he truly think that highly of himself or does Niall have a sense of humor? Must be his ego—I can't envision him ever laughing.

Over the next four days, the mood in the ship returns to almost normal. The little kids are no longer so upset and while there are still morose expressions, there is laughter as well. I help my parents and attend soch-time. Niall has reverted back to ignoring me and that's fine. It's more than fine. It's perfect. I play games and he sketches or reads.

The afternoon of the fifth day my mother tasks me with organizing the supply list. After a Warrior planet is discovered, DES sends a ship with all the needed equipment to establish a research base. They build the structures, unpack the furniture, and install the power so when the scientists show up, everything is ready to go. They also deploy the robotic diggers to excavate the pits. If the pit has collapsed, then they clear out the dirt and/or sand that has buried the Warriors. The pits are really underground caverns to prevent them from being exposed to moisture and sunlight. But they're called pits at Xi'an on Earth so they're labeled the same. However, once the construction crew leaves, they shut down the diggers as they need to be frequently maintained—sand gets into the mechanism and ruins the equipment.

In the meantime, my parents want to know exactly what is at the base. The list the construction team sent included every single thing, including how many nails they had. The problem— there are no categories. It's a mess, with the number of nails listed with the number of spoons. Ugh.

I glance at my bed. Perhaps a nap first? A chime sounds, signaling a visitor. Not an unusual occurrence. Muffled voices travel through my door and I return to my contemplation. Maybe I should take my pile of dirty clothes down to the washers first.

A knock on my door startles me.

My father pokes his head in. "Li-Li, there's someone here to see you."

There is? Odd. I follow him out and stop dead. Officer Radcliff is waiting with my mother. She doesn't look angry, but she doesn't look happy either. Does it matter? He's here to see me, which means I'm in trouble. Has security traced my worm into DES or has Niall ratted me out? Yeah, it was very stupid of me to do that in front of Niall, but still. My fear mixes with anger.

Dad stands next to Mom—a united front. That confirms it. I'm in big trouble.

"**G**o on," my mother says to Radcliff. "Ask her."

I brace for his accusation about illegal worming into DES's data banks—next time I see Niall, I'm going to break his pencil. Plus I won't be able to lie to Radcliff— not in front of my parents!

He tugs his shirt as if he needs something to do with his hands. Fear creeps back in. At least in the brig, I won't have to organize a supply list.

"We need your help," he says.

Thrown, I stare at him. "For what?"

"There are files missing from Xinji's reports during that last year. We think they might help explain why the planet went silent."

"And you want *me* to find them? Don't you have..." I gesture at his uniform. "People for that?"

"Of course we have people," he snaps.

Mom frowns at him and he draws in a deep breath. "Our

people were unsuccessful. We are hoping that your…unconventional methods will have better luck."

In other words, legal worming! I suppress a grin as I act like I'm thinking about it. Let him sweat a bit. "I'm going to need access to a better terminal."

"I'm under the impression that you don't need one," he says with a gleam in his eyes.

He knows about my activities during soch-time. Damn Niall—I'm gonna kill him. I wave a hand toward my room. "The terminals here are not up to the task."

Amusement relaxes his stern features. "You'll have access to *my* terminal on the bridge."

All moisture leaves my mouth. The bridge! Oh. My. Stars.

"Of course, I'll be monitoring you."

Oh. Not as much fun.

"Will you help us?" he asks.

"Yes."

Proud beaming emanates from both my parents. Guess there is a first time for everything. Officer Radcliff looks at me expectantly.

"Now?" I ask.

"Unless you have other pressing matters to attend to?"

His humor is so dry, I almost sneeze. I meet my mother's gaze.

"The supply list can wait," she says.

Oh joy.

Then she adds, "Lan's full report on the alien artifact is part of those missing files, Lyra."

In other words, this is important. Got it. I don't want all of Lan's hard work to be for nothing. I nod importantly and the adults appear satisfied.

I follow Officer Radcliff through the ship's corridors. He stays to the public areas and doesn't say a single word. I pay close attention when we enter through a door marked Restricted. Now the hallways are not as nice. Black scuffs mark the walls and the pipes and wires in the ceiling are exposed. The air smells of burnt rubber and oil.

We reach a set of metal steps that spiral upwards.

"Steps?" I ask as I follow Radcliff. "Why not an elevator?"

"Would you want the captain of the ship to be unable to reach the bridge if the power goes out during an emergency?" he asks.

"No."

"Plus they're easier to defend."

"Ah."

The steps empty into a landing. Two armed officers stand to each side. We cross into a large half-moon shaped room. The lights are dim. A handful of people work at terminals along the back wall that bookends the entrance. There's a giant screen covering the entire front curved wall. It shows... Pulled by an invisible force, I step closer. That's not a screen.

The Big Fat Frog doesn't have windows—or so I thought—for safety reasons, yet the blackness on the other side is alive. Points of light burst and swirls of yellow streak and reddish orange globs glow. I've seen pictures of the Milky Way Galaxy before, but they are a child's crude sketch in comparison to this... awesomeness.

"Beautiful, isn't it?" a male voice asks next to me.

I jump a meter.

"Sorry," he says then holds out his hand. "Captain Abraham Harrison."

I gape. He's exactly what an Interstellar space ship captain should look like. Tall, muscular, with just enough gray in his short brown hair to instill confidence, but not enough to worry he'd have a heart attack enroute to the next planet. Intelligence and competence fog the air around him and I realize I'm staring and my insides turn to liquid as I clasp his extended hand with my own cold fingers. "Lyra Daniels." I suppress a wince at the slight squeak in my voice. We shake and he releases my hand. It tingles.

"Welcome to my bridge, Miss Daniels. Thank you for being willing to help us. We're all worried about the people on Xinji as I'm sure you are as well."

Unable to trust my voice, I nod importantly—seems to be my go-to response when I'm overwhelmed and surrounded by adults.

The captain switches his attention to Officer Radcliff. I almost sway with relief.

"Tace, make sure she has everything she needs," Captain Harrison says.

"Yes, sir." Radcliff sweeps an arm out, indicating the far left corner. "This way, Miss Daniels."

Oh, so it's Miss Daniels now. I flash a grateful smile at the captain and just about faint when he grins back. He puts

Diamond Rockler to shame.

We approach a dark-haired man who is sitting at a terminal. His back is to us.

Radcliff taps him on the shoulder. "I'm back."

Without turning around, the man says, "There's a glitch in camera two-oh-seven. Do you want me to check it out?"

Recognizing the voice, I suck in a breath. Niall.

"Yes," Radcliff says.

Niall stands in one fluid motion, relinquishing the seat as he removes his tangs. He steps back and freezes when he spots me. "What is *she* doing here?" he asks with a hint of surprise in his voice.

Nice acting job. Niall knows exactly what I'm doing here. I glare at him.

"Miss Daniels is helping me. Go check on two-oh-seven."

Niall stiffens. "Yes, Dad." He brushes past me without another word.

Dad? I figured they were related, but Radcliff being Niall's father seems like a betrayal. I know, weird right? Although it figures. Like father like son.

Radcliff inserts his tangs and accesses DES's database. "Now what?"

"Your way didn't work, remember? Let me sit down," I instruct.

He faces me. "I'd rather you tell me what to do."

"It won't work that way. It's..." I search for the right word. "Instinctual."

"That doesn't make sense."

I shrug. "It's called worming for a reason. I find the small gaps in the Q-net by...feel. I'm like a blind earthworm in the dirt, and I just have to squirm my way through it without creating ripples so you don't know I'm there."

He opens then closes his mouth. "Squirm?"

"Yeah. There's so many layers that it's a tight fit to go from one to the other."

Radcliff sighs, but relinquishes his seat. I insert my entanglers. Wow, this terminal is like diving into the deep end of the pool.

"Can I trail you?" he asks.

"No. It's going to be tough enough for me to get through." As far as the Q-net goes, I'm spelunking in mostly unknown territory.

"Then keep the screen on."

I do as requested. Radcliff remains behind me as I worm into DES's files. It takes a fraction of the time compared to using the rec room's game system. After ten minutes, I find the cluster where the files should be. The gaps in data stand out like missing teeth. There's an...echo of them and, if I can follow that echo, I'll locate the files.

Except it's a strange echo. The tone is wrong. Foreign. The person who moved the files entered the Q-net from...well, I don't even know. He or she is good. Very good. And when I hunt down the files' new cluster, there's nothing there but a clean sheen, which means they've been deleted. I drum my fingernails on the armrest. Nothing is ever really deleted in the Q-net. And there's a...residue, but it's beyond my abilities to translate. I try a few tricks I'd learned. Nothing.

"Well?" Radcliff asks.

I explain.

"Do you know who deleted the files?"

"No."

"Can you speculate?"

In other words, can I rat out my cohorts? While I'm flattered he thinks I'm a member of one of the nefarious worming gangs, I'm just a dabbler. All my knowledge came from Jarren and his from Warrick. Thinking about them triggers a memory. When Jarren taught me that deleting just re-positioned files, he mentioned that a few people know how to bury the files deep, leaving only a residue, but I can't recall his actual instructions.

"Miss Daniels?"

"No. The identity of the person is beyond my skills, but there still might be a way to get those files."

"How?"

"I have a friend who might be able to help if he's not in transit to another planet." And if he even remembers me or wants to talk to me.

"I guess that will have to do." Radcliff moves to my side. "I'll locate him for you."

"No need." This terminal is rated at such a high level, I'm able to pinpoint his location without having to worm. Jarren is still on Planet Suzhou and he's thirty-seven A-years old. I send him a text message through the Q-net. It'll still take time—there's relays and space-time frequencies involved, but that's not my area of expertise. I'm just glad "real time" communications are possible. The bigger question mark is *if* he replies.

"I'll let you know if I hear from him." I stand up.

Radcliff grumbles. "See that you do." He tilts his head toward the stairway. "I'm sure you can find your own way out."

I can. Does that mean he trusts me?

"Don't worry if you get lost, Miss Daniels. I always know when someone is where they shouldn't be and will send one of my officers to *rescue* you."

And that would be a no on the trust thing. As he settles in his seat, I wonder if he realizes that he has just issued me a challenge to infiltrate those restricted areas without getting caught. The cameras and sensors that are installed throughout the ship are far easier to worm into than bypassing DES's security.

I grin at the back of his head. Challenge accepted.

Crossing the bridge, the Galaxy once again captures my attention. I slow to a stop as I marvel.

"This is why we don't have windows anywhere except here. No one would get any work done," Captain Harrison says in a joking tone.

"Really?" I ask even though I'm half-distracted and unable to tear my gaze away.

"No. All the bridge officers eventually get used to it. Safety is the real reason Interstellar Class ships don't have windows." He sweeps a hand out. "There's lots of bits floating around in the universe and when you're traveling as fast as we are, those small pieces become lethal projectiles when a ship hits them at speed. Our titanium hull can withstand the impacts, unlike glass."

"But your window…"

"Not glass. Transparent lonsdaleite."

"Lonsdaleite?"

"It's a hexagonal diamond and fifty-eight percent harder than a regular diamond. Expensive, but it won't crack."

Interesting. I turn to him. "Why do you even have a window on the bridge? You don't need it to navigate."

"No we don't." His blue eyes spark with humor. Captain Harrison leans closer and lowers his voice. "The DES's recruiters tell everyone if they join the fleet, they'll *see* the universe. If that wasn't here, I'd have a mutiny on my hands."

A few of his crew huff in amusement and I'm smart enough not to believe him.

"There's also a powerful magnifier in the lonsdaleite. What you see there is thousands of light years away." He straightens. "Were you successful, Miss Daniels?"

I explain about the files being deleted.

"That's more than we had a few hours ago." He studies me and I resist the urge to squirm. "Have you ever thought about becoming an interstellar navigator?"

Caught off guard, I blurt, "No. Why?"

"Navigators have to be experts in accessing and manipulating the Q-net. According to Officer Radcliff, you have an impressive skill in this area already."

"I…I never considered it."

"How about a bribe?"

What? Who is this guy?

He laughs at my expression. "If you'd like to learn more about what it's like to be a navigator, I'll introduce you to our chief who will arrange what we call short-term internships for teens who have potential. There are more and more Interstellar Class ships being built, but finding crew is getting harder and harder. We already recruited Tace's son Niall. He's been a ship rat all his life and he's going into security."

"No surprise," I mumble.

"Excuse me?"

"Ah... How long would the internship be? My parents—"

"Yours would only be for the rest of the trip to Yulin—sixty days or so for a couple hours a day."

"Is the bribe about not having to go to soch-time? In that case, sign me up."

"Sorry, no. The bribe is you can come up here and stare out that window whenever you want as long as you stay out of the way."

Wow. That is a heck of a bribe. "I'll think about it."

"Good. Now, if you'll excuse me..."

"Of course."

He strides over to one of his officers. I'm surprised he even took the time to talk to me. I gaze out the window one more time, drinking it in before I leave. How could anyone get used to that view? I've no memory of my trip back to our quarters. My thoughts swirl with all I learned. Why would someone delete those files? Me a navigator? Would Jarren reply? What happened to Xinji? A navigator?

When I enter our quarters, my mother is at the terminal, but she stops working.

"Where's Dad?" I ask.

"In a meeting with the chemists. How was the bridge?"

I'm impressed. She showed considerable restraint by not pouncing right away over the files. Then I gush over the view, the captain, the view and the captain again. Hey, I'm seventeen A-years old, I'm allowed. Her loving amusement fades when I mention the internship with the navigator.

Instead, a whole gamut of emotions flit over her face before she settles on a careful curiosity. "And what did you tell Captain Harrison?"

"That I'll think about it."

She winds a strand of hair around her fingers. "It's a wonderful opportunity. Are you interested in being a navigator?"

"I don't know enough about it. But I'm willing to find out just for access to that view. Have you ever seen it?"

"I did when we traveled from Earth to our first assignment on Taishan. The crew used to allow the passengers to take tours of the bridge during non-critical times."

I wait, but she doesn't elaborate. "What happened to make them stop?"

"It was a security thing. Not everyone can handle the realities of the time dilation. And now people are given a full psyche eval to see if they're cut out for space travel." Mom pulls me into a hug. "Whatever you decide to do, we'll support you,

Lyra."

I squeeze her back and she releases me. "Thanks."

"Just be aware that flight crews leave all their friends and family who are not on board their ship far in the past. We'll never see you again."

Ah, yeah. There's that. "I'm still going to Yulin with you. And if I do the internship, it will keep me busy and out of trouble."

Mom cocks her hips and crosses her arms into a familiar posture. "Why do I not believe that?"

"It's called denial, Mom. Once you embrace the concept, you can believe anything."

She laughs her light trill that resonates with me like I've been wrapped in a warm blanket. It's a sound I've only heard a few times since Phoenix left.

"Did you find those files?" she finally asks.

"Sort of." I explain.

"Let's hope Jarren comes through. In the meantime…"

I'm already heading to my room. "Yeah, yeah. The supply list isn't going to organize itself." I stop with my hand on the door handle. Why can't the list organize itself? From what I've just seen, the Q-net should be able to do it. I turn around. My mother has returned to work. Did she assign me busy work, or does she not know? I'd have to ask her after I complete the task so she can't accuse me of using delay tactics, which I might have tried a few times in the past. Without success. But this time, I'm looking forward to the chore.

Of course my terminal is useless for what I want to do. I

need deeper access, like through the forgotten terminal that's tucked away, but Officer Tace Radcliff would swoop down on me even though what I'm doing isn't illegal...or, at least I don't think it is. The urge to take a chance pulses in my veins. I could worm straight for the cameras and erase my passage to the terminal and then... But what if I'm caught? The captain would rescind his offer and I might end up in the brig after all.

Better not risk it. I guess I'll use the game terminal in the rec room. Huh. First time that I'm looking forward to soch-time.

The next day, I'm five minutes early for soch-time—a personal record. I even arrive before Niall and I briefly consider taking his seat. Normally, I would do it in a heartbeat just to bug him, but not today.

I hurry to access the Q-net and transfer the supply list from my terminal. Now what? Worming into an empty cluster that's deeper than the surface programs that do the basic plug and chug type work that everyone has access to, I drag the list down with me. Now what? I think *reorganize* and the cluster rips it into a million bits, but they don't go far, they fog around, filling the cluster. I concentrate on *kitchen*. Movement as lines of text form. Row after row of kitchen items. Woo hoo! Next is *construction* and the nails list with the hammers and screws. The *laboratory equipment* column goes on for quite a while. And then I no longer have to do any prompting as the Q-net "gets it" and takes over, putting the proper items in the right groups. In a heartbeat, it's done. Wow.

I save it to my personal cache then pull up Lan's research data file and spend the next hour developing a headache as I try to understand what those symbols mean besides the fact they're similar to the ones on my octagon.

"You can't disrupt soch-time," the babysitter's shrill voice cuts through my concentration. "It's illegal."

"I've permission from the captain," Officer Radcliff says.

Both are dangerously close. I quickly enlarge the game to cover the entire screen before I turn my head.

Officer Radcliff is standing by Niall's chair, ignoring the babysitter's flutterings. His gaze is on Niall's sketchbook—now closed on his lap. Radcliff's expression is ugly.

"Is this what you *do* with your soch-time?" Radcliff asks his son.

Niall doesn't say a word. He's still and holding his pencil with a death grip as if his father has aimed a weapon at him.

"You're supposed to be *socializing*." Radcliff's anger is clear.

"They are," Babysitter says. "They play games all..." She trails off when Radcliff turns his glower on her.

I use the opportunity to add another character to the game. Then I make a quick decision that I'll probably regret later.

"Officer Radcliff," I say, standing up.

"What?" he practically growls.

"Can you settle a dispute for us?" I ask.

His posture radiates suspicion, but he nods.

"Niall's sketching out the map of the dungeon under King Toad's fortress, and I think that's cheating. That the intention of the game is for us to be able to learn how to navigate the labyrinth as we go. Like with trial and error versus mapping it out. What do you think?"

"I...er...think that if you have a map, you should use it. Why risk running into trouble or a dead end—which would be bad if you're being chased—if you don't have to?"

"That's what I told her," Niall says, catching on quick. "We can save our lives for the final battle against Queen Mouse."

Niall's sketchbook is now open to the page that looks like a map, although I've no idea what it really is—I'm just glad I remembered seeing him work on it. I snatch it up so his father can't get a closer look. "Okay, okay, you made your point. I'll use your stupid map." Grumbling, I return to my chair.

"No more games today, Miss Daniels," Radcliff says.

My heart plunges to my stomach. Did he suspect? I wait.

"Your presence is required on the bridge."

Relief courses through me until I remember Niall's comment about the brig.

"Now?" the babysitter asks. "It's highly unusual and there's fifty minutes left."

Does soch-time trump captain's orders?

"Yes, now."

I turn off the game system. Before following Radcliff, I hand Niall his book—now closed.

When I catch up to Radcliff, I ask, "Has Jarren—"

"Not here," he says.

We arrive at the bridge without saying another word. I'm drawn to the window, but Radcliff grabs my elbow, guiding me to his terminal. He points to the chair. I sit.

"There's a message from your friend, but we can't open it."

Pulling up the file, I smile. In order to open the message, I have to answer a question correctly. *What did Belle inherit?*

I reply, *a terracotta vase.*

The message appears on the screen.

2522:022: Hello, Lyra! It was a nice surprise to get your message. The short answer to your problem is yes, those files are recoverable. The long answer, no, I can't tell you how to do it. It would be too complicated to explain to you from this distance. Plus you know how it's more of a... feel than following actual instructions. I can uncover them for you. However, I need permission to access the Q-net. My worming activities have landed me in detention a few <cough> dozens of times throughout the E-years (see what happens when you're not around with a handy passcode) <smirk>. Even though I'm not in detention at the current moment, I've been banned from anything deeper than basic communications. I heard about Xinji and really want to help.

"Passcode?" Radcliff asks.

"He's joking."

"Uh huh. I've looked into your friend's records. He's been in and out of detention for illegal worming most of his life. Are you sure he's the only one able to get those files?"

"Do you know anyone else?" I'm being serious, but Radcliff

shoots me a warning glare. "He has friends on Xinji, he's concerned about them, too."

"All right, I'll grant your friend access, but he's to direct those files to me and no one else."

I swallow a protest as I send Jarren a reply.

Radcliff dismisses me with a curt, "If you hurry, you can attend the last fifteen minutes of soch-time."

That is so not happening. I spend the time pressed against the window. Never seeing my family again might just be worth this view.

"See that little speck right there?" Captain Harrison asks.

I don't jump quite as high this time. How can a big man like that move without making a sound?

"There are millions of specks," I say.

"Billions just in the Milky Way," he corrects. "But..." He shines a laser pointer at a dot of white light in the upper right-hand side. "That's Yulin's sun. We'll be there in sixty-four days."

Wow. "What's next after Yulin for you?"

"We travel to Planet Theta to drop off supplies and then to Maoming to refuel."

"Why do you do it?" The question pops from my mouth before I can stop it.

"To explore the Galaxy. To see the future. To run away from the past. To have a grand adventure. Take your pick."

"But we haven't found anything exciting. Just those Warriors that were made on Earth."

"Allegedly. Someone transported them to all those planets. I believe we're going to run into them eventually."

If they aren't extinct. I'm smart enough to keep that thought to myself.

"Have you thought over my offer, Miss Daniels?" Captain Harrison asks.

"Yes. I'd like to learn more about navigation."

"Good. Chief Hoshi," he barks.

A woman bolts from a terminal and stands at attention. "Sir!"

"This is Lyra Daniels, our newest victim...er...potential recruit. See that she has a proper introduction to the fine art of flying through space without getting lost."

"Yes, sir."

He claps me on the shoulder. "Enjoy the view."

The captain leaves me with Chief Hoshi. She studies me and I assess her as well. Short auburn hair, green eyes and a few centimeters shorter than I am, she appears to be around thirty A-years old.

Without warning, Hoshi fires off a series of questions about the Q-net. I answer each one with what I hope is the correct response.

"You'll do. Report to my office at oh-nine-hundred hours every day."

"Where is—"

"Figure it out on your own, Recruit. And don't be alerting security either." Hoshi returns to her station.

Did she just give me permission to worm into security? I believe she just did. Fun. What isn't fun is encountering Niall when I'm spiraling down the stairs from the bridge. I move right to let him pass me, but he blocks my way.

"What?" I demand. I meet his gaze and my hostility drains away. There's a softness in his expression I haven't seen before.

"Thanks," he says. "My dad...doesn't understand about my sketches."

I'd say. "You owe me one."

"I do."

That was too easy. I squint at him. Is he trying to lull me into a false sense of security?

Niall half smiles. "King Toad?"

I half shrug. "You inspired me."

He presses a hand to his heart. "Ouch."

"You'll live."

He moves out of my way. "See you around, Queen Mouse."

2522:022

My parents exchange a concerned look when I inform them of my internship. We're in the main room of our quarters and getting ready to head to the galley for dinner.

"As long as your grades remain high," Mom says.

"And it doesn't interfere with soch-time," Dad adds.

You'd think I'm borderline feral the way everyone keeps harping on about soch-time. Believe it or not, I am able to hold a conversation with another human being. Sheesh.

After dinner—a disgusting grayish-brown lump that was supposed to be meatloaf, there is nothing worse than ship food—I go to my out-of-the-way terminal. My heart is beating fast with anticipation. Or it might be fear or anxiety—probably all three as I didn't want to fail my first assignment from Chief Hoshi.

As soon as I worm in to the Q-net, I tweak the camera so it shows an empty room and erase the prior thirty seconds of yours truly entering. Then I set up an alarm on the hallway in case anyone comes to investigate. I don't want any surprises this time. It doesn't take me long to find Chief Hoshi's office. Of course it's in a restricted area. I find the cameras along my route and set them to turn off when I'm going to be walking toward the Chief's office and return to a live feed once I've passed by and am out of sight. As long as my timing is right, I should be like a ghost to security. Fun.

Finishing up, I cover my tracks and leave, returning to my room. Even though the ship's lights mimic a twenty-four hour light schedule and it's dark, I can't sleep. Nervous excitement courses through my veins like data streams in the Q-net. Giving up on sleep at oh-five-hundred, I dress and wander through the quiet semi-dark corridors. It's only when I'm halfway up the steps to the bridge do I realize where I'm going. I freeze in place. Did I set off any alarms by being in the restricted area? An image of Radcliff bolting out of bed, strapping on his weapons and running to protect the captain flashes in my mind. It's a laughable scenario since that wouldn't be very effective. I could reach the captain before he—

"Are you going to stand there all night?" a female voice asks.

I look up the steps and a security officer is peering down at me. Oh. I forgot about them. "I...um..."

"While this is an unconventional time for a visit, you've been given permission to be here, Miss Daniels. Unless you're in need of assistance?" Her brown hair is short and is tightly curled and her skin is a lovely chestnut color. I guess she's in her early twenties.

"No, Officer…"

"Keir."

"I just…" I shrug sheepishly. "Want to see the universe."

She smiles. "Not a surprise. That's why I request bridge guard duty."

"Captain Harrison says you get used to the view."

"Not me. Not yet anyway and I hope I never do."

I agree. "Something that awesome should never be taken for granted."

"Well said." Keir returns to her post.

I finish the climb and enter. The room is at half-light…no. It isn't. Artificial light spills from the screens. The rest is from the universe. I thought it was bright before, but this is incredible. Pulled to the window by an invisible force, I walk by the crew, who ignore me as if I'm already part of the scenery. Finding a spot next to the window that is out of the way, I squirm into a comfortable position. And I marvel until I fall asleep right there on the floor.

Even though Radcliff's voice is pitched low, it's loud enough to rouse me from my dreams. "…sure about this? With the extra knowledge she might end up like her friend, spending the bulk of her life in a brig."

Fully awake now, I feign sleep. Is he talking about me?

"Not with the right guidance. I doubt her friend had the same opportunity," Captain Harrison says. "Besides, her school records indicate she excels at problem solving."

They do?

"Are you sure it didn't say she's good at *causing* problems?"

Hey!

"You're grumpy this morning, Tace." The captain sounds amused.

"Spent all of last night trying to track down a worm."

Oh no, I'd hoped to avoid drawing his attention.

"Oh?"

"She's getting better."

And I'd hoped he wouldn't notice that either. Strike two.

"That's good," the captain says. "She's going to need those skills to keep up with the Chief."

Radcliff groans. "May I remind you of this conversation when you order me to throw her into the brig?"

The captain chuckles. "I don't know why you're asking for permission. You know you'll remind me even if I say no."

"Someone has to keep your ego in check, sir."

"Don't you have work to do?"

"Yes, sir." And this time Radcliff chuckles.

The man actually knows how to laugh? Wonders never cease.

"If you hurry, Miss Daniels, you'll have time for breakfast before reporting to the Chief," the captain says.

Caught faking sleep and eavesdropping on their conversation, I open my eyes and meet his gaze. Humor and not censure stares back at me. I surge to my feet in relief.

"Thank you, sir," I say.

"That's what I'm here for. Most people think I'm in charge of an Interstellar Class space ship, but I'm really here to provide wake up calls for my passengers."

Ohhh. A nice touch of sarcasm. I flash him a grin. As I head for the stairs, one of his crew calls, "Can I put in a wake up request for oh-four-hundred, sir?"

"You're not a passenger, Hector," Captain Harrison counters.

"He's not?" another asks. "You mean he's *supposed* to be doing *work*?"

"Ha. Ha. Not funny," Hector says.

Their banter fades as I hustle down the steps. Do all the space ship crews have this camaraderie or just this one? Does it depend on the captain's personality?

I have enough time to eat, check in with my parents and sprint for the Chief's office. Entering the restricted area at precisely oh eight forty-five, I slow my pace to match the schedule I'd programmed for the cameras. I arrive at Chief Hoshi's office at oh eight fifty-nine. One minute early.

Her office is small and cluttered. There's a projection of a star map on one wall. She stands when I enter.

"This way, Daniels." She leads me to another room down the hall. There are a number of terminals inside, but no screens. A few people are already working. The place stinks of body odor and sweat. Ugh.

Hoshi sits in an empty terminal and pats the one next to her. "Have a seat, Daniels. Please access the Q-net."

I do as instructed and— Oh. My. Stars. There's no restrictions here. All the levels of the Q-net are available. It's like the entire universe is at my disposal.

"See me next to you?" she asks.

"Yes." My voice cracks.

"Okay. Show me what you can do."

Already overwhelmed, I freeze with panic.

"Relax. Start with communications. I assume you can access your messages?"

Oh. Taking in a breath, I access my personal account, then broaden to the ship's data files, security cameras, the captain's log—that ought to be interesting.

"Keep going," Hoshi orders.

I reach DES's main database and the wealth of information that is accessible makes my heart race like I just fell into a vat of sugar. It's like finally having the map to King Toad's dungeon when before I'd just been stumbling my way around in the dark.

"Not bad. Can you go deeper than DES?"

"Deeper? There is no—"

"Think of the Q-net like a giant ocean. Everyone can access the surface. Messages, basic plug and chug programs, some data clusters. Just underneath that shallow surface layer sits DES's data banks with all the information stored from all the planets, but they're still not that deep, and beyond that are the star roads. It's where the Q-net keeps track of where all the space ships are in space-time, where they're going, what areas of the Galaxy they're crinkling, and when they arrive. That's what you need to access in order to navigate and navigators must follow the star road mapped out for their ship by the Q-net."

That's cool, but... A question hovers on the tip of my tongue. I hesitate, then decide to risk upsetting the Chief. "If the Q-net is mapping out the course, why do the ships need navigators?"

"Would you trust your life to the Q-net?" Hoshi asks.

"Yes. People make mistakes all the time."

Her laugh is light and musical. "True. But what happens when someone like your friend worms into the navigation commands and changes a few parameters?"

"Uh, bad things happen?"

"An understatement. The consequences will be monumental. The ripple effect will destroy hundreds of ships if we're lucky."

"And if you're not?" I whisper.

"Everything."

And I complain about the pressure to get to soch-time on time. This is... Terrifying.

Hoshi is quiet for a while, then she says, "In order to prevent 'bad things from happening,' each ship has navigators to cross-check the information and ensure the ship is following the star road and to report any deviations so the Q-net can make adjustments to all the ships."

"Deviations?"

"Like when the engines don't keep the correct speed due to a maintenance problem or a strong solar wind knocks us slightly off course. Don't look so scared, Daniels. We do have some wiggle room and there are four of us so we're monitoring the parameters constantly."

It's hard not to be scared, especially when I consider all the holes in the Q-net. "What if someone tries to worm into your navigation?"

"That's why we have security. Not only to keep the people on board safe, but to prevent that from happening."

Uh oh. "But I've—"

"Been worming. We know. Officer Radcliff's been tracking your activities."

Not a comforting thought. "Am I going to get into trouble for rigging the security cameras this morning?"

"No. That's on me. I was curious to see if you could do it."

Lovely.

"Relax, Daniels. You've been mostly playing around on the surface and couldn't have gotten into any dangerous areas through the game system. If there was any chance of that, Officer Radcliff would have thrown your ass in the brig by now."

We still have sixty-three days until we reach Yulin. "Officer Radcliff's son thinks I'll end up in there eventually."

"I hope not. I've eighty credits on the line."

I stare at her. "You've bet on me not going to the brig?"

"Of course, we bet on everything. It helps pass the time."

"Navigating the stars not enough excitement?"

"That's just it. It's so exhilarating that anything else seems...dull in comparison." She leans closer. "And I'm pretty good at betting, so if you stay out of the brig, I'll give you ten percent of my cut."

"No promises," I say.

She laughs. "I like you, Daniels, you'll fit right in here. Now, let me show you the next level."

And with a few instructions, Chief Hoshi guides me past

DES's data banks and into the star roads. Well, not quite. I stand on the edge, peering into the bottomless depths.

After an eternity, she says, "Like I said, the Q-net does all the calculations and maps the roads that we follow. But the ship won't travel anywhere without a human navigator linked into the Q-net. It's like we're the key to starting the engine. I think the Q-net designers didn't want the net to have that much control."

An interesting fact. "How much control do you have? Can you ignore the star roads?"

"Yes."

My terror returns at the implications. "So wormers aren't your only problem?"

"No. However, navigators are frequently assessed for mental health problems. Plus the captain can override a navigator and, if it's not too late, send out a distress which will alert all the other ships."

"Has that ever happened?"

"Once very long ago. No need to worry, we're a quirky bunch, but we're dedicated and we've pledged to transport people across the Milky Way without harm. Not only is it our job, but it is our privilege." She brings me closer to the star roads and points out what a few of the icons mean. "Okay, that's enough for today."

Returning to reality, I blink at the solid walls around me. Was the room this tiny before? With my head spinning, I stand on wobbly legs.

Hoshi cups my elbow to steady me. "You'll get used to it

eventually."

"Does that mean I'll stop feeling like I'm a speck of nothing in comparison to the Q-net?"

"I'd have thought your first glimpse at the universe would have done that?"

I shake my head. Big mistake as pain pounds in my temples. "It's different. At the bridge's window, I'm looking *out* at the stars, but with the Q-net, I'm *with* the stars. Does that make sense?"

"To me and the other navigators, yes. I'm not sure anyone else would understand."

In other words, best to keep that to myself. I step toward the door, but have to grab a chair for a moment.

"Do you need someone to help you back to your cabin?" Hoshi asks.

"I'll be okay, thanks."

"Well?" my mother asks when I return.

"Star roads," I mutter, aiming for my room for a lie down.

She trails after me. "I've heard of them, but the ships are programmed to follow."

"Yeah, but the navigator has to ensure the ship listens."

"Well, I'm sure it's easier than getting a teenaged daughter to listen to her mother," my mother snarks.

If I'd the energy, I'd snark back. And that's a dead giveaway.

"Lyra, what's wrong? You're pale." She presses her lips to

my forehead. "No fever."

I admit to being in pain and she snaps into mother-mode. Giving me a pain-killer, she has me tucked into bed with a cool cloth draped over my forehead in no time.

"Thanks, Mom." Navigating the stars might be exhilarating and challenging, but nothing compares to having your mom take care of you when you're feeling sick.

She squeezes my hand and dims the lights before leaving. I try to nap, but every time I close my eyes, I either see the universe or the Q-net. It feels as though my skull has expanded and my thoughts are no longer content to stay inside my brain. Instead, they follow the star roads.

A few hours later, I drag my butt to soch-time. Niall is already there. He has his sketchbook, but it's closed.

"Hey, Mouse," he says when I sink into a chair.

"Toad," I say. All I can manage.

He huffs in amusement. I slide down in the chair, close my eyes and rest my head on the back.

"Early morning?" he asks.

Since when did he become so chatty? Or did his father tell him about me falling asleep on the bridge? I glare at him. But Niall's attention is focused on his sketchbook. Grunting, I return to my nap. Except I can't sleep now. I sit up straighter, but I'm soon bored. No way I'd access the Q-net right now, not even to check for non-existent messages.

"So what was that…map thing you drew?" I ask.

He opens the book and flips a few pages. "It's the bark of a tree."

"Huh?" I stand and peer over his shoulder. "It's really close up."

"That's pretty smart of King Toad to design his dungeon like the bark of a tree."

He laughs. "King Toad has many talents."

"And a big ego," I mutter. "What else have you drawn?"

"Here." He hands me the book. "See for yourself."

Sensing this might be a big deal for Niall, I act casual as I sit down and flip through the book. Flowers fill one page, a sleeping toddler clutching a stuffed bunny is on another. Flowers? A bunny? Who is this guy and what has he done with Niall? Then a realistic portrait of the captain catches my heart—I try not to drool on the paper. Next is a sketch of the Big Fat Frog orbiting a planet. There are a few sky-scapes of the universe. Guess I'm not the only one who likes to stare out the window.

I glance up and meet his gaze. "These are fantastic."

He shrugs away my compliment.

I reach the last couple pages and stop. He has drawn a few of Lan's symbols. He must have been watching when I scanned through her research. I thought I'd made that section of the screen too small for anyone to read. "Why did you draw these?"

"Curiosity."

"They don't mean anything," I say. "It's just a waste of time."

"Well, when I did a search of DES's database for them, I

found those symbols are on all the Warrior planets and not just on Xinji."

"They're not?"

"You seem really interested in something that is a waste of time," he counters.

"Fine." I draw in a breath to steady my emotions. "Lan was my best friend and those symbols were important to her. She made a huge breakthrough with them, and they might be key in finding out why Xinji went silent." Plus she deserved to be recognized for all that hard work.

"She was on Xinji?"

"Yes."

"Sorry."

Even he thinks they're all dead. Grief swells, lodging in my throat.

"Turn to the last page of the book," Niall says into the silence.

I flip to the end. There's a sketch of the markings on my octagon. I say, "Still think it's a hoax?"

"No. And I think your friend was on to something."

"Yeah, she found a way to decipher those symbols. I was hoping her notes would tell me how she figured it out." Then I realized he'd said he'd been looking into it. I lean forward. "Do you know what they mean?"

"No. But the handful of those symbols that I saw, I found out they're not on all the Warriors, just some of them. I checked DES's security logs, and Lan accessed all the Warrior planets' files. She must have dug through a million images of the

Warriors and found the ones that matched the ones on that octagon. It took her years to do all that research."

"Decades, actually." And wow, that's impressive.

"Maybe if I see the others she included in her research…" He turns his hands up.

Still not sure I trust him, I consider his offer. "Why are you so interested?"

"I've always been fascinated with the Warriors. Not enough to become an archaeologist like your parents, but it's a mystery and this is the only clue. Ever."

True. Plus it can't hurt to have another person look at the images. We scooch the chairs closer to the game screen and despite my earlier intention to stay off the Q-net, I pull up Lan's files. "I can send you the file."

"I'd rather copy them onto paper. There's something about…" He makes a vague circular gesture with his pencil. "…the action of marking paper that just… makes it more real. I know, it sounds stupid." He concentrates on finding a clean page in his book.

"I grew up surrounded by scientists so I've heard stranger things." I bring up the first of many of her research notes. "How do you want to organize it?"

"By shape. The easiest thing to do is find all the glyphs that match the ones in row one and put them together on the same page, marking which planet they came from. Then move on to row two."

"All right." I hesitate.

"What?"

"This would go faster if I use the Q-net to help us sort them. There's hundreds of symbols."

He stills. "That's not for—"

"Passengers, but I'm an intern now."

"You've had one session."

"I'm a fast learner."

He huffs. "If my father shows up with his team, I'm saying you forced me to help you."

"Good luck with that." I take Lan's file into an empty cluster and soon the symbols arrange themselves by which row they match.

Niall copies the swirls and loops of the symbols while I keep an eye out for the babysitter. When he's done with a row, I save the symbols in its own file. Prompted by a strange unsettled niggle in my stomach, I add another layer of security and bury the files deeper in the Q-net. We work in companionable silence until the tone ending soch-time startles me. That was a fast two hours. I shut down the game system.

"Do you want to continue this at another terminal?" I ask him, thinking about the one I used before.

"Can't. I have to report for my security shift and then I need to work on my school assignments. Other than soch-time, I don't have much free time." Seeing my expression, he quickly adds, "Boredom is a killer out here. Some people go crazy when they have nothing to do but think of who they left behind or worry about what might happen on Earth when we skip ahead in time."

Ah. That makes sense. "What happens if one of the crew or

their kids figure out living on a ship isn't for them?"

"If they haven't gotten into trouble before we reach the next destination, they'll go planetside."

"Trouble?"

"Yeah, like illegally worming into the Q-net," Niall teases. "Actually, people get pretty creative when they're bored. Not always a good thing."

"Have you ever lived planetside?"

"No. I was born on a ship and will die on one." He gives me a mock salute and heads to the bridge.

Routine claims the next three days. Mornings with the Chief, followed by staring at the universe, afternoons copying symbols with Niall, and evenings with my parents. On the fourth day, I receive a communication from Jarren. It's encrypted and I answer a bunch of questions in order to access the message.

> 2522:027: Wanted to let you know I found some of those deleted files for Officer Tight Pants—man that guy is Mr. By-the-Book. The files are missing chunks of data and are not complete. I'm still trying to dig more out. I'm sending them to you as well. I don't care what Officer Send-Them-To-Me-And-Only-Me orders. I don't trust him or anyone in security or DES for that matter. Do you really think they're going to tell the truth about why Xinji went silent? I also figured your parents will want to read

these, too. Many of the files are marked to their attention. Be careful, Lyra!

My stomach churns. I'm not supposed to have these files, yet they might help my parents' research. Opening one of them, I scan the contents. Jarren wasn't kidding when he said they're missing chunks—it's more like gaping holes. The file is about the positions of the Warriors—I think—it's almost unreadable. Maybe the others will be better. I'll wait until I have all the files before I decide what to do with them.

2472:034: <groan> I feel like I've just spent seven days chasing echos! This is the last of the files. The rest are gone, which I never ever thought I'd say. Whoever buried them has some mad skills. Better than me! <grumble> <pout> It's probably Osen Vee, she's my idol—that girl can worm and she's never been caught. Unlike me. Even though I was helping Officer Tight Pants, I enjoyed being useful and hopefully helping Lan. I might even be allowed to work in the Q-net again. Supervised, of course, until they trust me. I know what you're thinking, Li-Li! And you'd be right—just don't tell anyone!

I smile as I send him a reply, reminding him of the boring white walls of detention.

Over the next couple days, I debate what to do with the files as my insides turn into knots. My parents really should have them, they're important to figure out what went wrong on Xinji, but to send them to Mom is bypassing the security protocols and I'll be in trouble. What if DES is keeping vital information from my parents? Argh. I take the risk.

I sit at the terminal in our living room that evening. "Mom, I need to show you something."

"Be there in a minute." She's in her bedroom working on her terminal.

The screen fills with one of the missing files.

"What do you need?" she asks, coming into the room.

The buzzer from the door sounds.

"Just a minute." Mom looks at the video screen to see who's standing outside. "It's Radcliff."

In a panic, I clear the screen and retreat from the cluster where I stored all of the lost Xinji files just as Radcliff enters.

"Is Spencer here?" he asks my mom. "I need to update you."

Mom calls for my dad and I'm politely sent to my room. I figure he is finally consulting them about the files. The snatches of murmured conversation I catch with my ear pressed to the door—come on, you'd do it too—confirms my guess. The tightness in my chest eases and my appetite returns. Too bad the food hasn't improved over the last fourteen days.

Those incomplete files dominate my parents' days and all their conversations. I catch snippets of, "maybe they found a new pit," and bits of, "don't know what this means." Frustration laces their tense voices and I've learned not to ask if they've discovered anything new. Not if I want my head to remain attached to my shoulders. I stay in my room as much as possible over the next three days.

In fact, I'm working on some mundane task for my mother, when my dad pokes his head in. "Li-Li, Officer Radcliff wants to talk to you."

This time, I don't panic. After all, I haven't done anything illegal...lately. I follow Dad and stop. Niall is standing—not quite next to his father—more like a step behind as if he's hanging back. Niall's stony expression reminds me of the first time we met. Oh boy, this isn't going to go well.

"I've been informed," Officer Radcliff says to me in his heavy official tone, "that you can get information to...ah...rearrange itself into a more understandable format by using the Q-net. Is this true?"

The desire to glare at Niall burns up my throat, but I keep my gaze on his father. From the corner of my eye, I catch my parents exchanging a concerned look.

Unable to lie, I say, "Yes."

Officer Radcliff's neck muscles tighten and he clenches his fists.

I brace for the lecture if I'm lucky, the brig if I'm not.

"Then I'm afraid we need your help again, Miss Daniels."

My insides just about melt in relief, but I manage to ask, "For what?" with only a slight squeak in my voice.

"The recovered files from Xinji are a mess. They're utterly useless. We are hoping your skills with the Q-net could organize what bits we have into some coherence."

"I can try, but no guarantees that it'll work. It'll depend on the files."

"We would appreciate the effort, Miss Daniels." The words are nice, but his tone holds a sharp edge. And I have the feeling that if I'm not successful, I might still end up in the brig.

As the three of us trek to the bridge, my thoughts are on how I'm going to kill Niall without his father finding out. It might be near impossible, but I can be rather creative when I'm pissed off.

The captain is talking with Chief Hoshi. They glance at us, but continue their conversation at a lower volume.

Great. Probably deciding if my internship should be suspended indefinitely.

After a longing glance at the universe, I sit at Officer Radcliff's terminal. It doesn't take me long to realize that doing one file at a time isn't going to work. I need to access them all at the same time—a job too big for this station. "I need to use the navigator's terminal. The one in that room near Chief Hoshi's office," I say.

"No," Officer Radcliff says.

Shrugging, I stand. "Then I can't help you." I step away, but strong fingers grasp my forearm, stopping me.

"Explain."

"There's not enough data in each file. Many of the reports from the planet have a degree of redundancy and overlap. The Q-net can scan all the files at once and group all similar information together."

"Stay here." Radcliff joins Captain Harrison and Hoshi. They lean together like a bunch of teenagers gossiping.

I ignore Niall, opting to gaze out the window while the adults have their discussion.

But he can't take a hint and moves closer to me. "I'm sorry."

Apology not accepted. Shifting, I turn more of my back to him.

"I tried to keep you out of it by doing it on my own," Niall says. "But like you said, you can't do it from here and my dad...wouldn't give up until I explained how I learned about it. And I thought it was more important to find out what happened to Xinji...to your friend than protecting you."

He just had to go and ruin a good sulk with his logic. Of course Xinji was more important and I'm a selfish idiot. Facing him, I say, "If I end up in the brig, you have to visit me every day and bring me candy."

"Candy?" There's a half-smile on his face as if he doesn't quite believe me.

"Yes. And now you know my *other* secret. I love a good sugar rush."

He presses his hand to his chest. "I'll die before I tell my father."

I poke him in the shoulder. "See that you do."

He laughs. It's a rich deep sound—very manly—and all is forgiven.

Radcliff returns with the news that I can use the navigator's terminal. This time Captain Harrison and Chief Hoshi join our posse. Oh joy, nothing like an audience. We're all wedged into that small smelly room.

Once I'm in the Q-net, it takes mere seconds to rip the files apart into millions of bits of information. They spread out like ink from an octopus, clouding the space around me. For a moment I'm overwhelmed. Where to start? I catch a fragment that says Pit 32 and I concentrate, calling other Pit 32 fragments. In a blur of motion that makes me slightly nauseous, hundreds of bits fly together. Then I pick another fragment and repeat the process. After a dozen such repetitions, the Q-net takes over, organizing the data into new files. I close my eyes to avoid throwing up.

"Wow," Hoshi says. "I never thought to use the Q-net that way. It's like asking a genius to sort socks—a waste of valuable resources, but in this case..."

"There's millions of socks?" I ask.

"Yeah and it found a better way to do it."

I peek at the activity from time to time and after ten minutes there's a list of new files. And there's hundreds of them, but they're smaller in size. "Just to warn you," I say. "I've no idea if these are any better than the originals."

"Send them to me and Officer Radcliff *only*," the captain orders.

"Yes, sir." I do as instructed although I'm tempted to send a copy to my personal terminal. Too many witnesses. Besides, I think I can retrieve them later without alerting anyone.

"Thank you for your help, Miss Daniels," Captain Harrison says. "We'll ignore your prior activity as long as there won't be any more unauthorized access to the restricted areas of the Q-net."

Purposely misunderstanding his comment, I ask, "Does that mean you're authorizing me?" Yeah, I didn't need to see Niall's flinch to regret that comment as soon as it left my big mouth. But the captain laughs. "Only with proper supervision. And by that I mean myself, Officer Radcliff, and Chief Hoshi only and not some clever loophole you've found. Understand?"

"Yes, sir."

While the adults return to work on the bridge, Niall walks with me as I head to my quarters. The ship's lights along the corridors are dimming slowly, mimicking sunset. Not that they ever go completely dark, but the low light helps us stay on the same sleep/wake cycle as Earth.

I ask Niall about his work in security. "How long have you been helping your dad?"

He runs a hand through his dark hair. "All my life, or so it seems."

I wait but he doesn't elaborate and by his tense posture I guess it's a sensitive subject. "So you're more than an intern?"

"Yeah. Captain Harrison refers to me as one of his junior officers."

Stopping in my tracks, I laugh.

"What?" He takes one look at my expression and raises his hands. "No. No way. You'll get into huge trouble."

"Why? I'm just following the captain's orders, *Officer* Radcliff." I try to go for innocence, but I can't erase my gleeful smirk.

Niall groans. "No. Don't drag me into one of your crazy

schemes."

"I hate to tell you this…no, wait, this is actually gonna be fun, but guess what? You're already involved. Or have you forgotten the symbols?"

"That's not…" His shoulders droop. He sighs as he drops his hands. "How long until we reach Yulin?"

"Forty-seven days."

"It will be a miracle if we don't *both* end up in the brig by then." He strides down the hallway.

I rush to keep up. "Face it, you'll be bored when I'm gone."

That earns me a derisive huff. I wonder if I'm going to miss him when we arrive at Yulin. I jerk my thoughts from that dangerous path, replacing them with the reminder of my promise when I left Xinji. No. More. Friends.

When we reach my quarters, he pauses. "See you tomorrow, Mouse."

"Until then, Toad."

My parents ambush me the second I step through the door. I inform them about what happened.

"Do you think they'll share those files with us?" my mom asks me.

"If they're actually any good, I don't see why not."

But the days pile up and no one has contacted my parents about the contents of the files. Niall claims to be out of the loop and his annoyance over that appears genuine. Chief Hoshi just frowns at me when I try to bring the subject up. My parents' frustration is clear and they're getting nothing but typical delay tactics from Officer Radcliff and the captain. I offer to retrieve those files for them, but they won't allow it. According to them, spending the rest of the voyage in the brig would go on my permanent record. I don't have a problem with that, but they're worried about my future.

Five days after I helped with the files, my parents are called to the captain's office for an important meeting.

"Finally," Mom says.

When they return, their faces are drawn. My father pours them each a shot of whiskey—the good stuff they hoard for special occasions. His hand shakes and the bottle's tip clinks against the glasses.

Fear washes through me. "What happened?" I ask.

"I'm sorry, Li-Li, it's classified," Dad says.

I open my mouth to protest.

"For now," my mother adds, stopping me. "We still have a number of meetings with the captain before we can discuss this with you and the other scientists. Just give us a few days. Please."

The please worries me more than anything else. "Okay."

Two days later while my parents are in an important session with the lead scientists, there's a loud banging on our door. I'm working on some task designed to keep me busy so I'll patiently wait for the big, terrible news. 'Cause I've already figured it has to be horrible just from my parents' hushed conversations, significant glances and all the things they *don't* say out loud.

Niall barges in as soon as the door opens. Every muscle in

his body is clenched tight and his expression is exploding sun, supernova furious.

"What's going on?" he demands.

"I don't—"

"Don't lie to me." He grabs my upper arms in a tight grip. "You've read the files. You *had* to. No way *you* could resist."

"No. I haven't."

He stares at me as his fingers dig deeper into my flesh. Pain stabs down to my bones.

"Let go of me or I'm going to knee you in the balls. Hard."

That snaps him out of it and he jerks back, releasing me. I rub my arms. "What happened?"

"You sure you haven't—"

"I'll admit it's been killing me. But no. I haven't. What happened?"

All his fury rushes out of him and, in one smooth motion, he plops down on a chair, and cradles his head in his hands, resting his elbows on his knees. I brace for his news.

"My father is transferring to Yulin to head up the security on the planet."

Wait, what? "We have a security force." All the Warrior planets do. Not a very good one because scientists vetted by the company multiple times tend to be law abiding citizens. Then it dawns on me. "Oh."

"Yeah. Something in those files from Xinji has DES on high alert and your security force isn't equipped or trained for whatever it is."

"Oh."

Niall looks up and meets my gaze. "And guess who isn't eighteen A-years old yet and *has* to go planetside with him?"

I suck in a breath. "Your father wouldn't—"

"He did."

2522:047

No wonder Niall was so upset. This ship is his home. And he has to be very close to eighteen A-years old. "Did you talk to your father about staying?"

"Of course I did! He said no."

"How soon until you're eighteen?"

"Thirty-two days *after* we arrive at Yulin."

"That's...I can't..." At a complete loss for words, I just stare. Poor guy. Niall would never see the captain or the crew again. Ever. "Captain Harrison?" I try.

"Agreed with my dad." Hurt betrayal sharpens his tone and flashes in his eyes. Then Niall surges to his feet. "Oh, and you'll like this. According to the captain, they *need* me on the planet because of my experience and skills." He spits the words out. "Your nerdy security force is ill prepared."

"For what?"

"I've no fucking idea. That's why I'm here! I figured you would know."

Ah. I glance at my room. "All right. Come on." When Niall follows me inside, I'm already regretting my decision, but I can't...not help him. Not when he looks so shattered.

Closing my door, I sit at my terminal. As I expected, the files are not hard to find. It's almost like they've been waiting for me.

"I thought you have limited access to the Q-net from here," Niall says, standing behind me.

"I did, and, according to your father, I still do."

"If you're not triggering our security, you must be really good." A pause. "It's the Chief's training, isn't it?" Before I can reply, he says, "No. Don't tell me. I don't wanna know."

Smart. He's right. All those hours with the Chief have shown me just a fraction of what the Q-net is capable of and DES has only tapped into a small portion.

Pulling up the files, I ask Niall, "Where do you want to start? There's hundreds of them."

"Can you look for certain terms like *security* and *danger?*"

I initiate a search. Within seconds the files are sorted. "We're down to twenty-seven."

"Better. Let's start with the top one and go from there."

No way I'm going to put it on the screen, so when I open the first one, Niall inserts his tangs and crouches next to me. Suppressing a sigh, I scooch over and let him share my seat. The file is far from complete, but there's enough there to cause my insides to twist with fear.

...one thousand and forty-six Warriors destroyed... cameras show... piles of debris... hundreds missing...

...Dr. Gary Swenson, chief chemist, found dead at his

workstation... multiple lacerations... C.O.D.: exsanguination.

...unable to confirm...explosions...

...Keller, xenobiologist, found... sublevel... eviscerated...

...multiple perpetrators, weapons unknown...

...communications blocked... sabotage?

...unlocked... curfew and buddy system enacted...

A knock on my door sends me a meter into the air.

"Li-Li," my father says. "We need to talk to you. Got some time?"

"Uh, just a minute, Dad," I call, while working to hide the evidence. Then I realize I have more to hide than files. I lower my voice. "Um...I don't suppose you can fit under my bed."

"I'm not hiding." Niall stands.

"But..." I gesture to the terminal. "They'll suspect."

"Suspect what?" He pockets his tangs.

Is he purposely being obtuse? "That we're worming despite the captain's orders."

"We can use the Officer Radcliff loophole."

"Niall," I hiss.

"Is something wrong?" my dad asks. "I hear voices."

"Uh...be right out," I say.

Then Niall gets this evil little grin on his face. "Let's give them something *else* to suspect." He scrubs his hands through his hair, creating little spikes. He reaches for me.

I step back. But he's quick and grabs my shoulders, pulling me close.

"Oh no you—"

His lips press against mine, cutting off the rest of my

protest. They're firm and warm and sparks of electricity shoot through my body. He's had some experience with this and...damn...all coherent thoughts dissolve as his fingers weave through my hair. His clean scent of sage grass fills my senses and he tastes like mint. Wait... when did our lips part? When did I start kissing him back?

"Lyra, what's going on?" my mother demands.

We jerk apart.

"What the hell?" I ask Niall.

"You needed to look like you've just been kissed, Mouse."

An angry heat flushes my face. "You—"

"Mission accomplished," he says and opens the door. Both my parents are standing there. "Hello, Dr. Daniels. Mr. Daniels."

My father steps back to let Niall pass, but my mother blocks his path to the exit. A coldness emanates from her that makes absolute zero feel warm. "Hello, Mr. Radcliff. I didn't know you were visiting us tonight," she says.

"I just stopped by to see Lyra." He sidesteps my mom as if unaware of her disapproval. "Later." He gives us all a jaunty wave and is out the door before anyone can respond.

I'm gonna kill him. But first, I brace for the lecture. And they don't disappoint. Did you know an unwanted pregnancy can ruin a person's future? And that these *space boys*—my mother's term, not mine—have sex with girls all over the Galaxy because they know they won't ever see them again? I try to remind my parents that I'm a reasonably intelligent person, that I already know all this and they should trust me. But they *remind* me about my teenage hormones, and that reason, intelligence, and logic are all trumped by the chemical cocktail that is raging in my body. Yes, they used the word raging. And, thinking back to Niall's kiss...they sort of have a point.

So I cease trying to argue and endure the clichés and lame parental advice. All the while, I'm plotting to kill Niall in very painful and creative ways. It helps me not to flinch when my mother starts instructing me on various birth control methods while my father turns bright red with embarrassment.

Finally the talk winds down and I jump in and ask about what they'd wanted to discuss before they ask me to sign a virginity pledge or something. Don't laugh, it's happened before.

"Oh." Mom glances at Dad. "We wanted to let you know what happened on Xinji."

What I thought were problems with my parents and Niall dissolve into mere trivialities with the reminder of all those people on Xinji. Dread floods through me as the words *exsanguination, explosions*, and *eviscerated* flash in my mind.

"You better sit down, Li-Li," my dad says.

Realizing I'm clutching the back of the chair, I relax my grip and sink into the cushions while my parents perch on the edge of the couch facing me.

My mother draws in a deep breath. "The people on Xinji are gone, Lyra."

"Gone as in..." I can't say the word.

"Dead, yes."

My fingernails dig into the nubby material on the arm of the chair. "Everyone?"

"Yes."

"Are you sure?"

She covers my hand with her own. "A DES scan confirmed there are no life signs other than the local wildlife."

"All of them?"

"Yes."

Oh no, Lan. And her husband. And the archaeologists. And the geologists. And… A strange lightweight sensation sweeps through me and black and white static swirls in my vision.

"Lean forward, Lyra. Put your head between your legs," Mom says.

The room starts to spin, but I do as instructed.

Mom rubs my back. "Deep breaths."

Grief has a stranglehold on my throat and I can't draw any air. My eyes burn with tears that track up my forehead because my head's upside down. And that weird sensation is just the distraction I need to kick start my lungs. A sob breaks free and then I'm sucking in lots of hiccupy, snotty breaths. Grief isn't pretty.

After that, I'm not sure of the course of events except I end up in my dad's lap. He's holding me and I'm curled up against his chest like I used to do when I was little. Once I calm down, I untangle from my father and sit next to him on the couch. Mom hands me a wet cloth to wipe my face.

"What happened?" I ask.

"You almost fainted," Mom says.

"Not that. Xinji."

"Are you sure?"

"Yes." I press the cloth's cooling relief to my forehead. "That was…" Well, I'm not quite sure what that was all about. "I'm okay."

My mother exchanges a significant glance with my father.

I sigh. "Would you rather me find out at soch-time tomorrow?"

Mom stiffens, but then relents. "There's still a great deal of information missing, but DES, Captain Harrison, Officer Radcliff, and we believe it was looters."

Did I just hear that right? "Looters? But they just steal Warriors. They've never attacked, let alone killed anyone."

"It appears there is a new…gang for lack of a better word," Dad says. "This gang is ruthless. They appeared from nowhere and just attacked the base. No explanation and no mercy. We guess that the Warriors must be selling for a fortune on the black market, but there is no way to confirm that at this time."

"Have they attacked any other planets?" I ask.

"Not that we know, but DES is sending Protector Class ships to the Warrior planets to protect them. Of course it's going to take years for the ships to reach them all. Even though we're way out on the edge, there's a Protector Class ship accompanying an Exploratory Class vessel nearby and will be at Yulin in two E-years."

Fear blooms in my chest. "We're still going to Yulin?"

"Yes."

"But—"

"Don't worry, Li-Li. Captain Harrison assigned us his security force, they have a great deal of experience." Dad gives me a shrewd look. "Is that the real reason Mr. Radcliff was here? He must be happy to be going planetside with us."

I don't bother to correct him. Even if his kiss meant something, which it didn't, Niall would never be happy about being assigned to the planet. To him, it's the same as being banished by his family. "What about the ship? Won't they be defenseless?"

"Our security people will remain here. They're not picking up passengers in Yulin so they'll have some time to train and will get more personnel at their next stop. Speaking of the ship, Chief Hoshi asked if you could help her a few more hours a day. With the launch and re-routing of the Protector ships, DES has to make changes and it's complicating everything, including the ship's trajectory."

"Of course I'll help."

Assisting the Chief those extra hours proved to be an excellent distraction. Instead of my imagination envisioning the poor people on Xinji being murdered (eviscerated!), my brain was stuffed full of all the changes the ship needed to execute in order to arrive at Yulin without getting caught in the Protector ships' crinkle fields. To see a fraction of the Q-net map out the new star roads, set schedules, and plan supply drops in just our section of the Galaxy was like witnessing pure magic.

And then my parents needed help prepping for arrival. The construction team finished building the base and removed the sand from four of the Warrior pits before they left. For the second time during this voyage, I looked forward to soch-time. It was a break from work. Even though Niall spent the entire two hours brooding, I was happy to just sit and not think. Our project of organizing Lan's symbols was put on hold. No surprise. Niall's devastated over leaving his family and every time I think about Lan tears threaten. And I can't help but wonder if her discovery scared someone. Lots of people believe that the aliens are long gone and good riddance. What if she found evidence that the symbols tell us where to find them or something like that?

Yulin's sun grows bigger and bigger in the bridge's window as our remaining thirty-nine travel days slip by in a blur of activity. Captain Harrison grants me permission to remain on the bridge when the ship approaches the planet as long as I promise to stay out of the way.

On the morning of day ninety of our voyage, I sit on the floor next to the window as a yellowish-orange orb the size of my fist finally swings into view. Yulin. The color is a dead giveaway that the planet is mostly covered with sand. Ugh. The greenery must be on the opposite side, still in darkness. Over the next hour, the orb expands like a balloon, filling half of the window. Eventually the ship reaches orbit and the planet blocks out everything else. The bridge glows with a soft buttery light as the surface reflects the sun.

Staring at my new home, I listen to the officers' chatter.

"...see that blurry spot? That's a sandstorm for sure..."

"...nothing there...where's the trees?"

"…at least there are dunes, that helps block the wind…"

When Captain Harrison asks Officer Radcliff about other ships in Yulin's solar system, I strain to hear his answer.

"None detected so far," Officer Radcliff says. "But I won't clear a landing party until we confirm there's no one hiding behind the other planets or the sun."

"How long?"

"Twelve hours."

An unhappy grunt.

"We're not a Protector Class vessel, we don't have all the technology to—"

"I know. Any signs of activity on the planet?" the captain asks.

"No."

"I've linked with the power station. The base should be live in a few hours," Radcliff says.

"Double check the environmental systems."

"Aye, Captain."

Captain Harrison keeps up a steady stream of commands, but they seem like a mere formality since the crew is already one step ahead of him. I wonder how many planets they've "woken" for lack of a better term. With the time dilation and the Q-net determining star roads, some planets waited E-decades before settlers arrived. Or in our case, the scientists.

After an hour or so, I'm bored. The view remains the same—still yellowish-orange, still desolate. I return to our quarters to finish packing. Actually, I didn't start, but my meager possessions won't take long to stuff into a couple duffle bags. However, my parents pounce as soon as I enter. I answer their questions, telling them there were no signs of looters. Yet. And they thank me by hijacking me into helping them by schlepping equipment cases to the shuttle bay. Not fun.

Soch-time is a welcome break from the manual labor, except, for the first time, Niall isn't there. I stand next to his empty chair and wonder if his not being there is a bad sign. Do I need to be worried? And if so, what type of worried? Concerned he might be feeling ill or hurt—that and loss of a family member are the only acceptable excuses to miss soch-time. Or concerned something happened and the ship needs all its security personnel, including their junior officer, because looters are going to attack and kill us all (eviscerated!). That's a super big worry.

By the end of soch-time, I'm convinced we've been boarded and I hurry to our quarters to find...my parents deep in conversation with the meteorologists discussing sandstorms and the base's air filtration system. Normal stuff. Taking a deep breath and feeling silly, I enter my room and access my required daily school work. Even with working the extra hours with the Chief, I've still had to keep up with my lessons. Sheesh. The looters could be banging on my door, but I'd have to tell them to wait until I sent my homework. At least it keeps me from being a pack mule for my mother. That is, until I finish.

I swear two seconds after I disentangle, my mom's knocking on my door.

Poking her head in, she takes one look at my expression and says, "You can rest all you want when we're on the planet."

"Oh no. I'm not falling for that," I say. "I won't get a break until after we unpack and set up all the equipment and establish a routine." Which will take over a hundred days at least. "I do remember when we arrived at Xinji, Mom."

She smiles—not what I expected at all. "I remember watching you move a heavy case across the floor. It was twice your height and width, yet, even though you couldn't see where you were going, it didn't deter you. Your pigtails bounced with every mighty push."

Even recognizing what she is doing—using my younger self to make my older self feel guilty about being lazy (where did she learn this stuff? Mom school?)—I stand and follow her to the living area where a cart full of scanners waits for me to transfer them to the shuttle bay.

When I return, Officer Radcliff is talking to my parents. Well...sort of. My mom and dad are arguing and Radcliff's standing there, tugging at his shirt as if uncomfortable. I stop. How could I be in trouble? I've been too busy being helpful! Then another thought strikes me. It's been over twelve hours. Have the sensors located another ship?

"I'm going," my father declares to my mom. "You haven't finished packing yet." He sounds smug.

"And you haven't finished the shuttle schedule yet," Mom counters.

"That's easy, we'll just reverse the—"

"Going where?" I ask.

"With the security team. They're doing a sweep to make sure there's no one on the planet before we all go down to the surface," Dad says.

"Did you access the cameras?" I ask Radcliff.

"Yes, but they can be compromised." He gives me a pointed look.

Ah. Well. I clear my throat. "Do you really think someone is down there?" I ask him.

"All the evidence collected so far indicates that the chances are slim, but we have to follow procedures."

"And since I'm in charge of the base's operations, I know the layout the best and can show the team—" my father tries.

"*We* are in charge," Mom interrupts. "And *we* both know—"

"Actually, I know the base better than you both. I should go." The words pop out of my mouth before my brain stops them. I don't really want to go down there until it's safe.

All three adults turn to me and say no in unison. Impressive.

"Lyra." My mother gestures to another loaded cart. "You shouldn't even be a part of this conversation. Take that to the bay, please."

Now my brain has caught up and it's annoyed at being dismissed so quickly. "May I explain my logic before I go?" I ask.

Dad's torn, but my mom says, "The answer is still no."

"I'm curious why she thinks her reasoning is logical," Officer Radcliff says.

An unexpected ally. Nice.

"All right, go ahead," Mom says with a sigh.

"I grew up in the research bases. I've spent my life in them. They all have lots of hiding places where the cameras can't see."

"That's ridiculous, Lyra," Mom says. "The bases are rectangular, there are no hiding places."

"And yet you couldn't find me when Dr. Samell visited five years ago. Remember, your techs searched everywhere?"

"Lyra Tian Daniels, did you purposely hide from me?" Mom's tone drops near the dangerous level.

"No. I hid from *Dr. Samell.* He was creepy and I didn't like the way he looked at me." As if he wanted to eat me. "And he kept touching my arm."

"Why didn't you tell me?" she demands.

"You were too busy telling me he's the expert in Warrior reconstruction and I should be honored that he offered to show me some techniques. It was just easier to make myself scarce." I suppress a shudder. If you ask me, three days of avoiding his touch was an eternity.

"Next time, please tell us when someone makes you uncomfortable," Dad says.

"Good thing Samell is dead." Mom puts her hands on her hips. "Or I'd have him discredited."

"About the base," Radcliff says before Mom can launch into another lecture. "Lyra can tell us where the hiding places are."

"It won't work," I say. "I'm bound to forget some. And then there are the ones I've forgotten existed but once I see a familiar area, it'll trigger my memory."

"Still no," Mom says.

Despite the danger of the mission, disappointment swirls around my heart. Huh. Knowing when to abandon a fight, I grasp the cart's handles and push it toward the door.

"She has a point," Radcliff says.

Oh? I pause.

"Maybe she can watch the team through the cameras and give us directions," Radcliff offers.

"I'll still miss places, since they're not visible to the cameras," I say. "It's best if I go along."

Radcliff shakes his head. "Still no. But I'll talk to the captain about having you monitor us through the cameras."

Better than nothing. I maneuver the cart through the door and down the corridor. One wheel refuses to roll straight and the damn thing keeps veering off and smacking into the walls. I curse the laws of physics. We can build space ships with artificial gravity, but we can't invent an anti-gravity device to make things...float in it. Gravity is an all or nothing kind of thing. You either have it or you don't.

By the time I reach the shuttle bay, I'm sweaty and irritated. I pile all the cases next to the others before taking a break. The air in the bay is much colder than the rest of the ship and thinner as well. This area is only used when the ship arrives at a planet. In order to save energy, its atmosphere is set at the minimum required to keep the shuttle functional until needed, then it's heated and pressurized. Same with the storage bay, which is why my parents jammed all the sensitive instruments into our quarters.

When my body and mood cools, I push the directionally challenged cart back. Officer Radcliff is gone, but my parents sit together on the couch. They both look at me when I enter. Have they been comparing notes on all the times they couldn't find me over the last seventeen years? Am I about to get into trouble for all of them?

Instead, Mom points to the other cart. They've loaded it while I was gone. Yippee. At least this one rolls straight. When I return this time, Captain Harrison and Officer Radcliff are in our quarters. All conversation ceases when they see me. Tension fogs the air and I almost step back into the corridor.

"Lyra, can you give us some privacy, please?" Mom asks.

"Sure." I bolt for the safety of my room. And while the desire to press my ear to the metal door pulses through me, I'm wise enough to resist the urge. As I ignore the muffled conversation, I pack my stuff. It takes me all of three minutes. After a long look at the door, I stretch out on my bed. My muscles are sore and my mom won't wake me to deliver another pile of boxes tonight. Right? A girl could hope.

A knock rouses me from a light doze.

"Come in," I say.

When the captain enters, I just about hit my head on the ceiling as I launch to my feet.

"Sorry to bother you," he says.

"Not at all," I manage with only a slight squeak.

"We discussed your concerns about the base and I'm inclined to agree with you. The security team is unfamiliar with the layout."

I press my arms to my sides to keep still.

"I'd like you to accompany them tomorrow. The plan would be for you to stay in the shuttle until they finish the initial sweep, then you'll show them the hidden areas. The danger to you should be minimal, but I won't lie that there isn't any risk involved. Are you willing?"

"My parents—"

"Have agreed that it is *your* decision."

I consider. Have they agreed because they figured I'd be smart enough to say no, or have they truly left it up to me? Parents can be tricky that way. I want to help so I say yes. Of course this means I won't be able to hide on a research base ever again. Although I haven't needed to hide in a long time. And now I know my parents would trust my word more than some creepy famous scientist.

"All right. Report to the shuttle bay tomorrow at oh-six-hundred hours. One of the security officers will drop off a jumpsuit and boots for you later tonight."

"Uh. Yes, sir."

He nods, then leaves. I sway and plop onto my bed. Three. Two. One.

Right on cue my dad pokes his head in. "Li-Li?" Worry creases his forehead. "Are you sure?"

"Yes. I'll be fine." The captain did say minimal risk. Who am I to question the captain?

2522:087

My brave words last until the next morning when I struggle to pull on the one-piece jumpsuit. The black material is form fitting yet flexible and, according to my dad, puncture resistant, which doesn't help my nerves. It's one thing to talk about doing something, quite another to actually be doing it.

There's plenty of pockets and a belt with an empty holster. I wonder if they plan to give me a weapon. Would I *need* a weapon? Jerking my thoughts away from that speculation, I lace up my boots—also black with rubber soles. They are surprisingly light. Comfortable, too. I tie my long hair back into a French braid. My reflection is impressive. It says I'm ready for action. It says don't mess with me. I marvel a bit over the way the jumpsuit shows off my curves. I have boobs and hips. Who knew? My baggy shirts have been doing a good job of covering them up. I'm not super tall at one hundred and sixty-seven centimeters, but I tower over my mother.

My parents go with me to the shuttle bay. A part of me wants to complain—I know the way—but a part of me is secretly glad they're with me. Eleven other black-clad figures wait by a small shuttle—not the transport one that I'm familiar with. There are seven men and four women. Officer Keir smiles at me and my nausea eases a fraction. Nearby, Captain Harrison is talking to Officer Radcliff and my insides twist when Radcliff spots me and gestures me over.

Captain Harrison gives me an encouraging smile and my dad squeezes my shoulder.

"See you in a few hours," Mom says and my parents leave with the captain.

My feet are numb by the time I join Radcliff and the others. Their holsters have weapons.

"Here are the rules," Radcliff says to me. "You're going to be a part of Beta team." He points to a woman around my mom's age. She has bristle-short blond hair and ice blue eyes. "You follow Officer Morgan's orders without question, without hesitation. Don't think. Just do. Understand?"

"Yes, sir."

"Same goes for the other Beta team members. If they say to hit the floor, you pretend you're a rug. If they say freeze, you don't move, you don't breathe. If they say run, you become the Galaxy's fastest woman. Got it?"

"Yes, sir."

He pulls out a pulse gun, and sets it in my right hand so my fingers curl around the grip. "Hold it."

Shocked, I do as instructed.

"Don't drop it." He touches a button.

A light flares from the gun and I tighten my grip in surprise.

"Now it's set to your electromagnetic signature. No one can fire this gun but you. It also won't fire if it's aimed at any members of the security team, including you." Radcliff shows me how to shoot the gun. "Hold it in two hands, arms extended with your thumb resting on the button. You need to press down hard in order to fire." He takes it from my grasp and shoves it into my holster. "Only pull it if your life is in immediate danger. Understand?"

"Yes, sir." My throat is tight and I'm seriously considering hyperventilating.

Radcliff leans forward to meet my gaze. "Breathe, Miss Daniels. You'll be well protected. Captain Harrison threatened to demote me to galley cook if any harm comes to you."

That surprises a laugh from me. I draw in a few lung-filling breaths. Minimal risk. Plus this was my idea after all and I have a pulse gun, which, if I remember correctly, is a non-lethal weapon that renders a person unconscious.

"Load up," Radcliff shouts.

I follow the others onto the small shuttle. Two rows of seats line the sides, facing each other. There are no windows except in the front where the pilot is. It's a bare bones conveyance. Hard seats, no rugs and plenty of weapons stashed in netting. Not a passenger shuttle at all.

As I find an empty seat toward the back, I make brief eye contact with the rest of the security team. A few are curious, others appear bored, but they all have an alertness about them as if their bodies are coiled and ready to strike. They're wearing communicators in their right ears. Yet there's an awkward silence.

Keir plops down next to me. "How in the universe did you manage to become part of this mission?" she asks.

"An inability to keep my mouth shut," I say, half-serious.

Her laugh echos off the metal hull and sounds loud in the quiet shuttle. "Don't worry, we'll protect that pampered ass of yours." Keir elbows me to let me know she's joking.

Her comment releases the tension and I relax until I realize the man who is sitting directly across from me is Niall.

Not the Niall that ignored me in soch-time or the one who draws pictures. Not the annoyed Niall or the teasing one who calls me Mouse and tells me I'm going to end up in the brig. Not the Niall who kissed me.

No.

This man is an entirely different being. His shoulders are set with confidence and his posture oozes competence as if he'll have no trouble handling any situation that arrives when we're on the planet. There is no expression on his face and his gaze is flat when it meets mine. I've no idea if he's surprised or upset to see me. And, damn. The jumpsuit shows off his physical attributes as well. Memories of that kiss sear my insides.

The pilot's voice slices through the air. "Launch in ten, nine, eight..."

I scramble to buckle my five-point harness.

"...two, one."

The shuttle lifts off and soon after we are weightless. My stomach does a cartwheel and I would have expelled my breakfast had I been able to eat this morning. No artificial gravity. If it wasn't for the shoulder and lap straps, I would have floated off my seat. Instead, I hover in place. Thanks for the warning, Radcliff. Too bad he's sitting with the pilot and can't see my nauseous glare. But Keir is watching me and, with a glint of amusement in her dark brown eyes, she extends a vomit bag. I consider ignoring it, but the thought of throwing up in zero gee without it... Beyond gross. Taking the bag, I mutter a thanks.

It's not long before Yulin's gravity pulls my butt back in the seat. Then we're falling toward the planet. Fast. I can't call it flying as the ship's engine is the only thing keeping us from crashing. As I try not to imagine my life ending in a mangle of metal, we hit Yulin's atmosphere. Roaring noise, jaw-cracking turbulence and waves of heat are now added to the vision of my fiery death. The light turns orange and I clutch the armrests. I'm never gonna complain about the passenger shuttles again.

The others appear unfazed and right after I'm convinced we'll be cooked alive, the ride smooths and the air cools. The rest of the trip is pleasant in comparison.

When the ship slows, I brace for a rough landing, but we settle to the ground with a slight bump. The team unhooks their harnesses, but remain seated.

Radcliff enters. "We have three minutes until the port's temperature and air pressure are stabilized."

The port is basically a part of the complex that has a retractable roof for the shuttles. There's an air lock between it and the rest of the base. However, since Yulin's atmosphere is close to Earth's I've a feeling we will eventually acclimatize to the local conditions in order to save energy.

Radcliff turns to me. "You stay with the pilot for now. Alba will show you what to do."

"Yes, sir."

A tone sounds and Radcliff says, "Alpha team with me."

Five officers including Keir stand, draw their weapons and follow him out. Keir glances over her shoulder and winks at me.

Officer Morgan hops to her feet. "Beta team with me."

The rest head to the exit behind her. Niall gives me an encouraging nod before exiting with Beta team. I take a breath before fumbling to release my harness. My legs are a bit rubbery as I enter the small area for the pilot and co-pilot. Beyond the window is the port. Equipment crates are stacked to the side and a couple forklifts are parked nearby. Not unusual except there isn't anyone around. A good sign, but kind of eerie, too.

Alba gestures me to the empty seat and motions for me to put my entanglers in. I do as instructed.

Behind you is a screen, Alba's voice sounds in my head.

I swivel around. Pictures of empty rooms and empty corridors fill it.

As Beta team advances through the base, Officer Morgan will be calling in their location and status. You'll be able to track their progress through the cameras. When they clear a section, check it off on the map.

Map?

Bottom right. Focus on it to enlarge.

Oh. The screen fills with a diagram of the base. Some areas are colored red, others are orange.

Orange is Beta team's route. Red is Alpha's. I'll be tracking Alpha.

Understand?

Yes. I shrink the map back down.

If you see anything unusual in the cameras or anyone that is not a member of the team, let me know right away and I'll alert them.

Okay. I scan the feeds. Nothing. But it doesn't take long until the six members of Beta team show up on the screen. They move carefully and stay close to the walls, walking—not quite sideways, but they keep their bodies turned slightly as if trying to be a smaller target. Instead of going straight through an entrance, they first stand to the side of it as if expecting to be attacked, then, when they go in, it's done in an explosion of movement. Interesting.

Beta team. Microbiology lab cleared, Morgan says through the tangs.

I open the map and check off the area. It turns from orange to green. Then I return to the cameras. It doesn't take me long to get into a routine. I have to admit, it's kind of fun. Of course I'm safe in the shuttle. My team is out there doing all the work, taking all the risks. I smile over calling them *my* team. No doubt they wouldn't be as amused.

The research base is big and it takes the two teams four hours to clear all the labs and housing units. After a thirty-minute break, Alpha team will move on to the opened Warrior pits while Beta team returns to the shuttle. Alba offers to share her lunch with me.

My stomach growls a yes in response, but I ask, "Are we going to be weightless on the way back?"

"Yes."

"Then no thanks."

She grins at me, revealing straight white teeth and dimples. "I'd say you'd get used to it, but unless you decide to become a shuttle pilot..."

"No."

"...or a security officer..."

"No way."

Alba laughs. It's a sweet sound that matches her petite body. "Then you won't experience weightlessness enough times to get used to it."

Fine with me. "Are you coming planetside with the rest of the team?" I ask.

"No. I pilot the shuttles and they stay with the ship."

Soon Radcliff reports they're heading into the pits. I track my team. They're more relaxed and head straight back, but they still keep their weapons drawn. When they enter the port, Alba tells me to join them. She toggles a switch and the door opens, lowering a small ramp. The cool air fans my sweaty face and a musty dry smell fills my nose as I walk out of the shuttle. My heart jerks as the door clangs shut behind me.

Officer Morgan gestures me closer. She sweeps her arm out and does a little bow. "Lead the way to *your* hidey holes, Miss Daniels."

The desire to correct her—they're not mine—pulses through me. And from the smirks on a couple of the other team members' faces, it's obvious they also think my claims of hidden areas are ridiculous. I glance at Niall, but his expression remains neutral.

Fine. First stop, the emergency exit in the port. I point to the sealed door.

Officer Morgan raises her eyebrows. "That goes outside."

"Eventually." I agree. "There's a big room in there with pressure suits. No cameras."

"It's not on the map." Doubt laces her tone.

I reach to unseal the door, but Niall knocks my hand away. "Allow me."

Shoved back out of the way, the others take up positions to the sides and do their thing. They investigate the inside and return with an all-clear.

They wait for me to point out the next area. I meet Officer Morgan's gaze. I'm not moving without an apology.

"Right then, let's continue," she says.

That's close enough. I take them through the base and show them the weird triangle room, the basement under the astrophysics lab, the blind spots in the supply bay, the oversized ducts that crisscross the labs, the duct to nowhere, and a number of others. When we reach the farthest point from the port, I relax. We didn't encounter any hidden looters.

Officer Morgan holsters her weapon. "That was the oddest thing. Why doesn't the base match the blueprints?"

"The construction team must have altered the plans," one of the guys says.

"But the changes don't make any sense," another says.

"Maybe it was in the original plans and they were updated, but the advance crews didn't get the updated version," a woman suggests.

"Regardless of why, we need to mark all these on the map," Morgan says. "Radcliff."

"Yes, sir," Niall says.

"See that the changes are noted."

"Yes, sir."

I silently apologize to all the bases' kids.

Morgan turns to me. "Are there any hidden areas in the Warrior pits?"

"No. There are blind areas for the cameras, but Alpha team will see everything when they do their sweep."

We head back to the port.

Halfway there Morgan slows. "Change of plans. What's the fastest way to the pits, Miss Daniels?"

I take point and lead them to the archaeology labs. They are along the outer wall of the base and are below ground level. There's only one main entrance into and out of the pits and it's through the archaeology labs. There are other emergency exits installed, but they're only used if there's a cave-in. To prevent them, the caverns are braced with support beams. And the base pumps in clean dry air. It's not quite an air lock since it's the same air that is used in the base, but rather a decontamination area to keep the techs from dragging sand and soil in from the caverns. It doesn't work. Eventually sand will get everywhere and into everything.

Once we reach the entrance, Officer Morgan takes point and I'm surrounded by the others. A damp chill taints the air despite the base's dehumidifiers. A wet earthy scent mixes with a harsh mineral odor. White artificial light glows from the ceiling as we follow the tunnel to Pit 1. Then the ceiling disappears into the darkness.

An army of lifelike Warriors greets us. They're lined up in rows and are all just under two meters tall. Each pit contains one thousand, four hundred and forty-eight Warriors arranged in a giant octagon with a two-meter square hole in the center of each—another difference from the original army on Earth. The archaeologists have determined that each pit contains a battalion of Warriors led by a general.

The Warriors were crafted from the same red clay (terracotta) as those found in China, Earth. Even though they're hollow and one and a quarter centimeters thick, they weigh about two hundred and seventy kilograms each. Their uniform coats go down to their knees and are covered with armor. Chinese calligraphy and a variety of strange symbols decorate the armor (unlike the ones on Earth).

Impressive and daunting, the Warriors stare straight ahead. Their long hair is pulled into warrior knots on the top of their heads and a few have headdresses or caps on just like those on Earth. It's their faces that are the most amazing to me. Each one is unique. My ancestors.

A brief swell of pride inflates my chest.

The diggers also built a corridor that runs parallel to all the pits, connecting them. We pass through two more pits—identical to Pit 1—and meet up with Alpha team in Pit 4. I stop.

Pit 4 is a disaster area. Broken Warriors litter the floor. Others appear as if a giant has smashed them into pieces, sending bits out in a wave. The ground is scarred and lined with grooves.

"What happened here?" Morgan asks Radcliff.

"I'm hoping Miss Daniels might be able to tell us."

"Is it safe?" I ask.

"No one is here and the support beams are intact. Is this typical of a dig site?"

"There's always a number of pits that collapse. Understandable since they've been buried for thousands of years, but this doesn't look like one of those." Not that I'm an expert, but I remember when there is a cave-in, the Warriors are crushed in place, smashed down into piles, not flung sideways.

I step carefully through the debris trying not to break any more pieces. Some poor tech will be assigned to put this mess back together again. With my luck, it'll be me. I reach an open area. There are Warriors missing. Then I spot footprints and wheel marks. It appears they've been dragged away by heavy equipment. Where did they go? I follow the grooves to a mound of soft dirt and rocks. At first glance it looks like a cave-in, but the marks disappear under it. Which means...

"Your assessment, Miss Daniels?" Radcliff asks.

"Looters." I gesture to the pile. "They tunneled in here, stole at least five hundred Warriors and then collapsed the tunnel to hide their activities."

"How long ago?"

I consider. "The marks on the ground seem recent."

"I concur."

Which means the looters could still be here.

2522:087

I scan the others, but they don't appear as panicked as I am. Am I the only one to jump to the conclusion that the looters could still be on the planet? Obviously.

"Everyone back to the shuttle," Officer Radcliff orders.

As we jog through the corridor and then the base's hallways, I consider. The construction crew left many years ago. The looters could be long gone by now as well. When we reach the port, I'm not the last to arrive, but I suspect the two lagging behind me are supposed to be the rear guard. I am the only one out of breath— guess there is a downside to sitting and playing multiple hours of games a day. Who knew?

"Get your B-apps on, we're going outside," Radcliff says.

Everyone rushes into the shuttle. I move to follow, but Radcliff says, "Not you, Miss Daniels. You're to stay with Lieutenant Alba."

"Yes, sir."

The others return with masks on their faces and hard

rectangular packs on their backs. Ah. B-apps a.k.a. breathing apparatus. The team aims for the outer air lock and I join Alba in the cockpit. But I don't have anything to do except listen to the team's status updates as they search the surrounding area.

When the scientists settle into the base, they'll install cameras outside to record any indigenous wildlife. Not that any have been discovered on Yulin so far.

There's a crackle of excitement. Well, not exactly, but instead of a dry status update, Officer Radcliff actually sounds mildly interested. A big improvement.

"...found evidence of a ship... staging area... tracks... broken Warriors..."

Mom's not gonna be happy about that.

"...no signs of life... appears as if they've been gone at least a half a year..."

Good news. Hopefully, they crinkled far away and are not hiding in the solar system for another raid.

The team returns. Their faces are red either from the sun or exertion. Sweat shines on foreheads and dampens hair. And the smell—think boys locker room after a big game—a hot funky odor. Plus a peppery sweet scent that must be the outside air. It's breathable, but until the meteorologists certify that it's safe, everyone has to stay inside the base unless they wear the proper equipment.

Strapping into their seats, the team guzzles water. We've been on the planet for nine hours. I buckle in as the shuttle takes off. No one has the energy to talk and the ride up is the same noise, heat, and stomach-flipping turbulence—I clutch the vomit bag in both hands just in case. But this time, I know what to expect and that makes a big difference.

My parents and the captain are waiting for us in the bay. I'd be embarrassed, but I make the mistake of relaxing. Now I'm lightheaded and unsteady. My mom and dad thank the team for checking the base, the captain gives everyone a proverbial pat on the back, and Radcliff dismisses the team. The others break up and head for the exit as Radcliff, my parents, and the captain discuss...er...things. A loud buzzing muffles their voices.

Doesn't anyone else hear that? I swipe a loose strand of hair from my forehead. My hand is shaking.

"When's the last time you ate?" Niall asks from right next to me.

I jerk in surprise and just about fall over.

He grabs my arm to steady me. "That answers my question. Come on." He twines his fingers in mine and tows me from the bay.

I'd like to say I protested and insisted I could walk on my own, but the truth is that the trip is a blur. Eventually we stop and Niall pushes me into a seat.

"Wait here," he orders.

By the time I think of a snarky response, he's gone. Instead, I rest my head in my arms, not caring about the strange looks I've been getting from the other diners. An incredibly delicious aroma rouses me. It's meatloaf! The world must be ending if I think meatloaf smells that good.

Niall places an overflowing plate in front of me next to his own heaped portion. I just blink at him. "Go on, Mouse. Eat."

I wolf the loaf down along with a pile of potatoes and a bunch of carrots that go from yummy to rubbery pretty quick. I must be feeling better. Niall fetches us a couple glasses of water and two pieces of—

"Chocolate cake! I'm not dying!"

He grins. "Relax. It's part of the special meal for the disembarking passengers."

Oh right. A tradition for everyone at the end of the journey. A chance to get together with the crew and thank them and make empty promises to stay in touch.

"You missed it," he says.

"Good."

"Not a fan?"

"No."

"Me either. They're a waste of time. No sense getting friendly. Passengers come and go." Then his good mood drops and he slumps back in his chair.

No doubt realizing that this time he is leaving as well and there is nothing he can do to stop it. Having seen it on countless kids over the years, I recognize the posture and miserable expression. I wore it myself not that long ago. There are no words that I can say to make him feel any better. I squeeze his hand in silent support.

He meets my gaze. "How many times have you had to leave?"

"Three times, but only the last two...hurt."

Jerking his hand back, Niall pushes to his feet. "I gotta go. See you planetside, Mouse."

"Later, Toad." That earns me a weak smile.

He steps away, but pauses. "Not bad for your first mission."

"Thanks."

"You look good in that jumpsuit. Maybe you should consider signing up."

"Do you think your father would be willing to train me?"

That surprises a laugh from him. "No. In fact..." He yanks my gun from my holster. "I'm supposed to ensure this is returned to him."

"You're no fun."

"There will be a full security force on the planet. You don't need it."

"Need? No. Want? Yes."

He laughs again. I decide I like making him laugh. "Are there brigs on the planet?" he asks.

"Yes, except they're called detention centers, and, for the record, I've never been in one."

"Uh huh. Guess there's a first time for everything." He gives me a mock salute and leaves.

I watch his...er...back. The jumpsuit really is form fitting and he has a nice form. Once he's gone, I slouch in my chair. My stomach is super full and despite the sugar from the cake, I'm sleepy. I trudge back to our quarters, thinking of napping. As soon as I enter, my parents pounce with the questions. Do I know how many Warriors were taken? Destroyed? Radcliff didn't know. Neither did I.

But my mom is in full out fret mode. "How many heads did you see? Were there more than ten rows missing?" she asks.

"Mom, you're going to be down there tomorrow. Nothing's gonna change because you know the answer now versus later," I snap.

She gives me a sharp look, but then softens. "Sorry. You're right. You've had quite the day. What was it like?"

"Zero gee sucks," I say.

"Really?" my dad asks. "I thought it blows."

I groan at the lame dad joke. "I'm going to bed."

The next day is a flurry of activity as the shuttle transfers equipment down to the surface. My arm muscles ache from loading crates and containers. My mom and dad rush around checking things off and sending me on emergency errands. Once all the supplies are unloaded, the rest of the passengers begin to leave.

At the end of an exhausting day, our family is going to be the last to board. Captain Harrison arrives to give the official send-off. More thank yous are exchanged and handshakes.

The captain pulls me aside as my parents head to the shuttle. "You managed to impress both my Navigation Chief and Chief of Security. Tace said you handled yourself like a professional during the mission."

Wow. Not expecting that. Unsure of how to respond, I nod importantly.

"I hope you consider joining DES. I've already written you a letter of recommendation and added it to your permanent record."

I'm struck stupid. Did he just say... Oh. My. Stars. I finally manage to squeak out a thanks. The word seems inadequate and small for such a gesture. He waves it off and says good-bye. I'm halfway to the shuttle when he calls out, "Remember the view, Miss Daniels."

"I will." I don't think I could ever forget. When I board the shuttle, I search for Niall even though I know the security team went down first. The quartet of girls are sitting together, laughing. The rest of the scientists are chatty and their faces shine with eagerness, ready for a new planet to study. I plop into an empty seat.

My emotions are a strange mix. Despite my determination to not make friends when we left Xinji, I did. And while I'm looking forward to a change of scenery, I'm going to miss the captain and Chief Hoshi. Reconstructing artifacts will no doubt be dull in comparison to navigating the stars.

What about Niall? Will our friendship continue? Will it deepen into something else? What happens when the next Interstellar Class ship arrives in four E-years? We'll both be over eighteen A-years old. I close my eyes. Perhaps I should worry about it then? No. I need to protect my heart. It's already been torn into quarters at least. How much can it take before it's turned into tiny pieces that not even the best reconstructionist can fit back together?

The shuttle lifts off, jolting me from my thoughts. Perhaps the best thing to do is focus on figuring out my future so I have a direction in mind when the next Interstellar Class ship arrives.

A responsible decision. Very adult. It'll probably last until Niall kisses me again. *If* he kisses me again. I hope he does. My raging teenage hormones agree. So much for being an adult.

The first few days on Yulin are very similar to the last few days on the ship. Moving equipment, running errands, but unpacking instead of packing. Our housing unit is super nice. Mom and Dad both have offices with terminals and there's a conference room between them. My room is twice the size of the one on the ship and I have my very own washroom. My possessions are still meager, but I fill my extra-large screen with a collage of images, including the new ones of the captain, Hoshi, and of the Galaxy. My terminal is still a standard one, but after employing a few tricks I learned, I have wider access to the Q-net. I grin. Officer Radcliff is going to have a harder time tracking me down.

It takes a surprisingly short period of time for everyone to settle in and get to work. Good news for my parents. Me, not so much.

"The socialization area is operational, Lyra," Mom says at dinner that night. "You are to report there at thirteen hundred hours tomorrow."

Two hundred and twenty-one more days of soch-time left until I turn eighteen A-years old. Not that I'm counting.

"Don't give me that look," she says.

"You can't yell at me for a look."

"She's right," Dad says in my defense. "For once in her life, Li-Li didn't argue about soch-time."

"Hey!" He's exaggerating, but I play along. "There was that day when I was five."

"My apologies."

"It'd be nicer without the sarcasm," I say.

"It would."

"After soch-time I need your help in Pit 4," Mom says. "We need to assess the damage and determine just how many Warriors are missing."

"All right."

She studies my expression. "That was too easy."

"Maybe I'm maturing."

"Or maybe you're up to something."

I laugh. "Already? We've only been on the planet for five days."

"We have high expectations of you," Dad says.

"Don't encourage her, Spencer."

I arrive at soch-time at the proper time and sign in. On the research bases there's a specific set of rooms just for socialization. Not like the ship, which takes over the rec room for a couple hours. The younger kids run around and the quartet of girls hold court back in the far right corner. And sitting on a chair that's too small for him is Niall. His supernova glower keeps the others far from him. I know I shouldn't be surprised that his dad is such a stickler for the law, but his birthday is in twenty-five days after all. Poor Niall.

"Come on," I say to him.

He glares at me.

"Unless you'd rather stay here with the younger kids?"

Niall stands.

"Thought not," I say.

He follows me back to the game room. I step through the door half expecting to see Jarren, Belle, Cyril, and Lan waiting for me since the room is an exact duplicate of the one on Xinji. But it's empty and a pang squeezes my chest hard as I remember Lan is dead.

Niall scans the area as if assessing it for threats before he sits down.

"The game system is much better than the one on the ship." I point to the speakers. "It has surround sound. And during soch-time this place is teens only."

His demeanor doesn't change. It reminds me of when I first met him.

"Where's your sketchbook?" I ask, hoping to draw him out. Get it? Draw.

"My father has taken all my sketchbooks."

That's harsh. "Why?"

"Insubordination."

Not quite an answer. "Will he give them back?"

"No."

Okay then. I quickly change topics. "What do you think of living planetside?"

"I hate it."

"But it's only been—"

"Lyra, stop. I've no interest in making the most out of a bad situation. I'm going to serve my time here on Yulin and as soon as that Protector Class ship arrives, I'm enlisting." He gives me an icy smile. "My father always wanted me to go into security, and that's the ultimate experience."

I've a feeling that's not exactly what Radcliff wanted.

The Protectorate is a whole other beast.

"Just leave me alone."

"Fine." What else can I say? I've been there and I personally know there are no words, even well-meaning ones, that will ease his pain. He's viewing this assignment as a punishment. Time might help him or it might not. And I'm sure he didn't intentionally mean to hurt my feelings when he called me Lyra and not Mouse— but if he's dead set on leaving when the ship arrives in two years, it's probably best I keep my distance as well. Perhaps by then, my heart won't care. Because the stupid thing didn't listen to my "no friends" directive. Pah. I load up a game and spend the next two hours playing by myself.

The meteorologists have given the all-clear for the atmosphere and they slowly incorporate the ambient air into the base. A light peppery sweet scent fills the rooms and hallways, reminding me of Niall. Curse you, Yulin!

Despite what I said about leaving Niall alone, I'm

determined to distract him from his broody funk. Trying to entice his interest, I pull up Lan's files with the alien symbols through the game system. I wonder if he still has the sketchbook he used to copy them. As I attempt to pick up where we left off, Niall sits in stony silence.

So tonight, I'm on a mission. I'm taking advantage of one of the benefits to being my parents' errand girl. I search out the base geologist, Dr. Roy Carr, and confer with him about some minerals I found in the pits. Turns out they're limestone. Perfect. Then I visit the chemists for a little help in creating different pigments. My final stop is with the botanists. That's a harder sell and I'm told no. So close!

The next day I do a little research and discover an alternate recipe. After raiding the kitchens, I visit the chemists again. The process involves more effort than they're willing to give so I offer to help them in the evenings for six days in exchange. Free labor is always welcome and they agree.

You might be wondering why I'm doing all this. Niall's miserable. He's acting as if his time here is a prison sentence. He needs a distraction. He needs a friend. Plus his birthday is coming up. I know I'm probably setting myself up for a big hurt, but…I just can't…not help.

Exactly thirty-one days after we arrived at Yulin, I bring my gifts for Niall. Normally, the babysitters and all the kids make a big deal over a person's last required soch-time the day before their eighteenth birthday, but not for Niall. Everyone's been tip-toeing around him and they'll all be glad to see him go.

"What's this?" he asks when I set the package in front of

him. "I told you to leave me alone."

"And I have. After this, you won't have to see me again." I've never run into him outside of soch-time. I suspect it is on purpose.

"Promise?"

That nasty comment slices right through me. That's it. I tried my best so my conscience is clear, but I'm done being nice. "You're a jerk. I promise you can keep wallowing in self-pity all by yourself." I leave the room. I tell the babysitter I'm sick.

"Do you need to see the doctor?" she asks.

"No."

She glances at the monitor on her desk that allows her to see what's going on in the game room, but not hear. "He's having a hard time adjusting."

"He can go to hell."

A smile, then she sobers. "I'll have to report it to your parents."

"Fine. I'll go straight back to my room to lie down."

"All right, you can go."

Wow. "Thanks."

"I understand. I've been in love before."

"That's not...I'm not..." My stomach twists at the thought. Now, I really am sick. I bolt.

My mother has determined that there were two hundred and twenty-eight Warriors stolen and six hundred and twelve

Warriors destroyed. The base's engineers have deployed the robotic diggers to start uncovering Pit 5, and I've been drafted to help piece together one of the broken Warriors—I'm pretty sure it's the general. In fact, I'm working on reconstructing the lower half of him when I kneel on something hard. Not a surprise as there's shards and pieces littering the ground. But this is a smooth hard. Plus it's at the bottom of a long deep gouge in the sandstone that must have been made by the looters' equipment. Perhaps something is buried here.

I sweep the sand away and uncover a... I'm not sure. It's flat and gray instead of light tan like everything else and it has no markings. I wave my mother over and she, with much excitement, calls the techs to do their thing. Believe it or not you have to be trained to remove sand and dirt. They expose more flatness—it's about a meter under the Warriors. I've discovered a floor. Yippee for me.

But this doesn't deter them and like a dog after its bone—do they really do that?—they keep it up. For hours. And I'm curious why no one has thought to dig underneath the Warriors before.

"They did, on Xi'an and a bunch of other Warrior planets," Mom says when I ask her. "Not all sixty-four pits, but a random sample. For the rest they used Ground Penetrating Radar."

GPR is a device that uses radar waves to penetrate the earth. If there's something other than dirt or rock, the waves will bounce off it and alert the techs that there'd be treasure below, mateys...ah, sorry.

"Nothing has ever been found below and since it appeared all the planets matched, we stopped doing it. Plus we needed the funds for other things," Mom says.

The diggers take a break and the lead man consults with my mother. She returns to me and says, "We're waiting for the GPR. It's being used out in the desert to map the location of the other fifty-nine Warrior pits. Team two is going to bring it back."

"Do you think it'll work?"

"Probably not, but we have to follow standard procedures."

I stand and work a crick from my neck.

"Go to bed."

"But I..."

"Don't worry, I'll wake you if we find anything exciting," Mom says.

"Thanks."

Archaeology is not a fast-paced endeavor. It takes them two more days to figure out there might be a room or cavern below the floor, which, despite its name, the GPR can't penetrate. It's another three days until they locate a hatch. And that causes massive excitement because there's an octagonal shaped groove in the hatch about three centimeters deep. In the groove are eight different symbols. They're etched in the stone. Rather deep, I'd guess a centimeter at least.

My heart just about stops when I see the glyphs. "These are similar to the ones on that octagon I found," I tell my mom.

"Are you sure?"

"Can I access your terminal?"

We return to the archaeology lab and I shove my tangs in. My parents stand behind me as I bring up the photo of the octagonal artifact on the screen.

"Row three," Dad says. "They almost match the style."

I open file three, which is where the Q-net placed all the Warriors with that symbol together. "Lan sent this to me," I say before they accuse me of stealing the document.

"I know some of those Warriors," Mom says, pointing to a few statues. "The pathfinders. See, they hold scrolls. We think they're maps. And these are chroniclers. Each pit has one, supposedly to record the battalion's adventures." The Warriors hold a small rectangular object against their chest with one hand and grasp a strange knife with a thick block on the end with their other hand.

"With a knife?" I ask.

"No, it's a stamp. See the markings on the base? They press that into the wet clay. It's rudimentary, but if you're going to write the same thing on thousands of Warriors, it makes it easier to just use the stamp."

Oh.

"Can you pick out the ones that just have those eight symbols that we uncovered around the keyhole?" Dad asks. He's bouncing on the balls of his feet.

I drag the file into a cluster and make the request. The Q-net sorts the Warriors. Eight chroniclers remain.

"Pits 2, 3, 4, 5, 7, 24, 32, and 56," Mom says.

"But not all from the same planet," I remind them.

"Yes, but a scribe from Pit 2 on Xinji is the exact same as a scribe in Pit 2 on Ulanqab." Dad flings his arms up. "Which is why I think they were mass produced and not on Earth. The aliens used Earth's clay and asked the Chinese craftsmen to teach them. Then the aliens went their merry way and created all these."

"There's been no evidence of a factory on another planet," Mom says.

"And there's no evidence on Earth of such a massive endeavor," he shoots back. "The Emperor had eight thousand to guard his tomb, and it took a dozen men thirty days to create just one Warrior."

I ignore their argument because I can recite each of their responses by heart. I stare at the screen. Actually, I study the stamp. The markings are too hard to see. But I don't need to strain my eyes. Instead, I consult a map—Row 1, Column 16— that should be easy. I stand up.

"Where are you going?" Mom asks.

"Pit 2, to take a closer look at that scribe."

The Warriors in the pit stand in precise rows and columns. They also form a giant octagon, so the total number in each pit is one thousand, four hundred and forty-eight—there's an empty square in the exact center, that's about two by two meters. One general leads them, and I'm sure my mother can tell you what each of the Warrior's ranks and jobs are—archers, swordsmen, pike men, infantry carrying maces, and now pathfinders and scribes.

Row 1 is easy to find as they stand in front. I count the

columns and stop at 16. Like all the Warriors, he's close to two meters tall. His features are serene and his uniform is plain. Only a few symbols mark his tunic like the Chinese calligraphy that is the name of the artist who made him and those alien glyphs.

But it's the blocky base of his writing tool that I'm interested in. "Ha! Look at that." I point. "His stamp is one of those eight keyhole symbols."

My father peers closer. "You're right. I wonder..." He wiggles the stamp's handle.

"Be very careful," Mom warns.

With a skin-crawling screech the stamp slides free.

My father brandishes it about like a flag and hops around in circles. "It's part of the key!"

My mother and I exchange a do-you-want-to-tell-him-or-should-I glance. *He's your husband*, I mouth.

"Spencer, that may be so, but we only have scribes from Pits 2, 3, and 4. If we need all eight, it's going to be a few years before the other pits are uncovered on Yulin."

He stops dancing. "You're always being so practical. Well, guess what. We have an entire research base filled with talented scientists and I'm sure we can duplicate those other five keys. What's the sense of being in charge if you can't hijack a few people for our project?"

"Way to go, Dad!"

"And if that doesn't work?"

"There's always brute force and jack hammers for that lock," my dad says. "I'd hate to do it as it might damage something below, but this is too important to leave alone."

"Did those recovered files from Xinji mention anything about them finding a sublevel?" I ask my dad.

"I don't think so."

"Do you want me to look through them?"

"No!"

Surprised by the vehemence in her reply, I glance at my mom.

"There's an entire team at DES analyzing them. Plus they've marked them as highly classified," Mom says. "I can't even access them, and if you try to worm into them, you'll be arrested."

"Why did they do that?"

"Because everyone in the Galaxy has a theory about why Xinji went silent. These rumors can spread panic and distrust, especially if they take information from those files out of context. DES wants to do a full investigation and then release the facts."

At least I was able to help a little bit. But if I have to do some illegal worming to solve Lan's discovery, then I won't hesitate.

My mom and I are getting ready for dinner when my dad enters the kitchen holding eight stamps... er... keys.

He waves them about. "They're done! Come on, let's see if they fit!"

"Three days. That was fast," Mom says as she turns off the cooker.

We hurry to catch up to Dad as he's all but sprinting to the archaeology lab. The techs still on duty follow after us and those working in the pits join our joyous parade.

Dad yanks off the sheet covering the hatch with a flourish. We all crowd close as he matches the symbols and inserts each key. I don't have any desire to become an archaeologist, but I gotta admit, my heart's doing flips in my chest and I'm on my tiptoes trying to see better.

"Everyone back up a meter," my dad orders. "We don't know what will happen." He tries to turn the keys all at once. First clockwise then counterclockwise.

Nothing moves.

Then he pushes them all down at once. They give. We gasp, but nothing else happens.

"Maybe you have to push and turn at the same time," someone calls out.

"Then I need more hands," my dad says. Three techs offer to help.

They try various combinations. Nothing works.

Archaeology and frustration go hand in hand.

"Well shi—"

"Spencer," Mom interrupts. "You really didn't think it'd be that easy; everything's been a puzzle so far. You probably have to press down each key in the right order."

He sets back on his heels. "Okay, what's the right order?"

"Numerical. Pit 2 first then go from there." And when it didn't work, "Try going backwards, highest to lowest." And then, "How about in the order they appeared on the screen?"

As my father tries different patterns, I remember what Lan said in her one message. It's like a code within a code. I move away to a quiet spot, take a trowel and scratch the pit numbers into the sandstone.

2, 3, 4, 5, 7, 24, 32, and 56. I glance around. The aliens liked octagons so it makes sense that the number eight is important to them. There's sixty-four pits on each planet. And eight symbols for the key. But the numbers aren't all multiples of eight. Maybe if I add them all together...ugh...that's...one hundred and thirty-three and even I know that's not divisible by eight. How about subtraction...that's a negative twenty-one. Multiplication? Yikes—too big, and forget division.

Eight is key. Two times three is six, but two times four is eight. And five plus three is eight. What about seven? Uh...pass. Thirty-two minus twenty-four is eight. And...fifty-six divided by seven is eight!

When I return, my father is talking about trying sledgehammers before they move on to the jackhammers.

I interrupt him. "Try one more combination."

"No sense, there's millions of possibilities."

"Indulge me."

"Well, you've gotten us this far." He shoos everyone back. "One more."

Suddenly nervous and trying to ignore the techs' eye rolls and muttered comments, I say, "Push down five and three at the same time."

He does.

"Then the thirty-two and twenty-four at the same time."

"Next?"

"Four and two."

He gives me a wild-eyed grin. "And then fifty-six and seven! Addition, subtraction, multiplication and division all equaling eight!"

Dad presses the final two and a loud clunk sounds as the keyhole drops down ten centimeters, releasing a giant whoosh of air. We all jump back and my father scrambles away in case there's toxic gas escaping.

Yes!

Dad picks me up and twirls me around. "You figured it out! Using math!"

"Lan figured it out, I just followed her logic."

"But you used math!"

"Does this mean you'll stop teasing me about my mathematical abilities?"

He sets me down and considers. "Probably not."

"Can we open the hatch?" one of the techs asks. A group of them are edging closer.

"Not yet," Mom says. "Keep away from there. We need to sample the air and I'm sure Officer Radcliff would like to be on hand just in case."

"You think looters have been hiding down there?" one snarks.

"And that is why you're still a tech, Regan," Mom says coolly. "Booby traps are far more dangerous than looters."

They all back up a few more steps.

By the next day, all is ready. I join the group in Pit 4 right after soch-time. My parents are there along with the techs and a security team wearing their black jumpsuits and guns. Six of them, including both Radcliffs. Lovely.

Officer Radcliff hands me a B-app. "Always a pleasure to see you, Miss Daniels."

Do I detect a hint of sarcasm? Perhaps a smidge. "How are you settling in, Officer Radcliff?"

His gaze jumps to Niall before he says, "Just fine, thanks for asking."

Oh aren't we being polite? And I suspect things aren't just fine by Niall's hostile expression. Radcliff helps me don the heavy rectangular air filter. The weight rests below my shoulder blades. Then he shows me how to properly seat the clear plastic mask over my face. The peppery scent disappears. I glance around. Radcliff is the last to put on his B-app. Everyone else is wearing one.

I back away as my father gives the signal. He and a few techs muscle the thick slab of stone to the side, revealing a black hole.

Dr. Bernstein crouches next to it and lowers a device that tests the air. "It's stale and there's not enough oxygen." His voice sounds funny through the plastic. "We can install a few ventilation shafts and air exchangers down there and it'll eventually equalize to what we're breathing up here."

Officer Radcliff turns on a flashlight and shines it down. "Anything explosive or acidic?"

"No," Bernstein says.

"All right, let's go check it out," Radcliff says. "Four meters."

One of the men hands a small ladder to another. They pull it apart until it's about four meters long. Fancy. They insert it in the hole. Radcliff swings onto it while the two hold it in place. He motions to two others before he climbs down. They follow and the other three officers— who include Niall—take up positions around the hatch.

My mom makes a low derisive sound next to me.

I glance at her with my eyebrows raised.

"I should be going with them," she explains. Her voice is muffled by the mask.

"Booby traps?" I ask. My words bounce off the plastic—a strange almost echo.

"Yes. He's not trained to recognize them."

"Are you sure you're just not jealous he's the first to go down there?"

"Smart ass," Mom says, but she's smiling. No. She's grinning like a crazy lady. I haven't seen her this excited since we learned about Yulin.

Officer Radcliff shouts up an all-clear and my parents eagerly descend with Dr. Bernstein right behind. Two security officers follow them and I'm left with the techs and Niall. Guess he's the low man on the team. He keeps his focus on the ladder and the dark hatch.

We wait. And wait. And wait some more. Niall never relaxes, but I'm considering sitting down.

The ladder rattles and Niall holsters his weapon. My father

comes up first and Niall helps him step onto solid ground.

Dad is all smiles. He pulls his mask off. "There are rooms and rooms that extend out." He throws his arms wide.

"What's in the rooms? More Warriors?" I ask.

"No. There's strange—perhaps alien—machinery and work areas. There's evidence of people...or aliens who might have lived here! And we saw a...factory or something. It looked like they might have done something to the Warriors here!" My dad does a little jig.

Now that was worth the wait.

The rest of the team bubbles up from below and my mother is beyond thrilled. Even through her joy, she's shouting orders before she even steps off the ladder. "Spencer, send word to the other Warrior planets, letting them know about the lower level and how to open it, they need to test beneath every single pit. Del, schedule the cartographers, I want a detailed map as soon as possible. Yuki, go get the carbon dating equipment. Regan, I want you to schedule the techs to work in rotating eight-hour shifts. I want someone down there cataloging twenty-four seven. Lyra, go with Dr. Bernstein and the rest of the techs to get the air exchangers and pumps."

Everyone rushes off except me.

"Lyra?" Mom asks.

I glance at the hatch. Once the archaeologists get into full discovery mode, I'll just be in the way. Plus I'm already wearing the B-app. "Can I go down?"

Mom huffs. "We don't have time right—"

"I'll take her," Radcliff offers. "Come on, Miss Daniels. You, too, Niall. Gordy, hold the ladder."

If Niall is surprised, he doesn't show it. Radcliff turns the flashlight back on and leads the way. I'm next and Niall is last.

"Don't touch anything," my mom calls as we descend into an empty square room.

The walls are smooth and not dug from the sandstone. Dust motes float in the flashlight's white beam. Sand crunches under our boots as we follow Radcliff through a doorway on the right that leads to a hallway with multiple entrances on either side. The rooms are all different sizes and there are counters and strange silver colored machinery. The tall boxy...things have symbols and grooves, but they don't resemble anything I've seen before. A film of dusty sand coats everything.

Then we enter a cavern—definitely hewn from the sandstone. It's big and Warriors lie on long tables. There must be hundreds of them. It's creepy.

Moving deeper into the cavern, we pass more rows of tables. Far in the back is another table. This one is pushed against the wall and is loaded with terracotta... hearts? I stop. It's beyond creepy. But it's fascinating as well. I step closer. They appear to be shaped like human hearts, but I'm not an expert. And there's something written on them.

"Miss Daniels?"

"Can you shine the light here?"

Radcliff stands to my right while Niall comes up on my left. The light is almost swallowed by the deep black of the hearts—not terracotta, and there are silver lines visible on the surface. No. Not lines. Oh. My. Stars. I glance at Niall as my own heart jumps in my chest.

"What's that?" Radcliff asks. "Chinese calligraphy?"

They're the same symbols that are on the octagonal artifact. They're carved into all the hearts. And the desire to touch one burns hot inside me.

Ignoring the voice in my head—my mother's—warning me to stop, I pick up one of the black hearts to take a closer look at Lan's symbols, but it disintegrates in my hand. I yelp as a bone-numbing cold coats my fingers and sears my palm.

10

2522:127

R adcliff brushes away the bits of the heart left on my skin with his sleeve. "Is it burning you? Some kind of acid? Are you in pain?"

"No." The truth. The cold disappears as fast as it arrived. "It just...surprised me. I didn't think the heart would crumble like that."

"You're not supposed to touch anything."

"I know. I just...couldn't resist. Something about it..." I rub my right hand along my jeans. "Sorry."

"Well there are hundreds of these, I don't think your mother will miss one."

I give him a look. He should know my mother by now.

He sighs. "Yeah."

"Don't worry. I'll fess up."

"Will you get in trouble?" Niall asks, speaking for the first time.

The words *why do you care* push at the back of my throat.

But I reject the childish retort. "I'll get a lecture and be assigned the most tedious and mindless task in the lab so I learn just how crucial and valuable every single piece is in a dig site."

"Sounds like this isn't the first time you've broken something," Radcliff says. The humor in his voice is evident even through his mask.

"Let's just say I'm well past my first time and leave it at that."

He chuckles. "Let's go back before anything else happens."

I take one last look. It'll be dozens of days before I'm allowed in here again. Following Radcliff back through the rooms, I mull over the significance of those hearts. The Warriors are all hollow. They're life-sized and lifelike, but nothing's been found inside them. Well...not the broken ones. I rub my hand. If they're that fragile... then the hearts would have crumbled when the Warriors broke. But why didn't the digital X-ray scanners see the hearts inside intact Warriors? They did appear to soak up the light, maybe they don't reflect. Guess that will be a puzzle for my parents to solve.

At least my mistake will warn my mom about how fragile they are. I doubt she'll see it that way, but a girl can hope.

When we exit, my mother is still barking orders. She spots me. "What do you think? Isn't it exciting? Did you see they might have used an assembly line of some sort? We have *so* much work to do! Dr. Bernstein already left, but I need you to —"

"Mom, I..." I take a breath and tell her about the heart.

"Lyra Tian Daniels, what have I told you a million times since you were born?" she asks with barely contained fury.

"Not to touch anything. I'm sor—"

"It's such a simple rule, but it appears you are incapable of keeping your hands to yourself." Mom shakes her head. "That's it. You're banned from the pits. Go. Get out of here before I say something I'll regret."

I expected a lecture, but not to be scolded in front of the Radcliffs. Mortified, I take off the B-app and leave. The Warriors stare at me with censure as I cross through the other pits. If they have hearts, they've been well hidden. Wish I could say the same about mine.

When I reach the base, I pause. I don't want to go back to our quarters, I'm not hungry or tired. I just want to…hide. Except I promised to help the chemists again after dinner. Seems I'm good at preparing slides. Just great. All these useless talents add up to make me an expert in absolutely nothing.

Without a destination in mind, I wander through the corridors, passing groups of scientists and techs on their way to the cafeteria. Excited chatter about the new discovery buzzes in the air. They all know who I am, some have watched me grow up. I get hellos and smiles. But even with a research base filled with people, there's no one I can really talk to. No Lan to pour my heart out to. No Lan to tell me I'm being melodramatic and should know my mom will eventually relent. Instead, my chest hurts like there's a scream trapped inside. It's pushing so hard to escape that I fear I'm about to explode.

I arrive at the game room in the soch-area with no memory of my trip. It's empty—no surprise since it's dinner time and everyone is still settling in to labs and housing units. Plopping into one of the oversized chairs, I stare at the dark screen. Since Niall's "graduation" I'm not allowed in here by myself during soch-time, so I've relinquished it to the quartet of girls. But now there's no restrictions and I can play by myself. Except that sounds depressing.

Being banned from the pits doesn't bother me all that much. My parents need all the help they can get so I'll be shoveling sand in no time as punishment before Mom orders me to finish the reconstruction of Pit 4's general.

I wonder if Lan found the same hidden room on Xinji, if she discovered those strange black hearts and Warriors lying down as if waiting for…surgery or something. Was she super excited to see the result of all her hard work researching those symbols? Or was finding the room just the first step? Could there be more marvels to discover? I'd give anything to be able to ask her. I glance around at the still empty room. I can't ask her, but perhaps there's something in one of those files from Xinji.

Inserting my tangs, I connect with the game system. Hoshi has taught me so much, it's easy to bypass all the limits, worm into the security cameras, erase my passage through the corridors and make it appear as if the game room is empty. The difficult part will be getting into the classified cluster where DES put the files from Xinji.

In order to reach them, I need to find the smallest of holes to squirm through without causing ripples. It's a challenge and

I run into a number of dead ends. Argh. Going in a different direction, I try again. And again. And again. Maybe if I message Jarren... No. I'll figure this out on my own.

Those holes in security disappear the closer I get to those files, but maybe if I dip underneath and... Ah ha!

A nice little gap appears and I'm in! Now what?

I do a Q-net search for Warrior hearts and underground. A few files pop up and—

"Lyra!"

My name shatters my concentration. I turn and see Niall standing in the doorway. Bad timing is an understatement.

"Go away," I say.

"I've been searching for you for hours."

The lights are nighttime dim, it must be late. "Congrats on finding me. Now, go away." I've no desire to talk to him. He made his feelings about being friends with me clear.

Instead of listening he steps into the room. He's holding a white sheet of paper. "I checked all your hiding places. And the security cameras—"

Shit. I wait as he puzzles out the logic.

"You wormed the cameras! What are you doing?"

"Playing a game," I try.

"Lyra," he growls. Setting the sheet down, he inserts his entanglers.

Shit. I can't retreat or cover my tracks that fast or it'd alert DES.

He pales, which is impressive considering how pale he is from living on ships all his life. "That's... you're... how?... it's classified!"

"Looters never killed before Xinji, Niall. So why this time? We just made a colossal breakthrough. What if that same thing triggered the attack on Xinji? I'm just checking to see if Lan mentions anything about what we found."

Niall sinks into the chair next to me. He runs a hand through his hair. It's shorter than when he attended his last soch-time, but not as short as his father's. He's still wearing his black jumpsuit. He still looks good in it. No. Not going there. I concentrate on how much I hate him as I wait.

"It doesn't matter *why* you're worming. It's illegal and I have to arrest you."

Alarm sizzles down my spine. "You? But you don't—"

"I have the authority. I'm no longer a junior officer but a full-fledged member of the security team." Bitterness laces his voice.

Hate turns to fear. I'm already in trouble with my parents. If Niall arrests me, they'll go supernova and spending time in detention will be a vacation in comparison.

"How about if I promise never to do it again?" I ask.

Niall gives me a do-you-really-think-I'm-that-stupid look.

He's really going to do it. I try another tactic. "All those people died. You saw the reports of evisceration and exsanguination. I'm helping like I did for your dad by organizing those files. I'm not causing trouble like that girl Jarren mentioned...Osen Vee, I think."

"But that was before DES classified them. I know you're upset about Lan, but you need to let the experts figure it out."

"Okay. I will. Come on, Niall." My thoughts race, seeking a loophole or something. Then I remember. "You owe me one from when your dad caught you with your sketchbook at soch-time!"

"But this..." His shoulders droop. "All right."

Relief washes through me. I smile. "Thanks."

"Don't thank me. If your activities here are discovered by DES or my dad, I can't help you." He gestures to the cameras. "Plus there's no evidence I was ever here."

Which reminds me. "Why are you looking for me?"

He lifts the piece of paper he set down and flips it over. I stare at a drawing of a black heart with silver symbols. It resembles the one I accidentally destroyed.

Amazed, I ask, "Is that—"

"Yes."

"But how did you remember the symbols?"

"We used to play this memory game on the ship where you glance at something for a second and try to remember everything you saw. It's a good skill to have if you're a security officer. Plus I drew those symbols when we were deciphering Lan's files so I'm familiar with their shapes."

I'm impressed.

"You can give this to your mom so she has a record of the heart that you destroyed. Maybe then she'll let you back into the pits."

That's actually sweet of him.

He stands. "Now we're even. And this doesn't make us friends. If I catch you illegally worming again, I *will* arrest you.

Understand?"

"Yes, *Officer* Radcliff." Jerk.

He leaves and I copy those two data files to a hidden cluster. Erasing my tracks, I move with extra care. The threat that Niall's father or DES will sense me is not idle and I don't want to give Niall the satisfaction of seeing me get arrested. Once that's finished, I fix the cameras.

By the time I'm done, the base's corridors are empty and the lights are at their dimmest setting. It's close to oh-three-hundred hours. I'm halfway back to my unit when I realize that Niall drew the heart on a piece of the rice paper that I made for his birthday. Stopping in the middle of the hallway, I don't know whether to be glad he's using it or furious that he didn't even thank me. I settle on extreme annoyance—he did refrain from arresting me.

My parents are not back and probably have no idea I've been gone most of the night. Thinking about it, I doubt I'll see much of them in the next couple— probably more like dozens—of days. I lay the picture of the heart on my mom's desk and go to bed.

Warriors fill my dreams. They march through time. Their urgency, their need to fight presses on me. They grab my arm, pulling me along. We must protect. We must sacrifice our lives for—

A light tapping wakes me. My heart pounds in sync with my

dream Warriors' steps. My pajamas stick to the sweat on my skin. What the hell? I've never dreamt of them before.

"Lyra? Are you awake?" Mom asks.

"Yeah, come in."

I sit up as my mother enters my room. She's holding the picture. "Is this—"

"Yes. Niall drew it." I explain about his memory game.

"This is wonderful. He's very talented."

Yeah, a talented jerk. But he did help me out. "Just don't tell his dad. He doesn't...support Niall's hobby."

Mom presses her lips together, then sighs. "It's hard being a single parent. I'm sure Tace is doing his best."

I can't decide if my mother being on a first name basis with Radcliff is a good or bad thing.

"Lyra, I'm sor—"

"Don't say it, Mom. It was my fault. I know the rules. I just..." The desire to touch was so strong. It's hard to explain. An ache travels up my right forearm. I rub it.

"What's wrong with your arm?"

"Nothing."

"Don't lie to me. That's the fourth time you've rubbed it."

Fourth? "I...think I slept on it wrong. It's all..."

"Pins and needles?"

Close enough. "Yes."

She takes my hand and strokes my arm. "Once the circulation is restored, the pain will go away."

Her touch is gentle and I lean toward her. She sits on the bed next to me, putting her arm around my shoulder, tucking me close. How does she know what I need most? She'd probably say it's a mom thing. I inhale her comforting scent of lilacs and relax against her.

"I overacted yesterday," she says. "I'd like you to keep working on putting the general back together. It was his battalion that was taken and destroyed by the looters, I think it's the least we can do."

"Mom, you're not anthropomorphizing, are you?" I tease. When I was little, I used to name the Warriors and make up stories about them, pretending they were real. That's how I learned a fancy word like anthropomorphizing.

She squeezes me. "Well, there's a possibility that they have hearts. It's interesting how that changes the way I view them."

I straighten. "I thought the same thing—that the scanners can't detect the heart because of that black material. It'd be easy to confirm, you can carefully drill a hole into an intact Warrior and use one of those snake cameras to see if it's there."

Mom laughs. "We'll make an archaeologist out of you yet."

I press a hand to my chest in mock horror. "Oh no."

Another light laugh and it sings in my ears. "Get dressed. You have a microbiology exam at oh-nine- hundred hours."

Surprised, I ask, "How do you know?"

"I'm Mom. I know all, see all—"

"Hear all. Yeah, yeah, I've heard that a million times. I didn't think you had time to check my class schedule."

"The Warriors don't rule my life."

I look at her.

"Okay. They dominate my time, but I also keep up with

what's going on in your life."

Hmmm. I tuck that little nugget away.

"For example, I know you made the colored chalks and rice paper Niall used to draw the heart."

Not a big surprise. Scientists either drone on and on about their research or gossip about other scientists. It's hard to keep a secret in this small community.

"And I know you and Niall haven't been hanging out."

"He's made it clear he doesn't want anything to do with me." Jerk.

"He's having a tough time adjusting. I see him in the pits quite a bit. They're closed in like the ship. He really needs a friend."

I poke a finger at the paper. "I tried. He told me he doesn't want to be friends."

"Men get like that. You have to ignore his words and keep trying. He used the paper, that's a good sign. Plus his dad's really worried about him."

Then he shouldn't have taken his sketchbooks. "All right. I'll try again." My words are positive but not my tone.

"Remember that he's not mad at *you*, but at his situation. Try not to take it personally."

I stare at her.

"Yeah, I know how hard that is to do."

Try *impossible*, but I promise my mom I will make another attempt. She leaves and I connect to my terminal and take my microbiology exam. Halfway through I'm struck by how similar the body's microscopic world is to the Q-net. Kind of fascinating.

When I cross through the pits on my way to Pit 4, I spot Niall in Pit 2 and decide to talk to him. Except he disappears and I can't find him. Huh? Maybe he didn't see me.

After Niall evades me on two other days, I figure out he's avoiding me. Such a jerk move. How am I supposed to help him if he won't talk to me?

My brain works on that problem while I reassemble the General. Yeah, I decided he should have a capital letter. I'm also close to the hatch and I keep an eye on the scientists going up and down, exploring and mapping the rooms below—their excited chatter echos off the walls. There's always a few security officers with them just in case they run into trouble, but Niall isn't one of them. Well, not at that time. They're still working around the clock.

Once the adhesive in the General's legs cures, I stand them up. It just feels right. He needs to be on his feet again. His legs weren't too hard to reconstruct. I suspect his chest will be the most difficult because that's where he was hit. Plus I'll need a frame to hold the pieces together, because I'm not strong enough to hold them while they dry.

Happy with the progress I've made, I straighten and dust off my jeans even though I know sand is probably in my socks, boots, and underwear. It's just a fact of life. You either get used to it or it drives you insane.

On my way out, I debate between food and sleep. Since we opened the hatch, the Warriors have been haunting my dreams and interrupting my sleep. And the General has become an unrelenting presence in both my waking and sleeping life—if I'm not working on him, I'm dreaming about him leading his men. Lovely. I roll my stiff shoulder.

When I pass Officer Tace Radcliff, instead of nodding a greeting and continuing on like normal, he steps into my path. "Miss Daniels, do you have time to talk?"

I stop. Is he going to arrest me? "Uh...sure."

He pulls me away from the steady flow of traffic through the pits. "It's about Niall."

Oh no. My stomach churns for a different reason. "Okay."

Radcliff runs a hand over the stubble that is supposed to be his hair. A familiar gesture. I almost smile, but he is clearly upset.

"I've tried everything and I'm out of options." He presses his fists against his thighs. "Niall's miserable. He's surly, disobedient, and argues with me about... everything. I just found out from your father that he requested his own housing unit. Could you talk to him for me and find out why?"

Oh boy. "I've been trying to talk to him. He's avoiding me and told me he doesn't want to be friends."

He flinches as if I'd just stabbed him in the gut. Poor guy. I'd like to help and I promised my mom. So I dredge up my memories and emotions from when I've had to leave my home. I don't have to dig deep. Remembering my conversation with my parents before we left Xinji, I say, "Niall didn't want to come here, but he had no choice. Getting his own unit is something he has control over." Then I thought about what Niall said in soch-time. "Why did you take away his sketchbooks?"

Radcliff gives me a harsh look. "That's none of your business."

He's right, but I can't stop. "You took away his family *and* his sketchbooks. If that was me, I'd be surly and disobedient, too." And there would have been tears. I doubt Niall's the crying type.

"*I'm* his family," he practically growls. "And he can have his blasted books back if he behaves."

Niall said they were taken for insubordination. And it clicks. "But now you're his boss. Do you do that to the other officers when they fail to follow orders?"

Radcliff's gaze burns through me. I'm such an idiot. I'm arguing with the Chief of Security. Is that insubordination? Can he arrest me? Sweat trails down my back.

He blows out a breath. "What about you? Why is he pushing you away?"

"I think it's because he doesn't want to become... attached. I had four close friends on Xinji a hundred and thirty-six days ago. Now one's dead, another's thirty-seven A-years old and I've no idea what happened to the other two."

"But you can still communicate with them like you did with Jarren."

"Yes, except it's not the same. Jarren's twenty years older than me. Our lives are no longer aligned. And that's why Niall won't talk to me. If he did, it'd just hurt him more when he leaves in two years."

"Two—" Radcliff's face drains of all color.

I clap my hand over my mouth, but it's too late.

"He's going to join the Protectorate." Radcliff's stunned.

So I just made everything worse. Good going, Lyra. Guess I can take becoming a psychiatrist off my list of potential careers.

And I kind of know why Niall hasn't told his father. Parents want to hold on tighter when things go bad. I've seen it happen. Mine clung to Phoenix those last sixty days before he left and he told me he wished he'd given them less notice. He missed just being a normal family.

Radcliff recovers and straightens. "Thank you for your time, Miss Daniels."

Before he turns away, I touch his sleeve. "Can I ask a question?"

"Yes, but I can't guarantee an answer."

"Fair enough." That earns me a ghost of a smile. "Why are you so against Niall's drawing? He's really good at it."

A pause. Then he pulls in a breath. "My wife was a talented artist and, whenever I see him drawing…" He taps his chest. "It's like ripping open an old wound, reminding me she's gone."

"Oh."

"That isn't a good enough answer?"

"It's not that. I'm just surprised. I would have thought it'd be the opposite."

"The opposite?"

I circle my hand in the air as if I could pull in the right words. "That it would feel good to see a part of your wife in your son. He does have twenty-three of her chromosomes." Yup, it's official, I've been hanging out with scientists way too long. When he doesn't say anything, I add, "My dad cheats at cards all the time—it's just to see if he is smart enough to get away with it because he doesn't care about winning. My brother Phoenix does the same thing and my father is so proud of that. If we catch Phoenix cheating, Dad praises him and encourages him to cheat better next time so he doesn't get caught. Mom scolds them both. But her heart isn't in it because I think she likes seeing a part of my dad in her son."

Radcliff is looking at me with a strange expression. "Thanks for the warning about your father."

There's a touch of humor in his voice so I think that's not what he's really thanking me for. I play along, though. "My money's on my dad."

"That confident?"

"He's had years of practice."

"We'll see." Radcliff tilts his head. "Have a pleasant evening, Miss Daniels."

"You, too, Officer Radcliff."

Wow, I'm doing some serious adulting, I need to steal a bit of the hooch that the chemists brewed up—that I'm not supposed to tell my parents about—in order to get my miscreant card back. If you don't know what miscreant means, then you haven't been misbehaving enough in your life.

He continues on to Pit 4 and I hurry to the canteen because my stomach is threatening to go on strike. Family meals are not a priority right now and, like most of the scientists in the base,

I don't want to waste time cooking. I find an empty table and dig into the mystery meat covered with the brown colored goo—doesn't matter what it is, it all tastes the same.

A thud shakes the table. I glance up. Niall is sitting opposite me. He doesn't have a tray of food, but he does have an extremely pissed off glower.

"I saw you talking to my dad. What did he say about me?" he demands.

2522:132

Oh no. He doesn't get to avoid me and then demand I talk to him. "We agreed that you're a jerk. Now go away." I make a shooing motion.

"Lyra." His tone is low and dangerous.

"We're not friends. Remember?"

"Yes, I do. It's because I can't..." His forehead smooths. "Be like you."

That's unexpected. "Me?"

"Yeah." He gestures. "You're so well adjusted. You just lost a bunch of friends and it doesn't bother you."

Doesn't bother me? Anger and frustration mix and just about choke me. I tap my chest. "Do you know what's in here? Crumbs. My heart crumbled when I left Xinji just like that black heart I touched. And Lan's death..." A tight fist of emotion clamps around my throat, but I force the words through. "Just about swept all those crumbs away. The only thing keeping what's left together is finding out what happened to her and making sure all her decades of work weren't for nothing."

Bile churns in my stomach as I lean closer. "It bothers me. A. Lot. I've just had more experience at hiding my emotions. And I had more time to deal. My parents let me know we were leaving Xinji well before your ship arrived. You had what...thirty days? I understand *exactly* what you're going through, and I promised myself the same thing when I left Xinji—don't make friends because you will leave them or they'll leave you."

Niall stares at me, but his anger has dulled into a simmer. "But you made friends."

Friends as in plural? I think about it. I did. Huh. "I guess that broody-leave-me-alone isn't my style. Besides, it helped." The truth—a surprise. "You said boredom kills, well it's like the same thing. Being with others is a break from the pain. And, let's face it, no amount of anger or sadness is going to change anything. We're still stuck on Yulin." I pause. "Well, I am. You'll be gone when that Protectorate ship arrives."

Now my anger returns. I stand. "And do you know what?"

Niall tenses.

"Being an asshole and pushing me away to save yourself from future pain is a dick move. I'm the *only* one who understands what you're going through. You could have talked to me, instead, you hurt me. And guess what? When you leave, it'll still hurt me because it'll remind me of King Toad and how we'd once been friends."

Not waiting for a response, I walk away. Yelling at Niall probably didn't help him, but I can breathe easier now. And I did promise to talk to him. That counted, right?

I don't see Niall again until seven days later. I'm searching for pieces of the General in the debris of Pit 4. Even though there are still fragments missing and cracks zigzagging throughout, the General is as complete as I can make him from the chest down. You can see his pointed armor flap. Digging through a pile of rubble, I find what I hope is his left arm, but it's stuck under a section of another broken Warrior that's too heavy for me to lift. I'm about to call for one of the techs to help when Niall appears and hefts the Warrior as if it weighs nothing. Show-off. I tug the arm free and return to the General.

Niall trails after me. He's wearing his security uniform—not the jumpsuit, but the everyday one. The long-sleeved shirt is light gray. It has his last name and the word "security" embroidered on the left breast. The uniform also includes tactical pants, boots, and a weapon belt—all black in color. There's a pulse gun in his holster. I ignore him. There's nothing left for me to say to him.

"You're here late," he says.

The General's been insisting I finish him. Yeah, I know it sounds crazy, but I think, once he's finished, the Warriors will stop marching through my dreams. Of course I don't tell that to Niall. Instead, I continue to ignore him as I sit down and brush the sand off the General's arm.

Niall crouches down and grabs my wrists, stopping me. I

glare at him.

"My dad gave me my sketchbooks back," he says, releasing my wrists now that he has my attention.

Wow. Radcliff listened to me? Good thing I'm already sitting down.

"I know you said something to him. Thanks."

I grunt. "You're still a jerk."

"Yeah, well, I'm now getting lectures about joining the Protectorate, since you ratted me out. My dad and I are still fighting."

"Then you should have told me that was a secret... oh, wait...I believe you were telling me to get lost at that time." I regret my outburst when he flinches—because I'm not normally that mean. "I'm sorry it caused you more trouble. It was another poor attempt to help. Don't worry, I'm done interfering."

"Are you done illegal worming, too?" he teases.

Or he tries. I just can't banter with him anymore. "No comment, Officer Radcliff."

A pained expression grips his face. "Lyra, I'm..."

My mom once said that men are physically incapable of verbally apologizing. Now I believe her as I watch Niall squirm.

"I'm — "

"Lyra, do you know if your father's down below?" Dr. Bernstein interrupts us. His tone is harried and his gray hair is sticking up.

Niall straightens. "Something wrong?"

Bernstein eyes Niall's uniform. "I can't reach him and a sandstorm is coming. We need to close all the outside vents right away. It's a significant one."

"He went down a while ago," I say. Probably still there if they couldn't reach him. The extra layer of sandstone makes communications difficult.

"I'll get him and then contact my father," Niall offers. "Go to the Control Center and alert the teams in the field. We'll meet you there."

Bernstein nods and rushes off. Niall descends the ladder. I'm left wondering if he was going to apologize. Perhaps something like, *I am so sorry, please forgive me.* Or maybe confess? *I am so in love with you, I can't think of anything else.* Uh…probably not that one. Why would I even think that anyway? He's been such a jerk.

I sigh. However, he just lost his family and he didn't arrest me. I do miss teasing him at soch-time. Plus he made sure I ate after our mission to Yulin. And look at the way he just jumped into action to help. And that kiss… Argh. Why does everything have to be so… complicated?

I should be more concerned about the sandstorm. But we've had a few already and everyone who is involved knows the drill. The scientists outside hunker down in their protective tents. It's all good. Bernstein just panicked because he couldn't reach my dad.

Speaking of my dad, he and a handful of others climb out of the hatch one at a time and bolt toward the base. Niall is last and he glances at me and hesitates. I making shooing motions. He needs to alert his father and help prep the base. After he takes off, I can't help smiling. Pah.

During a sandstorm, I'm safer in the pits, so I finish cleaning off the General's arm. He's missing a couple fingers. I return to the debris pile and search. There's a bunch of smaller pieces that…resonate with me. Weird, I know. I grab a bucket and start filling it with bits of his armor, a finger, and a rounded section that might be a part of his shoulder. I dig through the fragments for a while. Then I find his face.

My blood turns to ice. There's something very familiar about his features. Granted, I've seen more than my share of Warriors and the General looks a little bit different than the regular foot soldiers. He has full lips and a mustache under a fleshy, almost pudgy nose. He has a little drop of hair on his chin. His beard is below his jawline and comes to a point in the front. The rest of his head has been broken off, but I'm sure I'll find it… eventually.

It seems creepy to be holding a face without a body so I set it down near his statue, arranging it so he can watch as I rebuild him. Even I'll admit that's bizarre. It's definitely time for a break and I realize I'm the only one still working in the pits. I stretch my back and turn to leave. A grinding noise sounds from the far side of the pit. Wow, that must be a big sandstorm if I can hear it down here. I investigate. The clamor is coming from the loose pile of sand that filled the hole the looters dug. There's movement from within and sand gushes out.

The wind? This deep? No. It's not the storm. Mind-numbing fear flushes through me, rooting me to the floor. The pit is collapsing! More noise rumbles from deeper in the pit. Clouds of sand fill the air. I sprint for the exit. Another grinding whine comes from Pit 3 and the Warriors in Pit 2 are shaking with a vibrating hissing. The tunnel's wall on my right disappears as a large metal blade rips through it. Metal? I skid to a stop.

It's a digging machine. And the only people who use them at dig sites are— Looters!

Protect the General is my first thought. Which I immediately ignore for the better advice of protect myself. Once those machines break through, the pits will be overrun with looters, who I can't stop and who will steal the Warriors. As I race toward the exit, another thought pops into my head. If the looters find the factory below, they'll destroy all those hearts. My reaction is instant. I cannot let that happen.

Argh! I change directions. At the hatch, I shove the ladder inside and… Think! The cover is too heavy. What else? I scan the room as the whine from the machines diminishes. There's a long table. I drag it over. It'll cover it, but the legs don't fit.

Please be a folding table. Please be a folding table. I lay the table on its side. Yes! I kick the supports to collapse the legs and then position it over the hole. It's not gonna work. I drag a tarp over the table. It's still too obvious. The pepper sweet scent of Yulin's air reaches me along with a haze of dust. Is that the crunch of boots?

Panicked, I sweep sand onto the tarp with my hands like a dog digging a hole. I grab a few big pieces of a random broken Warrior. Then I add my tools, adhesive and arrange them as if it's a workstation.

Voices call and echo through the pits. Time to go. Except

figures step from the hole in Pit 4. They're wearing gray coveralls with hoods and B-apps that have black masks. Only their eyes are visible behind clear goggles. They haven't spotted me yet, but will as soon as I move.

Nothing I can do. I sink to the "ground" and grab my brush as if they'd interrupted me at work. One person yells and points to me and my heart does somersaults.

I clutch the brush to my chest as if it'll protect me. Two of them draw weapons and walk slowly toward me. I don't move. There's no need to act terrified. Every part of me is numb with fear. My mind is screaming, *I'm dead. I'm dead. I'm dead* over and over and my insides threaten to turn to liquid.

The looters stop a few feet away. "Stand up," one orders, aiming the gun at my head.

It's not a pulse gun. It's a killing weapon. I stare at the barrel—it flares out like the end of a trumpet that's two centimeters wide. My legs are useless so I remain on the ground. He grabs my arm with his free hand and wrenches me to my feet. Yanking me close, he presses the barrel to my throat. I don't dare breathe.

"Sorry, no witnesses," he says.

Images of my parents and Phoenix flood my mind as the world freezes.

"Let her go," the other man orders. "She's just a tech."

"But she'll—"

"What? They'll figure out pretty quick what we're doing." He points to his face. "Besides, she can't identify us."

My captor lets go and my legs buckle. Once again I'm on the

floor. My throat eases a fraction and I suck in a thick breath coated with dust. I stifle a cough.

The "good" guy crouches down to my eye level. "We're here for the Warriors. If you stay out of the way and promise to behave, we won't hurt you." The B-app makes his voice sound artificial.

Yeah right. Tell that to the people on Xinji.

"Do you understand?"

Not trusting my voice, I nod.

"Guard her," he orders the other guy. "If she tries to run, you can shoot her."

Then he yells at the others—when did they all arrive?—to get to work. He must be the leader.

My guard stares at me as if daring me to move. He keeps his weapon in his hand. I've no intention of misbehaving—if I live through this, I'll never misbehave again. Instead, I watch as teams of looters throw nets over the Warriors before carefully tipping them over. They hook them to small four-wheeled vehicles that drag them up through the hole in the wall. They seem to be cherry-picking certain Warriors. They're coordinated and efficient as if they've done this many times before. It's amazing in a scary way. The rest of the Warriors in Pit 4 disappear. And it sounds like the same thing is happening in the other pits.

Hoping that the leader didn't lie to me about my chances for survival, I count looters—four dozen at least—and vehicles and scan for anything that would identify them—nothing so far. After an hour or so I wonder what's going on in the base. Do they know the looters are here? What about our professional security force? Then I remember the sandstorm. Could it be hiding all this activity?

I glance at my guard.

"Got a question, little girl?"

"Why?"

"An obscenely rich patron paid us lots of money."

"Why didn't you take more Warriors before?"

"That wasn't us. And the Boss is pretty pissed about it, too."

I gape at him. There's more looters? But more importantly, did this group attack Xinji? No. There is no way they could travel from Xinji to Yulin in two E-years.

"Is your patron even going to be alive when you return?" I ask. "The time dilation—"

He laughs. "It sucks. Well it sucks for *you.*"

Before I can even process what he means, a high-pitched whistle cuts through the air. The workers have finished netting Warriors. They draw their weapons as the vehicles all disappear through the holes.

"What's—"

A whomp sounds and a Warrior breaks into pieces and topples. No! Without thought, I'm on my feet. Surprised they support my weight after so much time folded under me, I step—

The guard jerks me back. His fingers dig into my right shoulder. "Flying debris will kill you, unless you're trying to run away?" He releases me. "Go ahead, I need to practice my aim."

I stop.

"Smart."

But more whomps echo and more Warriors break until the sound is continuous. Horrified by the carnage, I cover my ears. They're intent on destroying all the remaining Warriors and the assault goes on for hours and hours, or so it seems to me. When they finally finish the air is fogged with dust and debris. I cover my mouth and nose with the crook of my arm, blocking the grains with the fabric of my sleeve. My eyes sting and tear.

"Why did you demolish them?" I cry.

"Orders." My guard pulls me over to another who is standing near the General. "What do we do with her?"

Terror sizzles through me, but I stay upright. Go me.

"Leave her, she's harmless." It's their leader. The man who told me I wouldn't be hurt.

Every atom of my being hopes he didn't lie to me.

"But she'll tell them —— "

"What? She can't identify us. Unless you said something?" His tone is dangerous even through the mask.

"She doesn't know anything."

"Good." The leader comes close to me. "Don't follow us. Stay right here and you'll be safe. The sandstorm is still raging outside and your people will be digging through our blockade for another hour or so before they break through. Understand?"

"Yes."

My guard grunts. The leader calls for everyone to evacuate and watches the rest of his people file past us until no one is left.

"Let's go," he says to the guard before heading to the tunnel.

But the guy lingers and stares at me as if deciding if I'm a threat or not. I try to appear harmless, but our conversation replays in my mind and my throat squeezes shut.

"Don't say anything," he warns.

"I won't. I promise." My words are almost a whisper.

Apparently satisfied, he follows his leader. Shaking from the encounter, I'm torn between collapsing in relief or hyperventilating.

Before the man disappears up the tunnel he spins around with his weapon drawn. "Sorry, but I don't trust you." He aims at me.

I dive behind the General. But I'm not fast enough. An invisible force slams into me, sending me flying back. I'm in the air so long, I know I won't survive the landing. The darkness is instant.

Pain drags me from the comfort of oblivion. It throbs from the soles of my feet to the back of my head. Every centimeter of my body aches. I keep my eyes closed against the brightness stabbing through my eyelids. Groaning, I try to move my limbs to find a better position to ease the pain. My left shoulder flares to life with an intense agony. Unable to endure it, I cry out.

"She's regaining consciousness. Increase the dosage," a woman orders.

"Hold on, Lyra," my mother's voice whispers in my ear. "They're putting you back together."

Am I broken like the Warriors? As my world turns fuzzy and the pain dulls, I imagine the doctors reassembling the pieces of my body. I hope they found them all.

Voices wake me. Pain pulses through all my muscles— even the ones I had no idea existed—but it's not as sharp as before. Peeking through the slits in my heavy eyelids, I spot my parents talking to a doctor or nurse. They're huddled together, looking…worried. A vision of my body with cracks and holes fills my mind, but I don't have the strength to care. Instead, I drift back to sleep.

The next time I'm aware of my surroundings the lights are dimmer. My mom is asleep in the chair next to my bed. The smell of antiseptic and bleach confirm I'm in the infirmary. The small room has no decorations, just a night table, another chair, and medical equipment. Something beeps behind me. It's not a strident sound, more of a soft reassurance. *Beep—you're doing fine. Beep—you're breathing. Beep—you're good. Beep— everything's okay. Beep—your heart's beating.*

I take stock of my aching body. There's an IV in my right arm near the crook of my elbow and I wonder how long I've been out of it that I need fluids. A long black clamp is on my right index finger and a few wires and tubes snake out from underneath my blankets and disappear. It's probably best that I don't know where they're attached and what they're for.

My left arm is secured to my chest in some type of sling. There is a bandage wrapped around my head that itches my scalp. My lips are stuck to my teeth and my tongue has turned to sandpaper.

Other than desperately needing a drink, I'm glad to be alive. I gaze at my mother. Should I wake her? She'll want to know what happened. I try to recall the details, but a throbbing headache flares to life and I close my eyes against the pain. I'll wake her later when I have more energy.

I dream about the General. He stands alone in a silent field. His sadness wraps around me and I choke back tears. *I'll find your men*, I promise him.

My father's voice jolts me from the dream. "Has she woken yet, Ming?"

"No."

That short word holds so much emotion that I immediately feel guilty for not waking my mom last night.

I open my eyes and meet my mother's gaze. "Hi."

She hops to her feet and Dad joins her by my bed. They both have dark circles around their eyes and exhaustion lines their faces, but they still smile at me.

"How do you feel?" Dad asks.

"Like I'm one giant bruise. What's the damage?" I gesture to my body. "And don't sugar coat it," I add, because they're doing that silent communication thing about how much they should tell me.

"Concussion, four broken ribs, broken collarbone, dislocated left shoulder and a number of cuts and contusions on your back," Mom says as if repeating a supply list.

Wow. Considering my injuries, I feel pretty good. Or is it because of the miracle of medication? I ask my parents if I'm being given a painkiller.

"Yes. You'll need to stay on the pain meds for a while. The calcium accelerators are still repairing your bones. It's the concussion we're most worried about," Mom says despite Dad's frown.

"How long was I unconscious?"

Mom's grip on the bed rail tightens and, for a moment, her calm demeanor cracks as a brief flash of anguish replaces it. "It's been three days since they found you."

Three? The beeping behind me increases its pace and volume. Found? Then my memory creeps out from where it has been hiding. Now the strident sound is almost continuous as I remember what happened. I struggle to sit up. "The looters?"

A couple of nurses arrive and muscle past my parents. One nurse presses my shoulders down. "Lyra, you need to relax."

"Mom! The looters?" I practically shriek.

"They're gone."

I sink back. The beeping, while still agitated, is no longer screaming. The nurses fiddle with the equipment and a numbing heaviness flows through me. My eyes drift shut despite my best efforts to keep them open.

I float in and out of consciousness the rest of the day. Each time I wake one of my parents is there. I'm allowed a couple sips of water and I soak in lots of attention, but there are no questions. I'm grateful and, by the next day, I'm stronger. The doctor gives the okay for me to start eating and the soup is divine—I'll never complain about the base's food again. Well...don't hold me to that. I've a concussion after all.

By the evening, I've learned that the looters knocked out the cameras and communications in the base when they landed right after the sandstorm arrived. However, everyone blamed the storm and it took a while for security to discover the ruse. The looters blocked the entrance to the pits with a mound of sand, which delayed my "rescue" another couple hours. By the time security reached Pit 4, the looters were gone.

It's getting late. I tell my tired mother to go back to our unit and sleep in a real bed. "I'll be fine." I reassure her.

She's sitting in the chair and she takes my right hand—the black thing and IV are gone. "Officer Radcliff wants to talk to you in the morning about what happened in the pits. Do you think you're strong enough?"

"Yes."

She hesitates.

Now I'm worried. My mother is not the type to hesitate about anything. "What's wrong?"

"The doctor said no questions until tomorrow, but..."

I can't take the suspense.

"Just ask."

Her fingers tighten around mine. "Instead of running away, did you cover the hatch in order to hide it from the looters?"

Oh boy. I search for an excuse not to answer— headache, fatigue, pain—but it would just delay the inevitable. "Yes." I wait for the lecture on my incredible stupidity.

Instead, she releases her grip and buries her face in her hands. Muted sobs fill the air. My mother, crying? Those two things just don't go together.

Shocked, I gape for a moment. "Mom, I'm so sorry. I know it was dangerous and idiotic, but I..." What? I needed to protect the General. I didn't want them to find the hearts. That wouldn't go over well.

She straightens and meets my gaze. Tears streak her face and her nose is red. "But you believe those artifacts are more important than *your own life*," Mom cries. "Because I'm a terrible mother who is too focused on her work."

"No, Mom, it's not —— "

"Lyra, *you* are precious to me. All those Warriors that were destroyed or stolen, I don't care about them. When I saw...when you..." She sniffs. "Nothing is more important to me than you and your brother. I'm sorry I haven't been —— "

"Mom, I know you love me. That's not the reason I covered the hatch."

She studies me. "Then why?"

Ah hell. "The hearts. They would have been destroyed and...we're going to...need them."

My mom wipes the tears off her face with her fingers, waiting for me to continue.

I rush to fill the silence. "I know it sounds crazy. And it was probably due to my panic when I realized that looters were drilling into the pits. You know..." I wave my hand in the air. "Adrenaline. The fear response releases all those chemicals and people do some strange things while they are pumping through a body." Okay now I'm babbling and I'm sure my mother is going to ask the doctor to examine my head again to search for brain damage.

"Nice to know all those hours of school work haven't been wasted," Mom says. She stands and brushes the hair from my face. Her gentle fingers are warm against my skin. "Promise me that the next time you'll run away without trying to save any artifacts."

"There might be a next time?" I squeak in alarm.

"There is always a possibility. But other than the hearts we don't have anything left for them to steal... not until we reassemble the broken Warriors and the diggers open the other pits."

In both cases it will be a long tedious process. And now that I'm thinking about it... "What about the General? Was the part I reconstructed destroyed?"

"No."

The relief that flows through me is stronger than it should be.

"Well?" Mom asks.

"Well what?"

"You haven't promised me to run away."

Oh. "If I can, I will."

That seems to satisfy her. "Get some rest, Lyra. Your father and I will be here in the morning." She presses a kiss to my forehead and leaves.

Except for the various monitors doing their thing, I'm alone for the first time since I woke up in the infirmary. Considering

Mom's reaction over my covering the hatch instead of running away, I wonder how Radcliff and his security force are going to respond. I fully expect a lecture. Maybe I could beg off on the questions, claiming fatigue. Except I couldn't do that. Damn, I'm too conscientious.

Beep—you are.

"Thanks," I mutter to the machine.

After breakfast, the nurses help me. The wires are disconnected and the tubes are pulled out...don't ask from where. Once freed from the bed and the bandages, they support me as I shuffle to the bathroom. My body protests each movement with a squawk of pain, but I'm informed that my bones have finished healing but my muscles have not—they take longer. And we are going to work on getting my full range of motion back over the next couple days. It's too early in the morning for such enthusiasm. Plus *we* really means *me*. My grumbles fail to subdue their energy.

Once I'm in the bathroom and prove that I can stand without falling over, they give me some privacy. I peel off the sour-smelling gown. Unable to resist, I gaze at my reflection. Nasty splotches of purple and red bruises are scattered on my skin from my forehead to my shin bone. I finger a painful lump at the base of my skull. Ringed around my arm are bands of dark red from where my guard grabbed me. I've a black eye and my long hair is plastered to my head in greasy clumps. Sexy, I'm not.

MARIA V. SNYDER

The hot shower is an amazing restorative and, along with the clean pajamas Mom brought yesterday, means my view on life is looking up despite me being reconnected to a few of the machines. Then the posse arrives.

The nurses have just left when my parents enter my room followed by Officer Radcliff, Officer Morgan, and Niall. Every expression is serious and my first reaction is that the doctors have lied to me and I'm dying. Niall is holding one of his sketchbooks and I try to meet his gaze, but he avoids looking at me. Lovely.

Mom and Dad stand to my left, while Radcliff and Morgan move to the right. Niall hovers near the foot of my bed. No one sits down. Oh boy.

Radcliff clears his throat. "Miss Daniels, please let me offer you my sincerest apologies for failing to keep you safe. I tendered my resignation, but your father refused to accept it."

"The satellites didn't spot them and they managed to bypass the security monitoring equipment before they attacked," Dad says. "And the sandstorm was the perfect cover. You're not to blame, Tace."

I glance at Radcliff. "There is no need for you to apologize, it was *my fault* I was in danger. I had enough time to run, but I hid the hatch instead."

The muscles in Radcliff's shoulders tighten and I brace for the lecture. Both Morgan and Niall stiffen with anger. The silence stretches as I wait for someone to yell at me for being an idiot. The machine behind me beeps.

"Lyra, no one is going to scold you," Mom says. "You're

suffering from the consequences of your decision. I'm sure you learned from the experience."

No doubt about that. Funny thing, though. Even though I promised my mother I wouldn't, I'd probably save the hearts again.

"Please tell me everything you remember after Niall left the pits with your father," Radcliff says.

I describe the attack from the digging machines to being shot. "I don't think he wanted his boss to know, so he waited until we were alone."

"You're lucky that he only clipped you," Officer Morgan says. "If you'd taken a direct hit all your bones would have shattered, killing you."

I struggle to draw a breath. To think that such a lethal force came from such a small weapon... And it was pointed at me. A couple times. I shudder.

Radcliff faces his second-in-command. "No need to terrify the girl."

"I doubt that's possible," Morgan says dryly. "Besides, she needs to know what those energy wave guns can do, since she tends to be where the trouble is."

No one corrects her. I'd be insulted, but Morgan has a point.

Radcliff focuses on me. He tilts his head at Niall, who appears even more pissed off—something I didn't think was possible. "Can you describe them?"

That explains the sketchbook. "All I saw were their eyes."

"Human?" Dad asks, leaning forward.

Mom scowls at him.

"The aliens could return at any time," he says.

"Yes, human eyes," I say before they can launch into what they claim is a discussion, but is really an old argument—they have lots of those.

Radcliff asks me a bunch of other questions to clarify details. "At least there aren't that many people who are obscenely rich. We suspected there might be more than one outfit stealing Warriors, but didn't think there would be a second hit on Yulin. We're at least thirty E-years away from the closest colonized planet."

That comment sparks another memory. "My guard said the time dilation sucked for us, but not for them." That got everyone's attention. Questions pelt me from all sides. I hold up my hands. "That's all he said."

My dad sinks into the chair. "What if that obscenely rich patron developed a way to bypass the time dilation, but decided to keep the technology a secret?"

"Then we have bigger things to worry about than looters," Radcliff says.

2522:143

The consequences of someone having the ability to zip around the universe without worrying about the time dilation are overwhelming. Then add in the fact this person isn't playing by the rules...it's too much for my aching head to comprehend. If I go by the expressions on the faces of the five people in the room, it's bad. Yes, that's an understatement, but I am recovering from a concussion. Gimme a break.

"Let's not jump to conclusions," my mom says. "It was an off-hand comment from a murdering thug. Until there's proof, there is no reason to panic."

"I'll still alert DES to the possibility," Radcliff says. "Can you remember anything else, Miss Daniels?"

"No." Exhaustion sweeps through me and I sink back into the pillows.

"You'll let me know if you do?"

A question or an order?

"Of course she will," Mom says, sounding insulted for me. Go Mom.

The officers leave. A nurse arrives and shoos my parents out so I can get some rest.

Mom kisses my forehead. "I'll be back in a few hours."

Dad lingers. "Just give me a minute," he says to the nurse.

She's not happy, but she follows my mother.

He takes my hand in both of his. "What you did… covering that hatch was very brave."

"Really? I expected all of you to yell at me for being stupid."

"Being brave requires a certain amount of idiocy. If you think about it, self-preservation is not only an instinctual impulse, it's smart—survival of the fittest and all that. To do the opposite is brave."

"Thanks, Dad."

"Just don't do it again."

"Mom already made me promise."

"Good." He squeezes my hand and leaves.

The nurse returns. Fussing over me, she checks the tubes and whatnot. She fiddles with the machine behind me. Its voice softens. *Beep—no worries. Beep—go take a break, nurse lady. Beep—I'm watching over her.* I drift to sleep.

However, the comforting mechanical sound turns strident in my dream. The General is calling his regiment to take up arms, but they're gone. The enemy is approaching and no one is there to stop them. Armed with only a sword, he's all that is left.

Pieces of the darkness break away, transforming into

shadowy figures. They move with a strange liquid grace. Definitely not human, but I'm unable to compare them to anything I know. Surrounding the General, they advance. He stands his ground with grim determination. Shadow appendages form into sharp-edged weapons.

When they're within reach, the General turns to me. "It's up to you now, Lyra."

They attack, ripping into him as easily as if he's made of paper instead of hardened clay.

"No, don't!" I scream, jolting awake. Sitting up in bed, I grab the rails. The room spins as pain throbs in my head and blood slams in my heart, both keeping time with the frantic beeping.

Niall rushes into my room with his weapon drawn, but relaxes when he sees I'm alone. "What's wrong?"

I collapse back. "Bad dream."

He holsters his gun and turns to leave.

"Wait. What are you doing here?" I ask.

"It's my shift to guard your door."

My pulse jumps. The Shadow Army is here! But my brain, even sluggish from pain meds, dismisses that as ridiculous and goes on to the next threat. "The looters are back." I'd like to say that my tone is calm and not panicked, but I can't.

Niall hurries over to the side of my bed to assure me they're not. He meets my gaze for the first time. "You're safe."

"Then why are you guarding my door?"

"Orders."

I wait, but he remains silent. "I have a concussion so help me out here. Why do I need protection when I'm safe?"

He gestures to the ceiling. "Just in case the looters return, my dad ordered that you are to be guarded at all times."

I mull it over. "Why would they come after me?"

"When you were...unconscious, we were afraid they tried to kill you because you could identify them and if they discovered you were still alive..."

They'd return to ensure I didn't wake up.

"Now that you explained what happened, as long as that guard believes you're...dead, there's no reason for them to return."

So for the last four days the security team worried about another attack. "And I can't even identify them. No wonder you're all angry with me."

He stares at me a moment. "We're not mad at you."

"Really? You couldn't even look at me this morning."

Niall sighs. "That's because I abandoned my post in Pit 4 to help prep for the sandstorm. These bruises..." He trails a gentle finger along the side of my face and I have to fight from melting into a puddle. "Are because I wasn't there to do my job."

"They would have killed you right away." A terrible thought. One that hurts more than cracked ribs.

"My job is to protect *you*. Not the artifacts. I would have dragged you out of the pits long before the looters broke through. I'm angry at myself. And the entire security team is furious that the looters got the drop on us and harmed one of ours. We're determined that won't happen again."

Maybe I could help with that once I recover. I'm better at using the Q-net than Radcliff. "How long did it take before security figured it out?"

"Longer than it should. Three or four hours at least." He grabs the rail. Hard. "Before the storm arrived, we were dispatched to help seal the base and bring equipment inside. Then our communications died along with the cameras when the storm hit and everyone was focused on restoring it." Niall runs a hand through his hair. "Hell, I think your father discovered the blockade in the archaeology lab. We thought it was a collapse at first so we spent time confirming that all the techs were safe inside the base."

I'm not a tech. "Did anyone realize I was missing?"

"Your mother asked if I'd seen you. I remembered you were working near the hatch before the storm. I searched the *entire* base for you." His expression grows haunted. "You could have been buried alive, and your parents weren't even upset."

I jump in to explain so he doesn't think they're heartless. "After working at dig sites for years, they have plenty of experience with cave-ins. Once the pits have been excavated by the robotic diggers, a total collapse is very rare. Mostly they're minor and Pit 4 is pretty far from the base. Plus if I had enough time I could have gone down into the factory. Those walls are sturdy."

"Oh. Your dad organized a bunch of the techs to clear the sand without causing more cave-ins. I stayed to help. Word spread that you were trapped and a flood of scientists arrived."

My chest warms. They care.

"When there was a break in the storm, we heard the noise from the looters' machines and finally figured it out. Dad took

Alpha team outside to stop them, Beta team joined us in removing the blockade. Once we had an opening big enough for us to fit, Officer Morgan took point and we entered the pits."

"It must have been a mess."

Niall gives me a you-got-to-be-kidding-me look. "I wasn't focused on the Warriors. Or the looters for that matter. Although I would have been more than happy to shoot the bastards if we encountered them. My main concern was finding *you*. And I did." He closes his eyes as if enduring a wave of pain. "You were lying among the rubble, broken, bleeding. I thought you were dead."

His anguish is clear. Despite his previous actions and words, he cares for me. And I feel bad for causing him pain. Logically, I know the Warrior hearts were not worth the massive amount of worry my parents and Niall endured. Yet, I don't believe I did the wrong thing.

I'm an awful person.

I put my hand over his. "Niall, I'm sorry."

His eyes snap open. "You have no reason to apologize."

"But I knew what was going on and still returned to hide the hatch."

"Like you told your mother, it was a panic response. Many people do things they're convinced is the right thing when under extreme stress. Plus you're a civilian. You don't have the experience to handle a stressful situation. Why do you think we train so much?"

"'Cause you have nothing else to do?"

"Funny. It's so certain responses become automatic. So

when you don't have time to think, your body is already reacting properly."

"Oh." A tightness around my chest eases. And that explains why Officer Radcliff didn't yell at me.

A nurse enters to check on my vitals. Niall lets go of my hand. Huh? When did that happen? Must have been one of those automatic responses. Tingles dance on my palm as he returns to his post outside my door.

After a few torture sessions...sorry, physical therapy... and visits from the doctors, I'm declared... well... not healed, but good enough to ease back into my life. Officer Radcliff ends my security detail, but that doesn't stop Niall from escorting me back to my housing unit.

Of course my parents notice this. When I'm tucked into my own bed, Dad leans forward and says, "I think a certain officer will not be dismissed so easily." He tilts his head toward the entrance to our unit. "One who has worked extra shifts."

My insides do a strange little twirly thing.

"Niall is just feeling guilty," Mom says. "The boy will get over it soon."

Gee, thanks, Mom.

Before they retreat to their offices to get some work done, but be within hearing distance should I need anything, I ask about the Warriors. "How bad is it? Are all the Warriors smashed to pieces?"

"Pretty much. We're concentrating our efforts on

reconstruction and analyzing the factory, but we're not reporting everything to DES," Mom says.

"You think the looters wormed into DES's data clusters?" I ask. I was able to get to classified files and I'm not near as skilled as many others.

"It's a possibility. And, there's just something...off about their responses to us."

Another thing I can help with, searching for signs that someone wormed into the Q-net. Once I can read more than a couple paragraphs without a headache.

"And we found evidence that the Warriors do have those hearts." Mom's face lights with excitement.

I sit up straighter. "Did one survive?"

"No, but we found particles of that black substance in the chest cavity of a few of them. Not as much as we'd hoped. It breaks down very quickly once it's broken."

"Have you figured out what that material is?"

"Not yet. The chemists are working on it, but we do know it absorbs X-rays and a number of other rays so it doesn't show up on any of our scanning equipment. Once the diggers excavate another pit, we can examine an intact Warrior and confirm it."

Sounds like a lot of work.

"When you're feeling better, we'd like you to finish reconstructing the General," Dad says.

His comment reminds me that I haven't dreamt of the General since he was attacked by those shadow creatures. Irrational grief floods through me.

"Lyra, are you okay? Should we call the doctor?" Mom asks in concern. "I told you it was too soon, Spencer."

"She's going to have to face —— "

"I'm fine," I assure them. "Just tired."

They hurry to leave so I can rest. Except, I lie there wondering why I'm so upset about the first quiet night of sleep since I touched that heart.

I return to soch-time on the tenth day after the attack. Niall is waiting for me at the end of soch-time. I'm not surprised to see him. He'd escorted me to soch-time two hours earlier. Even though he's off duty, he's taken this whole protection thing pretty seriously. And I'm torn between touched, annoyed, and suspicious.

Niall falls into step beside me and he laces his fingers in mine. A pulse of surprise skewers me, and, amazingly, I don't trip over my feet. I try matching Niall's nonchalant attitude even though my lungs struggle to draw in enough air. Will he kiss me again? Do I want him to? The response from my body is a resounding yes, but my battered synapses are signaling a warning. I've seen his mood change as fast as a heartbeat. And my mom's voice sounds in my head, *Niall is just feeling guilty. The boy will get over it soon.*

"Are you going to the pits today?" he asks a little too casually.

Soch-time has drained all my energy. The doctors warned me that recovering from a concussion takes much longer than all my other injuries. "No."

Niall relaxes. I wonder why he didn't want me to go. When we arrive, Niall releases me and goes in first to ensure there's no one waiting to ambush me.

"It's safe," he says in his authoritative tone.

I can't resist a sarcastic comment. "Are you sure? Did you check under the bed for dust bunnies?"

He shakes his head as if disappointed. "That's a rookie mistake, Mouse. They might be cute and fluffy, but those dust bunnies can be killers."

"Duly noted," I say, trying to keep my smile from going too wide. He called me Mouse!

"Good. Now get some rest."

"But I have to catch up on my school assignments." Just the thought of all that work makes my temples throb.

"Wrong answer." He steps behind me and grabs my shoulders. Pushing so I either have to walk forward or fall flat on my face, he steers me into my room.

Niall points to my bed. "Sleep." He stands in the threshold with his arms crossed.

"You're not going to leave until I lie down, are you?"

A mulish stiffening of his jaw is the only answer I receive.

"All right. All right." I yank the blanket down and climb in. "I'm in bed."

"Right answer."

"You're obnoxious, Toad."

He pushes me down so I'm horizontal. "Sleep well." Niall pulls the blanket up to my chin, then leaves.

Of course I plan to get up right after I'm sure he's gone. But warmth envelops me as the mattress molds to my body. I'll just close my eyes for a minute.

I wake up a couple hours later. Damn it. I'd blame Niall, but I do feel better. Mom knocks on my door and announces dinner. What?

I join my parents in the dining area. We haven't had a family meal since the discovery of the factory. But there's my favorite pasta dish—manicotti—with bread sticks in the middle of the table. No doubt this is Mom's way to counter her guilt over not being the best mother in the universe. She's a better cook than the chefs at the canteen, so I'm not going to complain. Might as well enjoy it while it lasts.

The food has restored me and I return with the intention of doing my school assignments. Except, I bypass my school files and worm deeper into the Q-net. It feels different, as if someone had rearranged the furniture. Maybe it's the concussion or the fact I haven't wormed since we found the hearts. At least the shortcuts Chief Hoshi taught me are still available. Remembering that I could be arrested if caught worming, I'm extra careful. Lyra Daniels, ghost wormer.

For the looters to get all the way out here on the edge of Explored Space, they had to use a Crinkler engine. In order to not kill everyone in the Galaxy, they needed to avoid all the other areas of crinkled space, suns, black holes, and any massive planets. They had to worm deep into the Q-net to see the star roads. Plus they'd have to input their route. There should be some evidence of that tampering. And the fact DES didn't notice is terrifying. Or they did pick up on it and are keeping it a secret?

If the looters tried again, perhaps DES will ambush them. Maybe that's why they're acting odd.

Either way, I might find something that will help. Except I can't access it from my terminal. After three hours of being blocked—even through the shortcuts—I figure I need a better terminal. One of my parents'? I consider the risks. Perhaps Jarren would be up to the challenge of finding the looters. I message him.

As I cover my tracks on my way out of the Q-net, I'm...detoured—that's the best word I can come up with to describe it—to another cluster. Lan's symbols fill this area and it takes me a few minutes to realize that the Q-net has continued to organize her research notes despite the fact I didn't request it—I've been too busy to return to the project. Not only did it organize the remaining symbols, but it interpreted them. I read through the results.

Oh. My. Stars.

2522:150

Niall rushes into the game room. "I got your message, are you all right?" His feet are bare and he's wearing a T-shirt, black jeans, and his holster. His hair is adorably sleep-tousled.

"Mouse?"

I stop staring at his hair. "I'm fine." I point to the game's screen which shows Lan's symbols. It's just after midnight so no one else is here. And I hope my parents don't check on me and freak out when they discover an empty bed.

"Is that—"

"Yes. The Q-net has continued to organize the symbols."

A pause as Niall puts it together. "Did you—"

"No. I didn't ask it to."

"It could have been inadvertent. You weren't exactly going through the proper channels at that time."

A polite way to say I was doing it illegally. "Regardless, it figured out another part of the code."

"And?"

"It grouped eight different symbols together and matched it to a Warrior planet. These..." I wave my hand at the screen, "are the ones for Taishan."

"So when those symbols are together they're referring to the planet Taishan?"

"Yes."

"But Earthlings named it Taishan."

"The Q-net used the astral coordinates of the planets then matched it to our designations. The important thing is that the aliens had their own designations for all the Warrior planets."

"I just woke up, you're going to have to explain why that's worth getting out of bed for." He yawns.

I pull up a list. It has all the names of the Warrior planets, followed by a list of coordinates. "Those numbers represent a Warrior planet that is unnamed."

"Unnamed?"

"Because it's undiscovered."

"You mean there's another Warrior planet out there that DES hasn't found yet?"

I draw in a breath. "No."

"But you said—"

Holding up a hand, I stop him. "Look closer. There's more than *one* that is undiscovered."

He pales. "How many?"

"There are a total of sixty-four Warrior planets."

"You mean..."

"Yup. There are forty-two others out there and we have the

coordinates of where they are."

We stare at each other. I'm still in shock, but it's a relief to share the news.

"Wait," Niall says. "Why are you telling *me*? Shouldn't you let your parents know this right away?"

"Before that, I was...er...worming." His expression hardens so I add, "I was trying to figure out how the looters got here."

"Lyra, my dad already talked to your parents about asking you to help us with that. They said he has to wait until you're recovered from the concussion."

"Oh."

"Yeah. Oh."

Suddenly tired, I sink into a chair.

Niall crouches next to me. "This is too big to keep to yourself. You're going to have to fess up."

"I know. Guess I was hoping you'd have some grand plan on how I could do it without getting into trouble."

"It's not like you're a stranger to being in trouble."

"Hey." I try for outrage, but it's a token gesture.

He smiles. "I'll visit you every day in the detention center and bring you candy."

That's it. I can't stand it anymore. Standing up, I take a few strides to put some distance between us. "Stop it."

"Stop what?"

"Being nice. You're only doing it because you're feeling guilty."

Niall straightens. All his humor is gone.

"Once you realize that it's not your fault I was hurt— because it isn't—you're going to be a jerk again and tell me to leave you alone." Now that I've started talking, I can't seem to stop. "And you'll spend the rest of your time on Yulin avoiding me. Then that Protector Class ship will arrive and you'll be gone." And so will the remains of my heart.

"So you have the future all figured out." His tone is emotionless, but his hands are balled into fists and pressed against his legs.

"What else could it be?"

He meets my gaze and I'm facing the man who sat across from me in the shuttle—the confident, capable soldier. My heart picks up its pace. I've no idea what's next.

"All the stuff you said to me before about why I was being such a jerk was right. You nailed it. I was beyond furious at my dad and Captain Harrison for dumping me on this planet. That hatred just consumed me." He taps his chest. "Your heart crumbled, but mine burned. I couldn't get rid of it. It poisoned everything—even drawing. Then when I couldn't find your pulse after the attack, all that anger and hate—" Niall snaps his fingers. "Gone. You were dead. Nothing else mattered. It put everything in perspective."

Wow. I don't know what to say to that even though my heart thumps its approval so hard I think it's going to crack my ribs.

Niall steps close and takes both my hands. "That jerk is not coming back. And I want to spend more time with you."

"But I annoy you."

"Part of the appeal."

"And I have a habit of breaking rules."

"Nobody's perfect." He cocks his head to the side. "Are you trying to talk me out of it? If you don't want — "

"That's not it. It's just...are you talking about being friends or more? I can't do more with your plans to leave. Signing up for the Protectorate is not on my career list." Well, nothing is on my list at the moment, but he didn't need to know that.

"I'm not signing up," Niall says. "Captain Harrison was right, I'm needed here. It's what I trained for. Plus my dad...well, it's only been two A-years since my mother died, he still needs family around." Niall moves so he's centimeters from me. "And there's this girl, she's like a comet—makes the rest of the Galaxy seem dull in comparison."

Heat flushes through me. "A comet." I raise an eyebrow. "They can be pretty dangerous."

"Don't I know it. Guess I'm just one of those adrenaline junkies." He meets my gaze. "And I'm willing to take the chance. Are you?"

My heart yells YES, but my brain is being more cautious—not like a comet at all. "It's going to take me a while to get used to..." I hold up our intertwined hands. "All this."

"We can take it slow."

"And I don't think I could handle too much niceness."

"Duly noted."

"All right."

His grip tightens as he grins at me. A happy Niall is quite the sight, causing my head to spin and excitement to beat in my veins. And I won't even go into what it's doing to the rest of me.

I didn't expect this tonight when I messaged him. And that thought grounds me as I remember the reason I contacted him. I tilt my head at the screen. "You might have to visit me in the detention center in order to spend time with me."

He glances at the symbols. "Your parents might be so ecstatic over the news of those other planets that they'll probably forgive you for illegally worming."

I look at him.

"Will it help if I'm with you when you tell your parents?"

The moral support would be welcome, but there's no reason to involve Niall. After all, I did the deed. "No. It'll go better if I'm by myself. When do you think is a good time to tell them?"

"First thing in the morning."

"Ugh. How about — "

"No sense putting it off."

I try to look on the bright side. No school work or soch-time while in detention.

Niall releases me. "It's getting late and you should get some sleep."

That's not gonna happen, but I restore the game system to its original settings. Niall takes my hand and we walk through the mostly empty corridors. A few late-working scientists are also heading to bed and a couple hurry past as if on an errand.

I gesture to one of the cameras. "Is someone monitoring them?"

"Yes. We used to review them daily, but after the attack my dad ordered a security officer to be on watch around the clock. Guess who has the oh-four to oh-eight-hundred-hours shift."

His wry tone requires no response. "Three hours of sheer boredom, followed by an hour of watching everyone grab breakfast and report to work."

It's just past oh-one-hundred hours. "You're going to be beat. I'm sorry — "

"Don't worry about it." He squeezes my hand. "This was more important than sleep."

We continue to my unit in comfortable silence. I open the door. Half expecting a parental ambush, I pause in the threshold.

"Do you want me to check your room for dust bunnies?" Niall teases.

"No need. I've recruited them and now I have a cadre of dust bunny assassins at my beck and call."

"That's hard core. I see you're well on your way to a life of crime." He tugs me into the entrance area. Closing the door, he leans toward me. "Better kiss you while I have the chance."

When his lips meet mine, all sorts of tingles race through my body. His kiss is tentative at first, but soon deepens. I wrap my arms around his shoulders and I'm finally able to run my fingers through his tousled hair as I open my mouth. A low growl vibrates in his throat. His warm hands press on my back, drawing me closer until the space between us shrinks to nothing. The thuds from his racing heartbeat vibrate on my chest. Or is that my heartbeat?

Niall pulls away and I protest. He rests his forehead against mine. "It's late." His thumb traces my jaw. "And you're still healing."

"I see you're going to be the sensible one in this relationship," I mock grouse because he's right and step back.

"Someone has to be. Night, Mouse."

"Night, Toad."

After he leaves, the warmth of his touch lingers on my skin as I head to my bedroom. I'm dreamily replaying our kiss in my head when I'm jolted back to cold reality. All sweet thoughts are banished as fear's icy tentacles wrap around my stomach.

My mother is sitting at my terminal. She's wearing a robe over her night clothes. The screen is filled with Lan's symbols. I must have left it up in my haste to talk to Niall.

Mom swivels. Her arms are crossed and a dangerous expression is stamped on her face. "What is going on? Where were you?"

So much for waiting until morning. At least she didn't freak out and call security. "Is Dad awake?"

"No. Why?"

"He's going to want to hear this, too. And for the record, I planned to tell you both in the morning."

She studies me for a moment. "All right."

Mom goes to wake him and I sort the information into a logical format. I calm my nerves with the reminder that my parents are reasonable and intelligent.

When they enter my room, I'm ready.

"What's with all this fuss?" Dad asks, yawning.

They stand behind me as I explain everything, showing them the symbols and the Q-net's interpretations on my screen. When I finish, there is silence. I'm afraid to turn around, but can't stand the suspense.

My mom's left hand is clutching my father's forearm while her right is covering her mouth. Dad blinks at me. A half-smile tugs at his lips as if he's trying not to whoop out loud in joy.

Dropping her hand, Mom recovers first. "Send me the files." Her voice is higher than normal. She's excited but trying hard not to show it.

I do as requested.

"That's...wow...I can't believe...Li-Li, do you know—"

"Spencer, *we* need to discuss this in *private*," Mom says.

"But Li-Li has—"

"Has done something illegal to get this information." She turns to me. "Get some sleep. We'll talk to you in the morning." Mom practically pushes Dad out the door.

That actually went better than I'd expected. It's a relief to have come clean. I change into my pajamas and get into bed. My fate is no longer in my hands so instead of worrying, I think of Niall's touch.

The next morning, I'm "invited" to join my parents in their conference room along with Officer Radcliff, Officer Morgan, and Dr. Milo Jeffries and Dr. Kara Gage, who are the two highest ranked scientists on base after my parents. Oh boy.

"Lyra, we've been discussing Lan's discovery," Mom says in a formal don't-argue-with-me tone. "She had collected all the relevant information, and, by bringing it into the Q-net, you aided in the translation of some of those alien symbols. The credit for the discovery will go to you both."

I open my mouth to protest. Lan did all the work, I was just lucky, but a warning glare from my mother stops the words.

"Miss Daniels," Dr. Gage says. "We've also decided to keep this discovery a secret from DES and the rest of the base for now. We believe the looters have access to DES's database and the Q-net and do not want them to find out about the additional Warrior planets."

Understandable.

"We need you to promise not to divulge this information to anyone," Dr. Jeffries says.

I swallow as my blood rushes to my feet, leaving me lightheaded.

Seeing my reaction, Officer Radcliff asks, "Who else knows?"

Oh no. Taking in a breath to keep from passing out, I exhale slowly. I don't want to get Niall into trouble so I explain that I panicked and called him, but he advised me to inform my parents and escorted me home right away.

"Officer Niall Radcliff can be trusted with this information," Morgan says.

"Anyone else?" Radcliff asks.

"No, sir."

"Can we trust *you*, Miss Daniels?" Dr. Jeffries asks.

That question rubs me the wrong way. Angrily, I go from a defensive mode to offensive. Keeping my tone cold and voice even, I say, "The looters almost *killed* me, Dr. Jeffries. I'm not about to let them know there are more planets out there for them to pillage."

Although it's not visible, I sense my parents' approval.

"Fair point, Miss Daniels. Can you remove the file of Lan's symbols from the Q-net?"

"No. But I can bury it so it's very hard to find and add security measures to alert Officer Radcliff if anyone tries to access it."

"Good. Your mother informed us that you were...worming last night." Jeffries' lips twist as if the concept is distasteful to him. "Did you learn anything about the looters?"

"No, sorry. My terminal...ah...limits my reach."

"DES hasn't a clue either," Dr. Gage says in disgust. "They have the full power of the Q-net at their disposal, yet they are unable to find the looters let alone stop them from worming into the star roads."

With the mention of worming, the group looks to Officer Radcliff. Warning bells go off in my head and I brace myself for whatever's coming next.

Mom says, "Normally, when someone breaks the rules, the base leaders decide the punishment. However, since you're our daughter, we have a conflict of interest so we abstained from this decision. Doctors Gage and Jeffries have consulted with Officer Radcliff and agreed with his recommendation, which is not subject to change."

Meaning I can't argue. The strength in my legs ebbs, but I keep my knees locked as I meet Radcliff's gaze.

He doesn't smile. He's all business. "You're mine for the next ninety days, Miss Daniels. Go pack your clothes and any essential items you may require. Wait for me in the living room. I will escort you to your new quarters."

Every centimeter of my body goes numb and my thoughts jumble into gibberish with Radcliff's order. A glance at my parents' pinched expressions confirms that I did indeed hear him correctly—I'm going to spend the next ninety days in detention.

All six adults are staring at me, waiting for a response or a reaction. I do the mature thing. "Yes, sir." I turn on my heel and leave before I do the immature thing and burst into tears.

Back in my room, anger burns away the fear. Ninety days is excessive. I'm a first time offender…well, first time I'd admitted to illegally worming. Plus I've been nothing but helpful when they needed me to find Xinji's deleted files. Radcliff is an ungrateful jerk. Shoving jeans and shirts into a duffle bag with more force than needed, I vent my frustration. I include the security jumpsuit and boots—I've been meaning to return them. Argh. I'm way too nice. Hmmm…that could work in my favor. Maybe I'll get time off for good behavior.

It's hard to think of what essential items I might need to sit in a white room for days on end, so I toss in a few basics. My parents should be allowed to bring me stuff. Right? I only know what Jarren told me. Which reminds me. After I finish packing, I connect to my terminal. First I bury the file in the Q-net and mound protective measures over it.

Then I message Jarren:

2522:150: Well it finally happened. I'm headed to detention for illegally worming. Out of all my friends and family, I think you alone would be proud of me. I'll try to remember that when I'm staring at the white walls all day. Was it really that bad? I hope not, but I can't do anything about it now. What sucks the most is I was trying to help find the looters. At least I pieced together some of Lan's research for my parents. Poor Lan—I miss her so much. To me, it's only been a half a year since I last saw her. <sigh> My sentence is ninety days so if you discover any information about those looters, please send it to Officer Tight Pants right away. It's that important! Otherwise I'd ask you to send him a scrambler. Well... no I wouldn't. That's too nasty. Maybe a butterflier just to annoy him—let him chase it around the Q-net for a few hours.

I think about it and delete the last four sentences. No need to get Jarren into trouble too. Then I sign off. I sling my bag over my shoulder and scan the mess I left behind, seeking anything I missed. I try to do the look-on-the-bright-side thing. Ninety days isn't that long. It took us ninety days to travel to Yulin, and that...seemed like forever and I was busy. Great. I suck at looking-on-the-bright-side.

Radcliff and Morgan are waiting for me when I exit my room. Morgan opens the door and gestures me to precede her. I glance back to see if my parents are going to say good-bye, but they're deep in discussion with the others. An ache squeezes my stomach as I leave.

When we enter the security area, I slow, not sure exactly where to go. Believe it or not, I haven't spent much time in this part of the base before—all the kids avoid it—but I've done some exploring when I was younger. Enough to know to circumvent it if at all possible. We pass offices on the right and, after a long expanse of blank wall on the left, there are double wide doors propped open. Inside is a big area covered with mats. Punching bags hang from the ceiling and other workout equipment rings what is clearly the training room. A couple of officers are sparring. I catch a glimpse of black hair before we're out of sight.

Is that Niall? I've been avoiding thinking about him. Will he really visit me every day and bring me candy? Would his father let him? Would that be another one of those conflicts of interest? Guess I'll have plenty of time to ruminate about that.

After another couple of turns, I'm lost. We go left down another long hallway. Numbered doors mark both sides. Radcliff stops at three-oh-one, which is the last one on the right. He enters a code on the security pad and places his hand on the scanner. As light leaks from his fingers, my throat tightens.

This is it.

My cell.

Black and white spots swirl at the edges of my vision. My temples throb.

More beeps sound. "Place your hand here, Miss Daniels."

All moisture leaves my mouth, but I manage to say, "Call me Lyra, please." Being called Miss Daniels always sounds like I'm in trouble. Yes, I know I *am* in trouble, but the thought of being called Miss Daniels for ninety days would be...unbearable.

He studies my expression. "All right."

I splay my fingers and press my palm on the glass. Radcliff taps on the pad again and the door unlocks. He enters. Taking a steadying breath, I follow.

2522:150

Bracing for an assault of white, I slow to a stop in surprise. We've entered a housing unit. It's a little bigger than a standard size, but not as big as my parents'. I blink, staring at the common room, kitchen area—

"Something wrong, Miss...Lyra?" Officer Radcliff asks. The skin around his eyes crinkles as if he's amused.

"I thought..." I'm reluctant to say the word *detention* aloud just in case he forgot why we're together. Yeah, I know, it's silly, but a girl can hope.

"While it would be within my authority to have you confined to a cell, it would hardly be fair at this time." He gives me a weighty stare, implying it could be in my future. "You're on probation. You can stay in Niall's old room."

He leads me to a small bedroom on the right side of the unit. It's next to a washroom, but they're not connected like in my parents' unit. There's also no terminal or screen.

Radcliff notices my concern...okay my panicked expression.

"Your activities on the Q-net will be supervised at all times."

I'm not happy about it, but I understand why. "What about my school work?"

"That, too. You can do it on the terminal in my office. Also you're not allowed to leave this unit without an escort."

This is starting to sound like detention without the white walls. "Escort?"

"Me or one of my officers. That's what probation means."

I open my mouth to protest, but a hardness in Radcliff's gaze stops me.

"Do you understand, Lyra?"

"Yes, sir."

"Good. Because if you don't follow these rules, you'll be spending the rest of your probation in detention."

Radcliff leaves the bedroom so I can settle in. It takes me all of two minutes to unpack. Then I sit on the bed. The blanket and pillow smell faintly of Niall, but otherwise there's no other sign that he once stayed here. The walls are rather plain without the screen. I'm still a bit stunned about the turn of events. Uncertain how I feel about the situation, I wonder what's next.

Radcliff knocks on my door. "Your escort is here."

Well that answers that. I join him in the common room. "Where am I going?"

"Lunch and soch-time."

"Oh."

His eyes crinkle again, but he refrains from commenting. Instead, he tilts his head at the door. My escort. Right.

Niall is waiting outside. He's in uniform and has donned his serious demeanor so I suppress the urge to hug him. It takes effort, I could really use a hug right now.

Sweeping an arm out, he says, "This way, Miss Daniels."

I glance at Radcliff. He's watching us. Does he know about us? I've no idea and I'm not going to wait around to find out. Instead, I head down the hallway with Niall at my heels.

At the first intersection, I stop.

"What's wrong?" Niall asks.

"I don't know which way to go."

"But I thought—"

I just shake my head. "I'm not that familiar with this area— it's not off limits, but I never had a reason to be here...before." And I was more than a little freaked out on the way in, but I don't say that.

"All right. Follow me."

Niall navigates the turns without hesitation. We pass a handful of security officers. A few nod to Niall and give me curious stares. Some grin at me and one guy with spiky brown hair with the tips dyed blond, who appears to be around twenty-five or so A-years old, slaps Niall on the back as he walks by.

Unable to endure the silence, I say, "Do they—"

"Yes. *Everyone* knows."

Oh. "Because we held hands in the corridor last night?"

He huffs. "I wish."

I wait. "Is there something else?"

"Let's just say I became a little overprotective when you were recovering."

That's sweet. Once again the desire to hug him warms my chest.

He stops. "However, my father made it clear that when I'm in uniform, I'm to maintain my professionalism. In other words, no hand holding in public. Otherwise I won't be assigned to escort you."

I'm just happy that I can spend time with him. Maybe this probation thing won't be too bad. "All right."

He squints at me. "You don't seem that upset."

Ah, the male ego really is fragile. "Considering that I was convinced that I'd be spending the next eighty-nine days in detention, I'm just glad that you're not smuggling candy in to me through a slot in a locked door."

Niall laughs, but then sobers. "I think this is an excessive punishment." He swirls his hand, indicating the both of us. "But I'm happy knowing you're safe. At least for the next eighty-nine days." He continues down the hallway.

His comment worries me. "Should I be concerned? Is there a chance the looters will come back?"

Ah, there's that familiar scowl. I almost missed it.

"We don't know where they came from or where they've gone, so yes, there's a chance. Slim right now, but once those other pits are opened..."

There will be more Warriors to steal and destroy.

Niall reaches for my hand, but stops. "We'll protect you. No need to worry."

But what about the rest of the base?

After soch-time Niall escorts me to Radcliff's office where I use a terminal to work on the school assignments I missed that morning. When my head starts throbbing, I rest my forehead on the edge of the terminal. It's been ten days. Why does my brain still hurt? It's so frustrating that bones, muscles, and skin can heal so fast, but the medical professionals still don't have a quick fix for concussions.

A warm hand touches my shoulder.

"Time for a break," Radcliff says.

I want to protest, but I don't have the energy. We return to his unit and he gestures to my bedroom. "I've been ordered to ensure you don't overdo it until the doctor gives you the all-clear."

"What happens when I get the all-clear?"

"Training."

My brain tries to rally my thoughts to form a coherent reply. It fails.

"Officer Morgan made a very good point about you being in the middle of trouble. If you're going to be where the action is, you'll need to learn how to defend yourself. Now get some rest."

I go lie down. I'll worry about training later...much later. Although...I do look good in that jumpsuit. It might not be that bad. Perhaps I'll get to wrestle with Niall. That would be fun. Except I doubt my idea of wrestling matches Officer Radcliff's idea. Not as much fun now.

A knock wakes me from a light doze.

"Lyra, time for supper," Radcliff says.

I groan into the pillow. Who knew that just being able to go eat whenever I wanted would become so appealing. What was that saying...something about missing something only when it's gone? I run my fingers through my messy hair and consider pulling it into a ponytail for a half a second. Nah.

When I open the door, I immediately regret my sloppy appearance. My parents and Niall are in the common room talking. A lump grows in my throat and I'm going to blame the concussion for it—not the fact I'm overwhelmingly glad to see them. My mom spots me first and swoops in for a hug. I lean into it. I've been needing that hug all day.

"What are—" I ask.

"Tace invited us for supper," Dad says, taking a turn to squeeze me.

"We heard he's quite the cook," Mom adds.

Hurt, I stare at her.

But there's a glint in her brown eyes. "You didn't think we abandoned you. Did you?"

"Uh...I thought you were mad at me."

"Officially, we are," Dad says. "Unofficially, we're so proud of you, Li-Li! For someone who claims she doesn't want to be an archaeologist, you certainly have made a number of vital discoveries." He claps me on the shoulder and I almost topple over.

I meet Niall's gaze. He's grinning and mouths *Li-Li*. I'm about to scowl at him when I notice he's not in uniform. Instead, he's wearing jeans and a form-fitting black T-shirt. Oh my. I really should have fixed my hair.

"Food's ready," Radcliff announces.

My parents head to the kitchen.

"Did your dad invite you, too?" I ask Niall.

"Sort of."

"That's not an answer."

He hesitates, then says, "Since my mom died, my dad and I make a point to eat dinner together. Unless one of us is on duty or something big is going on. When I moved out, he asked me to continue the tradition." Niall shrugs. "Captain Harrison is...was his closest friend. Being down here has to be rough on my dad, too."

He has a point, and I regret all my unkind thoughts about Officer Radcliff...well, most of them.

Niall steps closer and lowers his voice. "Do your parents know about us?"

I shake my head. "I didn't know about *us* until last night."

He grabs my hand. "Then this should be an interesting meal. Come on, Mouse." He tows me into the kitchen.

My mother is talking about the new Warrior planets. She doesn't miss a beat when we enter, but she notices our laced hands before we break apart to sit down in the two empty seats at the table. Radcliff sets out a steaming white cheesy-looking casserole that smells divine and tastes even better. A man of many talents. I might actually enjoy this probation.

Conversation ceases as we all enjoy the meal.

"Too bad we can't use the Q-net to map those planets," Dad says before he shoves the last of several huge forkfuls into his mouth. "Not a single scientist on this base has an old-fashioned paper star map." He says it like it's an insult.

"Is there a way to discover how the looters are accessing DES's data? Or where they breached the security?" Mom asks me, changing the subject before Dad gets into full ranting mode. "I'm not comfortable with keeping critical information from them."

I consider. My activities last night focused on the star roads. Then I remember my message to Jarren. I tell them about it. They stare at me as if I'd done something wrong. Again.

"You reported the looters to DES right?" I ask to break the silence.

"Yes," Radcliff says. "Did you consider that asking Jarren to find information on the perpetrators might endanger him?"

Uh. No. "But he can't go that deep."

"With his record, I've no doubt he will ignore his restrictions and try."

"He's good enough not to draw attention, he should be allowed to search," I say. No response. "I'll send him another message. And, if I'm permitted, I can try to find the security holes they used to worm into DES and trace them."

"Won't that endanger you?" Mom asks.

"She's well protected," Niall says almost hotly.

My hero. Dad covers his smile behind a napkin.

"And we've already been hit," Radcliff adds. "The looters

might target Suzhou because of Jarren."

Never thought of that! I swallow. "I'll do it tonight."

Radcliff agrees. "Niall, take her to my office. Morgan's on duty, she can supervise."

Niall stands. "I can stay with her."

"No. You have an early shift tomorrow."

His shoulders stiffen, but he doesn't argue. "Come on, Lyra."

I glance at my parents. Mom says, "Don't worry, we'll be visiting again."

Relieved, I follow Niall out.

"Gotta make a quick stop," he says, pausing at entrance number three-oh-four, which is two doors down and across the hall from Radcliff's. Pressing his palm to the lock, he opens the door and hustles inside.

I trail behind him into a tiny housing unit. While he ducks into the bedroom at the back, I glance around. Large colorful paintings decorate the walls. Actual canvases. Not images. They're gorgeous and so different from each other. A field of yellow flowers hangs next to a painting of a nebula cluster. I'm drawn to the one of a blue and white ocean wave crashing against a steep cliff face.

"My mother's," Niall says behind me.

"All of them?"

"Just my favorites. She painted...hundreds."

"They're amazing."

I turn around. He's belting on his holster, but his gaze is focused on a painting of a ringed planet streaked with purple and blue clouds. His grief is still raw. Stepping closer, I wrap my arms around him. He freezes for a moment then draws me tight against him. Warmth and the scent of sage envelop me.

"We better go," Niall says in a rough voice.

I tilt my head back, hoping for a kiss. "You're not in uniform."

He laughs. "I'm armed. And there are cameras in the corridor, tracking how long we're in here together."

"They can be fixed." I'm kidding, but he gapes at me. It's kind of cute.

"Good thing I'm the sensible one." Niall releases me and gestures to the door.

"I could fix them when I'm worming tonight."

"Lyra." He uses his stern Officer Radcliff voice.

Now it's my turn to laugh. "I'm joking."

Shooing me out, he shakes his head sadly. "Do you know most of the officers are betting on how long you'll last before being sent to detention?"

Not so funny now. "No."

We head to Radcliff's office and I wonder... "Why are you armed?"

"Orders."

"Oh no you don't. Tell me why."

There's a tense silence.

"Does your dad think I'm going to run away? Or that I'm going to cause problems and have to be stunned?"

"I don't know."

I huff.

"Look, I'm the lowest ranked officer on this team. I'm not

part of the decision-making process, I follow orders."

"And your orders are…"

"To protect you."

I wait.

"Either from invaders or from yourself."

Great. Just great. I don't know why I'm upset and I think it might have to do with the officers betting on me or maybe the fact I'm being supervised all the time and it's like everyone is waiting for me to do something… stupid. When we enter, Niall explains to Morgan why I'm there.

Before he leaves, he leans close and lowers his voice. "My money's on you, Mouse. Ninety days without a hitch."

My bad mood dissolves in an instant.

I use the terminal while Morgan stands behind me with her thumbs tucked into her weapon belt. What does she expect me to do? Ignoring her, I worm into the Q-net.

First stop. There's a message from Jarren.

2522:150: Wow! I AM proud of you, Lyra. Major points for getting thrown into detention. And WOW again for the ninety-day sentence. You must have been worming deep into illegal waters. Go you! Was it because I sent you those recovered Xinji files? They were a mess. I doubt anyone harvested any good information from them. At least not any details that would compromise the almighty DES's security. Did Lan's research have anything of interest? I miss her too. I'm sorry to hear about the looters. I'd love to help you out, but I can't go that deep anymore. I've an Officer Even Tighter Pants tracking my activities. When I'm in a good mood it's kind of cute—like an over-eager puppy following me around the Q-net. Other times it's annoying— like an over-eager puppy following me around the Q-net. <smirk> I couldn't get permission to go further either. I was told DES's "experts" were looking into it. Yes, the quotes are mine. When you get out of detention, send me a message, we can compare notes!

Lamenting the loss of major points, I send Jarren a quick reply, telling him about my probation and not to worry about the looters. I downplay Lan's research, saying that she sent it to me before Xinji went silent and it isn't about anything important. I don't want him to get into trouble trying to access the files.

Then I worm deeper, searching for evidence of another. I encounter a few collapsed tunnels of worms who have covered their tracks...well, inexpertly. There's a number of abandoned holes from brand new worms. I'm amazed by how many people are worming into DES, but they're mostly digging into minor areas. Allowing my instincts to lead the way, I sink into the levels that are between the surface systems and the star roads.

The clear purity and sizzling fastness of the star roads call to me, but this terminal doesn't have permission to go that far. I glide above and eventually spot a smooth shimmer. I track it for a while and discover it's a collapsed worm tunnel. But it's so expertly done, it's almost invisible. And impossible to trace back to the worm. I wonder if this is the work of the infamous Osen Vee. Once I know what to look for, I find more. Many more. And these are going into highly secure areas. Unease tingles up my spine. That's scary.

Going a bit further, I almost trip over another worm. This one is active! That's even scarier. My pulse jumps.

"Officer Morgan," I squeak.

"What's wrong?" She crouches next to me.

I explain what I have found, pointing to the screen. "What should I do?"

"Can you follow it to the source without letting the worm know you're there?"

Can I? Before my time with Chief Hoshi—no. Now... "Yes."

"Do it. I'll contact Radcliff."

I trail the worm by staying below it, as close to the star roads as I can get without setting off DES's alarms. The fact that the illegal worm is this near to the roads sends bolts of panic along my nerves. This could be one of the looters.

Voices sound behind me, but I'm too focused on my prey to listen. Time passes, more voices arrive, and pain stabs my forehead. At one point the worm dips into DES's sensitive database. I edge closer to see which one, and—

"Shit!" I bang a fist on the chair's arm as the worm spies me and takes off, zigzagging and covering its tracks so fast I lose it. "Shit!" Disgusted, I turn and freeze. Radcliff, Morgan, and my parents are staring at me.

"Uh…sorry."

"What happened?" Radcliff asks.

I explain.

He exchanges a glance with Morgan before asking me, "Can you go back in and track it?"

"Not on this terminal." I rub my temples.

"What about mine in the Control Room?" Dad asks.

"No. You need—shit!" I swivel back, calculating how many days it's been. About sixty days. Would they be in a time jump? I quickly access the information and— Yes!

"What are you doing?" Radcliff asks.

I hold up a hand. "Give me a minute." I send a message and hope there's not too long a delay—depends on how the Q-net is routing it. It's out of my hands now. I relax and turn to the others. "We can't follow the worm, but Chief Hoshi or one of the navigators can from their terminals. As long as they do it soon."

"How soon?" Radcliff asks.

"Now."

He strides over to his desk and consults his terminal. "They're ten days away from a crinkle point."

Which means they're too busy getting ready to bring the Crinkler engine online to even see the message. If they do notice, they still won't have time to do anything. "Shit."

"Lyra," Mom scolds.

"Sorry."

"It's certainly appropriate." Radcliff sits down. Lines of exhaustion are etched into his face and his shoulders droop.

"I can set up an alarm on a few secure areas. If the worm encounters any of them, we'll know," I offer. Considering how vast the Q-net is, chances are slim.

"All right."

"Not now," Mom says in her it's-pointless-to-argue voice. "You've been worming for hours."

Hours? I glance at the clock. It's oh-two-hundred hours. No wonder my brain feels like it's turned into goo.

"Okay, I just need to erase my trail." No way I'd want that worm to follow me home. And since the worm is an expert, it takes me another hour to ensure my tunnels have disappeared.

Just as I finish, I get a message— "Hoshi replied!" I shout.

Radcliff is next to me in an instant. "And?"

"She tracked the worm."

"And?"

Oh. My. Stars. "It came from Xinji."

15

2522:151

Stunned silence. I read the message again just in case my tired eyes missed a word or two. Or skipped something that would result in a different answer. One that made sense.

"That can't be," Mom says. "Did the Chief make a mistake?"

"Hoshi doesn't make mistakes," Radcliff says.

"Then that means there's still someone alive on Xinji," my dad says.

More silence. Everyone looks as exhausted as I feel. It's oh-three-thirty-hundred—well past my bedtime.

"While it is possible," Radcliff says, "it's not probable. DES did a remote scan for life."

"But that was..." Dad makes a circular gesture with his right hand. "...about a year and a half ago. Maybe the Xinji looters returned."

"Or never left," Officer Morgan adds. "There are ways to hide from a life scan."

True, the satellites in orbit can't penetrate bedrock.

"What about using the satellite relay to confuse a trace and lead us to the wrong planet?" Mom asks.

"It's possible," I say. "And if that's the case, then..." Everyone is staring at me.

"Then," Dad prompts.

"That worm is far better than Chief Hoshi and will be impossible to find."

No one has the energy to react.

I glance at Radcliff. "Jarren mentioned a wormer named Osen Vee. Have you heard of her?"

"Unfortunately. She runs with a dangerous crowd of wormers. Did he mention Warrick Nolt, Ursy Bear, or Fordel Peke? Along with Vee, they've been a menace in the Q-net for a couple E-years now."

"No, but Warrick Nolt taught Jarren how to worm long ago." I pause. Now that I understand the consequences of illegal worming better—messing with the star roads which might cause a catastrophe, looters stealing Warriors and killing people—I know what my next action should be. Yet reluctance causes me to hesitate. It'd be the same as telling security about all the hidey holes in the base, but this time it's in the Q-net. From worm to rat. Then I think of Lan. I'm an idiot for even questioning it. Pass me that cheese!

I point to the terminal. "DES has a bunch of security holes that I can mark."

Radcliff glances at Morgan and I wonder if they'd been hoping I'd suggest doing this during my probation.

"That's a generous offer," Radcliff says. "If you're willing to flag those areas, our staff can fix them."

"You'll have to do that at another time," Mom says. "Lyra needs to get some sleep."

The door to the office opens. Niall strides in and then jerks to a stop. He's in uniform and holding a steaming mug of coffee. Oh-four-hundred hours already?

"What happened?" he asks.

He slept through all the fun. I stifle giggles.

"I'm sure your father will fill you in," Mom says to him. "Come on, Lyra, let's get you to bed."

Standing requires more effort than my body is willing to give. But I gather what strength I can and... Ta da! The room tilts under me. My father hooks his arm around my waist, supporting me.

"Should we call the doctor?" Morgan asks in concern.

"Yes, please. Tell him to come to Tace's unit. I want to ensure she's all right." Mom drapes my right arm over her shoulders.

"I'm taller than you," I say to her with a smirk.

"Yes, you've been reminding me of that since you were fifteen A-years old." She uses the patient I'm-humoring- you-because-you're-not-feeling-well tone.

Wow, my mother's vocal range is phenomenal. I could probably tell you her mood from just one spoken word—almost telepathy. I swallow more giggles.

My parents half carry me the endless distance to Radcliff's unit. By the time I collapse in bed, my goofy stage of exhaustion is gone and I go right into the passed out cold stage.

When I wake, I've no idea if the doctor visited or not. Enjoying the comfortable warmth under the covers, I snuggle deeper. My heavy eyelids are almost shut when I spot the time. I'm on my feet without having any memory of the trip.

I'm late for soch-time!

But...this isn't my room. And...I'm supposed to... I've no idea. A horrible headache pounds all the way down to my ears.

I sink back to the bed, sitting on the edge, cradling my head. A light tapping interrupts my misery.

"Come in."

Niall enters with a bowl of soup. "Thought you might be hungry."

Am I? Not really. I take it anyway. "Thanks." The warmth soaks into my finger bones and the smell of chicken broth stirs my appetite. "Why didn't you wake me sooner?"

"You're on bed rest. Doctor's orders."

I'd complain, but my mouth is filled with yummy soup— guess I was hungry after all. After I suck down every last drop, I ask, "How long?"

"Two days."

This time I groan.

"What did you expect would happen after staying up all night chasing a worm?"

"I'd get a medal and my probation would be suspended."

He smiles. "And here I thought you were awake, but you're still dreaming."

"Funny," I deadpan.

He takes my empty bowl. "Now, back to sleep." Niall waits.

"Are you going to stand there until I lie down?"

"I don't know why you're unhappy. I'd love to have two days to do nothing but lie in bed all day."

"There's too much to do." I flop back.

Pulling the covers over me, he brushes his lips over mine. "Let someone else do it."

I relent...for now. "If I sleep, will you come back later with more soup?"

"I'll go one better and bring some of my dad's casserole. Deal?"

"Shhh, I'm sleeping."

Two days of bed rest isn't half bad when you have a handsome nurse/guard, bringing food and providing entertainment. Playing cards, people! We just started dating after all. Niall didn't seem to mind the make-sure-Lyra-stays-in-bed duty. Although I think we were both very happy when the doctor said I could return to soch-time and my *normal* activities. Which we all knew I'd ignore.

At soch-time on that third day, one of the quartet of girls comes up to me.

She whispers in my ear, "Lyra, there's a...message for you."

Wait, what? "Really? Where?"

Her young face creases as if in pain. "In the game system."

Oh boy. This can't be good. "Ah...all right." I unfold my legs and trail the girl to the game room.

The three others turn to us when we enter. I probably should learn their names. Nah.

"It won't let us play," whines the blond girl.

"And we don't know the password," another chimes in.

Password? I insert my tangs and see the problem. Jarren has sent me another secret missive. Such drama. I answer his question and words fill the screen. Shrinking it down quickly, I step closer to read his message.

> 2522:153: Lyra! Stop searching for those looters. From what I've been able to piece together about Xinji's final days, they're dangerous killers. And there's rumors they're hunting for a worm who got too close and they may have hired Ursy Bear. He's one of those nuts who think the star roads should be available for everyone to access and not just DES. Please let DES do its own dirty work and stay out of it! I already erased all the Xinji files I sent you so they can't trace those to you. I beg you to delete the research notes Lan sent you as well—your life is at stake!

If he wanted to scare me, mission accomplished. My initial reaction is to bury Lan's research so deep even I can't access the files. Yet, they're the result of decades of her hard work and I'm reluctant to part with them. Plus I'm surrounded by security officers.

I send Jarren a quick note, thanking him for the warning, but I can't lie to him and tell him I'm going to stop. Instead, I assure him I'll cool it for a while and be extra careful. Then I reset the game system and apologize to the girls for the disruption. I return to the main area, but am unable to sit still, so I grab some of the modeling clay the little kids play with to keep my hands busy.

What if my activities bring the looters back? Would our security team be able to fight against a greater force armed with those energy wave weapons? Pulse guns are no match for those. Now my fear is not just for myself, but for everyone on the base.

The tone sounds, ending soch-time.

One of the younger kids peers over my shoulder. "Uh...that's an...interesting looking...blob?"

"It's a space fart," another says. "Nature's own propellant!"

They laugh as if it's the funniest thing they've ever heard in their lives. Boys. I glance at my clay creation and...they're right. Definitely blob-like in appearance. Although, if I tweak it here and pulled this side out just a little—I drop the clay with a small cry. It reminds me of those shadow creatures in my last dream of the General. The same ones that have been popping up in my other dreams as well.

"Something wrong?" Niall asks, striding up to us.

No longer chortling, the boys edge past him and bolt. Chickens.

I smash the creature into a ball and stuff it into the air-tight container with the rest. "My dream of becoming a famous sculptor has just died." Another career off my list.

"I'm sorry to hear that, but I'm not surprised." His tone is serious, but there's a glint in his eyes.

"Oh? You don't think I'm artistic enough?"

"Your creativity is more suited to another career."

"And that would be?"

"Criminal mastermind," Niall says matter-of-factly.

He's teasing, but I play along and rub my hands together. "Lyra Daniels, Criminal Mastermind. I like the sound of that."

He huffs in amusement. "You would." He helps me to my feet.

My good humor fades as we traverse the corridors. Laughter and voices float from the open doors. Smiles of hello greet us whenever we pass others. I realize I know almost everyone in this base. Maybe not by name, but at least by profession. A sudden desire to protect them all floods through me. I wonder if this is how my parents feel about me. It would explain quite a bit— especially about all the nagging to be cautious.

"Niall, what would happen if the looters attacked the base?" I ask.

He glances at me and when he sees I'm serious, he says, "We added more sensor arrays to the outside of the base to scan the surrounding desert. We'll spot them before they can get close and deploy outside and stop them."

"How? Pulse weapons—"

"Are for when the threat level is low. We have others that pack more firepower, including those energy wave guns. That satellite in space has a few surprises as well. Plus there has been no sign of the looters in the solar system."

Which, while a relief, is odd. The safest crinkle point in this area is seventy days away. Unless they've found another way to travel. Or another crinkle point. I like the second option the best. Then they'd be far away in space-time.

A tightness inside me eases, until… "What if they're hiding on the planet or have control of our sensing devices or the satellite and can sneak inside the base?"

"Beau—Officer Dorey—checked the security clusters for the base and satellite twice. No one has tampered with them since the storm and he's keeping a close eye on them. We scanned the entire planet, and unless they're hiding deep underground, they're not here."

"And if they're underground and attack us again?"

"Then we scramble to the breach and fight them. In that case, there will unfortunately be some civilian casualties."

"What if you can't stop them?" I hug my mid-section, thinking of those poor souls on Xinji.

Niall stops and faces me. "What brought this on?"

I tell him about Jarren's warning.

"There is a reason to be worried. But not *too* worried. Chief Hoshi told my father you did an expert job erasing your worm tracks. Plus our team isn't your typical base security. An Interstellar Class ship's security force is as well trained as a Protector Class ship's. Trust us, we're not letting them get the drop on us again. Okay?"

His reassurance is well…reassuring. I nod and squelch the desire to take his hand as we continue to Radcliff's office. After a few moments, I say smugly, "Expert job eh?"

He sighs. "Out of all the stuff I said, that's your takeaway?"

"I could focus on how the team is atypical. Is that better?"

Niall just shakes his head and mutters under his breath about me being the death of his career. I laugh.

When we reach Radcliff's office, we interrupt a meeting. Morgan and another man sit in front of Radcliff's desk.

Radcliff waves us in. "Lyra, this is Officer Dorey."

Dorey stands and I recognize the spiky-haired man who slapped Niall on the back a few days ago. He's good looking and knows it, flashing me a bright smile. His bronze skin complements his amber eyes.

"Can you show him those unsecure areas you found?" Radcliff asks.

"Sure." They're all waiting, expectant. "Now?"

"If you don't mind," Dorey says. "Unless you'd rather do homework?" He winks.

"No. Now's fine."

"This way." He opens the side door that I've wondered about and sweeps a hand out. "After you, my lady."

I glance at Niall. He's scowling at Dorey. Jealous? Yeah, I'd bet he's the jealous type. I enter the narrow room. There are rows of screens on both sides. Silent images of the base's public areas, labs, and corridors fill them and two officers sit and watch. Ah that's why Niall was headed here for his early morning shift. We cross through and exit into another office. It's small, but it has a dual Q-net terminal. Sweet.

"We'll go in together and you can show me the holes. Are there a lot?" he asks.

"Yes. And I probably won't be able to work too long today,

Officer Dorey. I'm still recovering."

"That's fine, we can take it slow. And call me Beau."

"All right. Also we can't follow the proper channels like you're used to. Do you know how to worm?"

"Oh yes. And I'll tell you a secret, Miss Daniels. Many of the security officers whose job also involves securing the Q-net were caught illegally worming before they turned eighteen. Those caught enough times get a choice to go to the brig or to help out."

"And let me guess, you were one of those miscreants." I grin at him, sensing a kinship.

"I *might* have had an adventurous youth." A glint lights his eyes. "But once you get hooked on helping others...it's not a hard choice to make."

Ah. I suspected as much. "That means my probation is more like an internship."

Beau beams as if proud. "That's a positive way to look at it, Miss Daniels."

Great. "Call me Lyra."

"All right, Lyra. Shall we get started?"

"Yes."

He pushes up the sleeves of his uniform, revealing spider web tattoos on both forearms. I briefly wonder what they mean before my attention is captured by his expert navigation of the Q-net.

After a couple hours my vision blurs, but I don't want to stop. I can't believe I'm saying this... It's fun working with Beau. It reminds me of when Jarren taught me how to worm.

Eventually, though, I can't concentrate and we call it a day. Beau escorts me back to Radcliff's unit.

As we near the door, Beau says, "You have a unique way of navigating the Q-net."

"Is that good or bad?" I ask.

"It's good. That's why you spotted those holes. I can see all the others that are made the...traditional way for lack of a better word. It's like you're looking at everything from a different angle."

I mull over his comment. "Well...I've had lots of practice putting broken terracotta pieces together. But no matter how well those fragments fit, there are always gaps. I think that has helped my worming the most." I press my palm on the lock. The door opens, and my mother's voice spills out. I lower mine so only Beau can hear. "Just don't tell my parents that, or I'll never hear the end of it."

He laughs. It's a light pleasant chuckle. "Your secret is safe with me." Winking, he strides away.

I turn in time to see Niall hide his frown. Yup, jealous. He's sitting next to my mom with his sketchbook in his lap. She is showing him something on her portable. I debate if I want to know what they're doing, or go nap. A heavenly scent wafts from the kitchen. Dinner first. Then nap.

Settling on the other side of Mom, I see Lan's symbols and various Warriors on her portable. "What's this?" I ask. "While the diggers are finishing Pit 5, I decided to analyze the groups of symbols that represent the different Warrior planets—there's five hundred and twelve of them in all. Last time we had dinner

Niall told me that he spotted some of those symbols on our Warriors. I'm trying to find their actual locations in the pits. We managed to catalog the Warriors in the first two pits before the looters attacked."

I watch as a surface program compares each Warrior to the symbols. "Uh, Mom. The Q-net can do that in seconds."

"I know, but I don't want anyone to see what I'm doing." Her frustration is evident by the tight way she holds herself.

Good point. "I can bury the results with Lan's research. If a worm goes near, an alarm will go off."

"But what if I need access to it?"

Hmm. Another good point. Guess she's stuck doing it the slow way.

Niall flips to a clean page of his sketchbook. "We can make a grid on paper and mark the location of the Warriors with those symbols on the grid. After we do Yulin, we could do the other planets to see if there's a pattern."

Excitement pulses, energizing me. "That's right. Lan only found the symbols, she didn't figure out where they were in the pits."

Mom taps her foot as her gaze turns inward. "That's twenty-two planets with sixty-four pits each, that's over fifteen hundred pits. Quite the task."

"You can recruit help," I say. "The chemists can manufacture more rice paper and one of the engineers can create a grid template for the Warriors—they're set up the same way in all the pits. All we need to do is mark the square with a symbol." My heart taps a fast rhythm, but I don't know why I'm pushing for this. I've a ton of school work to catch up on. Perhaps it has to do with spending more time with Niall.

"I'll discuss this with your father," Mom says.

Radcliff pokes his head into the room and announces dinner. Mom pushes to her feet, wasting no time going to the kitchen.

Niall lowers his voice. "If that was my mom, that would be code for no."

"My mom is *never* that subtle. Trust me. If she's going to use the base's resources she needs to consult with my dad."

We join my mom at the table.

"Where is Dad?" I ask Mom.

"Dealing with a dispute over equipment. I swear scientists can be like a bunch of children sometimes."

Radcliff dishes out a stew that is the best thing I ever tasted without sugar. I'm going to gain a zillion grams if I keep eating like this.

At the end of the meal, Mom says, "About those symbols, let's do Yulin since only two pits were cataloged." Which is why after we finish, Niall and I are in Radcliff's office. He's drawing a grid that matches the rows and columns of the Warriors as they stand in their octagonal formation. He does this on two separate pages of his sketchbook—one for each pit. I pull my mom's scans of the Warriors from Pit 1 deep into the Q-net and let it tear it apart and put it back together. Niall marks the grid with the location of the Warriors with those symbols. Then we do the same for Pit 2. While I'm burying and protecting the results, he finishes up.

"Amazing," he says.

I glance over. "What is?"

"Pit 1." He points to the page spread out on Radcliff's desk. "Right around that square hole in the middle of the pit are twelve Warriors in a somewhat octagonal shape. The Warriors on each side of that small octagon have the same symbol. There are eight sides so there are eight different symbols."

"Octagon equals eight, I get it. I'm not *that* bad in math," I say.

He ignores me as he's flipping through his sketchbook. Turning to a page with rows of eight symbols next to names of planets, he scans the list.

"Is that from the other night? Lan's discovery?" I ask, surprised.

Niall glances up with a sheepish smile. "I figured the file would be locked down once your parents found out the significance of it so I spent the rest of the night making a copy."

Oh so he can do a little worming as well. "Devious. I approve."

"Ah, there!" He runs a finger along one of the rows. "The eight symbols in Pit 1 are the same one for planet… er…UK 23."

UK, meaning one of the forty-two unknown planets. "What about Pit 2?"

He checks. "Planet Chaohu."

"So each pit represents a planet?"

"Looks like it, but we'll have to analyze the other planets to be sure."

"That's great, except what does it mean?"

"Not our job. Don't you have cryptologists to decipher this?"

"Yes." But Lan had said there were codes within codes, so there was probably another level to this discovery. "Did you know the ancient Chinese considered the number eight lucky?" I ask.

"No, but it's certainly lucky for us." Niall taps his pencil on his chin. "No doubt your mother will want us to do the rest of the planets."

No doubt is right. She has it approved within the hour.

While the chemists work on supplying the necessary paper and grids for our symbol project, my life lapses into a routine. School work in the morning, lunch with Niall followed by soch-time. Then to Beau's office for a couple hours of worming. Dinner with Radcliff, Niall and, on occasion, one or both of my parents—which is sadly more time than I spent with them prior to my probation. After the meal, I head back to the office to catch up on my missed school work.

Each day I last longer before my head explodes. Okay, that's an exaggeration, but I definitely reach a point every night where my thoughts drag as if swimming in mud.

After five productive days, I've finally finished all my missed assignments. To celebrate, Niall is taking me out on a real date. Well, sort of. Since he's not wearing his uniform or a weapon, I'm still required to have an escort. Unless we stay in Radcliff's unit. While I'm not about to turn down potential making out on the couch (only if Radcliff's in his bedroom and stays there), Niall wishes to go out. He has the next day off so he can sleep in. Plus he even wore a nice button down shirt with gray stripes. It's tucked into black pants. I'm wearing my nicest navy blue blouse with a delicate yellow floral print that Mom dropped off this afternoon (who packs nice clothes when you're facing detention?) and jeans.

However, first is dinner with his father.

Except after Radcliff sets down a lovely baked ziti, he suddenly remembers some work he needs to do. Before he leaves he says, "Curfew is at zero-hours, Lyra. Not a second after." He gives Niall such a piercing look, I half expect Niall to topple over. "Officer Menz will be here in an hour." Then he's gone.

"What was the death-stare about?" I ask Niall.

"His way of reminding me that I'm not allowed to sweep you off your feet, carry you into the bedroom and ravish you for the next hour."

Heat blooms in my chest and spreads to places I'm not going to name. "Oh." I'll admit it's not the snappiest of replies.

"Relax, Mouse. This is going to be a *proper* first date."

"Oh." Is that disappointment I hear? Stupid hormones. "What does a proper first date entail?"

"You haven't been on one before?"

I think back. Cyril and I spent some time in the kissing zone. We played games together, but that's about it. "No."

"Well then you're in for a treat." He stands and fishes out a set of candles from the cupboard. Lighting them, he sets them down on the table. "First, a candlelit dinner served at the finest eating establishment on base." Niall sweeps a hand out with a flourish. "Before you can protest, you know my father can cook the pants off the chefs in the galley...er...canteen."

True.

Niall uses a spatula and scoops out two heaping portions. He sets one down in front of me. Spicy garlic wafts off the steaming ziti. We clink our water glasses.

As expected, the meal is top notch.

"What's it like growing up on a ship?" I ask.

"It's probably similar to growing up on a base. You explore every inch including the off-limits areas, boredom gets you into various degrees of trouble, you have not one mother and father, but an entire crew of mothers and fathers nagging you, and you need permission to leave."

That sounded about right.

"There are a few differences," he adds. "If you go outside, you're dead, and you learn the hard way not to make friends with the passengers."

"You mean you didn't want to become my friend?" I ask with mock surprise. "I never would have guessed."

"Oh, man, don't get me started. When you tricked the game system that first time...I figured you'd be in the brig within days. When that didn't happen, I fully intended to ignore you for the rest of the journey." He throws his hands out wide. "But you just wouldn't... stop."

I laugh. "I enjoyed bugging you. Still do."

That earns me a wry grin. "Yeah, I got *that*, but that's not what I'm talking about."

"Then enlighten me."

"Stop is probably not the best word. What I mean is you never hesitated to help out or offer your opinion whether it was wanted or not. You even volunteered to go down to the planet after knowing what happened at Xinji. Basically, you refused to be ignored."

"Ooh...I like that. Lyra Daniels, Refuses to be Ignored."

"What happened to criminal mastermind?"

"I think refuses to be ignored has more weight. Anyone can be a criminal mastermind, but those who refuse...scary stuff."

"Hmmm...I think you have something there. *Those who Refuse.* We can start a club, create a logo, develop a mission statement."

"I suspect you're making fun," I say.

He widens his eyes in an attempt to appear innocent. "Hey, I'm just glad criminal mastermind is off the table."

"For now. And for the record, Those who Refuse would not have some lame club."

"Duly noted."

"It would be better without the sarcasm."

"It would."

Pouting is not my style so I ask about dessert. When he hesitates, I say, "Don't tell me—"

"Don't worry, I'll have plenty of sugar for you later." He leers suggestively.

It's so overdramatic I can't help it, I laugh.

He joins in. "Yeah, I didn't think I could pull that off."

"Seriously, though. There's dessert right?"

"My stars, woman, you have a one-track mind. I'm running this date, so you'll just have to trust me." Niall clears the dishes and cleans up.

Even doing domestic chores, his movements are fluid. I'm content to watch.

There's a light knock on the door.

"And that would be our escort. Time for part two of a proper first date." He grabs my hand and tugs me to my feet.

Officer Menz waits in the corridor. His pained expression just about shouts that he didn't become a security officer to watch a couple teenagers on a date, but he remains professional, offering his hand when introduced. Menz's auburn hair is buzzed short like all the other officers. He studies me with dark green eyes as if assessing my threat level. I'm tempted to bare my teeth at him.

Niall holds my hand as we walk through the base. The heat from his palm travels up my arm, driving away the cold that has lingered there since I touched that heart.

There's a fair amount of people out and about. Most of the scientists get days off, but not many actually take the time. They're all a bunch of workaholics, which is why they were hired in the first place.

Niall steers me into the recreation room. It's about half filled. Every single person stares at us. Or more accurately, takes note of Officer Menz. It's unusual to have an armed officer in here. Plus the security team has its own rec room. Niall ignores them and heads straight for the game system. He pulls up *Mutant*

Zombies from Planet Nine.

"Okay, Mouse. Let's see if you can hold your own against *me.*"

"This is gonna be easy, Toad."

He settles next to me on the overstuffed orange couch. "I don't think so. I've seen you play during soch-time."

"You ain't seen nothin'. You were too busy drawing bunnies and babies."

He tsks. "Already trash talking. Let's see what you can really do. Ready?"

"Always."

The battle begins. Niall's mutant zombie army launches an offensive right away. It's over the top and I suspect it's to test my defenses. I counter with a standard boring move, but, while he's distracted, I set up a couple surprises for later. I learned a few tricks while playing with Cyril and Jarren and I plan to use them all. No space boy is gonna beat me.

The battle transforms into an all-out war. It extends. Damn, he knows what he's doing. I'm suddenly retreating, losing soldiers left and right as they turn into the enemy, joining Niall's zombie horde. He's driving us toward a huge pile of dangerous building rubble blocking the street. A dead end.

"It's not looking too good for you. Are you ready to give up, Mouse?"

"Giving up is not an option."

"Then prepare to become the mutant zombie queen."

My dwindling army retreats further.

"Being a zombie queen is really not so bad, there are perks," he says. "Living forever for one, which is how long I'm going to gloat about this."

A pathetic handful of survivors form a shield around me. We're almost to the barricade. Come on. Just a little bit...there!

"What? Hey!" Niall shouts.

I grin as the pile of rubble turns into soldiers. Lots of them. Now his zombies are outnumbered and surrounded. In a matter of minutes his army is routed. Game over.

"Yup, I'm the queen all right," I say with a touch... oh, all right, *a lot* of smugness.

He shakes his head. "I gotta admit that was a sweet move. But you owe me a rematch."

"Now?"

"No, it's time for part three." He takes my hand and we cross to the canteen. There's a queue of people, talking and laughing. We join the end of the line.

"How are you enjoying your first proper date so far?" Niall asks.

"Very much. The highlight, so far, was luring you into my ambush."

He lowers his voice to a husky whisper. "You can lure me in anytime."

A tingling warmth races up my spine. Purposely misunderstanding him, I say, "I'll remember that the next time I have one of my crazy schemes."

I'm rewarded with a groan. We're inching along, but Niall won't tell me what we're waiting for. I don't mind. Even though Menz is hovering nearby, it's just nice to stand close to him and talk about nothing important.

When I finally spot the reason for the line, I almost squeal. Thank the stars, I don't. I'd forgotten it's ice cream night—a rare treat from the chefs. Bonus, it's my third favorite flavor—butterscotch.

"Does this count for dessert?" Niall asks.

"Yes!"

We each get a bowl and Niall grabs one for Menz. The three of us return to the rec room.

"Now for part four." Niall turns on a video show and we return to the couch with our ice cream. Once we finish the frozen goodness, Niall puts his arm around my shoulder. I lean against him, soaking up his warmth, breathing in his scent. Content.

I'd stay there all night, but I have a curfew. Plus there's a bored security officer yawning loudly behind us. We return to Radcliff's unit. Menz waits until we enter before leaving. Niall's father is sitting in the common area, working on a portable. He makes a show of glancing at the time. We are four minutes early.

"Now that you're back, I'm going to bed," he says, stretching. "Good night."

"Good night," we say in unison.

When Radcliff's bedroom door shuts, Niall turns to me. "I've been looking forward to part five all night."

"Part five?" Only a slight squeak mars my voice.

He steps nearer. "Actually, I've been thinking about this since I escorted you home back before your probation."

I haven't forgotten either. Heat races through me as Niall closes the distance between us. His lips are on mine. His fingers are in my hair. The combination of sensations sends shivers along my skin. I wrap my arms around his neck and deepen the kiss.

I lose track of time, but Niall eventually breaks away. "If I don't leave soon, my father will poke his head out the door to check on us."

I'm a bit breathless so instead of talking, I just pull him in for another kiss. His hands press on my back until I'm against his chest. And I have to admit, part five is my favorite of the night.

Niall once again ends it. "Right now, I really hate being the sensible one."

He moves away and I stifle my groan of protest.

"Did you enjoy your proper first date?" he asks.

"It was perfect. Thank you."

"We're almost ready," Mom says at dinner two days after our date. "I'm just worried pulling the files from the other planets will tip off the looters that we're searching for those symbols."

"It shouldn't," I say between mouthfuls of chicken corn soup. "It's part of your job. And, as long as I bury the Q-net's results, the looters or that worm won't know what we're doing with the data."

Mom drums her fingers on the table—a nervous habit. "All

right. All the materials will be ready in three days. We can start work on it then. I suspect it'll take us a number of sessions to go through all those pits."

She peers at me with her Mom-X-ray-vision set to maximum. Uh oh. This isn't going to be pretty.

"How are you feeling? Still getting headaches?" she asks me.

"I only get an occasional headache. Why?"

"I'd like you to keep working on the General. That section of Pit 4 is the only place that the looters haven't destroyed. I know you have separated out some pieces so it's best if you're the one to reconstruct him." She leans forward. "But *only* if you're feeling better."

The thought of someone else putting him together is almost painful. I wonder if he'll return to my dreams once he's complete. I glance at Radcliff. "As long as it's okay with the boss."

Radcliff's lips quirk into a smile before he smooths his features. One of these days, I'm going to get him to laugh. "It's fine with me," he says. "I can arrange an escort for you. There's already plenty of security in the pits. When do you want to start?"

I catch Niall's eye. He's unhappy but doesn't say anything. Lately he's been staying after everyone leaves and we play cards or talk for a bit before Niall's too tired to do more—poor guy has to get up oh-so-early. Other than that, I don't have anything planned tonight. "Might as well start now."

"Let me check the schedule." Radcliff heads for the terminal in his bedroom.

My mother stands. "I better get going. I've a meeting with the geologists." She kisses me on the temple. "Don't overdo it tonight. An hour or two is fine. Promise?"

"Yes." That earns me another kiss before she's gone. I turn to a still frowning Niall. "What's wrong? Is it because we're not going to hang out together?"

"No." He moves to sit next to me. "Are you sure you're ready?"

Confused, I ask, "Why wouldn't I be?"

Stroking the side of my face with his fingertips, he rests his hand on my shoulder. "You almost died there."

He's concerned for me. That's sweet. "I'll be fine."

Radcliff returns. "I can have someone here in an hour — "

"I'll take her," Niall says.

He pauses a beat. "All right. Then inform Beau he can bring her back when his shift is done. Will two hours be enough time, Lyra?"

"Plenty."

"Good."

Niall leaves to get changed. And I switch to my old work clothes. By the time Niall reappears, I'm ready to go. Too bad he's in uniform. As we walk side by side, the desire to hold his hand grows with each step.

"Do you get many days off?" I ask to break the silence and to distract my itchy fingers.

"Right now, it's eight days on and one day off."

"That's a lot."

"We're still on high alert. Once the threat level is reduced, we'll go back to a six and two schedule."

"Are you still on high alert because you don't know where the looters are?"

"That's my guess, too. Plus my dad tends to be overly cautious."

We cross through the archaeology labs. Many of the archaeologists and techs are still at their desks or bent over equipment. However, everyone stops to greet me and tell me how fantastic I look. Guess I haven't been down here since I was carried out bloody and broken.

There are a few workers in the pits sorting through the rubble. It's...a disaster area. My stomach sours as I scan the debris. The once neat lines of Warriors are now broken heaps. Pieces of clay too small to be identified crunch underneath my boots. The techs have filled in the holes dug by the looters, and repaired the walls.

At least the 3D laser digitizers are being used to scan the fragments. Perhaps I can drag all the data into the Q-net where it could reassemble the shards. That would speed up the process somewhat. Of course, it might be years before they finish scanning.

When we enter Pit 4, I stop. Memories threaten to overwhelm me, the edges of my vision turn fuzzy.

"Are you all right?" Niall asks.

"Yeah, I just need a minute." I suck in dusty air until the floor steadies. Then I stride over to the General. He's still half completed and the area around him remains the same as before. The rest of the Warriors are either gone or destroyed.

I find my bucket of pieces and his face. But when I sit down to get my bearings, another memory tugs at the edges of my mind. Something about the way the looters moved through the pit. I try to concentrate, but the idea slips away.

Niall crouches down next to me. "You're pale."

"I'm just upset by all the damage." I tilt my head at Beau and Menz who are standing by the hatch. "You can go, I'll be fine."

"I'm not going anywhere."

"But — "

"I'm going to help you."

I stare at him. "Why?"

"This is our time together. I don't care what we do. Where do you want to start first?"

He's serious and a strange mix of emotions flood me. "First, I want to drag you behind that large pile of debris where the cameras and those officers can't see and kiss you until you can't breathe."

"What about the General?" his voice rasps.

"He won't mind."

"I'm in uniform."

I leer. "Not for long."

"I'm the sensible one. I'm the sensible one," Niall chants under his breath while taking in deep breaths.

"Would you rather go down below?"

"My stars, Lyra. You're going to get us in trouble."

"You started it."

"How?"

I open my mouth to answer, but movement catches my eye.

Something dark near the back of the pit. Odd. I don't think anyone is working there. The lights don't reach all the way so it's hard to see. I stand to get a better look.

"What's wrong?"

"I saw..." I take a step.

Niall grabs my arm and pulls me behind him. "Me first." He draws his weapon. Beau and Menz are hurrying over to us with their guns in hand.

"Where's the trouble?" Beau asks.

Feeling silly, I point to the back corner. "I thought I saw something move. Probably nothing."

"Menz, stay here with Lyra," Beau orders. "Niall, with me."

They advance to the area, moving slow and keeping the piles of rubble between them and the back wall. Beau signals Niall and they split up, each going around a stack of broken Warriors. When they disappear from sight, a large shadow darts out.

"To the left!" I shout.

Both men burst from cover then stop.

Beau signals.

"Where is it?" Menz asks me.

The shadow is crouching behind another pile, hidden from the men, but not from us. "Can't you see it?" I ask Menz.

"No."

I tell Menz and he relays the information via hand signals. Beau and Niall creep up on the shadow without making a sound. Impressive since there is sand and rubble everywhere.

When they get close, the shadow breaks cover and runs

straight at me. For a second I'm thinking it's man-shaped, but then it transforms into one of the shadow creatures from my dreams. And it's a meter away.

Terrified, I grab Menz's arm. "There!" I point.

"I don't see anything."

I backpedal as it advances. "Shoot it!"

"Shoot what?"

It brushes against me, knocking me down. I yell as something sharp rips my shirt. Then it reaches the bright light and between one blink and the next, it's gone.

Niall is standing over me in a protective stance. "What happened?"

"Did you see it? See what clipped me?" I ask Menz.

"No." His voice has an odd tone. "There was nothing there."

2522:160

From the ground I stare at Menz. Nothing there? Nothing there? Is he blind? "It knocked me over."

"It?" Niall asks. He's still standing over me.

"Yes. A shadow-blob thing. It ripped my shirt." I push up onto one elbow.

"Stay down," Beau orders me.

"What should we do?" Menz asks.

"Call the boss."

It didn't take long for Radcliff and six members of his team to arrive. Using bright spot lights, they do a thorough search of all four pits. Unable to participate, I remain in Pit 4 with Niall.

"Can you describe the shadow-blob thing?" Niall asks while we wait.

I have to give him credit for not teasing me or treating me like I'm insane. "No, but if I get the molding clay from the soch-area, I can try to shape one for you."

The security team finds nothing. Dusty and sweaty, Officer

Radcliff approaches and asks all the same questions Niall did. My answers don't change, except now that I'm no longer scared, I sound insane. But I pull my shirt away from my stomach and show him the rip. The shadow's blade didn't cut my skin, which I was relieved about before, but now I'm thinking a little blood would go a long way in my favor.

Radcliff runs a finger along the tear. "It's clean. Could be from a blade."

"Or a shard," Menz said. "She fell into a pile of them."

The rest of the security team avoids meeting my gaze. Except Keir, she tilts her head at Menz and rolls her eyes. Nice that someone else supports me.

"There's nothing here now," Radcliff says. "We'll double the guard in the pits. Niall, Keir, Beau, and Menz, you'll remain here."

"Yes, sir," four voices say in unison.

"Morgan, set up a new schedule for the pits."

Yes, sir," Morgan says.

"Those on duty can return to your posts, the rest, as you were," Radcliff finishes.

There's a bit of muttering as they leave.

Keir comes over to me and lowers her voice. "If you need to chat, let me know. You're surrounded by all that testosterone and they just don't get it. You know?"

I did. "Thanks."

She touches my shoulder and joins the others.

"Miss Daniels, come with me," Radcliff says.

I'm back to *Miss Daniels*. This can't be good. Niall's

conferring with Beau and has his back to me. I follow Radcliff through the pits. I scan the dark areas. Not that I have any desire to see another shadow-blob, but spotting one would prove to everyone it exists. My parents are waiting for me in the archaeology lab along with two more security officers. That's the entire team. Great.

Of course they pounce with the questions. And of course they don't like the answers either. My mom presses a cool hand to my forehead, checking for a fever. Then they escort me to the infirmary for, you guessed it, a brain scan and cognitive tests. Afterwards, I lie in a darkened room, listening to the hushed voices just outside.

"...too soon...concussions...slow to heal..."

"...post-traumatic stress disorder..."

"Couple days..."

"...better...some rest..."

I'm discharged with orders to limit my activities for the next few days. No extra projects, just soch-time and school. Mom and Dad say good night, giving me supportive hugs before I trail Radcliff back to our unit. Huh? Did I just say *our*? I've only been on probation for ten days.

When we return, it's late so I go to bed. Except I can't sleep.

Did I imagine the shadow creature? Could it be just a manifestation of my dreams because of my concussion? Like a waking dream? Menz was standing right next to me. If he didn't see it... But I felt the blade. Or did I? Could it have been just a shard? I know from experience that if they're broken just the right way those little suckers can slice open a finger. By the time

MARIA V. SNYDER

I drift off hours later, I'm convinced it was an overactive imagination due to trauma. Sounds better than going crazy.

The next day, no one says a word to me about what happened in Pit 4. I do my school work in Radcliff's office. And Keir escorts me to lunch. Of course, I can think of a million reasons why Niall doesn't want to see me. I probably embarrassed him and pissed off the entire security team.

In the canteen, she fills her plate until it's almost overflowing, while I take a few pieces of cheese and some crackers. The heavy mass rolling in my stomach since yesterday has destroyed my appetite.

She points to my meager rations. "You gotta eat more than that. It keeps your strength up."

I glance at her pile. "You must be very strong then."

Keir lets out a hearty laugh. "You bet your pampered ass. I can take down half the security guys and boy do they hate it."

"Pampered ass? Do you not know I'm on probation and can't do anything without an escort?"

"Yup. You have us all running around attending to you like you're the Queen of Yulin," she teases.

I can't help it, I laugh. "Lyra Daniels, Queen of Yulin has a nice ring to it. Perhaps you should start calling me Your Majesty." I add Queen of Yulin to my career list along with Criminal Mastermind and Refuses to be Ignored.

"You wish." Keir spoons some of her meat onto my plate. "Eat. Once your doctors say it's okay, you'll be burning calories like crazy."

"Uh, why?"

"Training. Officer Radcliff wants you able to defend yourself and guess who's gonna be your instructor."

"You?"

"You bet your —— "

"Pampered ass?"

"You catch on quick for a spoiled lab rat."

"So says my glorified babysitter," I shoot back.

"Ooh, nice. You'll fit in well with the team. Well, once we get you into fighting shape. You'd be surprised how much confidence you gain when you can take down a man twice your size."

What about shadow-blobs? Then I realize what she's doing. "Is this about yesterday? To help me so I don't jump at every shadow and cause the entire security team to rush to my rescue?"

She studies me. Long dark eyelashes curl from beautiful oval-shaped eyes. "Partly. But the training has always been included with your probation."

"Do they do that for everyone who gets probation?"

"You're the first person *ever* to get probation. Officer Radcliff usually tosses the person in the brig for a few days for a first offense. I don't know what this is all about, but I'm second to last on the hierarchy. I'm given orders, not asked for my opinion."

I wonder how the others rank so I ask her.

"Your lover boy is last." She grins. "Then me, Zaim, Menz, Dorey, Rance, Ho, Bendix, Vedann, Tora, Morgan, and Radcliff at the top."

"Is it based on experience or age?"

"Both are a factor, but also ability. Rance and Bendix are blockheads—muscular by-the-book guys, but not leaders. Once you show you can keep a cool head in a dangerous situation, you're moved up in the ranks."

It sounds like the labs. You start as a tech once you graduate and work your way up to scientist. The smarter and hardworking ones tend to be promoted faster.

Having lunch with Keir was fun, unlike soch-time, and, instead of worming with Beau, I'm escorted back to Radcliff's unit to rest.

Keir stops me before I shut the door. "You want me to stay?"

"Huh?" Confused, it's all I can manage.

"My last assignment, my team was ambushed—for lack of a better word—by Shredders—these big doglike creatures on Planet Epsilon. Big teeth, acidic drool and hooked claws. Nasty things. We fought our way out and no one died, but for many days—and I'm talking close to a hundred or more—I had nightmares of those Shredders ripping into me. I'd wake stabbing my pillow with my knife." She shudders. "My security partner figured out what was going on and he—the stubborn fool—camped out on the floor of my bedroom until the nightmares stopped."

Now I understand what she's doing, but I can't help ask, "How long did that take?"

"Only a couple nights."

Ah. "Thanks for the offer, Officer Keir—"

"Elese, that's my first name."

I smile. "Elese, but I'm not having nightmares about the looters."

"That's good." She slaps me on the back. "You're pretty resilient for a spoiled lab rat."

"And don't you have other work to do? Like guarding the toy chest in the rec room?"

"I like you." She waves and heads out.

The feeling is mutual, causing guilt to squeeze my chest as I wasn't completely honest with Elese. Shadows and not looters haunt my dreams.

Dinner is a sad affair. Niall and my parents are a no show and Radcliff has to work so I'm on my own.

By the third day of this, I invite Elese in to play cards. She's easy to hang with and she fills me in on the security gossip. "Menz needs to deck Dorey right upside his spiky head, but Ivan's too nice, which is why Beau keeps picking at him."

"Beau's nice to me," I say in his defense.

"Oh yeah, he's just testing Ivan, like he does to everyone. Sees how much they can take before they get angry enough to deck him. It's always good to know a person's snapping point. We go into some dangerous situations and these people are protecting your back."

"How long did it take before you decked him?"

"I didn't have to. Every time he started that nonsense, I gave him my hard stare." Elese demonstrates. It's chilling. It's a don't-even-think-about-messing-with-me-or-I'll-tear-you-in-two expression. "He stopped picking on me soon after."

"Impressive. Can you teach me?"

"Definitely, but don't try it on Radcliff, he's immune and he'll respond with his own stare that'll about knock you across the room."

Remembering Radcliff's glare on my first date with Niall, I say, "I think I've seen it."

"And you're alive to tell the tale?" Elese says with mock amazement.

"It was aimed at Niall."

"Ah. He's not immune to his dad's killer stare, but he's not *as* affected as the rest of us."

Once Elese beats me at Sevens five games in a row, she heads out and I'm left standing in the middle of Radcliff's common area. It's sixteen-hundred hours and since no one has joined me for dinner the last three days—don't bother the crazy woman—I figure I've eight hours of nothing ahead of me. And to think detention is *all day* of nothing—I would have gone insane. I shuffle to my room and crawl under the covers.

A knock wakes me.

"Lyra, dinner," Radcliff says.

"I'm not hungry. I'll eat later." I pull the blanket back over my head.

Another knock, but then my door opens.

"I said I'm not—" The material is pulled down and reveals my mother's concerned face.

"Are you okay?"

No, everyone thinks I'm crazy. "I'm fine, Mom."

"Then why aren't you hungry? You've had three days of rest."

"Resting doesn't exactly work up an appetite." I didn't mean to snap at her. "I'm sorry. I'm just bored."

"Then you'll be happy to know we have all the materials for the symbol project. You can start tomorrow."

Energized, I sit up. "Really? You'll let me work on it?"

"Why not?"

I tap my temple. "Brain damage."

"Don't be ridiculous, Lyra."

"And Niall might not be interested anymore."

"Let's ask him before you assume."

"Ask?" I squawk.

"He's having dinner with us. Unless you'd rather stay in here and pout?"

"But—"

She sits down next to me on the bed. "You were almost killed in Pit 4. It's not unusual to have an adverse reaction the first time you return. We shouldn't have asked you to work on the General so soon. Everyone understands. Now get up and join us."

Typical Mom—comforting softness followed by bossy orders. Just what I needed. I change out of my rumpled clothes and fix my hair. The conversation at the table doesn't even pause when I join them. Niall flashes me a smile and I about melt into a Lyra puddle.

Eventually talk turns to the symbol project.

"Of course I'm in," Niall says, sounding offended by my

question.

"When's the best time to work on it?" Mom asks us.

Niall glances at his dad. "Are we still—"

"For a couple more days."

"Evenings are best," Niall says to me. "Will that work?"

Considering everyone knows my schedule, it's nice of him to ask. "Yes."

"I'll bring the supplies to dinner tomorrow." Mom spears another piece of meat with her fork.

I gaze at Radcliff. Did he expect to have a full table when he put me on probation? He did invite my parents that first night and he appears to enjoy their company. The man left his ship family to protect us on Yulin. Perhaps I shouldn't give him such a hard time... Nah. Where's the fun in that?

After the adults leave, Niall and I snuggle on the couch. He drapes an arm around my shoulders. I lean against him and tuck my feet up underneath me. His body heat soaks into me and I would be content to remain here all night. There's a couple of his sketchbooks on the table along with a small box. I wonder what's in the mystery container. His chalks?

"I can't stay long," he says with regret. "My shift starts at oh-two-hundred hours."

"Why so early?"

He tenses. "Ah..."

I sigh. "Your dad is still doubling the guards in the pits."

"Yeah."

"I'm sorry I freaked out," I say. "Does the entire security force except Keir hate me?"

Niall pulls away. He looks me in the eye. "Not at all. They understand. In fact..."

"What?"

He scrubs a hand through his hair. "I'm not supposed to tell you."

I straddle his lap and grab his T-shirt in both my hands. "Oh no. You can't do that to me. Out with it, Toad."

"Or what?"

Ah, hell. Didn't expect that. A memory from my childhood bubbles to the surface—my brother's sure fire way to get me to talk. Releasing his shirt, I bend my fingers so they resemble claws. "I find out if you're ticklish."

He gives me a sly smile. "You *do* know where my hands are right now. Don't you?"

They're resting on my waist. Under my shirt. Skin on skin. Oh my stars.

"I'll bet that you're a lot more ticklish than I am." Niall moves his thumbs.

Instead of bursting into uncontrollable giggles, my breath catches as heat spreads over my stomach. His hands move upward, brushing my ribs. Fire races across my skin. All thought of tickling him for information dissolves when his thumbs reach higher. They slide under my bra and I gasp as they graze my breasts.

"So much for that bet," he whispers before kissing me.

The combination of his lips on mine and the soft strokes of his thumbs create a pulsing desire deep inside me. I tangle my fingers in his hair. Then it's all raw sensations and lustful thoughts. The need to be in contact with more skin drives me to pluck at his shirt. I want it off. Now.

Niall groans and breaks away. He grabs my wrists before I can pull him back for another kiss. "My father... return...anytime," he pants.

Cold reality douses me. The rest of the world rushes back in. Somehow I ended up underneath him on the couch. My bra is above my breasts. Niall moves to the far end. I straighten my shirt and fix the annoying undergarment. Sitting up, I settle on my side of the couch. Is it bad that I'm considering not wearing a bra the next time Niall and I have some alone time? Probably.

Once I recover my breath, I ask, "Why did you bring your sketchbooks?"

"To test a theory."

I wait.

He scrunches up the end of his T-shirt as if trying to gather courage. "I watched the camera feed of us in Pit 4."

Oh boy.

"Other than the four of us, there's nobody else there," he says.

Now I have proof of my insanity. Great. I sink lower in my seat.

"However..."

I risk meeting his gaze. "However?"

"Unless you're a skilled actress, something knocked you down."

Did he just... Hope wells. "Does your dad think that, too?"

He gives me a sour look. "Of course not. I'm biased due to

my relationship with the witness."

And hope dies. I huff. Sounds like Radcliff.

Niall leans forward and picks up the mystery box. He taps it on his leg before turning to me. "After the... incident, you told me you couldn't describe the shadow-blob, but could shape it." He hands me the box. "I don't want to upset you. If you're okay with the PTSD diagnosis for what happened, give me the box back and it's all in the past—never to be mentioned again. But if you're not okay with it, then open it."

I rub my stomach, remembering the sound of ripping fabric. Definitely not okay. Inside the box is a fist-sized glob of molding clay. Fear swipes my heart, but also warmth. Niall believes me. And just like that, the ever-present tightness in my chest lessens. But now I have a new problem. What shape do I show him?

Deciding to start with the first form, I work the clay until it's an approximation of what I saw.

"Wow, it really is a blob," Niall says when I show him.

"Well, it's a shadow. It doesn't have... density... thickness, just a shape. Does that make sense?"

"Sort of. How tall was it?"

"It changed height as it moved, going from a meter to two meters or so—like a giant amoeba." I pull the clay, creating appendages. "And the...tentacles... arms, turned into long sharp blades when it got close to me." Adding edges to my sculpture, I try to duplicate what I saw, but fail. In my hands is basically a blob of clay.

Niall stares at it with a furrowed brow, which is way more

effort than really needed for El Blobbo. It's sweet. Then he pulls the top sketchbook off the pile and pages through it. When he finishes, he puts it aside and takes another and then another. For once, I'm content to wait...well, not really, it's killing me and I'm itching to peruse one of his books. Would he mind...I'm reaching for the discarded pile when Niall makes a small *ah* sound.

He flips over a bunch of pages, revealing a drawing of one of the Warriors. It's impressively detailed and written on one corner is Pit 2, Row 33, Column 4.

"I liked this guy's expression," Niall explains.

The Warrior has a fierce, scowling countenance. Figures.

He turns the page. "And here's the back of him."

Another accurate sketch, including the man's short hair.

Pointing to the bottom of the Warrior's coat, Niall says, "There's a line of symbols here."

I peer closer. "That's Chinese calligraphy—it's the craftsman's name. All the Warriors are marked by their creators."

"But at the end is a blob. Maybe *your* blob."

I have a blob. Lovely. It did indeed appear to be a blob, but it could easily have been a smudge of dirt, a blemish, or the date the piece was crafted. All of which I mention to Niall.

He responds by finding two more Warrior sketches with signatures and a blob—another in Pit 2 and one in Pit 4.

"How many of these did you draw?" I ask.

"I had to do *something* while I was dodging you," he says.

I punch him on the arm. "I knew you were avoiding me.

Jerk!"

Laughing, he grabs my wrists. I try to free myself, but he's stronger and soon I'm pinned under him on the couch. Now we're both a bit winded, although I suspect his reasons are different than mine. I need to get into shape.

"Once you start training, I'm going to have a tougher time wrestling you," Niall says.

"You bet your...uh...ass."

"I see you're already learning from Elese. So I better take advantage of it while I can." He dips his head closer, kissing me.

All my worries fade into the haze of bliss. If this is going to be the downside of getting pinned, he can pin me all he wants.

He breaks it off with a sigh. "I hate being the sensible one."

"Then don't be." I reclaim his lips and he responds. He releases my wrists and his fingers are in my hair, pulling it away from my neck. Then he moves to suck on my earlobe. When he nips it, I just about jump as a shock of pleasure spikes through me. From an earlobe! Who knew?

A shuffle of boots sounds and we jerk apart, turning to the door. Thank the stars it's still closed. Radcliff's muffled voice reaches us. We rush to straighten our clothing and smooth our hair. Niall picks up his sketchbook just as Radcliff enters.

He studies us for a moment. "Niall, don't you have an early shift?"

"I do," Niall says, but doesn't move.

Radcliff grunts then says good night, disappearing into his bedroom. We share a smile, but then Niall sobers.

He taps a finger on his sketch. "I think we should see if one of these signature-blobs survived the looters' attack. Get a better look at it."

Anxiety swirls in my stomach. "We can look at the images in the Q-net. They scanned and catalogued the first two pits."

"I think it'd be better to see and feel the real thing if we can."

"You want to search through the rubble?"

"Yes." He rushes on. "We have an approximate location and some of the broken pieces are quite large."

"But what if I see the shadow-blob or have a panic attack?"

"We'll take it slow. If you're uncomfortable, we'll leave."

I consider. Eventually, I'll have to go into the pits again. And the thought of being afraid to enter is unacceptable to Lyra Daniels, Refuses to be Ignored. Besides, I might not see anything and that would put the entire shadow-blob thing behind us. "All right. When?"

"Tomorrow after soch-time. I'll work it out with my dad."

Not expecting it to be so soon, I frown.

Niall takes my hand. "Don't worry, Mouse. I'll be with you." He picks up the clay blob and crushes it into a ball.

The next day I'm a bit on edge during soch-time. My thoughts keep circling back to the pits and what I might or might not see there. If we even go. Officer Menz escorted me this afternoon in his usual silence, which I'm learning is just his easy-going nature to be quiet and it's *not* that he's annoyed with having to guard me. Plus Radcliff didn't mention Niall at all this morning.

But when soch-time ends, Niall and Beau are waiting for me

outside. Niall's familiar glower is back.

"Your father has conditions," I say by way of a greeting.

"Yup," Beau says even though I wasn't talking to him. "You two get to bring along the best-looking officer on the team." He gives me a little bow. "And you have to promise that if you feel at all anxious, you're to tell us right away and we'll skedaddle."

"Skedaddle?"

"An official term. In layman's terms it means to leave with the utmost haste."

"Ah."

"Do you promise?" Beau asks.

"Uh, yes, I promise to tell you when I need to...er... skedaddle."

"Excellent. Shall we, my lady?" Beau sweeps a hand out.

"We shall."

Beau and I take point while Niall trails behind. Beau keeps up a one-sided dialogue the entire trip to the archaeology lab. I suspect it's either to keep my mind off of where we're going or to annoy Niall. From Niall's ever-present scowl, I'm leaning toward the latter.

Of course my parents are working in the lab. Their pleasant chit-chat is just a façade. Underneath, they're scanning me with their parental powers of observation, seeking any signs of distress. I think calming thoughts, but it's hard to stay focused when two officers guard the entrance into the pits.

My dad claims he needs to go into the pits to check on progress with the hearts. "They're closing in on a method to move them without destroying them."

"That's great," I say, half-distracted, as our little group enters. Not much has changed in the pits. Teams of archaeologists work to reconstruct the Warriors. The faintly glowing lights cast multiple shadows. None move. A relief. I can do this.

At Pit 2, Niall pulls a large flashlight from his belt. My father hesitates, but then says, "Be careful and don't break anything."

We all turn to him with incredulous expressions.

"Don't break anything *more*. How's that?"

Not much better. I wave him off.

"Are you—"

"Go. Shoo," I say.

Niall and I share a smile of affectionate tolerance that says *fathers*. He toggles on the flashlight and a beam of white light pierces the dusty air. Now it's his turn to take point as we carefully traverse the rubble. Stepping over an arm and avoiding a head, I edge around a jumbled mess of body parts. I check the shadows. Frequently. They move with the light, but don't appear abnormal.

Or should I use the word sentient?

Only if I want an extended stay in the infirmary.

We arrive at the approximate location of Column 4, Row 33. The debris isn't as thick in this area. Beau hands me his flashlight so Niall and I can search while he stands guard.

I take the right side, while Niall goes to the left. Sweeping the beam over the nearby pieces, I scan the clay for the artist's markings. After an hour of finding nothing, Niall suggests we check the other Warrior. And when that has the same results, we head to the site in Pit 4.

Both officers tense when we enter. There are four guards near the hatch, so it's not because they're worried about an attack—half the security team is in here. No, they're bracing for me to freak out. Lovely. I remain calm despite the increased thumping of my heartbeat. No shadow-blobs. Not yet.

The Warrior Niall drew was in the last row. As we navigate through I notice there's not as much rubble in this section. Probably because close to five hundred Warriors had been stolen before the attack. Memories of the looters' actions replay in my head. They moved as if they had a plan, which makes sense. But what doesn't is that they didn't just take the Warriors closest to the tunnel they dug. They moved along a row, but then skipped some. It was as if they were—I suck in a sharp breath.

Niall's next to me in an instant. "What's wrong?"

I gesture around me. "I just remembered. The looters cherry-picked certain Warriors. Do you think they chose the ones with Lan's symbols?"

"It's possible, but..." He illuminates the mess with his light. "It'd be hard to say for sure."

And I didn't see what happened in the other pits. We continue our search, but are unable to find any signatures or blob marks. Gathered around the General, we discuss our next move.

"Guess we'll have to check those files," Niall says. "Good thing we're working on the symbol project so we'll have access to them."

Beau strides over from where he'd been "guarding" me, but it appeared like he was talking to the other officers by the hatch. "Are you done?"

"Yes," I say.

"What were you looking for?"

"Just some calligraphy," Niall says brusquely. Is he jealous?

"You mean like these?" Beau points to a spot behind the General.

We quickly join him and sure enough there's a small row of Chinese characters along the bottom of his coat— the artist's signature and a blob. I lean closer. Yup, still a blob or a squiggle or a doddle. I trace it with a finger, but it doesn't trigger any associations. Niall pulls out a piece of paper, presses it against the row of characters, and uses a piece of his chalk to make an etching—very old school.

The discovery worries me. When Niall showed me his sketch, I didn't remember that the General had a blob as well. Then again, when I do a reconstruction, I'm looking at the shape of the pieces, not what's on them. But I must have seen it. Perhaps my subconscious tucked the image away. I gaze into the distance as my thoughts tumble over each other. What if my concussed mind created those shadow creatures, making them into a shape that I'm somewhat familiar with?

Except—

There's a shadow-blob moving along the back wall. No, wait, there's two.

Three.

2522:164

My vision shrinks until the three shadow-blobs are all I can see. The sound of Niall's chalk rubbing on the paper matches my pulse. Panic climbs my throat. Drawing in calming breaths, I try to view the situation logically. Are they a figment of my imagination or deadly creatures who are invisible to everyone else but me? As much as I'd love to believe my parents, surely I'm not that special.

But what about the attack? The ripped shirt? I clutch the flashlight tighter as I replay what happened the last time. It only came at me after Niall and Beau flushed it out. So if I don't bother them…they won't bother me. After all, people have been working in here without any trouble.

Except…

What if the workers get too close and…they attack? Ah hell.

"Lyra?" Niall asks. "Something wrong?" He peers in the direction I'd been staring.

"Do you see anything back there?" I ask in a steady voice—go me!

After a moment, he says, "No."

"Beau?"

Beau steps closer to us. "No." A pause. "Do you?"

I swallow. "I do. Same as before, except there are three of them."

Both men pull their weapons.

"Can you shine the light on them?" Beau asks.

Oh! I forgot. Toggling on the flashlight, I aim the beam at the shadow-blobs. As soon as the light hits them, they vanish.

"Are they — "

I interrupt him. "They're gone." I switch the beam off. When my eyes adjust to the low light, I scan the shadows. Nothing.

When I return my attention to my companions, Niall and Beau are staring at me as if I'm about to explode.

"That settles it." I tap my temple with a finger. "It's a concussion-induced delusion that is easily banished. Remind me to use my night light when I go to sleep tonight," I joke. No one laughs. Tough crowd. "Come on, let's skedaddle, I'm hungry."

They follow me from the pits. My mother is still in the lab.

"How did it go?" she asks carefully.

"Fine," I answer. "Niall, where's the etching?"

After a brief hesitation, he takes it out of his pocket and unfolds it.

I take it from his hands and show my mom. Pointing to the blob, I ask, "Do you know what this marking is?"

"Why do you want to know?" she asks in that same cautious

tone.

"Just curious. It's on the General."

"Oh. We suspect it's a way for the craftsmen to keep track of how many Warriors they've built."

"Craftsmen?" Niall asks. "I thought the signature was the artist's name."

"It took a team of eleven to make one Warrior. The name on the Warrior is the leader of the team, or so we believe."

"But that mark isn't on every one," I say.

"Right. We think they marked every two hundredth. Considering they constructed two point three million, it was easier to keep track that way."

Beau whistles. "Damn. I didn't know there were *millions* of Warriors!"

"Math," Niall deadpans to Beau. "You should try it."

Mom and I share a glance. Once the news is made public that there are another forty-two planets out there, the number will officially jump to roughly five point nine million. Don't be too impressed, I did the math the night the Q-net revealed the results of Lan's research.

I hand the paper back to Niall.

"The grid papers were delivered to Tace's office this afternoon," Mom says. "Are you still planning to start mapping out the symbols tonight?"

I'm getting tired of everyone acting so *careful* around me. "Yes," I say without snapping at her because it's not her fault. I'm the one seeing imaginary shadow-blobs.

"Should I send you the Warrior files?"

"No. That would look suspicious. I'll access them through your account."

Mom crosses her arms, shifting her weight. "How long have you been able to do *that*?"

"Oh, look at the time," I say. "I have to go or Officer Radcliff will..." I make a vague motion with my hand. Somebody help!

"Chew us out," Beau says, coming to my rescue. "He's a stickler for punctuality. Come on, Lyra." Beau hooks his arm in mine and we head for the exit with Niall right on our heels.

"We'll discuss this at dinner, Lyra," Mom promises as the door closes.

Beau chuckles.

"You can laugh," I say sourly.

"I just find it funny that she never thought of that even when she watched you chase that worm."

"I would have liked to keep it that way." Accessing other accounts was one of the first things Jarren taught me. I never tapped into my parents' files, but I doubt they'd believe me now.

Beau laughs again. "Sounds like it's going to be a fun dinner. Can't wait."

"You're not invited," Niall says.

We both turn our heads. Niall's supernova glower is back and it's focused on our linked arms. We stop.

"Easy there, Junior," Beau says. "I'm not trying to steal your girl."

Except Niall is not mollified. If anything he appears more pissed off. I should unhook my arm. Instead, I can't help asking, "Junior?"

"It's a nickname," Beau says. "Because of his dad." He swipes his palm over his spiky hair. "Mine is Hedgehog. We all have them. Niall's just sensitive about his."

The man in question tenses as if he'd like to punch Beau in the face. Beau raises his eyebrows in a I'd-like-to-see-you-try invitation. I suspect there's history between these two idiots.

I drop Beau's arm, mutter, "boys" and stride down the corridor, forcing them to hurry to catch up with me. Then I ignore them. My thoughts loop back to the confirmation that my brain is still not working properly. It's worrisome, but not as scary as dangerous shadow creatures haunting the pits. At least I'm not having as many nightmares about them. My recent dreams have been focused on a certain person, who I'd like to lose another wrestling match to.

After we enter the security wing, Beau stops outside Radcliff's office. "Lyra, now that you're feeling better, can we continue plugging those worm holes?"

I glance at Niall, but his face is a stone mask. "I'll have to check with Officer Radcliff and probably my doctor, but I don't see why not."

"Great. Later." He ducks into the office.

Niall and I continue to Radcliff's unit. When I press my palm to the lock, Niall asks, "Do you really believe you imagined those shadow-blobs?"

I sigh. "What else could it be? No one has seen them but me. It has to either be the concussion or PTSD.

Doesn't that make more sense than shadow-blobs?"

"Remember Xinji."

Remember Xinji. Remember Xinji. Remember Xinji. Those two words repeat over and over in my mind during dinner. I've lost track of the conversation as I struggle to recall the little bit of information I'd read about Xinji. One descriptor stands out. *Eviscerated.* I rub my stomach. No. The *looters* killed the scientists. Not shadow-blobs with razor-sharp blades.

As if reading my mind, Radcliff pulls my attention back to him when he says, "DES performed another scan of Xinji. This one more comprehensive. Still no life signs. If anyone is there, they're deep underground."

"Then that worm must be exceptionally talented to use the planet's satellite to hide his or her tracks," Dad says. "Are there...super wormers in the Q-net?"

"It's possible," Radcliff says. "There's been no indications of one, but if the person is *that* good then he or she wouldn't leave behind a trail."

Mom shoots me a glance. She's been quiet during dinner. Too quiet.

"Any leads on who has the resources to fund the looters?" Dad asks Radcliff.

"DES has narrowed it down to three people. Madrea Javier, Anders Knut, and Hudson Tsang. Anders has hired Osen Vee in the past, and Madrea funded Warrick's campaign to free the star roads. Hudson is our prime suspect, but he very recently left Earth and is in a time jump—very convenient for him. We'll be able to interview him in twenty-four years when he reaches

Planet Beta."

"That gives DES plenty of time to build a case against him," Niall says.

"His lawyers are already causing problems, protesting everything, finding loopholes." Radcliff's disgust is evident in his voice.

"Was there any evidence that points to Hudson in those recovered files from Xinji?" Dad asks.

"Not that we could find. There may be something in the files from Xinji's last ninety days, but the files from that time period are almost useless."

"Wait. I thought those files were classified."

"To everyone except DES security, who I work for," Radcliff says.

"That's great!"

"They're still off limits to you," he says dryly.

"Of course." I consider the information. "It makes sense that the looters wanted to erase the data and they used that super worm to do it. It's only because of Jarren that we have any info from that time at all."

Niall gazes at me. "And you almost caught it. Can you dig up the rest of those missing files? The ones Jarren couldn't access?"

Everyone is staring at me. And I've a sudden feeling Niall's question isn't due to the current conversation, that he's been doing some extracurricular research.

Remember Xinji.

"I can try," I say into the silence.

"How dangerous would it be, Tace?" Mom asks.

He considers. "It might alert that super worm—make him or her more cautious. Other than that, I don't see how anyone could harm Lyra."

"What about the looters?" Dad asks.

"They're always a concern, Spencer. And if they're still hiding in our system, I'd love to draw them out."

Mom slams her fork down. "You're not using our daughter as bait."

"I was not suggesting that," Radcliff says in an even tone. "I merely wish to be more proactive. Waiting for another ambush is...tough."

"I understand," Mom says. "But I don't want Lyra to draw attention until we have a better idea of who we're dealing with."

"If I do it right, no one will know," I say.

"Not even that super worm?" Radcliff asks.

Good question. "Depends on if he or she has rigged the buried files with alarms, which considering they're about what happened to Xinji, then the worm would be an idiot not to. But..." I drum my fingers on the table. "If I assume there are alarms, then I might be able to bypass them." It would be an exciting challenge.

"Not worth the risk for a might," Mom says.

My excitement fizzles.

"Do you think you could teach Beau?" Radcliff asks me.

I consider. The man is good with closing the security holes, but isn't subtle when he worms. "I don't think he'll have the right...touch."

"Then we'll just have to wait on that for now." Mom

resumes eating, ending the conversation.

Too bad we have no clue where the looters are. If we can prove they're in a time jump, then my mom wouldn't be so worried. Neither would I.

Niall meets my gaze. And from his half-smile, I know the matter is far from settled. At least if I get thrown into detention, I'll have company.

After dinner Niall and I go to Radcliff's office. Under the watchful eye of Officer Morgan, we access the Warrior files for Xi'an—might as well start at the first Warrior planet that was discovered. The Q-net rips through the first pit, then the second and the third. Niall draws the symbols on the grid paper. Like with Yulin, each pit represents a Warrior planet—sixty-four in total. But Pit 1 and Pit 2 of Xi'an don't match the planets represented in the two pits on Yulin.

I say, "We should do Planet Anqing and see if it matches Xi'an."

As we work through Anqing, once again each pit represents a planet, but the pits don't match the order of either Xi'an or the two on Yulin.

"It's still pretty significant," Niall says. "There must be a reason. It's important."

True. Too bad I'll probably never learn why in my lifetime. Pah. I can't believe I just thought that! My parents would be signing me up for archaeology school if they heard that.

"Do you want to start Bazhou?"

Niall glances at the clock. "Not tonight, I'm beat."

We say good night to Morgan and head back. Niall's still in

his uniform. Poor guy doesn't get much time off.

"I've read through those recovered files from Xinji, too," Niall says oh-so-casually.

I tense. "Legally?"

He huffs. "I *am* on the security team." A pause. "There's not much there."

"Is that why you suggested I dig for more?"

"Yes. Also it's hard to tell for sure, but I think the looters didn't kill everyone. There seems to be a gap in time and people died later."

That's terrible. "Because of their injuries?"

"Hard to say for sure. But I found a reference to an unknown assailant with a knife."

Oh boy. I stop and turn to him. "Niall, that's sweet that you believe me about those shadow-blobs, but, think about it, it's insane."

He reaches to touch my arm, but catches himself. "You need to watch the feed of us in Pit 4." Before I protest, he asks, "Have you seen any of those shadow-blobs in the base?"

"No." Thank the stars.

"So if it's trauma-induced, you won't see anything since you won't be in the pits."

He has a point. "All right, I'll watch the feed."

Niall smiles and I think I'd do just about anything for one of his smiles. Besides, what harm can come from watching myself freak out?

We continue down the corridor. I mull over Niall's comments about the files. Having all the information would certainly answer a ton of questions.

"Would your dad let me search for those deleted files if my parents agree?" I ask Niall.

He doesn't hesitate. "Yes."

Guess they've been discussing this. "What if they don't approve?"

"No. Not until you're eighteen A-years." He glances at me. "When's your birthday?"

"Not for another one hundred and fifty days." Which doesn't sound that far away but... "I'll talk to my parents. Maybe if I promise to back off if I think I'll alert that super worm, they'll agree."

"Couldn't hurt."

When we arrive, Niall follows me in. Radcliff is sitting in the common room and Niall asks him permission to show me the feed.

"Why do you want to see it?" he asks me.

Ah. "I think it'll help convince my brain that what I saw wasn't real." Lame. Really lame. I try not to squirm when Radcliff studies me.

"All right. You can use my terminal." He tilts his head toward his bedroom.

Now? For some reason panic snakes around my throat.

"Thank you," Niall says. "Come on, Lyra."

But... I reluctantly join him. Guess I didn't think Radcliff would agree. Radcliff's bedroom is rather utilitarian. The bed is bigger than mine, which makes sense since he's taller and broader. There are almost no decorations except for one painting of dense dark green foliage. A thin vine of tiny orange flowers weaves through the leaves. It's very soothing.

Niall catches me staring at it. "The Pavartian Jungle on Planet Gamma. It's one of my mom's." He lowers his voice, "You've been a good influence on him."

"Me?" I squeak in surprise.

"When we lived on the ship, he wouldn't enter my room because of her paintings. He refused to look at them. A few days ago, he asked me for this one. His favorite."

"I still don't understand how I'm connected."

"He told me you said something that got him thinking."

"Did he say what it was?" Could it have been when I talked to him about Niall's sketchbooks?

"Nope. I was just happy he wanted the painting."

Niall sits at the terminal and soon a picture of Pit 4 fills the screen. "Ready?" he asks.

Am I? Worst case, it's another confirmation that I'm seeing things. Best case... Actually there is no best case. "Yes."

I stand behind him as he starts the feed. Everything looks normal except for the shadow-blobs. Grabbing the back of the chair, I lean forward. There are more than the one I spotted. My fingernails dig into the fabric as I count. Four. No, five. My attention focuses on me standing next to Menz. And sure enough the shadow-blob knocks me down as it slashes at me—just like I remembered.

Niall turns around. "Now do you understand why I believe you?"

"Yes." But it's not for the reason he thinks. "Can you play it again?"

"All right."

When the shadow-blobs do the exact same thing, I know they're not in my head. My memory just isn't that good. I have him play it a third time just in case. Yup. Not my imagination. So what does it mean?

That there are invisible and dangerous alien creatures in the pits. The thought is terrifying.

"You've convinced me," I say to Niall. "But we're not going to convince anyone else without proof. How does this help?"

"We really need those deleted files. Consider this extra motivation to persuade your parents to agree."

"My mother can be quite stubborn," I warn him.

"But you're Lyra Daniels, Refuses to be Ignored. Use your superpower."

I laugh.

Early the next morning, I'm woken by a loud knock. Before I can even comprehend that the sound came from my door, it's flung open. Radcliff storms into my room. Uh oh, what did I do wrong?

"The files are gone. What did you do to them last night?" he demands.

Confusion clouds my thoughts. "The Warrior files?"

"Don't pretend you don't know."

I push up on my elbow. "I'm not. What's gone?"

"The Xinji files."

Jerking up to a sitting position, I clutch my blanket with both hands. "Are you sure?"

He ignores my question. "Nice try, Daniels. I knew you were up to something. Distracting Niall with symbols and octagons. Really?" Radcliff gestures to me. "Get dressed."

Nothing is making any sense, but after he leaves, I throw on a pair of jeans and a shirt. Radcliff's waiting in the common room.

"Why—"

He grabs my wrist and drags me from the unit. I stumble along just behind him with my thoughts whirling. The only thing that might explain this is that the super worm wiped the files and framed me for it. At least Niall can vouch for me. But then again Radcliff's comment about octagons doesn't bode well for my alibi. Perhaps he's under suspicion as well. All the speculation in the universe isn't going to do me any good right now. I'll just have to wait.

Radcliff practically shoves me into his office. Niall and Morgan are standing behind Beau, who's sitting at the terminal.

"What's this?" Radcliff demands.

"Relax, Boss," Morgan says. "I asked Hedgehog to verify a few things."

Radcliff appears far from relaxed. Tension fogs the room, making it difficult to breathe. Questions push up my throat, but Niall meets my gaze and shakes his head a tiny bit, warning me to keep quiet.

After hours of standing there...okay more like fifteen

minutes, but each minute drags like an hour—trust me…Beau faces us. "It's a masterpiece, but it wasn't done by our girl."

My legs weaken with relief, but I keep my stiff posture.

"Are you sure?" Radcliff asks.

Seriously? After I helped them with the holes? I scowl at him.

"Yes. And there's another problem."

"Do tell."

Despite the fact I'm hating him right now, I'm impressed by Radcliff's sarcasm.

"The files that Lyra buried—the ones about the symbols that her friend researched—they're gone as well."

Gasping, I cover my mouth. This is bad. This is really bad. If it was the looters' super worm, then they know about the other undiscovered Warrior planets. Then I think about it. "I set an alarm on those files. Did it trigger?"

"No. But your secondary security measure picked up on a ripple and alerted Officer Radcliff just like you set up." He gives me a sardonic grin. "It's what caused this…" He sweeps a hand out, indicating everyone in the room. "Impromptu meeting. The boss checked to see what was going on and saw the Xinji files had been swiped. And you know the rest."

Yeah, he automatically assumed I'm guilty. After shooting him another dark look, I ask Beau, "How did you figure out it wasn't me?"

"I found your shortcut."

"Shortcut?" Morgan asks.

"She set up a way to access Lan's files without having to

disable the security measures each time. If she's the one who deleted those files, she wouldn't have triggered the alarm."

"That's equally irresponsible," Radcliff says. "What if the super worm found your shortcut?"

I shove my hands into my pockets and keep my mouth shut.

"Technically it did," Beau says. "But once you get into the shortcut, it acts like a trap so the super worm backed off and used another method to get to those files. When it backed out, it triggered that secondary alarm."

While I'm happy my trick worked, that super worm still stole the files.

"Can you trace the thief?" Radcliff asks.

"No. But I think Lyra can."

I step back with my hands up. "Oh no. Not me. Go find someone else. I'm done."

2522:165

I head for the door. But it's really hard to storm from a room when you're on probation and need a chaperone to go anywhere. Hesitating at the threshold, I debate if my anger is worth being thrown in detention.

Without turning around, I say, "Officer Dorey, would you be so kind as to escort me back to my room?"

There's a moment of silence. I imagine he's looking to Radcliff for permission. Then he says, "Uh, sure."

He joins me. Anger fuels my steps and it's not long before we're back at Radcliff's unit.

I go inside. "Thanks."

"Lyra—"

I close the door before I say something I'd regret.

Later, instead of helping Beau after soch-time, I head to the pits. He's required to follow me and he's not happy about it. Too bad. My mom and dad aren't in the archaeology lab, but that's okay. Taking a steadying breath, I enter the pits. I keep my gaze trained on the pathway and not on the dark shadows as I walk to Pit 4.

The General is just how I left him. I sort pieces with a single-minded determination, blocking out all distractions like the shadow-blobs flitting at the edges of my vision. The desire to yell at everyone to evacuate the pits because the shadow-blobs might attack builds in my chest, but no one would believe me, and I'd be escorted to the infirmary faster than a grain of sand in a sandstorm.

Instead, I work on putting the General back together. My fury at Radcliff fizzles with the exertion that it takes to muscle heavy pieces around. But that just means there's more room for a mix of hurt and betrayal to fill my heart. I thought I was part of the team. This will teach me to let my guard down.

Despite my best efforts, my thoughts drift to the timing of the theft. The super worm could have taken those files at any time. So why now? Because Niall's been reading through them? Or because we were sorting Warriors by symbols? No. I will not try to figure this out. The security team can do it.

"Lyra!" My father's happy voice breaks my concentration sometime...later. He climbs from the hatch and gives me a quick hug. "I didn't know you'd be here today."

That's because the General never falsely accused me of deleting files. I swallow that thought.

Dad gives me the parental once-over. "Are you okay?"

No. We're surrounded by shadow-blobs. "I'm fine. I've been here for..."

"Two hours," Beau supplies dryly.

Wow. "Without any problems." Which is true.

"Do you want to see what's going on with the hearts?" Dad asks.

"Sure."

"Come on, then."

Beau and I follow my father down into the factory. It's darker and cooler. The air smells damp. I brace, expecting a profusion of shadow-blobs, but there are none. In fact, the heavy pressure on my shoulders lifts. It's a relief to be down here.

"We've gotten 3D digital images of them all," Dad explains as he leads the way. "Except for the backs of course. But we confirmed they're indeed modeled after human hearts and are life-sized as well. The symbols on the hearts match the one row of your octagon. And there are exactly eight symbols on each one. I'm hypothesizing there will be eight on the back as well."

More proof the number eight is very important. Did the creators just like the number or is there a mathematical or scientific reason?

"Dad, did you figure out what substance the hearts are made of?"

"The chemists listed a bunch of unpronounceable chemicals, but there were a number of unknown substances, too. Best they can match it to is a form of pumice."

"Not helpful."

"No. But at one point they were...wet, then molded and dried...somehow. Plus they're as old as the Warriors so that's why we think they're so brittle."

We enter the large cavern and weave around the tables until we arrive at the back. There are a number of techs with protective gloves on who are hunched over the hearts, but no one touches them. There are a few empty spaces.

"What happened to them?" I ask.

"Failed attempts to move the hearts. All we want to do is look at the back of just one! Even if there aren't more symbols, there might be something else equally important. We tried to slide a metal spatula under one, it crumbled to dust as soon as it was touched. Same with using glass, plastic, and even paper. The techs are measuring to see if we can use controlled air cushions."

"Air cushions?"

"I've no idea how it works, but the engineers offered to build it and said it would be gentle enough." Dad watches the workers. "The creators had to lift the hearts to put them into the Warriors. Maybe they used antigravity devices or had some advanced tech."

I think about the General. There's nothing on the inside of his chest that would hold a heart—unless it broke off, but then I'd see where it did and I'm sure the experts would have picked up on that long ago. Besides, the heart doesn't have to be in the chest. Just because everything else is lifelike, doesn't mean that it has to be. Yet...they made a point to build everything to life-size. So if the hearts are in the proper position, then they would have to be attached to— "Terracotta," I blurt out.

"What?" Dad asks.

"Did you try using terracotta to move them?"

"Yes. I thought of the same thing, that maybe the hearts stick to the clay since we haven't found any evidence of how they're attached to the Warriors. It didn't work."

How else would they do it? I mull it over. "What about before the Warriors were fired? When the clay was still wet and soft? Maybe it sticks then."

My father beams at me. "It's worth a try." He hums to himself. "We would need to find clay on this planet, though."

"Can't your chemists mix up a batch?" Beau asks.

"No. It needs to match the terracotta used for the Warriors."

"In that case, you'll need to import some from Earth," I say. "Should only take a hundred and forty-five years—plus or minus a day or two."

Dad gives me this funny look as if he's holding back a sneeze. I study him with my daughter's power of observation— it was included with the birth package. He's trying to keep something secret.

"Beau, can I have a private word with my father please?"

"Uh, sure."

I grab Dad's arm and pull him away from Beau and the workers, but still within sight. "Okay fess up," I whisper.

"About what?" He tries for innocence, but he's fidgeting with his cuffed sleeves, smoothing the folded fabric.

Sweeping my arm out, I indicate the tables with the Warriors lying on them. "You discovered that they manufactured Warriors on Yulin, didn't you?"

He wilts. "I'm not saying anything until we have proof."

"Did you find a clay deposit?" I ask.

His gaze returns to his cuffs.

"Dad." I match Mom's tone when she's caught you doing something you shouldn't.

It works. "The geologists think they have, but the chemists haven't confirmed it yet."

"That's promising. And it would prove you're right that the aliens learned how to make the Warriors from the Chinese."

He frowns. "Yeah, but we can't report any of this until we have a secure channel to DES. I haven't even reported about the factory and hearts yet."

That's a surprise. "But that was before the looters attacked."

"I know," Dad says. "I just had this...feeling and with Xinji and all...I just couldn't do it. Your mother agreed to wait until we have proof that no unauthorized people are reading our reports to DES."

I open my mouth to offer to try to create a secure channel for him, but close it. Instead, I say, "Ask Officer Radcliff to have one of his security officers look into building one for you."

"They can do that?"

I showed Beau plenty of techniques. He might be able to design a channel that ensures there are no gaps. "Maybe." And before my father can ask more questions, I say, "I'm starving. Let's go eat."

"Not tonight. Your mother and I have a dinner meeting. We'll catch up with you tomorrow night."

Dinner with just me, Radcliff, and Niall. Ugh. I'm no longer starving. Maybe I should work on the General instead. We return to the hatch and climb up to the pits. Immediately, the air thickens around me. The shadows jump to life. After the peace of the factory, I don't have the stamina to ignore them. It's a quiet trip to the lab where my dad hugs me and asks me to keep our conversation private.

"I know the drill, Dad."

He pauses. "You certainly do, Li-Li. We'll make an archaeologist out of you yet."

"You think so? I've been contemplating another career option."

"Security?"

I huff in derision. "Please. What do you think of criminal mastermind?"

Dad glances at Beau. The man isn't amused. Too bad.

"Considering you're on probation, do you think it's wise to announce that?" Dad asks mildly.

They already believe it...or, at least Radcliff does. But I'm smart enough to keep that thought to myself. "I think it will add to the challenge."

Dad laughs. "Good luck with your new career."

"Thank you."

We part and I reluctantly head toward security with my escort.

"No need to be mad at me," Beau says into the silence. "I vouched for you."

"I'm not mad at *you*."

"You sure could have fooled me."

"I'm just angry."

He's quiet for a few steps. "That super worm matched your

style."

That's scary. I slow. Jarren taught me how to worm and he learned from Warrick Nolt, but eventually we all develop our own styles. So to match one is just more evidence that we are dealing with an extremely talented person who may have bypassed all security in the Q-net. "I'm listening."

"Niall asked me to investigate, and, I'll admit after seeing your worm tracks, I was pessimistic about finding any proof of your innocence."

A bit of softness cuts through my ire. Niall trusts me. Unlike Beau and Radcliff. "At least you still looked."

"Yes. Niall owes me one." He flashes a cocky grin. "And that shortcut of yours is a thing of beauty."

Ah, appealing to my ego. Good man. Still mad, though. "Except for Niall, did *any* of you question that I would do something like that? Yes, I've wormed illegally—I *am* on probation after all—but have I ever done anything *on that scale* before?"

Beau has the decency to drop his gaze.

"No! Not one of you gave me the benefit of the doubt!" A fresh wave of fury swells and I increase my pace.

We're almost to Radcliff's unit when Beau touches my elbow. "I'm sorry, Lyra. I won't do it again."

His sincere apology cools some of my anger.

"Still friends?" he asks.

Ah, hell. I couldn't hold a grudge even if it had handles. But I'm not above doing a little manipulation. "Only if Niall no longer owes you a favor." When Beau hesitates, I add, "He was right to ask you to dig deeper."

"Okay, okay." Then he grins. "Well played, Daniels."

I smirk.

When we reach Radcliff's unit, he asks, "Will you resume helping me with the security holes?"

Will I? "It depends on Officer Radcliff."

"Good luck with that."

After I open the door, Beau gives me a jaunty wave goodbye. Radcliff's in the kitchen so I duck into my room. And when he knocks to announce dinner, I tell him I'm not hungry. I'm not. At all. Who are you calling a coward?

A second knock sounds just before the door opens. Niall steps in and closes it behind him. He's not in uniform, so I don't hesitate to wrap my arms around him and pull him in for a kiss.

"What's that for?" he asks a bit breathlessly a long time later.

"For believing in me." I explain about Beau and the favor.

"Nice. Now can you do me a favor?"

I've a feeling I'm not going to like it. "What is it?"

"Come have dinner with me and my dad and save me from enduring an unpleasant meal by myself. I'm mad at him, too. He accused me of being duped by you and then covering for you."

"Sounds like you're not hungry either," I say. "We can stay in here."

"For another two minutes if we're lucky."

We glance at the door, expecting Radcliff to barge in at any moment.

"We can glare at him together," he says. "Solidarity."

"Oh, well, when you put it *that* way…"

He swoops in and gives me a kiss before we trudge out to the kitchen. The meal is a vegetable and ham casserole. We eat mostly in silence. Radcliff is either oblivious to our censure or very good at ignoring us. Halfway through, he receives a call and goes into his bedroom.

When Radcliff returns, he's wearing his black jumpsuit and holding a pulse gun. "Another big sandstorm's coming. We're on alert."

Niall jumps to his feet while my heart jams up my throat. Will there be another looter attack? There's been a couple other sandstorms since that one, but all have been minor.

Niall squeezes my shoulder and says, "Later," as if it's a promise, before he bolts.

Radcliff hands me the weapon. "Can you assist Officer Dorey?"

"Doing what?" Yup, my voice trembles as much as my legs.

"Monitoring communications, ensuring no one compromises them."

This morning I vowed not to help Officer Radcliff anymore. Now, with the possibility of the looters attacking the base, that particular drama seems so small and petty. "Of course."

"Change into your jumpsuit and wait here for Dorey."

"All right."

Radcliff leaves. Hurrying to my room, I search for the garment. It's one thing to put it on when you're relaxed and have time, quite the other when you're rushing and so not relaxed. First my foot gets stuck, then my arm, then I do this strange hopping wiggle to get it up over my shoulders. By the time I'm dressed, I'm out of breath and sweating.

A knock just about sends me a meter into the air. Clutching my weapon, I peek at the screen—something I haven't done since living here. Beau waits outside. He's also in a jumpsuit and wow, the man's been hiding some serious muscles.

I open the door and tuck the pulse gun into its holster.

"Keep it in your hand," Beau says. "Just in case."

"Oh...kay." I pull it out.

"Breathe, Lyra." He waits while I suck in a few deep breaths. "Better?"

"Yes."

"All right. Let's go." He sets a fast pace and we're soon in the room next to Radcliff's office.

There's only one officer watching the camera. She's also in a jumpsuit and armed.

"Go on, Tora. We got this," he says to her.

She takes off. Beau locks the door. "I need you to monitor the cameras. If you see anything or anyone who doesn't belong on base, let me know right away."

"What are you going to do?" I ask.

"I'm going to monitor security through the Q-net. If the cameras go down, come join me. I'll need your help."

"Okay." I sit on the chair. It's still warm from Tora's body heat and I get a whiff of a flowery perfume.

He heads to his office, but pauses in the threshold. "Oh, and Lyra, if an unauthorized person enters *this* area, shoot him or her."

"Unauthorized?"

"Anyone not on the security team. Got it?"

"Yes. Don't shoot Officer Radcliff no matter how much I want to."

He laughs. "He deserves it, but that weapon won't work on him or anyone on the team."

"Pity." Settling in, I scan the various screens on the right wall, before swiveling around to check the other bank. After a few minutes, I realize this is harder than it looks. I can't watch them all at the same time, so I have to prioritize them. Of course the ones in the pits get the most scrutiny—oh, look, shadow-blobs—then the ones just outside the base, next are the ones inside the base's entrances, and the interior ones get a brief glimpse before I start at the beginning.

Most of the security team is rushing to the pits. I spot Niall's lean muscular form and a tight ball of worry joins the turmoil already sloshing in my stomach. Radcliff and two team members are in the port, donning B-apps in preparation for going outside. With Beau in here with me, that leaves eight of them to deal with any looters in the pits. Not nearly enough.

The scientists clog the corridors as they head to their units—the safest place for them. I search the cameras for my parents. They're in the Control Center, directing the storm response teams. And…I peer closer. They're armed! Way to go, Mom and Dad.

Soon after, the visibility on the outside cameras becomes limited by the blowing sand. Surrounded by other rooms, I can't hear the wind, but sand grains pelt the roof. The officers reach the pits and fan out—two in each pit. Niall's in Pit 4 with Keir.

Memories of the attack flash in my mind. At least four dozen looters invaded. Trained or not, our security team in the pits is still outnumbered six to one.

On the edge of my seat, I scan each monitor. Then again. And again. Each minute that passes increases my anxiety level. After an hour, I'm actually wishing for something, *anything* to happen or I'm going to explode.

Right here.

In this seat.

But all remains...normal. The labs are empty. No looters invade the pits. The storm passes the base and the outside cameras show drifts of sand, but nothing else. Another hour passes before an all-clear signal sounds throughout the base. The officers in the port remove their B-apps as the eight in the pits head back.

Wilting in the chair, I finally relax.

Beau joins me. "False alarm."

"You don't sound surprised."

"They already used that trick. I really didn't expect them to try it again."

"Then why go to all the trouble?" I gesture at the cameras.

"Just in case. Their leader might think it's worth another shot. Plus, it's always better to be prepared than caught unaware."

True.

When everyone returns, the security team has a debriefing in the conference room. I man the cameras while they have their meeting. Tora returns with another man—I probably should learn all their names—to take over my post. Niall is waiting in Radcliff's office to escort me back. My parents are also there, getting an update.

"No problems this time," Dad says to me. "Such a relief."

"Except for the GPR team's shelters," Mom adds.

"What happened?" I ask in alarm.

"Their shelters were damaged by the storm. They're coming back for repairs in a few days."

Oh.

Dad frowns at Mom. "Like I said, no *real* problems. We're in the middle of a desert, sand is always going to be a nuisance for the field teams."

I gesture to their guns. "And you were ready."

"Tace suggested we have more armed people on base in case of an emergency," Mom says. "Your father and I volunteered to go through the training. There's a few others as well."

Niall stifles a yawn. It's close to twenty-two-hundred hours. I say good night to my parents.

It's a quiet walk back, but once we get into Radcliff's unit, Niall draws me in for a rib-cracking hug.

"What's the matter," I ask into his neck.

"Just glad that this time, I didn't have to worry about finding you broken and bloody."

I squeeze him back. "It was scary watching you go into the pits."

He pulls back to meet my gaze. "Thanks for helping."

"Of course."

"Does that mean—"

"No. Not until your father apologizes to *both* of us."

"But what about today?"

I huff. "That was an emergency, I'm not that petty. But I'm still pissed at him."

Niall cocks his head to the side. "If I was a betting man...my money would go to you relenting instead of my father apologizing."

"Your father's that stubborn?"

"No. You're that curious. Plus could your ego stand it if Beau found those stolen files instead of you?"

I growl at him 'cause he's right. Damn it. I try to step back, but his hold is like being wrapped in iron.

"You're pretty when you're pretending to be mad, Mouse."

That's cheating. He can't call me pretty while insulting me...can he?

"And that jumpsuit shows off all your lovely curves."

He runs his hands down my sides. His electric touch races over me. I shiver.

"You're just trying to distract me."

"If that's what you want to call it..." Niall leans in and kisses me.

I decide that he can distract me all he wants. But I'm the one to break it off many long minutes later. "You have to get up at oh-so-early tomorrow."

"I thought we agreed I'd be the sensible one."

"Consider this a one-time thing. Besides, if your father believes I'm *distracting* you from your duties, he'll make it harder for us to be together."

Niall sighs. "It didn't take you long to figure him out."

"Well, I've been on probation for fifteen days." Huh. That went pretty fast. "Although I think I should get time off my sentence for helping out. Maybe when I'm asked to assist Beau again or if he needs me to search for those files, I can negotiate."

Niall's forehead crinkles as he gives me a pained look. "I'm enjoying having you close by and knowing you're safe."

"Yeah, but having no privacy and being escorted everywhere sucks."

"With the cameras and with you living with your parents, we won't have much privacy then either."

"Ah, but you forget who you're dating," I say. "Once I'm back on my own terminal, those cameras are mine."

Niall just shakes his head. "I'm too tired to lecture you. Besides, you're almost eighteen A-years, I'm willing to wait."

"And Officer Sensible is back."

He sports a lopsided smile. "Miss me?"

"Go to bed before you fall over."

"Not until I get a good-night kiss."

I'm happy to oblige and I run my fingers through his hair, leaving behind spikes.

Stepping back, Niall arches an eyebrow at me. "Was that necessary?"

"You needed to look like you've been kissed, Toad."

"Why do I have the feeling I'm going to keep paying for that?"

I beam an innocent expression, which he doesn't buy at all. "Do you want me to recite the lecture I received after you left?

Or do you just want the highlights—like how *space boys* have sex with girls at every planet because they know they won't ever see them again?"

He rubs his face with his hands. "I really need to get some sleep. Night, Mouse."

"Chicken," I call after him.

Over the next couple days, Niall and I confirm that each of sixty-three pits on a Warrior planet represents another Warrior planet, and one represents itself. The alien designations don't match ours, which makes sense. The first pit we open on a Warrior planet has always been numbered one. I've a feeling that, in the future, the pits will be renamed. Instead of a numerical label, it'll reference the Warrior planet's name.

I continue to work on the General although I'll admit it takes all my courage to go into the pits. The shadow-blobs hover at the edges of my vision. They haven't hurt anyone nor have any of the techs reported seeing anything. Niall and I agreed not to try to convince my parents and his dad about them. After being accused of stealing the Xinji files, our credibility is shot.

The techs have reassembled a number of Warriors in Pit 1. They're missing pieces and cracks zigzag through their bodies. And I wonder why we even bother. They're dead.

Yes, I know that sounds...strange. But, to me, they no longer have that essence. Their hearts are broken. Even the

General. His chest is about as complete as I can make it, but it won't matter in the end.

This afternoon, Niall is helping me assemble the General's arms. The pieces need to be held in place until the adhesive dries, a two-man operation. The fact that this is his day off and he's with me instead of drawing, sleeping or hanging out in the rec room with his friends fills me with a strange buzzy warmth. It's hard to stay focused on the delicate work and keep from brushing against Niall.

When we finish the General's left arm, I step back and almost jump out of my skin as a shadow-blob grazes my shoulder.

Niall grabs my arm, steadying me. "What's wrong? Is it—"

"Yes." I glance around and they appear...thicker... than before. "Let's take a break."

He peers at me. "Your skin is like ice. We should leave."

"No. I want to get his other arm done. Let's go down in the factory."

"Why?"

"I just need...can we go? Now."

"All right."

Beau and Menz are guarding the hatch. Keir is my escort and she says, "Field trip, woo hoo!" before following us below.

As soon as I near the hearts, I relax. There's that peace. The workers glance at us, but then return to whatever it is they're doing. As long as we don't get in the way, we'll be fine. I tell Niall about the eight symbols on the hearts.

"We should see if they match the pattern of the planets," he says. "How many hearts have been found?"

Good question. I scan the closest table and count them, then I multiply by the number of tables for an estimate. "Well, more than sixty-four."

Then without warning, a bone cracking cold seeps into my body. "Freezing," I chatter, stepping closer to Niall who wraps his arms around me and pulls me against him.

"Wow, you're not kidding. We should—"

He never finishes his sentence. Two things happen at once.

All the lights go out.

And Beau cries out in pain.

2522:167

Everyone is stunned into silence. Niall's hold on me tightens. In the complete blackness, I see impossible things. I squeeze my eyes shut and open them again just to make sure they're not a figment of my imagination. But standing next to the rows of hearts are rows of ghost Warriors. Yup, they resemble the ones in the pits above, but these guys are white and a bit translucent. However, they don't float. Actually they don't move at all. Creepy, but not in a shadow-blob way. Oh great, I'm using shadow-blobs as a point of reference. Just kill me now.

A second cry galvanizes everyone. The techs all start talking at once.

Keir turns on her flashlight. "Remain here, I'll go check—"

"No," Niall says, releasing me. "You're required to stay with Lyra, I'll go."

"You're not armed," she says.

"We should all go," I say. I sense rather than see their

objections. "I'm the only one who can see them."

"Them?" Keir's voice is incredulous.

The emergency lights click on. The dim yellow bulbs are weak in comparison. But better than nothing. The ghost Warriors disappear.

Another yell is followed by the sizzle of a pulse gun discharging. Both Keir and Niall run for the ladder.

I turn to the techs. "You're safe down here. Stay here until you hear an all-clear." Then I race to catch up to Keir and Niall. "Keep your flashlight on," I shout to Keir as she reaches the top. "Aim the beam at the shadows." Which really sounds idiotic.

Niall steps off the ladder and crouches as if ready to fight. When I poke my head above the floor, he says, "Stay close to me."

The light is just as dim up here. I scan the scene in front of me. Beau is lying on the ground. His arms are pressed to his stomach and his shirt is soaked with blood. Fear sweeps through me, leaving behind a numb panic. Menz is standing astride Beau as if protecting him. He's firing his gun, but not hitting anything. There's a long cut down his right arm dripping blood.

The shadow-blobs have them surrounded. Instead of listening to my advice, Keir dashes to join Menz. Before I can warn her, she collides with one of the shadow-blobs. It moves so fast, it's just a blur of motion. She yells as two long gashes crisscross her arms and chest. Dropping the flashlight, she collapses back, firing her gun, but the pulse goes right through the blob without any apparent harm. Shit.

I yell to Menz and Keir, "Your pulse guns don't work. Use your flashlights!"

Menz spins around to face me, but just stares as if I'd spoken another language. Keir's panicking and shooting as she scrambles to get away. Except she's heading toward more shadows.

Niall curses and steps toward Keir. I grab his arm. "They're in a circle around the guys about two meters away from them. And there's another circle about a meter behind Keir."

"Got it." He rushes to Keir.

"Stay low," I call.

Niall dives for the flashlight. He scoops it up, switches it on and swings the beam in a circle around him. The shadow-blobs back up. A few disappear in a poof. Nice.

"Keir, rally around Beau," Niall orders. His harsh commanding tone snaps her from her freak out. "Go now!" He aims the light at Menz.

She lurches to her feet and bolts over to them.

"Lyra, you, too!"

I finally climb from the hatch and hurry over to the group. Beau's eyes are squeezed shut. He's conscious but in lots of pain.

"Hold on, Beau. You can do it." I take his flashlight. Keir reaches for it, but I yank it away. "Grab Menz's." The man is still standing there. He's no longer firing his weapon, but by his death grip on the handle he's not going to release it anytime soon.

Niall joins us. "Back to back."

Keir spins so her back is to Niall's. Oh. I turn so they're

behind me.

"Lyra, where do we aim?" he asks.

I check. The hole Niall created has disappeared as more shadow-blobs have moved in. "They're all around us. Keep sweeping the light in an arc."

Keir, Niall, and I swing the light back and forth.

"Is it working?" Keir asks after a few minutes.

"Yes, they're keeping their distance." And I poofed a couple of them, but I've no idea if they just reform in the darkness and come back.

Sometime...later, Beau groans in pain.

"We can't wait for the lights to come back on. We need to get him to the infirmary," Niall says. "Any ideas?"

As long as we keep the flashlights in motion we should be able to move. "Menz, can you carry Beau?" I ask.

"Huh?"

"Officer Menz, pick up Officer Dorey. Now," Niall orders.

"Uh...yes, sir."

There's a grunt and a cry of pain. "Sorry, Beau," Menz says.

"Next?" Niall asks.

"We walk our protective circle toward the hatch," I say. "Keep sweeping the lights."

"We all take exactly one step on my count. Understand?" Niall asks.

The three of us say yes in unison. A good sign.

"All right. One."

I'm facing the hatch so I step forward. The crunch of clay under the others' boots is reassuring.

"Two. Three. Four."

It takes twelve steps to reach the hatch.

"Now what?" Keir asks.

I move to the other side of the hatch. "We can't leave the techs down there. They can join our protective circle and help carry Beau. Then we move our circle to the exit."

"Niall?" It's Keir again.

"She's right," he says. Niall calls down to the techs to come up.

They emerge and start asking questions right away.

"Be quiet!" Niall uses the same voice he used to get Menz to pick up Beau.

They shut up and I wish I could see their expressions, but I'm too busy keeping the shadow-blobs away.

"Follow my orders, no matter how strange, and we'll explain everything to you when we reach the lab. Understand?"

A general yes amid some mutterings.

"Good. I need two of you to help Officer Menz carry our injured man."

There's a shuffling of feet and a grunt of pain from poor Beau.

"Does anyone have a flashlight?" I ask.

A few have head lamps. Niall adds them to our circle and instructs them on what to do. Then we move toward Pit 3 in the same step-by-step fashion. Halfway through Pit 2 the emergency lights go out. Everyone freezes.

"Keep moving," Niall says. He calls the steps.

With the added darkness, the shadow-blobs increase in

number. "Sweep faster," I call as one darts between the swings of the light and slashes. A tech cries out and drops his light.

"Lyra, status," Niall says.

"There's lots more. We need to move faster."

He doubles the pace. After two more people are injured, he triples it. A couple of the techs start pushing to go faster.

Niall uses his command voice. "Stay together."

It works until we reach Pit 1. A faint glow from the archaeology lab beckons in the distance, and, except for the two holding Beau, the techs all bolt. Niall keeps his flashlight's beam trained on their retreating forms, while Keir and I cover more area.

"Keep moving," I say as I duck a shadow-blob that snakes around my light. It clips my shoulder. Pain burns, but there's no time to think about it. I aim the flashlight into its core and it poofs.

Niall resumes counting and now we're jogging with him in the lead. Menz and his helpers pant with the exertion and I'm now "running" backwards. As we near the brightness of the lab, the bulk of the shadow-blobs drop back into the darkness, but a few still find gaps to attack. The cuts on my arms, legs and sides add up, but I'm too focused on keeping the shadow-blobs at bay to register pain.

Confused and shouting voices drown out Niall's and there's a shuffle of feet. Beau groans. I glance behind me. A group of people carry Beau into the lab. Keir and Niall are at the entrance. And I'm...not. How did I get so far behind? Breathing is hard as fear presses all the air from my lungs.

"Lyra, come on!" Niall shouts.

He aims his light at me. A good idea until Keir copies him. The added brightness sears my eyes. I turn around, but my vision is just a white haze. Backing up, I keep swinging my light, but I'm blind. A sharp needle of pain pierces my left hip. Stumbling, I fall on my butt with a cry. A blurry motion alerts me and I thrust my light in that direction, bracing for another attack. But there isn't one.

Shouts finally penetrate the buzz of terror in my ears. I recognize my name before strong hands hook under my arms and lift me to my feet. Another person joins us and they half carry me to the lab. It's only a few steps, but each one hurts from my feet to my shoulders.

Only when I'm safe in the lab do I see who's holding me. Niall and Keir. They're covered in cuts. Blood stains their ripped clothes. Dirt streaks their faces.

"Wow," I say, lightheaded with relief. "You guys look terrible."

They exchange a glance.

"You should sit down." Niall guides me over to a chair.

But sitting hurts too much. Black and white spots swirl in my vision and the loud buzz is back. "I need..." I slide to the floor.

"Lyra!"

"...to lie down." It's better on the cool ground. Niall kneels next to me. I wave a weak hand, shooing him away. "Go help Beau and the others. I'll be fine."

He disappears for seconds...minutes...hours... hard to tell

when the base is spinning around. There's lots of noise and commotion in the lab, but I'm happy to stay in my spot despite the burn and throb of my injuries.

It's not hard to miss when the rest of the security officers arrive. Radcliff's voice cuts through the din, demanding an explanation. I debate if I should pretend to be passed out or not to avoid talking to him. But he's soon shouting orders, and the ruckus fades to an abstract noise—something that doesn't concern me.

Niall returns to my side...later...with a nurse in tow. The nurse crouches beside me and examines me. When he touches the wound in my left hip, I yelp and slap his hand away as a hot poker of pain explodes inside me.

"This injury is severe," the nurse says.

Ya think?

He gestures and two white-clad helpers rush over.

"Take her to the infirmary."

"No, no," I protest. "Beau first and Keir!"

"Officer Dorey is already in surgery," the nurse assures me.

"Is it bad?"

"No need for you to worry about him."

Does that mean that other people are already worried? It's one of those frustrating non-answers that adults use so you don't get upset. And you know what? It never works.

Before I can call him on it, he says, "Off you go."

The two men scoop me off the floor and dump me on a gurney. I struggle to sit up. "I can walk." Pain stabs into my hip so the words come out weaker than I intended.

Niall grabs my hand. "Relax, Mouse."

His cuts are still raw although they've stopped bleeding.

"As long as you come with me," I say.

"Of course."

"And let them tend to your injuries."

"My father already ordered me to report to the infirmary."

There's a...glint in his eyes. "How long ago?" I ask.

Instead of answering he says, "Let's go."

The men wheel me into the hallway. Niall keeps pace, holding my hand and not meeting my gaze. Which means he should have gone before and probably refused. I squeeze his hand and he glances at me in concern.

"Thanks," I say.

"For what?"

A list of reasons spring to mind: for staying with me; for getting me out of the pits; but the most important one pops out first. "For believing me about the shadow-blobs." If he hadn't, then the encounter would have gone in a deadly direction.

"Anytime."

After we arrive at the infirmary, I'm separated from Niall. Which is a good thing because the first thing the two nurses do is cut and peel off my ripped and bloody clothes. In the harsh light, my skin resembles scored raw meat. Except for the ugly red puncture mark oozing a reddish liquid—that just looks nasty. The room spins and I take a deep breath to steady my overworked heart.

I swallow a scream when the doctor presses his fingers into the wound. "This is going to need surgery. Where are your parents?" he asks me.

I've no idea.

"Prep her," the doc orders a nurse and sends the other to find my mom and dad.

I quickly learn that *prep her* really means *torture her* by cleaning all the cuts with a substance that stings like a son of a bitch and smells just as bad. By the time my mother bursts into the room demanding answers, my eyes are squeezed shut and I'm seconds from crying or passing out or throwing up. It's hard to tell as my body cycles through all of them. Fun, eh?

The doctor's competent voice responds to my mother's questions. There's lots of medical lingo and soon there's a sharp pinprick on the inside of my left forearm followed by sweet oblivion.

At least this time when I wake up in the infirmary, I'm pain free and remember why and how I arrived. Progress! The lights are dim and the clock on the wall reads oh-two-hundred. I crinkle my nose over the antiseptic smell and discover the growly sound is my dad snoring in the chair next to my bed. Which I take as a good sign. If he was worried, he wouldn't be asleep. Right?

"Good thing I didn't die," I say loudly. "You would have slept right through it."

Dad jerks upright. "You're awake!"

I don't think that requires a response.

He arches his back and stretches. A tuft of his brown hair sticks up on the side of his head. "How are you feeling?"

"I'm fine. What's the damage this time?"

"I should probably wait—"

"Dad." I use my sternest voice, mimicking my mother.

He sighs. "Mostly minor cuts and bruises. A few deeper lacerations that might scar. And one stab wound that punctured your intestines, but they were able to repair the damage. A few days of rest and you'll be good as new."

A relief until I remember Beau. I grab the rail. "Beau?"

"Alive."

I wilt back into my pillows.

"He's weak and lost a lot of blood, but should recover."

"And the others?"

"Fine."

The tightness around my chest eases just a fraction. "The pits?"

"Locked. We also installed bright lights to shine on the doors around the clock."

And now I can breathe normally. "Have you figured out what they are?"

"No. When you've recovered your strength, Tace is going to talk to you about what happened."

At least I've been warned. I shoo my dad out, telling him to go to bed.

In the morning, my mother and Niall stop by and I reassure them about my health. They both appear as if they haven't slept. Although Niall has changed into clean undamaged clothes. Too bad it's his uniform.

Mom gives me a penetrating stare. Her Mom-X-ray-vision is turned on maximum. "We need to discuss your propensity for being at the wrong place at the wrong time."

"But I did as I promised. I ran away. We all did."

She drops into the chair. "You were supposed to be safe while on probation. Tace assured us."

Niall stiffens, but keeps his lips pressed firmly together.

"Not his fault," I say. And yes, I can't believe *I'm* defending *him.* "It's mine. I should have made more of an effort to convince everyone about those shadow-blobs." Then Beau wouldn't have been injured.

Mom cocks her head. "And that would have landed you back in the infirmary. Lyra, you're not to blame. No one is. I'm just being a mom." She hops to her feet, plants a kiss on my forehead and tells me to rest. "I'll be back later to check on you."

When the door closes behind her, Niall asks, "Is that a promise or a threat?"

I laugh, which is a bad idea because it hurts.

He takes my hand. "Sorry."

"You can make it up to me by helping me get out of bed."

"Are you allowed?"

That doesn't deserve an answer. I yank the covers down and swing my legs over the side. He grabs my other hand and pulls me to my feet. Then steadies me as a brief wave of lightheadedness affects my balance.

"Lyra?"

"I'm fine. Let's go."

Now he's alarmed. "Where?"

"To visit Beau. I want to make sure he's okay."

"He's still under heavy sedation."

"Oh."

Niall eases me back down. I reluctantly recline and he pulls the covers up.

"Tucking you into bed is becoming a habit, Mouse."

I pat the space beside me. "There's room for you."

"I'm on duty."

I pout. "Did you get any sleep last night?"

"Not much." He shrugs. "All part of the job."

"Really? Does that include fighting shadow-blobs?"

He gives me a wry smile. "If that's what's required to keep you safe, then yes, it includes fighting blobs of shadows. Plus it'll look good in my dossier. I can get a job anywhere in the Galaxy."

Even though I know he's joking, a cold fist of fear clamps around my heart as I remember Xinji. We might not live that long.

The next day I'm discharged with a list of instructions and orders to return for a checkup. Niall escorts me to security's conference room. I've been "invited" to the debriefing. When we enter, it's an effort to walk through the tension that fogs the air. Keir gives me a nod of encouragement when I meet her gaze. But Menz avoids looking at me. Niall takes the empty seat at the far end of the table. It appears my seat is next to Radcliff's.

Yippee for me.

I'm asked to describe what happened, starting with the lights going out. Drawing in a breath, I hesitate. Do I tell them about the ghosts? The attack proved I wasn't crazy, but ghosts?

"You need to know why we were in the factory," I say, then explain about feeling safer down there, the ghosts, and then the attack.

After a moment of silence, Morgan asks, "Niall, did you see these...ghosts?"

He straightens. "No, sir."

"So why can you see them and the...shadow-blobs, but we can't?" Morgan asks me.

A great question. Too bad I don't have a great answer. "Maybe it's because I had a concussion."

"So we're all supposed to get concussions now so we can see the damn things?" a burly officer sitting near Niall asks.

Radcliff ignores the comment. "Lyra, have you seen any of the...shadow-blobs in the factory?"

I think back to my two visits. "No."

"Do you think it might be because of those... ghosts?"

"I don't know. They didn't move. They just stood next to..." The hearts. I rub my right arm as a memory stirs to life of an icy cold coating my fingers and traveling up my arm. The sudden extreme chill that hit me just before the shadow-blobs attacked Beau.

"They stood next to what?" Radcliff prompts.

"The hearts. And I touched a heart. Remember? And I can see the shadow-blobs." I'm on the edge of my seat. "Maybe that's why I can see them! And it's the reason the shadow-blobs aren't in the factory. Because of the hearts!"

No one shares my excitement. Niall appears interested. Officer Burly scowls at me while the others crinkle their noses as if slightly nauseous.

"That sounds a bit...farfetched," Radcliff says into the silence.

And that just pisses me off. I've had it with their significant pauses. "Oh, so invisible shadow-blobs with razor-sharp tentacles are not...farfetched?"

Radcliff frowns. "No need to be sarcastic."

Oh there's every need, but I hold my tongue. For now.

"If we can get into the factory, we can test her theory," Niall says. "I volunteer to touch a heart."

"No," Radcliff snaps. "No one is going into the pits until we figure this out. As far as we know, these beings are afraid of the light. Is that correct, Lyra?"

"Yes. They recoil from the light and when the light beam is really close, it...poofs."

The tension in the room eases a fraction as many of the officers struggle to keep a straight face. I'd like to hear them explain it better, but I have to admit it does sound pretty silly.

"Poofs?"

I describe it as best as I can. "I didn't have time to count, so I can't confirm if poofing is a permanent condition or a temporary banishment."

Again a ripple of suppressed laughter.

"Regardless, we're going to need brighter light sources that cover more area and are portable," Radcliff says.

"How about lasers?" Menz asks.

"We've no idea if it will work. We need to consult with the physicists," Morgan says. "They might have some ideas."

Radcliff gives his approval. "Take Menz and...Tora, didn't you almost become a physicist?"

"I said I *passed* physics," Tora says.

"Good enough. You and Menz will assist Morgan. As for the rest, we'll have three guards in the archaeology lab armed with flashlights at all times. Six-hour shifts. First team is Bendix, Vedann, and Radcliff. Second team is Rance, Zaim, and Ho."

Keir glances around in dismay. "What about me, sir?"

"You are assigned to protect Lyra."

I need protection? That doesn't sit well with me. Keir glances at me and mouths *pampered ass*, which strangely makes me feel better.

"First team report to work," Radcliff orders.

Niall stands along with Officer Burly...Bendix and a tall thin woman who must be Vedann. They hurry out, but Niall meets my gaze before he leaves.

Radcliff dismisses the second team, but when I stand, he grabs my wrist. "Not yet."

I resume my seat. After the conference room clears of everyone but me, Radcliff, and Keir, he turns to me. "It's critical that we learn *exactly* what happened on Xinji. We need those deleted files."

"My parents—"

"Have already given their permission. Plus Keir and I will

be nearby at all times."

Am I a bad person if I have the desire to say something petty? Something like, oh so you're trusting me now? Or, aren't you afraid I'll steal more files? Of course I don't *say* those things because Beau is still in the infirmary and there's a chance another person could join him or worse.

"If I have any chance of finding them—and I can't guarantee anything—I'm going to need access to a high clearance terminal."

Radcliff studies me for a moment. "Your father said you can use his terminal in the Control Center."

Sweet.

We head to Radcliff's office. Before Keir and I continue to my room, Radcliff says, "You won't be seeing Niall as much."

Yeah, I already figured that out. "I understand. Too bad you can't recruit more people." And to think I once thought twelve officers was excessive. Now I'd be happy with a hundred more.

"Your mother is lending us her techs."

The memory of them panicking and bolting for safety replays in my mind. "At least they can help monitor the cameras."

I surprise a laugh from Radcliff—finally! "Yes, their unfortunate behavior was noted in Niall and Keir's report."

Good.

As I step away, Radcliff adds, "Their report also noted *your* behavior, Lyra."

Oh? I turn to look back at him. Am I in trouble?

"You're credited with saving Officer Dorey's life."

I am? Stunned, I stammer, "But Keir...and Menz... and Niall all—"

"Were fighting an invisible opponent. If you hadn't remained calm and aided them, they'd all be dead."

Wow. That's...I'd like to think they all would have been okay, but Menz and Keir were rather freaked out. "Niall—"

"I know. He's getting a commendation in his record."

"Keir—"

"Her, too. Now get some rest." Radcliff shoos us away and disappears into his office.

I walk beside Keir. "What about Menz? He carried Beau."

"He refused recognition. He feels guilty for freezing, which happens to everyone at some point during their career. And is understandable in this situation. I barely held it together, but I wasn't going to let some spoiled lab rat show me up." Amusement quirks her full lips, but then fades. "Truthfully, if I hadn't seen Beau lying there bleeding, I might not have believed you."

"Truthfully, I'd rather those shadows be a symptom of PTSD."

"Yeah, a couple of sleepovers with yours truly and you'd have been fine."

Too bad no amount of sleepovers will solve this problem.

My parents join Radcliff and me for dinner.

"I can't believe we've encountered alien life in our lifetime,"

Mom says. "I don't know whether to be excited or terrified."

"My stomach is battling between awe and nausea," my dad mutters.

Remembering the conversation with my dad, I ask, "Have you notified DES?"

"Of course!" Mom stabs her fork into the air for emphasis. "I don't care if the looters are listening in, this is light years beyond our authorization." She sets the utensil down with a clatter. "We need a better classification for those creatures."

"Shadow-blob not technical enough?" I ask, somewhat offended.

"How about Lyra's Shadow Army?" Dad asks.

"Ugh. No. I don't want my name attached to them. If they were shadow-puppies that licked your face, I might be more inclined to be a part of their discovery."

"We're calling them Hostile Life Forms," Radcliff says. "HoLFs for short."

HoLFs? I still like shadow-blobs better.

"Has anyone else touched the hearts?" Radcliff asks as I clear the table.

"Not with bare skin," my mother says, giving me a significant look.

"Can we access the factory without going through the pits?"

My father leans back and taps his fingers on the table. "It extends below the pits. We could dig down in a safe area, then dig over to the factory."

"The hatch is still open," I say.

Radcliff peers at me with his security officer expression.

"You said the HoLFs won't go down there."

"No. I said I didn't *see* them down there. I *speculated* that the hearts might scare them. But, I have no idea if it's true."

"And there's no reason to believe that a door or hatch would keep them out," Mom adds.

Lovely. My desire for dessert dies.

After soch-time the next day, Keir escorts me to the Control Center. My father is in his terminal, but he relinquishes his chair when he spots me.

"DES has sent instructions about those..." He lowers his voice. "HoLFs."

"And?"

"We've strict orders not to engage with them."

I almost laugh. "Did DES message the shadow-blobs, too? 'Cause the last time I checked, they *engaged* with us first."

Dad ignores my sarcasm. "Of course they tagged all information about the HoLFs as classified and when the Protector Class ship arrives, they will handle the situation."

"Aren't they freaked out by the fact there's hostile aliens out here?" I am.

"It's DES. They're not going to admit to being 'freaked out.' Also there's a chance they don't believe us. We could have been exposed to a mind altering gas and are all hallucinating. Then there's another possible explanation—they already know about the HoLFs."

"Then why wouldn't they warn us?"

"In that case, it would be because DES deemed we didn't need to know. Their communications have been carefully worded lately—probably due to the looters worming into their clusters. But I did see a few more exclamation points in these last few messages."

That didn't help. "What are we supposed to do in the meantime?"

"I believe we're doing it."

Somehow I'm not reassured. He pats my shoulder as if that will help. I appreciate the gesture and cover his hand with my own for a moment. After he leaves, I sit down in his terminal. Keir stands behind me.

I do a little worming to gather some information. I mark the security breaches for Beau to fix once he's better. Then I nose around and find the super wormer's trail. I don't want to alert him/her to what I'm attempting to do, but I can't help being impressed. Jarren's right, that guy/girl has some mad skills. I wonder if it is Osen, Warrick, Ursy, or Fordel.

Perhaps it's all of them.

Oh my stars.

I straighten. Why not? Beau and I wormed together. I trailed Jarren. Chief Hoshi and I worked in tandem. And the bridge crew...I'd bet they operate as a unit in the Q-net.

Another thought almost knocks me over. If those super wormers teamed up, they could take control of the Q-net. I imagine they'd rename DES to OWUF or WOUF or something like that. Either way it's a terrifying thought.

But it also gives me an idea to increase my chances of finding those files.

"You want to do what?" Radcliff asks, incredulous.

I explain it again. It's after dinner and everyone has left. "It's like that sorting socks thing—using valuable resources that are needed elsewhere," he says.

"But that worked," I try.

"I'll think about it. In the meantime, just keep looking for those files."

I'm hopeful that once he recovers from the shock, he'll see it my way. But he's not in our unit the next morning or in his office. Morgan's not there either and Keir doesn't know where he is.

She escorts me to soch-time and waits outside while I spend the next two hours trying to figure out the best way to find those files.

In fact, I'm so distracted, I'm halfway down the hallway before I realize Keir isn't following me after soch-time ends.

Huh? I return. No Keir.

Unsure what to do, I stand there. Did she need to use the washroom? Or was she called away? Or does Radcliff finally trust me enough to let me go around unescorted? Nah. He might trust me more, but with those— Oh no! I hope it's not another shadow-blob attack. At least the base's lights are on.

With anxiety churning in my stomach, I debate my next

move. I figure the best thing to do is to go to the Control Center as planned. This way Keir can catch up with me there and I can ask my dad what's going on.

I enter the center cautiously, but there's no tension and everyone appears calm as they perform their duties. My father isn't there and I ask his assistant where he is.

"He's in the port with your mom," Gavin says. "One of the field teams arrived an hour or so ago. They're having some equipment trouble. That sand just gets into everything."

"Was there another sandstorm?" I ask. That would explain Keir's absence.

"No, but being out there in the desert, it's hard to avoid."

True. I sit at my father's terminal and hesitate. If I access the Q-net without supervision, I'll be in violation of my probation. Just coming here on my own was a violation. I ask Gavin if there's been any trouble.

"Nope. Except for the pits being sealed off, everything else is going well."

Then where is Keir? Drawing in a deep breath, I worm into the cameras. If she's in a public area, I should be able to find her. First place I check is the archaeology lab. Three bored security officers stand guard. I about wilt with relief. No problems with shadow-blobs. Too bad it's team two. I'd like to have seen Niall.

As I'm checking hallways, labs, and the security areas, everything appears normal. But there's a niggle of worry scratching at the back of my mind. Something about Niall... Wait. I sit up. Team one is supposed to be on duty in the lab this afternoon. Not team two.

I apply logic before I panic. Maybe Radcliff changed the lab schedule. I check the camera feeds twice. And the answer is the same. In fact, it's all too much the same. Like Officer Rance scratching his nose in the same place three times in a row.

There's only one explanation.

A worm has altered the camera feeds.

2522:171

Panic bubbles up my throat. The cameras have been altered to show another time. I check through and pinpoint the time to around eleven-hundred hours. So anything that has happened after that time hasn't been recorded. Why? Obviously to hide something. Something bad. I glance around the Control Center. All still appears normal.

Okay. Just relax. How do I see what's going on in the base without tipping the worm off? It'll be tricky and I can only do it for a couple cameras. I pick a camera in the archaeology lab. With the utmost care, I split the feed into two images; one goes to the monitors in security, the other to me. It takes forever. Then I remove the bogus image of team one and—

The lab is empty. The guards are gone. I suck in a breath, trying to keep my fear to a simmer. At least the lights are still blazing. And everything looks okay— no blood stains or overturned equipment. So where is everyone? I can't check all the cameras, that would take too much time and I've a terrible feeling I'm running out of it.

Where else? I wish Radcliff had one in his office. There's too many cameras in the hallways of the security area. Think. What happened today that's different?

The port! I repeat my careful manipulation of a camera in the port. The large area is empty as well. No field team working on broken equipment. But I spot a pulse gun on the ground. And a couple of large metal racks have been knocked over. I stifle a cry. No sign of my mom or dad.

A crazy scenario plays in my mind. The field team wasn't really one of ours, but the looters. They blocked the cameras, gained access and... What? There's only ten rows of exposed Warriors in Pit 5. Why would they invade the base? Maybe it's easier to take over the base and then steal the Warriors once the diggers are done uncovering Pit 5. And the first target would be the security team. And then they'd go after the people in charge.

My parents!

I assume the worst. The security team has been compromised. Since the looters haven't announced their presence to the rest of the base, I'm guessing they want to keep it quiet. For now. No one in the port means they've taken them to another location. And they probably have my parents, too.

A horrible thought turns my fear into a full boil. What if they and the officers are all dead? Breathing is difficult as all my blood rushes to my feet. Black and white spots swirl as a weakness flows over my arms. I rest my head in my hands. The desire to yell for help pushes against my chest, but I swallow it down. There's nothing anyone can do until I figure out exactly what's going on. And I can't do that while having a panic attack.

Get a grip, Lyra. You're a criminal mastermind in training. You refuse to be ignored. I pull in lung-filling breaths one after another. The looters claimed no fatalities on Xinji. Don't assume the worst. Pretend you're a looter. You just captured the base's security team and leaders. What do you do next?

You'd want them out of your way. You'd put them in a secure location like— Detention!

I find a camera in the detention center, but after an eternity to strip the fake image, I'm rewarded with a view of an empty hallway and two rows of doors on each side. I go to another camera and start the process again. Except this time, the Q-net kicks in and does it for me in a fraction of the time. Stunned, it takes me a moment to register what the camera reveals.

There's Keir and Menz in a detention cell. To say they appear to be upset is a vast understatement. The Q-net once again anticipates my moves and all the cameras in detention show me real images. I count. Ten security officers in five rooms. Niall is with Morgan. She's sitting on the bunk appearing calm while he's pacing with short agitated strides— all that's possible in the small room. There's a nasty cut on his cheek, bleeding. Some of my fear turns to fury. How dare they hurt him! Anger is more motivating than panic, so I instruct the Q-net to clear all the cameras. While I wait, I wonder if not seeing my parents in detention is a good or a bad thing. Radcliff is missing as well.

When the Q-net finishes, I check the rest of the base. Strange figures are in security's halls and in the training room.

They're all wearing gray coveralls and masks that are similar to the B-apps. Only their eyes are visible. Looters. Lots of them. I count. Ten...twenty...thirty-five...forty-eight. Oh boy.

Breathe. Just breathe.

They're also armed with pulse guns and another weapon that I don't recognize—probably lethal.

Breathe. Breathe. Breathe.

They're patrolling the hallways in security. A few are playing cards in the officers' rec room. A couple are milling about the training area. What are they waiting for?

I need to show this to an adult. "Gavin," I say with only a slight tremor.

"Yeah?"

"Can I borrow your portable?"

"Uh...aren't you on probation or something?"

"This is for Officer Radcliff. It's very important. Please."

"Uh...okay, but—"

I snatch it from him. "I'll take full responsibility." I transfer the camera feeds to the portable so I can see the looters' location, but I can't go deeper in the Q-net on the device. "Do you know where Dr. Jeffries or Gage is?" I ask Gavin.

"Gage is usually in her lab at this time. If you hurry you can catch her before dinner. Jeffries is probably in his office."

I bring up a map of the research base. Both are on the opposite side of the base from security. Just my luck. The geology lab is a public place, so I check the camera. Dr. Kara Gage is there talking to another scientist. I'd better run, but I pause. Do the looters have access to the real views? Why not?

That worm could have easily done the same thing as I did. Plus it makes sense for them to have eyes on the base. They've probably been watching me in the Control Center. A creepy thought. And that also means they'll see me running through the base.

Shit. Shit. Shit.

Think. I drum my fingers on the terminal. If I can get the real feeds and have the ability to turn them off for the looters, then I'll control what they see or not see. Worming the worm!

I've no idea if it'll work, but I entangle with my strange...perceptive cluster in the Q-net and create a bypass for one camera, then another; by the third, the Q-net understands what I'm doing and finishes it for the rest of the cameras in seconds. I move all the feeds to the portable. I'm in the process of creating a worm hole so I can control the cameras with the portable, when a message pops up for me.

It's from Officer Tace Radcliff.

2522:171: Hello, little worm, you are in violation of your probation. Please report to my office immediately.

Ice flushes through my veins, leaving behind a numb terror. The looters know what I'm doing. I check the portable, but it appears my feeds are still good. Then I take a peek at the camera near Radcliff's office. Someone leans out the door and waves at a couple people nearby. They disappear.

Maybe they don't know the extent of what I'm doing. But now I don't have time to get to Dr. Gage or Jeffries. Although

I'm not sure what they could do besides order everyone to hide—

That's it!

The safest place for everyone is in their units. And the only way to get them there is to… I worm into a different part of the Q-net and trigger a base-wide sandstorm alert.

The strident siren sounds very sweet to me. Gavin curses, but he follows the procedures. I grab the portable and head for the door. Before opening it, I tap in my route, programming the cameras through the portable to hide me from sight, using the worm hole. Hoping like hell that my actions don't alert the looters, I leave. There's only one person left who will know what to do.

I check the portable frequently as I race through the crowded corridors, timing each turn to match the route I programmed. The alarm screeches overhead as I weave through the scientists and techs heading for their units. I reach the infirmary just in time to see Beau limping from his room.

He's buttoning his shirt and arguing with a nurse. "…have to help."

"I'm sure this is another false alarm. Return to your bed before you pass out," the nurse orders.

I grab his arm. "I'll help Officer Dorey back to bed."

Beau looks at me. "You will?"

"Yes. Radcliff sent me."

He pauses a beat, noting that I'm alone. "All right."

The nurse huffs. "You won't have time to go to your unit, Lyra. You'll have to stay with him. And lock the door."

Should I be concerned that I'm on a first name basis with the medical staff? Probably. "I will."

Beau lets me guide him back inside. I lock the door as promised.

"What's going on?" he demands.

"You might want to sit down for this."

"Lyra." His tone is dangerous.

"Okay." I explain as fast as possible. The words gush out of me in a torrent. Beau doesn't say anything, but his face pales to an unhealthy color—and he wasn't exactly in peak condition before.

When I'm done he says, "You're right."

"About what?"

"I need to sit down."

I help him over to the bed. He perches on the edge and rubs a hand over his face. I shift my weight from foot to foot, silently urging him to hurry up and come up with a brilliant plan.

"Sounding the alarm was a good move, Lyra. We need weapons. And then we need to rescue the others."

"Okay. Where are the weapons?"

"In storage lockers."

"The looters have probably already confiscated them."

He smiles. "Radcliff is smarter than the average criminal. The lockers are at various locations throughout the base. Not just in security."

"That's sneaky." Color me impressed.

"He can be. And as long as the looters haven't changed who has access, I can open them."

"And if they have?"

"There's the master override. But only three people have that code."

I groan. "Let me guess, my mom, my dad, and Radcliff."

"Yup."

Huh. And they didn't tell me. "I can worm into their accounts—"

"It's not in the Q-net. It's not written down. They have to memorize it so it can't be stolen."

Wonderful. "Is the override common knowledge?" In other words, would the looters know about it and change it.

"It should be limited to security personnel and the upper levels of DES."

Who have a ton of security holes for worms to wiggle through. We exchange a glance.

"Yeah, the looters probably know about it," Beau admits.

And all I have is a portable so I can't check for sure. "Then let's hope you can still open the weapon lockers."

On the map of the base, Beau shows me where the closest arms locker is and we plot a course. I set the cameras to hide us as we travel at a much slower speed than I'd like, but Beau, while able to stand, is still not fully recovered. The fact that he rests his hand on my shoulder for support tells me more about the state of his health than his efforts to mask his pain.

The hallways are empty. I hold the portable out so we keep pace with the cameras. The sandstorm alarm stops in mid-shriek and we freeze. It's a relief to my ears, but another level of anxiety twists in my guts.

"It's okay," Beau says after a moment. "It's supposed to stop when the storm arrives. As long as the all-clear signal doesn't sound, everyone should remain in their units."

We reach the weapons locker after a hundred and one years. I hold my breath as Beau presses his palm to the scanner. My heart is hammering against my chest. Probably trying to escape. I don't blame it. I've certainly put the poor thing through its paces.

The lock turns green with a click. I about faint with relief. There's a black duffle bag inside and Beau hands it to me. I hold it open as he fills it with a combination of pulse guns and other nasty stingers. When he's done, I zip it up and sling it over my left shoulder.

"Here." He shoves a pulse gun into my hand, and touches a button.

It flares to life, but I'm prepared and don't drop it. "They have other weapons besides the pulse guns."

"Do you want to kill someone?"

Ah. Good point. "What about you?" I gesture to the weapon in his hand.

"This gives me options."

"Okay. What's next?"

"You need to plan us a route to the detention center that avoids the looters, and then sync up the cameras to hide us."

"Is that all?"

"I didn't say it would be easy."

"Oh yes, 'cause everything up to this point has been a breeze."

"That's the spirit," Beau says, ignoring my sarcasm. He claps me on the back.

I long for a Q-net terminal, but I search for a safe route. And I realize we have a problem. "I can plan a route based on what I see now. But what happens when the looters move around? I can't anticipate where they'll be twenty minutes from now."

"Can you do it in stages? You know...just the next couple moves first. This way we don't have to guess that far out."

"Yes, but it'll slow us down considerably."

"Better than getting caught."

True. I keep working, but I scan ahead. When I reach the detention center, I spot yet another obstacle. "There are two guards outside."

Beau leans over my shoulder. "Hmmm. Are there any cross corridors nearby? Places we can hide behind until we reach that hallway?"

"No. It's in the middle of a long expanse."

He curses. "We need a way to sneak up on them."

My thoughts churn. Turn off the lights? No. Not with shadow-blobs in the pits. A distraction? That would announce our presence to everyone else. What did Jarren say about detention? Boring white walls. Maybe we can camouflage ourselves in white. I stifle a giggle over the image of pouring white paint over my head. What else did Jarren say?

"The duct to nowhere."

"What?" Beau asks.

"It's one of those weird design glitches I showed to Beta team. Jarren used to complain that it's a meter away from the ducts that cross over the detention cells. That he would have loved to use it to hide in and let the security officers panic when they saw he was gone." Well, he used cruder language, but I didn't think I needed to repeat it.

"Can we access it? Is it big enough?"

I check the base map again. Of course the duct isn't marked, but I use it to help jog my memory. If we could get into housing unit three-oh-eight, then we can. I tell Beau, "I don't how big it is or if there'll be a vent to the hallway. Oh, and we need to get into that unit." I glance at him. "I don't suppose it's yours?"

"Our luck isn't that good. Let's just hope you have decent aim."

"Me?" I squeak. "I've never fired one of these."

"There's always a first time."

I gape at him. That is so *not* comforting.

He jabs a finger at the screen. "We don't have any other options. Let's get started."

We move slowly. I check our route and knock out the cameras as we go. Sweat soaks my shirt. The hallways are deserted—as they should be, but it's still eerie. I jerk at every little noise. Our check-first-move-second plan alerts us to a couple looters in a corridor on our route.

Beau and I freeze and press against the wall—not that it makes us any less visible, but trying to squish my body flat is better than standing there in the middle of the corridor like an idiot. The looters cross the intersection without glancing our way. I just about sink into a puddle. We wait a few more minutes before moving on.

The route to detention is out of the way and a bit roundabout, but it avoids the populated center of security. The second to last hallway we need to traverse is through the officers' housing unit wing. A brief wish to stop in Radcliff's and don that jumpsuit flits through me. Probably wouldn't save me from being stunned, but I'd feel safer.

Halfway down the hall, I check the cameras. My heart does a somersault and has a bad landing. "Beau," I whisper. "Incoming. Four looters around the corner!" I draw the pulse gun with my free hand. We'll be caught for sure.

Beau grabs my arm and yanks me to the next door. He slams his hand on the lock screen. The door opens, he pushes me inside hard enough that I sprawl onto the ground, dropping the portable while the pulse gun skitters from my fingers and out of reach. What the—

"Stay out of sight," he hisses.

By the time I scramble to my feet, other voices are shouting outside and the door closes.

Beau's still in the hallway! The muted crackle of a pulse gun on the other side stops me from opening the door. Plus his order. Instead, I toggle on the screen in time to witness Beau jerk and tumble to the ground as he's hit.

2522:171

Horrified, I watch through the view screen as three men stand around Beau's prone form. I bite my knuckle to keep from crying out as I search for signs of life. Is his chest moving? Did his eyelids just flutter?

Then I debate if I should throw open the door and shoot them with my pulse gun. I have the element of surprise. But I've no experience. Beau only managed to incapacitate one of them—at least I think the bottom of those boots on the far side of the screen is the fourth man—so what are my chances of getting all three before they get me? Zero.

"Where did he come from?" one man asks, toeing Beau with his foot. His voice sounds buzzy and is dampened by the mask, but still clear. Because he's standing right on the other side of the door.

I wrap my arms around my chest. Did they see Beau push me inside? I duck down even though I know they can't see me through the view screen.

"Must be the officer in the infirmary," another male answers. "Guess he wasn't as injured as they let on."

"What do we do with him?" the third asks.

"Dump him in detention with the others. I'll go tell the boss."

"What about Stan?"

"Leave him. He'll wake up eventually."

There's a rustling noise and I straighten. Two of the men haul Beau to his feet and wrap Beau's arms around their necks. They half-carry, half-drag him down the hall and out of sight.

A part of me is relieved that they didn't see me. Another part is cursing me out that I didn't do something to help Beau— I've a duffle bag full of weapons at my feet for stars' sake! A third part is terrified. Another part recognizes that Beau protected me, otherwise I'd have been caught, too. After a few shaky breaths, I'm... better. Still freaked, but not curled up into a ball, sucking my thumb. Not yet.

What do I do now? Should I stick to the plan and try to rescue the team? Could I incapacitate those two guards? Probably not. I'm not suddenly going to have perfect aim when I've never shot a pulse gun before. Plus I can't even get my heart to stop acting like an unruly toddler jacked up on sugar.

So what can I do? I can worm. All right. That's a start.

I glance around at Beau's unit—it has to be his, he couldn't open anyone else's. It's number three-oh-five and the same size as Niall's. A knot twists in my throat. Best not to think about Niall right now. The living room is neat with minimal decorations. Blue and navy are the main colors.

Gavin's portable is lying on the floor cracked and broken. If I survive this, I'll probably get into trouble and have to pay for a replacement. Funny how I'm looking forward to that time.

I'm sure Beau has a super nice terminal somewhere and I find it in his bedroom along with lots of hair care products. It doesn't take me long to worm deep into the Q-net. That master override might not be written down or in a file, but there's a part of the system that has to know what it is in order to respond to it. And I'm going to find it.

Sometime...later—I've no idea what the code is. I groan with frustration. The code slips out of my reach every time I get close. Doesn't the Q-net understand this is important? I may have to give up. While I'm this deep, I send a few hidden messages to Drs. Gage and Jeffries that I'm pretty sure won't be spotted by that super worm. I explain what's going on and hope for the best. I'm tempted to reach out to Jarren, but I don't want the looters to go after him. And much to my surprise, I can't reach DES through the normal routes. That super worm has blocked communications from the entire base. We are totally cut off from DES! I'd be more impressed by their skill, but fear is dominating my emotions at the moment.

Instead, I descend to the star roads, getting as close as the terminal will allow me, then search for a navigator. I connect with an interstellar navigator and am told to get the hell out before he/she reports me to DES. *Go ahead. Please do. And please help me.* The connection is terminated. I try really hard not to let that affect me, but curling up under Beau's bed is looking more enticing by the minute.

Come on, Lyra. Think! I need a navigator so I try again and again and again. Each time, I take a different path until I reach Chief Ritsa. At first she thinks I'm a glitch and I have seconds to convince her otherwise.

2522:171: Chief Ritsa, please look through DES's records, I interned with Chief Hoshi, she taught me how to reach this deep. I'm only seventeen A-years old and am desperate!

Finally, I receive this message:

2522:171: You're right only a person trained by an interstellar navigator could reach me in this particular fashion. What can I do to help?

Those last six words are pure magic. I ask for the master override code. While I'm explaining why I need it and what's been going on to Chief Ritsa, another message pops up.

2522:171: Hello, little worm. You've been busy. Your attempts to reach Jefferies, Gage, and DES have failed. And, no offense, but that's a really stupid move as none of them can help you. No one on Yulin can. But you can help your parents stay alive. They're sitting here with me in Officer Radcliff's office. If you don't come here within the hour, unarmed, I'll kill your father. Then you have one minute before I kill your mother. Don't be late.

The room tilts and spins around me. I dig my nails into the fabric of the chair as nausea burns up my throat. Stumbling to a trash can, I dry heave into it. One benefit from not eating in hours—no chunks. When the painful contractions cease, I lie on my side, curled around the can just in case.

After…who knows how long, my thoughts creep out from where they've fled in terror—I can't blame them. And frankly, I'm surprised they returned. I would have been okay with becoming a mindless zombie, I could have just—

Oh. My. Stars!

I hop up and re-read the message. It doesn't say anything about Chief Ritsa.

Fifty minutes left.

Re-connecting, I get the override code from Ritsa. And then cover my tracks. Or I pray to the universe that I did. When that's done, I ransack Beau's unit, searching for supplies.

Come on. Come on. Come on.

He has to have a portable somewhere!

It's in his sock drawer. Seriously?

I use a precious minute to transfer the camera feeds. Then I shoulder the duffle bag of weapons, peer into the hallway, and dash across and down to unit three-oh-eight. I hold my breath as I punch in the master override code.

The unit's door opens. I don't waste time thanking the stars.

Forty minutes left.

Moving furniture, I stack a chair on top of a table. It is just high enough for me to reach the vent. I use Beau's all-purpose tool to remove the cover.

Did you know a duffle bag full of weapons is heavy? Like sweat popping, muscles straining, back hurting heavy? Well it is. I struggle to get it into the vent and out of the way. Pulling myself up is no easy task either. My legs flail and kick as I try to get my hips into the duct—it's tighter than I hoped. Note to self: work on upper arm and body strength as soon as you live through this.

Drenched and out of breath, I lie on the cool metal.

Thirty-five minutes left.

I grab the portable from the pocket of the bag and activate step two. The shrill sandstorm alarm once again echos throughout the base. Such a loud, obnoxious, dominating noise. It's music to my ears. I slide the bag forward as I wiggle behind it as fast as I can in the small space. All the sounds of my passage are masked by that lovely siren.

When I reach the vent in the hall, I encounter my first unexpected surprise—the guards are not standing in the hallway, but are inside the detention center.

Thirty minutes left.

Committed to my plan, I keep moving. When I reach the second vent, their shouted voices can just be heard above the din.

"…still locked…return…post."

"…can't we…here? Quieter…"

"…can't see…boss…go."

Two dark heads pass under my vent and I flinch, but they keep going and the outer door shuts. Able to breathe again, I slither/slide to the next vent and remove the cover. I tie a sheet to a handle of the bag and ease it down until it reaches the floor. Too bad there's no one else in the vent to hold onto a sheet to help me. I go out feet first and then hips. The idea was to hang from my hands and drop gracefully down, but once the bulk of my body is unsupported, it drags the rest of me with it. Ducts are slippery.

I land on my feet, but my right ankle twists painfully and my butt hits the floor. A small shock wave slams up my spine. Woah. That's intense.

Twenty-five minutes left.

Checking the portable, I confirm that the guards have returned to their posts. I scan the doors surrounding me and find cell number three. Standing sends darts of fire up my leg, but I limp over. I key in the override, unlocking the door and—

It bursts open. I'm tackled to the ground. Knees press on my chest and hands wrap around my throat as my head bounces off the floor. Through vision blurred with tears, I gaze up at Niall.

He's staring at me in pure astonishment, but his iron grip on my neck eases. Too bad his weight is still suffocating me. I punch his thigh. Hard. He gets the hint. As fast as he knocked me down, he picks me up and hugs me.

The room spins so it's a good thing he's holding me. The pain in my head matches my ankle. Morgan is standing behind him. She's grinning and shaking her head in disbelief.

"What— How did you—" Niall says. His lips brush my neck.

"No time to tell you everything." I break from his hold. I've eight minutes before the siren stops. Waving Morgan over, I point to the duffle bag. They lean close so I can speak right into their ears as I explain my plan to them and give them the override code.

Niall shakes his head no. "We have weapons. The code. We can—"

"No. I'm going to be in your dad's office in…" I glance at the portable. "In less than twenty minutes. That's non-negotiable."

"You will not endanger yourself anymore," Morgan says. "I'm in charge now and you're going to stay safe inside detention while—"

"Mutant Zombies from Planet Nine," I say to Niall.

He meets my gaze. Within those blue-green depths are a riot of emotions—fear, pain, amazement, and the desire to protect.

I caress his cheek, careful not to touch the cut. "Trust me, Toad."

He nods and kisses me. Then he laces his fingers together. I step into them with my left foot and put my hands on his shoulders.

"Promise you'll stay safe and come back to me, Mouse."

"I promise to do everything I can to get through this."

He boosts me up into the duct. I scramble into the narrow opening.

Fifteen minutes left.

Sliding and wiggling is much harder to do with an injured ankle. And the beat of pain with every push slows my movements. The siren stops mid-way. While I try to advance without making noise, I can't avoid the hiss of my clothes rubbing on metal. Each one sounds louder than the last.

I peer through the open vent. A sweat slicked tendril of hair hangs down. The pile of furniture I left in unit three-oh-eight doesn't look as stable from this direction. But I have no time to worry about it. Once again, I lower my legs. This time, my feet touch the chair and I ease my weight onto it. Nothing collapses under me. A small victory. The rest of the climb is awkward—graceful, I'm not.

Discarding my pulse gun and the multi-purpose tool onto the couch, I check the hallway—it's empty— before adding the portable to the heap.

Five minutes left.

With fear skittering up and down my limbs, I leave the unit and limp toward Officer Radcliff's office. I don't get far before a couple masked looters round the corner and rush me. They press me up against the wall. Hands pat me down, searching for weapons. It's hard to breathe around the tight lump in my throat.

They each grab one of my arms and "escort" me. Locked between them, I'm suddenly convinced I've just made the biggest mistake in my very, very short life. Infinitesimal actually. Why did I ever think I might get through this? The looters are adults, with years of experience. They got the drop on the base's highly trained security team. Twice. And I'm... A little worm.

As we near Radcliff's door, I'm seriously considering getting sick or passing out or hyperventilating or screaming. I doubt any of them would help, but it might relieve the immense pressure building up on the inside of my body.

The door opens. At that moment, I'd rather face the shadow-blobs. Unable to alter my fate, I'm pulled through the threshold.

"Lyra!" My mom's anguished cry cuts right through me. "You shouldn't have come."

I turn. My parents and Radcliff are sitting on the floor along the left wall. Their arms are pulled behind their backs and two looters stand nearby them with weapons drawn. Mom and Dad appear unharmed, but Radcliff's uniform shirt is torn and a large bruise is purpling on his cheek. I'm surprised his supernova glower hasn't set the looters on fire by now.

"He was bluffing, Li-Li," Dad says. His shoulders are hunched.

I try to step toward them, but my captors drag me over to Radcliff's desk. Sitting behind it is another looter who's almost indistinguishable from the rest. But when he stares at me, I recognize his eyes from the attack in the pits—he's the leader.

As my legs threaten to collapse under me, I remember he didn't want to hurt me back then. I cling to that small tendril of hope and gather what's left of my courage—a pathetic amount.

"Two minutes to spare, Little Worm. Don't you love your parents? Or did you really think you could summon help? Out here? Thirty years from nowhere?" He laughs, it's a short bitter bark. "I gotta give you credit, reaching out to the navigators. Rather smart."

The last bit of my bravery flees. Does he know everything? "Why are you here?" I ask instead. Yes, my voice sounds like you'd imagine a terrified girl would sound like. I'm not proud.

388

"The diggers—"

"I came here for you, Little Worm. Too clever by far. I can't have you figure it all out and tell DES."

"I haven't figured anything out!" I back into the wall of muscles that is my guards.

"Give it time," he says in disgust. "No help for it. You're coming with us."

Stunned to my very core, I gape at him. "I am?"

"Yes."

Unable to pull enough air from my lungs, my words wheeze out weakly. "Are you going to—"

"No," he snaps. "I'm not going to kill you. You'll be well cared for." He stands and comes around to my side of the desk. "Now say good-bye to your parents. You won't be seeing them again."

Talk about confused. My mind is celebrating the fact I'm not going to die...well, not yet anyway, but my heart melts with sadness, filling my stomach with dread. "I'm not?"

"No." He grabs my right elbow and pulls me over to my parents. "Say good-bye, Little Worm. You won't get another chance."

"No, you can't take her!" My father struggles to his feet.

Radcliff and my mother stand as well. Their guards move closer. Radcliff shoulders one, slamming him into the wall. The other raises his gun.

I lunge, knocking his arm aside. The pulse goes wide. My guards quickly rush to their friends' aid and my parents and Radcliff are once again subdued.

The leader yanks me back. "Why would you help him?" he demands. "When those files were stolen, Officer Tight Pants didn't give you the benefit of the doubt. He was so quick to accuse you."

Officer Tight Pants? He just called Radcliff Officer Tight Pants. There's only one person—

Oh. My. Stars.

2522:171

arren must have recognized my expression, because without warning, he clamps a hand over my mouth and drags me out of the office and into the camera room. I'm too flabbergasted to resist.

"Leave us," he growls at the two looters monitoring the cameras. "Close the door behind you."

Without question, they bolt from the room. When the door clicks shut, Jarren releases his hold on me.

I sink into one of the empty chairs. "Wow," I whisper. "It's you."

His hard expression softens. With a sigh, he removes his mask. His brown hair is pulled back into a bun and sweat stains his well-groomed beard. How could I not recognize his eyes? Perhaps because, even though these are the same light brown color, the bitterness and fine lines around them are new. Well, new to me. Jarren appears to match his age of thirty-eight, but with the time dilation, you can never be certain.

"How…why…" A thousand questions push up my throat.

"Why?" He huffs in amusement. "Because instead of nurturing my gift, they locked me away. Because DES ruins lives. *All* our lives, including yours, Lyra. Because I can. And because once I've reached my end point, the Galaxy will be mine."

Lots of overwhelming and scary statements in that rant. I focus on the Jarren I knew. "What about Lan? All those people on Xinji. They didn't do anything to you."

"Lan." He says her name with reverence, but his fists are clenched, matching the anger in his gaze. "Her research unlocked the key. And with her relentlessness, it was just a matter of time before she put it all together."

I cover my mouth with a hand. "Is that why you killed her?"

"*I* haven't killed anyone. Neither have my people. We've stolen and destroyed Warriors. That's all."

"But…"

He waits with a half-smile.

And that's all I need. The answer pops into my head. "The shadow-blobs! When you take and destroy those Warriors they can no longer protect us. And those… creatures come through from…wherever they live. They're the ones that killed the people on Xinji."

"Like I said, too clever by far."

"It's still your fault. If you purposely—"

"I didn't know about those—what did you call them—shadow-blobs? That's a rather accurate name considering no one can see them. But I didn't know they existed until after we raided Xinji. If you want someone to blame, then blame DES."

Another thought propels me to my feet. "They'll kill everyone on Yulin. My parents!"

"Relax, Lyra. Your Officer Tight Pants seems to have a handle on it. They might survive until the Protector ship arrives."

"He's not mine."

"You're working with him even though he put you on probation. Then when I stole those Xinji files, he automatically accused you. I read his report about the incident, he treats you like a criminal."

"He's nurturing my gift, you idiot." The truth of that statement makes me pause. Huh. Who knew?

"I taught you how to worm." He steps closer to me. "Look, you're coming with me regardless, but I'd rather not force you and have to lock you up for the rest of your life. If you promise to cooperate, I'll explain everything to you. You'll be astounded. It's fantastic and when it's all said and done, we'll be heroes."

That's actually rather tempting. But also so very wrong. Behind Jarren, the images in a couple cameras flicker. His focus is on me so I hope he didn't notice. I need to prolong this as long as possible.

"All right, Jarren. I promise to cooperate with you. I'd rather help out than be confined."

He grins. "Just like old times."

"I've a couple requests."

The smile vanishes and he stiffens. "Go on."

"I want to be able to communicate with my parents on a

regular basis." I hold up a hand, stopping his protest. I didn't include Niall because I'm reluctant for Jarren to know about our relationship. I sense that would upset Jarren. "You can read all my messages. I won't reveal any of your secrets or tell them where I am. Promise."

"All right. And?"

"You send Officer Radcliff all the information you have on those shadow-blobs so he can figure out how best to fight them."

"I don't have much, but I'll do it. Anything else?"

"You release my parents so we can have a proper hug good-bye and you allow me to pack a bag to take along." When he hesitates, I add, "My unit is just down the hall." And that will eat up more time. Bonus.

"Okay. But you are not allowed to tell anyone my name. Not even my men."

Interesting. "Why not?"

"I'll tell you later, along with everything else."

Shoot. "Fine, I won't say your name. What should I call you?"

He flashes me his cocky grin. In that moment, he is *my* Jarren. The one who was my prank-pulling partner. "The Boss."

At least he hasn't named himself King of the Universe. Not yet. "Can I call you *The* for short?"

My comment surprises a laugh from him. "I've missed you." He sobers. "Do we have a deal?" He holds out his hand. I shake it. "We do."

He dons his mask.

There's a knock on the door. Jarren opens it.

"The shuttle's here," a looter says.

"Good. Prep for departure."

"Yes, sir." The man hustles out.

That's my second unexpected surprise—they're leaving on a shuttle. I shouldn't have assumed they planned to stay on the planet. This isn't good.

Jarren strides into Radcliff's office. He gestures to my parents. "Take the binders off them," he orders the guards. "After they're done saying good-bye to their daughter, take the three of them to detention."

I gaze at the floor, willing my expression to remain sad and scared despite my heart's dancing beat. Considering how much still has to go right for my plan to work, it's not hard to appear frightened. With four guards keeping their weapons trained on us, I hug my mom.

"I'm sorry, Lyra," she says in my ear while squeezing me tight enough to hurt.

"What for? None of this is your fault."

"For bringing you out here. If I'd let you stay with Lan and gone to the university on Planet Rho like you'd wanted, you'd be safe."

True. But I wouldn't have learned how to navigate an Interstellar space ship, or met Niall, or Beau and the others. "I'm really glad you did, Mom."

She draws back to study me. Unshed tears shine in her eyes. "You are, aren't you?"

"Yup. Now I know you'll worry anyway, but I'll be fine. I

worked out a deal and we'll be able to message each other."

Her tears overflow and streak down her face. "What kind of a deal?"

I almost laugh at her suspicious tone. "Nothing bad. I won't be harmed."

Mom releases me after another rib-cracking hug and my father pulls me tight.

"We'll come for you," Dad promises. "They don't get to keep you. Not for long."

"Thanks, Dad."

He releases me and it takes everything I have not to rush back into his strong arms.

"We're proud of you, Li-Li. We love you." Now he's tearing up.

"Love you, too," I say to both my parents as my own liquid sadness drips from my eyes and clogs my nose.

The guards escort them to the door. But Radcliff pauses before leaving his office. He turns to Jarren. "If she's harmed, I will hunt you down and tear you apart with my bare hands."

Oh my. That's... Wow.

The looters push him through the door.

"Seems you made an impression on Officer Tight Pants," Jarren says, seeming unperturbed by Radcliff's threat. "Let's go pack your bag, we don't have much time."

He walks with me through the hallway. The warmth from my parents' hugs still lingers on my skin. I'll see them again. I have to believe it or I'd crumple into a tiny ball. Jarren follows me into my unit. He rests his hand on the weapon on his belt.

"Relax. I've been staying with Radcliff." I explain the details of my probation. I open the door to my room. "See? No terminal. I'll be right out." I go to close it.

Jarren sticks his boot between the door and the jam. "Leave it open."

"I want to change out of these dirty clothes."

He peers into my room, scanning the walls, floor, and ceiling. Probably looking for vents.

Annoyed, I say, "I said I'd cooperate."

"Five minutes."

After the door closes, I lean on it for a second. I need a moment to just...be. Then I stay true to my word and pack a bag. It takes a minute. A sudden pang grips me. I wish I had something of Niall's—a drawing or T-shirt— to take along just in case I never see him again. No. Not going to think bad thoughts.

Changing my clothes, I take another minute to wrap my ankle. It's already starting to swell. Does Jarren have access to medical supplies where we're going?

Jarren barges in just as I'm slinging my bag over my arm. I glance over my shoulder when we leave the unit. I've only been living here twenty-one days, but I'm going to miss our nightly dinners. I clamp down on my doubts. It has to work. Jarren walks beside me as we head toward the port. There's a few looters ahead of us and a number of them behind.

Once we exit security's area, I brace for the ambush, but the corridors are empty except for us. Just as I suspected, but fought hard to deny, the security team didn't have enough time to get into position. My plan failed. And that's the last unexpected surprise. Although it shouldn't have been unexpected. Jarren did see my communications with the navigator. My denial just made it possible for me to function this last hour by delaying my terror. At least the scientists will be spared and I'll be...with Jarren. For the rest of my life. I shudder.

"That was smart of you to trigger the sandstorm alarm," Jarren says, sweeping an arm out. "It did me a favor, too, keeping the corridors clear. Wish I had thought of it." He pauses. "See, we make a great team."

That's not a comforting thought. "Where did you come from? You couldn't have traveled here from Suzhou."

"I left Suzhou after ten years of working as a tech in the Warrior pits. Well, in between my stints in detention." The bitterness is clear even through his mask. "Of course DES doesn't know I'm gone as I erased all my tracks. They still think I'm there, but I've been invisible to them for the last nine E-years."

"So our messages..."

"I'm deep in the Q-net, Lyra. Manipulating messages and creating bogus security officers is as easy as deleting files."

"Then why did you send us some of Xinji's files?"

"To keep you all occupied. I never thought you'd get anything from those. I didn't bother to check on it. When I did, it took me a while to figure out what you'd done or I would have taken you when we raided the pits."

"Instead you came back just for me." Why don't I feel special? "Why didn't you send your men to get me right after soch-time?"

"That was the original plan, but the security officers were harder to subdue than anticipated. By the time we had them secured, you were already in the Control Center. You left soon after I sent you that message, but then you disappeared from the cameras. What tipped you off?"

"The fact that Officer Keir wasn't outside the soch-area." No reason to lie. "Officer Radcliff would never have left me unprotected."

"Did he suspect we would return?"

"I think so. Plus he was worried about those shadow-blobs escaping the pits."

"Ah."

When we reach the port, I slow. A large shuttle sits in the middle. The roof of the port is already opened, revealing the yellow sky streaked with sunset colors. The strong peppery scent of Yulin fills the air. This can't be happening. But there are more looters around the shuttle and not a single security officer in sight.

Jarren grabs my elbow and pulls me along. Sand crunches under our boots. "You're not having a change of heart and thinking of doing something stupid, are you?" he asks.

Yes I am. I've changed my mind. I don't want to leave my parents and Niall. I didn't get a chance to say good-bye to him. But there's nothing I can do. I'm surrounded with no way to escape. Plus I gave my word. I consider. Does a promise under duress still count? And I'm not eighteen A-years either. Wouldn't my parents have to agree as well? I fixate on the legal issues. Better than thinking about my new future.

"Open the door and load up," Jarren orders his men near the shuttle. "Start the engines."

They turn toward us. Their weapons are drawn. One word pops into my head—mutiny—right before the sizzle of a pulse gun streaks by me.

Cries and chaos erupt around us. Jarren curses. He yanks me in front of him. Now I curse as he uses me as a shield. Good thing no one is aiming at us. Yet.

"This way," he says, edging us from the line of fire.

I catch a glimpse of two groups of looters shooting at each other before Jarren maneuvers us to the side of the port. Then he pulls me around to the opposite side of the shuttle. The large vehicle is now between us and the fighting.

"Come on." He enters a code and a ramp of steps opens, peeling down from the side of the shuttle. When the tip settles on the ground, he pushes me up them.

My stomach twists into a knot. We're in the shuttle.

It's empty. He closes the hatch and secures it.

This is happening.

This is really happening.

Oh my stars. Lightheaded, I grab the top of one of the seats.

"No time for dramatics," he says, propelling me toward the front. He shoves me into a seat right behind the cockpit. "Stay here."

Through the narrow doorway, I watch Jarren claim the pilot's seat. His hands fly over the controls and soon the hum of the engines rattles to life. I clutch the armrests with a death grip.

Four-seven-nine-three was the code he entered. If I hurry, I could—

The faint rustle of fabric draws my attention. Behind me, a looter—no, Niall, wearing the gray coverall of the looters—rolls out from underneath the seats and stands without making a sound. I bite down on my cry of joy as he puts a finger to his lips, signaling me to be quiet. His demeanor is focused. Confident. Drawing a pulse gun, Niall creeps up to the cockpit. Frozen in place, I hold my breath.

Niall aims through the doorway, but Jarren surges up and knocks him to the side. The gun clatters to the cockpit floor. Without thought, I dive out of the way as they wrestle. The desire to help presses on me, but Niall is between me and Jarren and I can't reach the gun. What else can I do?

I yank on my scattered thoughts, pulling them into a logical line. The security team must be dressed as looters, which means there's more help outside. Breaking my word, but not caring in the least, I race to the hatch and key in the code. With a hiss of air, the metal steps descend agonizingly slow. Millimeter by tiny millimeter. Didn't it move faster before?

A loud thump precedes a groan. I turn just as Jarren yanks his pulse gun from his holster and shoots Niall in the chest. He jerks, then slumps to the floor. *Niall!* Jarren's gaze meets mine.

The door is halfway down.

Jarren steps over Niall, aiming his weapon at me. "Don't make me stun you. Remember your promise."

I hesitate. There's movement behind Jarren, but I don't dare look. Then Jarren is knocked to the ground face-first with Niall on top. The gun skitters under the seats.

"She promised me first," Niall says, banging Jarren's head on the floor. Hard.

Jarren goes limp. I step toward Niall, but he waves me off. "Go. Get out of here."

The ramp is open, but I refuse. "Not without you."

The door on the other side of the shuttle—the one facing the fighting—hisses open.

"The rest of the security team?" I ask hopefully.

"They don't know the code." He scrambles to his feet. "That's our cue to go."

We hurry down the ramp. There's still no one on this side. Shouts and pulse blasts sound nearby.

Niall automatically reaches for his weapon, but it was lost in the shuttle. "Shit." He points to an overturned metal container that is about two meters tall. "Cover." Tucking me behind him, he backs us away from the shuttle.

He blocks my view. We crouch behind the container even though it's tall enough to protect us.

Niall peeks around the side. "They're retreating."

"Can't we stop them?"

"There's still too many of them left."

Sure enough the shuttle roars, sending a blast of air as it rises through the open roof.

Once the noise dies, Niall straightens and pulls me to my feet. Hugging me tight, he says, "That was too close, Mouse. We almost lost you."

"You saved me. Thank you." The enormity of everything

that happened crashes into me. I bury my face in his shoulder as shudders ripple through my body. "I thought…"

"Deep breaths. You're safe now."

So why was I falling apart? I managed to keep it together all during— "My parents?"

"Should be around here somewhere."

That snaps me out of it. I pull back. "Really?"

"We needed all the help we could get."

"That's what happens when you don't follow my plan," I tease.

"There wasn't enough time so we had to improvise."

"Well, I'll admit disguising yourselves as the looters was a pretty neat trick."

"Thanks," he says dryly. "It's not like we do this for a living or anything."

"Exactly."

"Can I interrupt." Radcliff's rough voice makes it sound more like an order than a question. He's holding a pulse gun, but it's pointed to the ground. His overalls are ripped and bloody. "Why didn't you answer?" he asks Niall, tapping his ear. "We thought you both were taken."

Ah, that explains the extra gruffness. I'm starting to figure him out. Sort of. The grumpier he is, the more he cares about you.

Niall releases me, but keeps his hand on my arm to steady me. "My communicator was fried by a point blank pulse."

That reminds me. "How did you shake off that hit?"

He pulls down the collar of the coverall, revealing the black jumpsuit underneath. "The fabric neutralizes the energy, but it still stings. How's the team?" he asks his father.

"Intact. Come on, Lyra's parents are frantic with worry."

Oh right. We emerge from our cover and within two steps, I'm squished inside a parent sandwich. I soak in the love, letting their happy words fill me. Once we break apart—well not quite as both my parents keep an arm around my waist—I scan the others. They're a ragtag group. Wounds bleed, sweat drips, bruises purple, and stains pepper their coveralls. But wide grins greet my gaze. Keir's curly hair is a wild mane around her head and Menz is clutching his arm to his chest. Everyone's there except Beau. I ask about him.

"Still sleeping it off," Morgan says. "He's going to be pissed he missed all the fun."

A number of prone forms litter the floor. Looters who were stunned and will eventually be put in detention.

"All right," Radcliff says, "let's—"

Air blasts through the port. Grains of sand strike my face. I shield my eyes with a hand, peering into the sudden cloud. A sandstorm? A rumble rattles my bones as another powerful gust of sand hits me. Talk about bad timing.

"Get inside," Radcliff orders.

My dad grabs my hand and my mother is already holding his other hand. The three of us head toward the base. A roar reverberates in the air around us. That doesn't sound like a storm.

"Lyra Daniels!" a loud voice shouts from above.

I glance up and almost trip over my feet. The shuttle has

returned. Its engine wash swirls the sand around us. The noise vibrates down to my toes. Or is that my fear? Because Jarren is standing on the open hatch. And he's pointing a weapon at me. Not a pulse gun.

"Can't let you live. Sorry!" he yells.

Purple fire explodes from the weapon. I yank my hand from my dad's just as someone tackles me. When I hit the ground, all the air whooshes from my lungs. But it's the daggers of pain that sizzle along my skin that claim my full attention. It's excruciating. As if every centimeter of the fabric of my clothes has turned into sharp tiny needles, digging deep into my flesh.

If I had any air, I would scream. Instead, tears flood my vision. The weight on top of me compresses my chest. Black and white spots dance in front of my eyes along with arcs of purple lightning. Passing out would be very welcome at this point. Static buzzes, replacing the shuttle's roar.

"Don't touch them," Radcliff orders. "Wait until the crackling stops."

The swarm of spots condense into one solid circle of blackness that grows until it fills the world. Everything stills. Pain dissolves into the peaceful silence. I'm untethered, floating free. Then I'm flying along the star roads, crossing trillions of kilometers in seconds.

It's exhilarating. The universe's infinite tangles twist and swirl and spiral and circle and dip and jump and cross and pulse and zip—a living, breathing organism all around me. It's as if all the molecules in the air suddenly became visible. And I'm swimming through them with ease. All the answers I seek are here, within reach.

Then the sharp acrid odor of burnt hair intrudes on the beauty. A fog of light encroaches, erasing the links of time. Pain returns, but it's sullen, broody, hiding in my muscles. Ice touches the back of my neck, shocking me toward consciousness with greater speed.

Another icy kiss jumps my heart and it beats with quick annoyed thumps. Noise drills into my head. A pulsing, pounding rhythm.

Lyra. Can you hear me? Lyra. Answer me.

Lyra. Please answer me. Can you hear me?

Please. Please. Lyra. Answer me. Lyra. Please.

It's relentless.

Sand coats my mouth, clogs my throat, fills my nose. I cough. Hard. Loud cheers erupt. Then I'm tipped to my side as a coughing fit racks my body. I curl, trying to expel the grains irritating my lungs. Gritty saliva pools under my cheek.

When the spasm releases my muscles, I wilt, sucking in deep breaths of air. I crack open one eye. My lashes are heavy with grit. Dr. Edwards peers at me. We're almost nose to nose.

"Welcome back," he says.

The burning pain in my throat prevents speech. Which is a good thing, because I desperately wish to return and I suspect the good doctor went to quite a bit of trouble fetching me from the depths of the Q-net.

I close my eye, letting that last thought—the depths of the Q-net—sink into my memory to be inspected and ruminated on later.

Adult voices discuss logistics over me. A bit of strength sweeps the fatigue and pain into the corners. I doubt it will stay there long so I open both eyes. Legs. Boots. Piles of sand.

Lifting my arm, I reach… Fingers intertwine with mine. I recognize the touch. My mother's. No need to see what a lifetime of seeking comfort from her has ingrained in my soul. My contentment lasts until the legs shift, giving me a better view of…a white sheet covering—

Niall! Memories flash. He'd tackled me right before I was shot and killed. He was hit. Murdered! A raw cry of anguish erupts from me as I surge forward, reaching for the fabric. Mom calls my name, but I'm determined. If I came back, he sure as hell can, too. I will make him.

2522:171

Yanking off the sheet, I freeze. Menz's not Niall's body is underneath. His, not Niall's, eyes are flat and lifeless. Two equally strong emotions grip me at once. Menz saved my life. It's not Niall. Menz died *because* of me. It's not Niall. A man is dead. And it's not Niall. I'm an awful, awful person.

Mom pries the sheet from my fingers and re-covers Menz. "The doctors tried to revive him, too, but he'd gotten the brunt of the hit."

I glance around. The security officers appear exhausted and sad. However, they smile at me, happy I'm alive despite the fact I caused Menz's death. My gaze snags on Niall. His expression mirrors mine—pained relief.

"Wearing that jumpsuit under your clothes saved your life,"

Mom says to me the next morning. "Why did you put it on?"

Shrugging, I say, "I felt safer."

I'm in the infirmary, again, waiting for Dr. Edwards to release me from his care. This time I'm in no hurry. Lying here doing nothing suits me just fine. According to DES and ninety percent of the people in the base, I'm officially dead.

Being dead means no school work. No required soch-time. No access to the Q-net. Avoiding the cameras. All preventive measures in case Jarren is searching for me. I'm no longer on probation, but I'm still going to stay with Radcliff for protection. I'm not dead, but I might as well be. Jarren has neutralized me as effectively as if he killed me permanently—according to Edwards, my heart stopped beating at one point.

If I'd just kept my word. Once Niall was clear of the shuttle, I should have returned and gone with Jarren. Menz would still be alive.

"...listening to me?" Mom asks.

"Uh..."

"That's all right. We can talk later. Get some rest." She kisses my forehead and leaves.

Sleeping is now my full-time occupation. Jealous? And I plan to do a damn good job of it. I roll over on my left side, squirm into a comfy position, and... I can't sleep. Lovely.

Yeah, I know what you're thinking. That I'm moping and pouting and I should be grateful that I'm alive. That I should focus on the positive. I did rescue the team from detention. Except they're not...complete. If I hadn't interfered, Jarren and his men would have left with me and without hurting anyone.

Menz would still be alive. And really, what do *I* know about security? Nothing really. What a huge ego, thinking I could outsmart the looters.

And this is the time you say that it's not my fault. That Jarren fired the weapon. He's to blame. That no one asked Menz to tackle me. That he died doing his job. That he understood the risks.

Yes, I agree with you. They are all true statements. Factual. My brain is in total agreement. Too bad my heart's not on board. And you can't force the heart.

I flip to my back and stare at the boring ceiling. The tiles are lined up in straight rows and columns just like the Warriors. But very unlike the Q-net—where everything's interconnected, just not in straight, predictable lines. There are many theories out there about the afterlife—in fact the Terracotta Army on Earth was created to protect the Chinese Emperor in the afterlife. Maybe the shadow-blobs are demons from the afterlife who found cracks into our existence. In that case, I would have encountered them during my brief visit to the afterlife. Instead, I flew through the Q-net—my own personal heaven.

Which makes sense, I've a knack for worming. Good enough to bring Jarren from wherever he's been hiding to stop me and kill Menz. Makes a girl not want to use a terminal ever again. But the more I mull it over—'cause let's face it I have plenty of time to do just that—this all started when I pieced together that alien artifact. The symbols intrigued Lan and she figured it out and must have told Jarren. Perhaps she sent her research to him as well. He's had years to decipher it, plus he worked in the pits. Something must have clicked for him. I doubt I'm really clever enough to understand what it means.

My mom returns in the afternoon as promised. "Dr. Edwards says you'll be released tomorrow morning."

I guess a change of scenery would be welcome. She hovers next to my bed and I suspect there's something she needs to tell me but is reluctant. I speak fluent Mom. "What is it?"

Mom studies my face. "They're having a funeral for Officer Menz in two days. You don't have to go if you're not feeling well."

"I'll go."

She squeezes my hand. "We'll be there, too."

When she leaves, I wonder if it will be the same as the funerals we had for our time-traveling friends. I doubt it. This is real, while then it was just play acting. We did it because it hurt to watch your friends leave and it was better to think that they were gone than to think they were living their lives without you and loving other people. That we were just *that* important to each other. Same when you left the others behind. From experience you knew that they'd eventually continue on just fine without you. It just makes it quicker if you cut all ties. We convinced ourselves it was easier that way.

But it was just fake. Because in the back of our minds, we knew they lived and loved and some had children. Denial in its purest form. I wasted so much time pretending, when I could have been exchanging messages, learning about their lives and joys and trials. Menz and Lan are truly gone and the pain is nothing like we pretended.

Beau visits me later. He moves with care and a nurse hovers at his elbow, but he waves her off before sitting— slowly—in the chair next to me. His color is better, but it's obvious he needs more time to heal.

"I hear you completed our mission. Well done, Daniels."

"Then you haven't heard all of it," I say. "Jarren escaped. It was an utter failure."

"I have to disagree with you. Our mission was to rescue our team members from detention and that is exactly what you did."

"Which wouldn't have been possible without your gallant sacrifice."

"Oooh...gallant. I like that!"

Despite myself, I grin. "You would."

"Is that your way of thanking me?"

"Yes, thank you."

He remains quiet for a while, but then laughs.

"What?"

"All those bets on when *you'd* wind up in detention, and it ends with all of *us* in detention first. You should do some major gloating over that."

"I'll think about it."

Beau cocks his head at my unenthusiastic response. "Do you know Niall bet you'd get through the entire probation without going to detention?"

"Yes. But it probably would have been better if I did go."

"Lyra—"

"What was your bet?" I ask before he can make a lame attempt to improve my spirits.

He pauses. "Thirty days." Beau holds up his index finger. "I figured the first five days, you'd be pretty freaked out over the whole probation thing." He adds a finger. "Then the second five, you'd be on your best behavior." His ring finger flicks up. "By fifteen days, you'd become comfortable with being around us." The pinky finger is next. "And by day twenty, you'd figure out all the weak spots in our organization. Around day twenty-five..." He adds his thumb to the rest. "Boredom sets in and roughly thirty days after you were placed on probation, you'd try something that lands you in detention."

I mull it over. "Sounds about right."

"Oh? No bragging that you wouldn't have been caught worming that soon?"

I shrug. "That was before." Now, it sounds childish.

"Lyra—"

The door opens and Radcliff strides in with Niall, Morgan, and Keir in his wake. "Why aren't you in your room?" he demands of Beau.

"I had to check on my partner. Make sure she's okay."

Niall's frown deepens, which is the reaction I suspect Beau was hoping for with that partner comment.

"Did you want something, sir?" Beau asks when no one says anything.

"Yes. We need to do a debrief."

"Now?"

"Yes. Niall, Keir, fetch some extra chairs."

I sit up. They're doing it here? I'm not sure I'm ready to talk about what happened. But I don't have a choice. They return with chairs and my parents slip in. Soon everyone is sitting in a half-circle around my bed, facing me and Beau.

Radcliff meets my gaze. "All right, Lyra. Let's hear what mischief you were up to while we were distracted."

Interesting choice of words. I tell them everything. Beau adds a few details about the time we were together.

Radcliff leans back. "Quite the story. That's an interesting theory about the HoLFs. But you shouldn't have endangered yourself by surrendering to Jarren. Niall shouldn't have helped you leave detention either, but it worked out."

Anger swells inside me. "It worked out? Jarren escaped and Menz is dead. How is that *working out?*"

"Calm down, Lyra," Mom tries to soothe.

But I'm feeling an emotion other than grief and it energizes me. "And don't you dare blame Niall, he trusted me. *My* plan failed. *I'm* the reason Menz died."

"That's enough," Mom says, standing. "No one blames you, Lyra."

I press my lips together, seething. Of course they do. Their hearts know as well as mine.

Mom glances at Radcliff. "I told you it was too soon for this."

He makes a noncommittal sound, staring at me. I glare right on back.

"All right. We'll continue this at another time," he says.

Good luck with that.

The next morning, I'm released and Keir and Niall escort me to Radcliff's. No one says a word. It's nothing but awkward silence the entire trip. I mumble a thanks and close the door to my room with relief. My jumpsuit is folded on the bed. It smells clean. I finger the material. It saved my life but not Menz's. The clothes I wore over it were singed beyond repair and my bag is still on the shuttle unless Jarren ejected it into the universe by now. Radcliff believes he and the men that escaped are off the planet, but with Jarren's superior ability to manipulate the Q-net, he could be parked right next door. Not a comforting thought. And no one has been able to answer how Jarren managed to get to Yulin in the first place.

Next to the jumpsuit are a pair of jeans and two shirts—the last of my clothing. Mom promised to scrounge for more, but I told her not to bother.

During dinner that night, my parents and Radcliff discuss…things. I'm not listening as I pick at my food. Niall isn't there and I wonder what he's doing, but I don't have the energy to ask. Plus I've more important things to do, like sleep.

Menz's funeral is the next day. It's nothing like the mock ones we held. They were a party in comparison. It's horrible. I'm not going to relate the details—they're too painful. However, I'll say this—I barely knew Officer Ivan Menz before the funeral. During the funeral, I learned what a loving, generous and kind man he'd been. Afterwards, I had to force air into and out of my lungs because of the crushing weight gripping my chest. Each breath is a conscious effort. I've never felt this terrible in my life.

Crawling under the covers of my bed after pretending to eat dinner, I'm starting to think Menz is the lucky one. He's flying through the Q-net and I'm struggling to remain upright.

A few days later—no, I've no idea how many—Niall joins us for dinner. I haven't seen him since the funeral. Dark smudges line his eyes and his hair is in need of a cut. He gives me a tired smile.

After we finish eating and the adults all leave, Niall and I sit together on the couch. He tucks me close and drapes an arm around my shoulders. I soak in his clean scent of sage. His warmth eases grief's hold on me just a fraction. Enough to say more than one word at a time.

"Can you draw a picture for me?" I ask him.

He glances at me. "Sure. What do you want me to draw?"

"Your choice, but make it small so I can keep it with me." But I think about it. Paper doesn't hold up very well. Then I remember Beau's tattoos. "Does anyone in security do tattoos? You could draw one for me, and it'll be with me forever. That'd be perfect."

Shifting slightly so he can see more of my face, Niall asks, "What's this really about?"

"When Jarren...when I packed my bag, I didn't have anything of yours to take with me. And I want something..."

"In case I die?"

"No!" I jerk away, horrified by the thought.

He takes my hands. "It could have been me," he says in a

quiet tone. "But Menz was faster even with a broken arm. Nothing I could do but watch you both die."

Remembered anguish flares in his eyes. I'm not the only one suffering.

"Were you glad it wasn't you though?" I ask.

"Yeah, of course. Part of me feels guilty about it, too. But I can't change anything and I wouldn't do anything different."

"Not even locking me in detention?"

"No. That was the right decision," he says with strong conviction.

Lucky him.

Radcliff returns and orders Niall to get some rest before his shift in detention. There are sixteen looters occupying the ten cells where they will remain until the Protector Class ship arrives. I assume Radcliff interrogated them, but I don't care. I return to my room for another marathon sleeping session.

It's another couple nights before Niall and I have some more alone time. Once again on the couch, since I can't be seen by the scientists, he pulls me against him. As I snuggle in, I realize I'm finally curious as to what happened after I rescued the team from detention. I ask Niall.

"Morgan yelled at me for letting you escape, but her heart wasn't in it. We released everyone and waited for the cameras to go dark. Then we ambushed the guards." He pauses. "It was Morgan's idea to disguise ourselves as the looters. The four guards escorting my dad and your parents were quite surprised when they showed up at detention. I know how they felt. Probably as shocked as I was when I realized I was choking you instead of one of the looters. I'm glad the bruises are gone."

Niall's fingers brush along my neck, sending a tingle down my spine. Since I haven't been able to look at myself in a mirror, I didn't even know I had bruises. "Was your dad surprised?"

"Not that we were free. In fact, he grumped at us for taking so long. He took the news about you in stride. Almost as if he expected you to go and do something like that. Of course, he reprimanded me for letting you go as well. But when I think back, there was no way we could have gotten enough looters without you surrendering."

That's new. "What do you mean?"

"Once Jarren had you, they prepped for departure. The small groups in the halls made it easier for us to neutralize them and to get to the port before them. And there wasn't a lot of chatter between them so they didn't realize some of their men were missing. If you didn't show up, they would have searched the base for you. That would have been more organized and it would have resulted in us being discovered. Plus if they went out into the base that would have put more people in danger. Of course, my father disagrees. He thinks that despite being outnumbered four to one, we would have won in the end."

Of course. "Did he assign you to hide in the shuttle?"

"Yeah. We had orders not to shoot you and Jarren, hoping he'd take you into the shuttle and leave his men behind." The disgust in Niall's voice is clear. "Too bad he spotted me right away. I was hoping he'd be too preoccupied with the controls." Niall rubs a hand over his face. "Good thing he didn't shoot me in the head or I'd have been stunned for sure."

And we'd have been Jarren's guests. But Menz would be alive. Would Jarren have killed Niall? I doubt it as he seemed reluctant to kill until the very end when he thought he had no choice. However, he didn't appear to care that the shadow-blobs might wipe everyone out. The bright lights at the entrance to the pits are keeping them from accessing the base. But for how long? I shake my head. Not my problem. Not anymore.

A few days later (in the morning... afternoon... evening? Hard to tell since I keep my room dark), Radcliff comes in without knocking. He flips on the lights. The brightness hurts my eyes so I pull the blanket over my head. Radcliff yanks it off the bed. I squawk in protest.

"All right, Lyra. You've had enough time to recover. No more moping. Time to get up." He is unaffected by my supernova glare. "Here." Tossing clothes onto the bed, he says, "Get dressed. You have five minutes."

"And if I'm not ready?"

"Then you'll go in your pajamas."

I know it's not an empty threat. Ugh. "Go where?"

"To your funeral."

24

2522:182

My what? Did he just say my funeral? Radcliff leaves my room before I can ask him for more details. He shuts the door behind him. I stare at my blanket on the floor, not really seeing it. Am I leaving Yulin? Has the Protector ship arrived? It isn't due for another year at least. Have I really been moping that long? A scary thought. And how did he find out about *those* funerals?

Guess I'd better get up and get dressed so I can find out. I freeze in shock when I recognize the clothes Radcliff threw onto my bed. It's a security uniform. Gray shirt, black tactical pants with a weapon belt. There's no name on the shirt and no pulse gun. Is this a joke?

I doubt Radcliff has that sick of a sense of humor—or a sense of humor at all. So I change into the uniform—it fits. I pull on my boots and comb my hair. Feeling like a fraud, I go out into the main area.

Radcliff's waiting for me. He nods at my appearance then

yanks open the door. "After you."

"Where?" I ask.

"I told you."

"But—"

"Come on. You don't want to be late." He hurries me through the hallways until we reach the officers' rec room.

It's the same place they held Menz's funeral. I hesitate outside the door, but Radcliff puts a hand on my shoulder and propels me inside. Just like last time, the pool table, game system, couches, and ping-pong table are pushed to the sides and there are four rows of chairs lined up in the middle facing a podium. All the security officers are there—Beau's hair is once again spiked— along with my parents, Gavin, Dr. Gage, and Dr. Jeffries. Niall sits in the front row next to my parents. He's trying to look sad, but I recognize the spark of humor in his blue-green eyes. Everyone is staring at me. The desire to duck behind Radcliff and hide flushes through me, leaving me hot and sweaty and if I'm truthful a little queasy as well.

Radcliff directs me to the armchair next to the podium. He hovers over me until I sit down. There's a picture of me on an easel. I'm smiling, but there's a bit of a snark to my smile and a mischievous glint in my eyes. It's hand drawn in pencil. It's lovely. I glance at Niall. He winks at me.

Radcliff stands at the podium and the slight buzz of conversation ceases. "We are gathered here today to remember Lyra Tian Daniels. She was a good friend, a loving daughter and a colleague. Although in the beginning, she was a very *reluctant* colleague."

A smattering of chuckles erupt over that comment.

I'm not amused.

"When I first met her, I pegged her for a troublemaker and thought she'd be in the brig by the time we reached Yulin. And I know many of you shared my assessment even when she made it to Yulin. Those who bet she wouldn't make it through probation need to pay Niall."

My father hands something to Niall and there's another round of laughter. Still not amused.

"But Lyra never once hesitated to help even when she was pissed off. And let me tell you, she was angry at me quite a bit over the short time we've known each other."

More laughter.

"I will admit, I did deserve her ire the time I accused her of illegally worming when she was on probation and I never had a chance to apologize for that."

I shoot a glare at Radcliff. Is that an apology? Ignoring me, he continues on with my eulogy and lists all the stuff I did to assist the security team. I'm surprised by how much I did. And when he chronicles my rescue of the team from detention, I sink down into the cushions in embarrassment. I thought he didn't like me and here he is thanking me for my efforts.

I'm relieved when he finishes, but then he says, "Would anyone else like to speak?"

My father hops up and takes Radcliff's place. "Lyra's mother and I are very proud of her. Although she insisted she wasn't interested in archaeology, she has made a number of crucial discoveries."

Dad continues to detail my achievements. Then he switches to a few of my not-so-stellar moments throughout my life. And no matter how hard I try, I'm unable to turn invisible.

He pauses for a moment. "A part of us has died with her. Our bright beautiful daughter is gone and I'd give anything to have her back." Dad swipes his tears.

And they're not fake ones. Mom's face is wet as well. My stomach churns. Guess I haven't been much of a daughter lately. Plus I still might leave and they'd lose me for real—like with Phoenix, they'll never see him again, yet they supported his decision. My parents are the best.

My dad rejoins my mom. They hold hands. Next up is Beau.

"I had the privilege of working with Lyra on a number of occasions. For all intents and purposes, she was my partner. We plugged security holes, tracked a super worm, and outsmarted the looters together. Menz died trying to save her. If only she lived and Menz's sacrifice wasn't in vain. His parents' grief might be just a little less knowing their brave son saved a life in his final moments."

Suddenly very uncomfortable, I squirm in my seat.

"But *Jarren* killed them both. He knew her mad worming skills were a threat to his plans and he neutralized her. He won this round. Without Lyra, it might be a long time before we can discover what he's up to and by then it might be too late to stop him."

I wrap my arms around my waist. Beau and the others are smart. I'm sure they'll figure it out without me. Right? Plus I can't worm or Jarren will come back and kill more people.

"Lyra and Niall saved my life in the pits," Beau continues. "Her ability to see the HoLFs and his trust in her are the only reasons I'm standing here today. I'm not going to *waste* my second chance. I've learned a few worming tricks from Lyra so I'm going after Jarren with all the skill and cunning I have. Too bad I won't have a partner to be there with me." He sits down.

The desire to melt into the cushions presses on my shoulders. I'm not wasting my second chance. I'm playing dead like I'm supposed to. Big difference. Although I did have fun working with Beau. Maybe I could teach him a few more tricks.

"Anyone else?" Radcliff asks.

Dr. Gage rises to her feet. "We are posthumously expunging her probation from her permanent record and giving her a commendation for her brave actions that led to her untimely death." She sits down.

That's cool. If I'm ever listed as living, that would help for my future career. Huh. That's the first time I've thought past my next nap. And just what would be my future career? Based on what I've enjoyed, it would be an interstellar navigator slash crime fighter slash archaeologist. I doubt that's listed under occupations. And Lan still needs her recognition. Perhaps I could add cryptologist to that job description.

No one else volunteers to speak. Radcliff ends the service. "Lyra Tian Daniels, may you rest in peace."

There's a moment of silence. I don't have a will. I've nothing to give them. Is this like the kids' funerals? Am I supposed to leave without saying good-bye? Cut all ties. I find the thought very alarming. I don't want to leave. I don't want to say good-bye. I blink back tears. I want my family back. *All* of them.

Radcliff clears his throat. "While I have all of you, I'd like to introduce our newest member of our security team."

Grateful for the distraction, I scan the faces again, looking for the unfamiliar one I must have missed. Nope. He/she must not be here.

Radcliff continues. "Since she's not yet eighteen A-years old, she'll be a junior member. If she accepts this commission, she'll be assigned to work with Officer Dorey to track down Jarren, and she'll be part of the team dealing with the HoLFs—she has a theory that the Warriors are protecting us from them that needs to be explored. Of course, once she turns eighteen, she'll have the option to continue working with us or go into another field."

Is he talking about me? Radcliff meets my startled gaze. Yup. I swallow.

He says, "It's a dangerous job and everyone will understand if she declines the commission. I will be sad, though, as she's like a daughter to me and I consider her a part of my team."

Oh my stars!

"Will you accept the position?" Radcliff asks me.

Will I? This is my second chance. Hell yeah. I stand and shake his offered hand.

He turns back to the now grinning crowd of people. "Please welcome our newest recruit, Junior Officer Ara Yinhexi Lawrence."

Cheers and claps greet my new name, which is a nice surprise. I'm sure Radcliff will be able to alter DES's records and

I'll be able to get on the Q-net again as long as I'm careful not to attract Jarren's attention. But I am curious…

"Ara?" I ask Radcliff.

"Your dad picked your first name. I believe it's a constellation. Your mother chose your middle name—it's Chinese and translates to Milky Way Galaxy. And your parents asked me to select your last name. It was my wife's maiden name."

Wow. He meant what he said about being like a daughter to him. "Thanks."

"But that doesn't mean I won't be hard on you, Junior Officer Lawrence. I have high standards for the behavior from *my team*. Understand?"

In other words, don't expect special treatment.

"Yes, sir."

My parents pounce on me right after Radcliff beams with approval. I'm embraced and fussed over.

But I stop them. "I still feel responsible and guilty for Officer Menz."

"We know," Mom says. "You need time to work through it. We understand, but if you start sleeping twenty hours a day again, you're going to have to talk to Dr. Jeffries."

"Why him?"

"He has some experience in that area—both personal and professional."

I glance at him. He's talking to Keir.

"Okay," I say.

Mom clutches her chest in mock surprise. "That was too

easy."

I grin. "Well I am a different person now."

Dad laughs, but Mom peers at me with her Mom-X-ray. "Uh huh. I'll believe when I see it."

"Come on, Ming, have a little faith," Dad says.

"Are you willing to bet on it?" she asks.

And that reminds me. "Dad, about that—"

"Oh, look at the time," he says. "We have to get back to work. See you at dinner." Dad pecks me on the cheek and pulls my mother away.

"Don't think I'm going to forget," I yell after him.

"Forget what?" Beau asks me.

"My dad betting on when I'd end up in detention."

"Yeah, I thought he shouldn't be able to bet since he has insider knowledge."

"That's not the point."

"Are you sure?"

I huff.

He grins. "Let me be the first to welcome you to the team." He holds out a hand and I shake it. "Nice to have a partner again."

After Beau, I end up shaking hands with the other members of the team as they welcome me one by one. Doctors Gage and Jeffries thank me and congratulate me.

Morgan squeezes my hand harder than necessary and says, "Training starts tomorrow, Recruit."

Ugh. I should have known there was a catch. She laughs at my sour expression. Which dissolves when Niall approaches.

He's the last one and I suspect it's on purpose because there's no one else in the room.

His hair is trimmed and he's looking more than fine in his uniform. The clean scent of sage reaches me. My heart jumps into double-time when he's within kissing distance.

I tilt my head at the picture. "Is that for me?"

"No. That's for me. This…" He reaches behind the picture, pulls out a smaller piece of paper, and hands it to me. "This is for you."

It's a drawing of a toad and a mouse, both wearing crowns, and fighting mutant zombies together. "It's perfect. Thank you."

"Welcome to the team," he says.

I raise an eyebrow. "No handshake?"

"I've been strongly reminded about being a professional while in uniform."

"And when isn't a handshake professional?"

"When I know if I touch you I won't be able to let go."

Ah.

He gives me a wry grin. "And I'm supposed to pass that along to you, Junior Officer Lawrence. While you're in uniform, you need to maintain your professionalism as well."

"Is that so?"

He nods.

This is going to be fun. "Please follow me, Officer Radcliff." I go to the far left corner of the room.

Niall joins me. "What—"

I place my hands on the sides of his face and draw him in for a kiss. A deep, passionate, curl-your-toes type. I know my toes are curling. After his initial surprise, he moans and responds in kind. I tangle my fingers in his hair. The rest of my body ignites. My new uniform feels tight and hot, the material abrasive against my skin.

Niall breaks away, panting. "We're going to get into trouble."

"No, we're not." He waits.

"This is a blind spot, Officer Radcliff. The cameras can't see us."

A wide grin lights his face. "Welcome back, Mouse."

THANK YOU

Thank you for choosing *Navigating the Stars* book 1 in the Sentinels of the Galaxy series. The second book, *Chasing the Shadows* will be out in December 2019!

If you like to stay updated on my books and any news, please sign up for my free email newsletter here:

http://www.mariavsnyder.com/news.php

(go all the way down to the bottom of the page). I send my newsletter out to subscribers three to four times a year. It contains info about the books, my schedule and always something fun (like deleted scenes or a new short story or exclusive excerpts). No spam – ever!

Please feel free to spread the word about this book! Honest reviews are always welcome and word of mouth is the best way you can help an author keep writing the books you enjoy! And please don't be a stranger, stop on by and say hello. You can find me on:

- Facebook: https://www.facebook.com/mvsfans
- Goodreads: https://www.goodreads.com/maria_v_snyder

ACKNOWLEDGEMENTS

From the moment I sparked on the idea of space explorers finding Terracotta Warriors on other planets, this book has been quite the departure from my usual fantasy novels. As with most new things, it was a scary prospect. However, I had several people to help me along this journey and make it not so scary (at least until the reviews come in!).

When I told this idea to my agent, Robert Mecoy, he was super excited about it and has been my staunchest champion for the project. Thanks, Bob, for being my cheerleader and for all the hard work you do on my behalf.

This project also had a number of unique challenges with factoring in the time dilation and keeping track of actual time versus Earth time and all the rest of the math (ugh). Without access to the Q-net, I relied on my Chief Evil Minion, Natalie Bejin, to keep the timeline straight with one of her magical Excel spreadsheets. And as one of my beta readers, she found all the inconsistencies. Thanks, Natalie!

Speaking of beta readers, I also need to thank Lynette Noni, who took time out of her insanely busy schedule to read through my manuscript and provide fabulous feedback. I also want to thank my sensitivity readers, Tien Ha and Ningji Hu, who ensured my depiction of the Terracotta Warriors was respectful and accurate.

Being accurate is always a priority for me. As part of my research for this series, I attended Launchpad Astronomy Workshop for Writers at the University of Wyoming for a

MARIA V. SNYDER

week-long intensive class (and I mean intense—long days learning about all the wonders of the universe). Thanks to Dr. Mike Brotherton and Christian Ready for teaching the workshop and to SFWA for funding the program.

This book went through several revisions, each one making the story stronger and better. For that, I have to thank my fantastic Australian editorial team: Rachael Donovan, Julia Knapman, Laurie Ormond, and Annabel Adair. You ladies made me look good. Next time I'm in town, the first round's on me!

As for looking good, I must thank Josh Durham for that gorgeous cover! It's perfect, Josh, thanks so much. And thanks to Louise Summerton who drew Lyra's crinkled space graphic—I love the Big Fat Frog, he's so cute!

Thanks to my publicity team here in the US: Michelle Haring of Cupboard Maker Books who has hand-sold a bazillion copies of my books (okay, not quite a bazillion, but close), to Sarah Weir for designing bookmarks, to Jaime Arnold for hosting my blog tours, to Carrie Miller and Mindy Klasky for helping with the daunting task of self-publishing, and to all my readers who have recommended my books to their friends/family/strangers on the street (that's the best way to keep an author in business).

The cliché of saving the best for last is quite true when it comes to acknowledgments. My family and friends have all been so supportive of me and my books and I appreciate their help and their patience as I disappear for hours to write or fly off to yet another conference or book signing. Thanks to my daughter Jenna for her honest feedback on my stories and wardrobe. And, as always, the biggest thanks goes to my husband, Rodney. I know I've said this in all my books, but without him I wouldn't be sitting here writing my sixteenth acknowledgments. Thanks so much!

ABOUT MARIA V. SNYDER

When Maria V. Snyder was younger, she aspired to be a storm chaser so she attended Pennsylvania State University and earned a Bachelor of Science degree in Meteorology. Much to her chagrin, forecasting the weather wasn't in her skill set so she spent a number of years as an environmental meteorologist, which is not exciting ... at all. Bored at work and needing a creative outlet, she started writing fantasy and science fiction stories. Over a dozen novels and numerous short stories later, Maria's learned a thing or three about writing. She's been on the New York Times bestseller list, won a half-dozen awards, and has earned her Master of Arts degree in Writing from Seton Hill University, where she is now a faculty member for their MFA program.

When she's not writing she's either playing volleyball or traveling. Being a writer, though, is a ton of fun. Where else can you take fencing lessons, learn how to ride a horse, study martial arts, learn how to pick a lock, take glass blowing classes, and attend Astronomy Camp and call it research? Maria will be the first one to tell you it's not working as a meteorologist. Readers are welcome to check out her website for book excerpts, free short stories, maps, blog, and her schedule at MariaVSnyder.com.

CPSIA information can be obtained
at www.ICGtesting.com
Printed in the USA
LVHW111433060219
606606LV00001B/113/P